DEATH SAILS
AMONG SHADOWS

WRITTEN BY ATHENA MATTHEWS

Registration No. 1141766
ISBN: 9781096570189

Dedication

This book isn't just dedicated to my friends and family who love and supported me through these years, helping me get through many hardships in life, and forcing me to push through with this novel in general, but it is also dedicated to all those out there who felt small, and out of place. Too weak and afraid to take their lives in their hand. Always remember you are never alone, even if you feel that way.

Death; Sails Among Shadows

The sky was clear on this late-winter night, as the moon was full and bright. It illuminated the sandy shore in a soft blue hue. Two sailors hurried back to the dock, where their Captain was waiting for their report; their Captain promised that their source was good, they were supposed to find something great along this beach, but as the midnight hour was fast approaching, they were still empty-handed.

The younger of the two was a pretty red-haired lad, he tied his medium length hair back with a bandana across his forehead, his eyes were incredibly bright, blue, he was thin, barely any muscle holding him together.

He led a few leads away from the other; an older sailor, a dirty, dust grey beard, strong structured physique, dark foggy eyes, and balding under his old rimmed hat.

The red-haired one's boots were tied in a knot and flung over his shoulder; he ran barefoot the ice-cold ocean waves softly brushed against his ankles.

Something caught his eye and he came to a halt. He cocked his head to the side slowly approaching what seemed to be a corpse. The waves must have brought it in, and it found itself stuck in the sand. He studied the body, it was a man, and they had been stripped of their clothing. Deep red gashes covered the body, bruises indicated that their hands had likely been bound at some point, he had been badly beaten, and a large open gash on the back of his head was still bleeding. He hadn't been dead long. The young sailor bent down next to the corpse, brushing some wet hair out of the man's face, only to jump back in a panic, falling ass first into the sand as the corpse's chest moved up and down. The red-haired lad blinked widely, studying the corpse again. Now watching closely as once again the 'corpses' chest moved up and down, *he's breathing?* He rolled the corpse over onto his back and pressed his ear against the corpse's chest.

"Ahoy, get away from that. Who knows where it's been!" The man huffed, quickening his pace.

"He's breathing," The lad called back.

The older man rolled his eyes and adjusted his hat, "Bah, ye be jus' hearin' thin's." he hustled over to his shipmate.

The young lad mimicked the other silently, untying his cloak and tossing it over the naked man. "Come, check for yourself then." He grumbled, turning his head towards the sailor approaching.

The older man disbelief towards the fact that the man lying in the sand was alive, was tested as he bent down to feel the body's pulse.

The stranger's eyes shot open! He coughed salt water, sitting up as he took a deep breath. He looked up at the two men staring down at him and crawled slightly away, shivering from the cold, fear and confusion. The stranger clung on tightly to the cloak, covering himself before placing his arms up in defence. He was terrified. His dark, shoulder-length hair stuck to his face, as blood trickled down the back of his neck and shoulders.

The two sailors also took a step back before freezing, unsure what to do. They looked at each other as the younger of the two spoke with a reassuring smile, "We aren't going to harm you, are you hurt? Do you require some help?" Clearly, he was, and clearly, he did.

Horror filled the strangers face as he went to

respond to the sailors, his lips moved, and yet no sound came out. He covered his mouth with his hand, pulling the cloak tighter around him, the wind howling against them, cutting right through the naked man.

The older man spoke, he was feeling sympathetic towards the young man, who was in clear distress. "Why don't ye come wit' us? We can get some clothes on yer back 'n headed where ye needs t' be?"

The younger one spoke again, taking a slow step forward, his hands out showing he meant no harm, "Come on, you can trust a couple of honest sailors."

The older of the two rolled his eyes at the innocent white lie, it was true the stranger could at least trust them. Though the stranger didn't have much of a choice in coming with them or not. His eyes rolled to the back of his head and he fainted, falling face first into the sand.

The two looked at each other before picking up the poor unconscious stranger and carefully carried him back to their ship.

With the help of some other shipmates who rushed to their aid when they came into view. They carefully laid the stranger down on the main deck of the ship, the older sailor barked orders to the crew, "Go get th' lad some clothes, 'n call th' Captain. Captain Far'mel shouldn't be th' last t' know about our guest."

Hours went by; the crew had dressed the stranger's wounds and clothed him before taking him down to the crew quarters under strict supervision of the two who had found him, Captain's orders.

The younger one sat on an old, dusty chest, arms crossed and head down, growing more and more tired as they sat there in near silence.

Morning Dawn was nearing as the ship rocked them softly against the uneased waters.

"We should 'ave jus' left 'im, bad luck bringin' a stranger aboard a pirate ship. Bad luck bein' a corpse comin' back t' life." The older of the two grumbled, scratching his long, dusty grey beard, while adjusting in the spare cot across from the still sleeping stranger.

The young one smiled looking up from the floor, "It would have been wrong to leave him there, and it was your suggestion, remember?"

"'n yet ye took th' blame fer it."

"No one would have believed if I said that grumpy ol' Daric offered to bring a stranded man aboard." The younger one laughed, he untied a bandana that was holding his hair out of his face, and fluffed it out, brushing his tangled hair with his fingers, "How mad was the Captain?"

Daric crossed his arms and puffed out his chest. "Captain didn' seem mad, jus' ordered that we report back when they wake up."

"If he wakes up." The younger one stated grimly. "Aye, if." Daric nodded.

A few more hours passed; the sun was shining and beaming through the small porthole. Daric had fallen asleep, snoring obnoxiously in his cot, while the younger one tugged at the ties to his leather arm bracers that covered him from wrist to elbow.

The strangers moved his arm, placing it over his eyes, shielding him from the light, shifting in the cot and covers.

The young man froze, not wanting to scare the stranger as he just observed him in silence, waiting for the right moment to make himself known.

The stranger opened his eyes and raised his hand above his face, he was studying his own hand as if it was a foreign object. The stranger must have caught the sight of the younger man watching him in the corner of his eye, he sat up quickly and backed away into the corner of the cot trying to get away from the kid.

"It's alright, I mean no harm." He spoke with a

smile, raising both hands up, "I'm Iggy, Iggy Dawning, and the sleeping grey-bearded beauty is Daric Greymorn."

The stranger's tension didn't ease as Iggy could see the man's chest pounding up and down in a panic.

"You are currently below deck of the ship called the Shadow's Blade. Do you have a name?" Iggy asked.

The stranger swallowed hard and went to speak, his lips once again moved, but no sound came out as he placed his hand over his throat, a sharp pain had pierced right through him, with a lingering burning sensation.

"Don't worry, stranger, it will all be alright." He smiled genuinely.

But the stranger did worry, he couldn't manage the smallest little sound, he couldn't scream, he couldn't call out. His heart was pounding hard in his chest, his head was a jumbled mess. *Who am I?* The stranger asked himself, he continued to panic. *Where am I? How did I get here? Where is here?!* Questions began to fill and pile up in the poor stranger's brain, as no answers were coming to his absent mind.

Iggy took off one of his boots and tossed it at the sleeping Daric, who quickly stirred up from his sleep, wiping the drool from his lips, he grumbled.

The stranger in defence cowered, pulling his knees

to his chest watching the two of them intensely.

Daric looked over the man quietly, in partial shock, he wasn't expecting the stranger to wake up. "I'll go get th' Captain, ye try 'n calm th' stranger down afore we get back."

"Aye," Iggy answered, Daric stretched and left the room, closing the door tightly behind him.

What's going on? Why can't I speak, where is my voice? The stranger screamed in his own head, placing his hands on the side of his head, trying to think, trying to remember… Remember something, anything! Everything was just black. He had no memory of who he was, where he was or even how he got where he was now. The clothes he was currently wearing were foreign to him, the room was foreign, the man staring at him, studying his every move, it was all a foreign mystery. *I don't even know my own name!* The stranger knew words, he had the urge to speak aloud, to scream, but nothing would produce except pain.

Iggy could see the stranger getting lost in his own mind, his panic at the situation, so Iggy tried to bring him back as he asked, "Do you know your name?"

The stranger looked up at him and paused. It took a lot for him to fight the urge to speak the words, but finally, he took a breath and shook his head answering the question with a no. His face filled with defeat.

Iggy scratched his head, "Can you speak?"

Again taking a minute to collect himself he finally shook his head no.

"But you understand everything I am saying?" This time the stranger shook his head yes to Iggy's question. Iggy smiled, "That's a positive at least, right?" The lad was overly cheerful over the ordeal. The stranger looked away, holding his arms crossed and biting down on his bottom lip.

Iggy and the stranger must have been distracted as they didn't hear the clicking of boots approaching until the door to the cabin slammed open. Iggy jumped up from his seat and dropped his hands to his side as the Captain of the Shadow's Blade entered the room.

The stranger's mouth went dry as he tried to swallow the fear away.

Thick, dark brown leather boots, with a large brass buckle, a dirty old, blood red coat that hung down past the Captain's knees, a thick black cotton blouse, slightly unbuttoned at the top, with matching black trousers. Long, thick, messy curl's trailed down and framed their tanned, toned face, thin pink lips pressed together, envy green eyes stared down at the stranger. The stranger couldn't help but stare up at the beautiful woman.

"The great Captain Jane Far'mel honours you with her presence, 'n who are ye?" She asked, crossing her arms over her ample chest.

"Captain if I may speak?" Iggy waited, Captain Far'mel nodded, "He seems to be a mute."

She stepped towards the stranger who cowered away trying to get farther away from the powerful woman. The heels of her boots clicked against the old wood planks. She studied him and smiled coyly, "What, did you sell your voice to a sea-witch for legs?" She chuckled, her crewmen behind her followed her lead in a short-lived laugh. She raised her hand in an order of silence, they did as she commanded. "This could be an issue. How am I to be sure you do not have ill intentions towards myself and, or my crew?" Captain Far'mel pulled out a dagger that had been hidden in her boot and sat on the edge of the cot, leaning in another inch towards the stranger. "Are you here to harm me, or my crew?" She asked, twirling the blade against her index finger.

The stranger shook his head no, as quickly as possible as she continued her questioning, "Do you know why you were on the shores of Duggar?"

He shook his head no, *I don't know who I am, how*

am I supposed to know why I am here? The stranger said this in his own head, almost forgetting that no one else could hear his thoughts.

She cocked her brow studying the stranger closely, before placing her dagger back in its hidden sheath. She watched as he let out a soundless sigh of relief as the woman spoke to Daric and Iggy. "When you found him there was nothing else on the beach alongside him? No clothes, supplies, anything with a clue to who he is or where he came from?"

Daric waved Iggy to silence before he could even begin to speak, "Nothin' Captain. He be covered in many large gashes 'n bruises, possibly from bein' toss around th' large coral reef."

"Hm, Karlic any other ships in the area?"

Karlic, a tall brutish man with a shaved head spoke with a smokers cracked voice, "No ship's in th' last few days, Captain."

The Captain pressed a finger to her lip, "Where could you be from, stranger?" She questioned aloud, but the crew knew not to answer with speculation. She stood up and walked away from the stranger speaking just before she stepped out of the room, "Take him to the brig for now,"

"Is he our prisoner then?" Iggy asked out of line as the Captain glared coldly back. He saw his mistake as he placed his arms back down at his side and spoke again, "My apologies Captain."

She honoured him with a response, he knew she didn't have to give him one. "He is and he isn't. He will be there until we get an idea of who he is. I can't have a stranger freely roaming my ship until I know he is not a threat to anyone aboard. We will take good care of him; don't you worry about that, Iggy."

Daric and Karlic approached the stranger as their Captain strutted away from the scene.
Daric spoke calmly, "Come wit' us. If ye do nah struggle or resist, everythin' will be alright."

The stranger tensed up but did as he was told. The two large men grabbed him by the arms and led him out of the room.

Iggy stood his ground; he knew better than to follow Daric or the Captain.

The stranger's eyes scanned the halls, the two men lead him through the ship in silence. He couldn't focus on just one thought as every question muddled together in his head. *What is going to happen to me? What are they going to do to me? Why can't I remember anything?*
Daric and Karlic placed the stranger in a poorly maintained cell, clearly, they did not have prisoners often as he sat down on a dusty old cot. Daric locked

the cell door behind the man, before dismissing Karlic. He sat down on a small wooden bench watching the strangers every move, making the poor confused man uneasy.

"I be goin' t' ask ye a few riddles, simple aye or no's if that be alright wit' ye, stranger."

The stranger sat up on the edge of the cot and nodded inspecting Daric, just as much as the man was inspecting him, he placed his hands on his knees.

"Good, at least I know ye understand wha' I be sayin'" The stranger nodded, unsure if he actually needed to respond to that question. "Do ye remember wakin' up on th' beach?" The stranger shook his head no, with a puzzled expression, "Do ye remember meetin' Iggy 'n I afore ye woke up on th' ship?" Again, he shook his head no, Daric was surprised in the fact that the stranger didn't remember their first encounter. Daric thought for a moment before explaining what he had forgotten, "Iggy 'n I found ye, naked, th' waves had brought ye in from th' sea. Ye be covered in cuts, bruises as if ye had been beaten, I assumed ye were dead. Ye woke up in a panic, we tried t' calm ye down, but ye blacked out again. So, we brought ye back here t' our ship th' Shadow's Blade. Do ye remember how ye first got in th' water?"

The stranger wanted to roll his eyes and yell, *how many different ways do I have to tell these people I don't remember anything!* But when he actually took a moment and thought about the question, a glimpse, a shimmer of a memory crossed his mind. Him tumbling under the surface of the water, his lungs filled with the cold salty liquid as he took in another breath, if somehow, he was hoping it would be air. The stranger shook his head and the little memory escaped him. *What terrible thing did I do in my past to deserve such a fate as this? Stuck with no memory and no voice to defend myself with...*

"Ye somehow hit yer head on somethin', possibly comin' into shore." The stranger placed his hand on the covered wound, while Daric continued to speak, "Thar be a good chance yer memory will slowly come back t' ye once it starts t' heal. 'twill take time, so rest, 'n try nah t' worry too much about it all. Captain Far'mel promises that 'tis temporary." The stranger nodded, pulling his legs up on the cot, "I be sure ye will gain her trust 'n ye'll be allowed on deck, supervised or she'll let ye off at th' next port. Fer now, rest up. Maybe thin's will clear themselves out in yer head aft a good sleep."

I hope you're right. The stranger said to himself,

curling up on the cot, rolling away from the old pirate, as he stood up and walked out of the room, leaving the stranger to his thoughts. The stranger closed his eyes and listened. The large pirate ship rocked and tossed against the sea. Drifting to sleep, he thought, *maybe my dreams will hold some hint of my past...* The stranger felt almost hopeful, drifting into the darkness of sleep.

Chapter 2

Even if our stranger had dreams of his past life, revealing everything he had forgotten, it was useless and wouldn't have helped him. When he finally woke the next morning from his restless slumber nothing that he had dreamt of held in his still fussy, confused mind. He sat up, hanging his feet off the edge of his cot, running his fingers through his long, tangled hair. *I still remember nothing.* Even trying to think of the last few hours some things remained misplaced, names and faces. The stranger placed his hands on the back of his neck and looked up at the ceiling, taking a deep breath. He closed his eyes and took in the sea air around him. He could smell the salt, and the musty old bones of the ship, and in that moment, he felt no panic. He eased himself into the dark silence.

His moment of silence was just that, a small moment as the door to the brig slowly creaked open and Iggy poked his head through the door. The young man waved and entered with a smile, taking a seat on the bench next to the cell. He reached out a half loaf of bread, and a mug with water to the stranger, "I brought you this, and Captain Far'mel asked me to bring you up to the main deck."

The stranger took the bread and water, smiling, knowing that it was his only way he could thank the young pirate. He finally took a moment to study Iggy, swallowing the bread as fast as he could stomach without choking himself. He did not look like a storybook pirate. He had delicate features, a beautiful face, a charming smile, a slim figure, piercing blue eyes, and his body appeared hairless. There were no visible tattoos on his body, but if you looked closely, you could see the whites of many old scars mostly on his chest.

He was dressed in well worn, fitted brown pants, the knees and bottom hem were blown out, he had a dark coloured vest and a torn grey shirt that was completely unbuttoned, with the sleeves rolled up revealing the same arm braces he was wearing the day before. The same dark bandana held his hair in place, as well as another green bandana around his neck. Iggy smiled as the stranger finished the last crumb, "Sorry if I knew you'd be that hungry I would have brought you more." He laughed lightly, trying to keep the mood easy going, "Do you remember your name, yet? I feel bad calling you Stranger." Iggy's smile was genuine, but the stranger shook his head no. Iggy shrugged and leaned back placing his hands behind his back. "Maybe we should think of a really cool pirate name for you. Like the Voiceless Butcher!" He laughed enthusiastically.

The stranger raised his brow and tried not to smile at the ridiculous suggestion. *Is this guy serious?* Shaking his head, no, and waving his arms out in front, trying to state firmly that he was rejecting the name completely.

"Okay, okay that was mostly a joke, but I do think it would be good to make a name up for you." He combed his hair back with his fingers once again, thinking to himself, "Captain made a joke about you selling your voice to a sea-witch, why not go with Ari?" Iggy cocked his head to the side and smiled with a nod, "I could see you being an Ari."

The stranger rolled his eyes and shrugged, *Ari? It's simple. It's a lot better than the Voiceless Butcher...* He nodded.

"Wait, you are actually agreeing to something I said?!" Excitement filled Iggy's face, he couldn't contain his exactment, jumping up from the bench. Iggy unlocked the cell door and stuck his hand out,

"Nice to meet you, Ari."

The newly named Ari cocked his brow as he hesitantly took the young man's hand and shaking it softly. *You are way too excited about this...* He thought to himself, *a temporary name...* Ari pushed back his thoughts for a moment, and he put on a smile. He didn't want to crush the man's excitement with his inner turmoil.

Iggy stepped back and headed towards the door, "If you are ready, the Captain wants you up on the main deck. She wants as many eyes on you as possible, so you'll probably get to stick with me." The way Iggy made his last statement was so overly excited Ari was under the assumption that he was being sarcastic in his emotion towards what the day was going to hold for them.

Ari nodded and followed Iggy out. He placed his hand on his throat as a small burning could be felt in the muscles of his neck. *Maybe this was just temporary?* He thought hopefully as he kept his head down, his eyes scanning their surroundings.

The Shadow's Blade was an older, smaller pirate ship; he could tell by her smell and the way the boards creaked, but to the surprise of those who dare face her in battle, she was sturdy, well armed, and the crew were well trained and ready for battle.

The two finally reached the door leading to the main deck, Ari stopped in his tracks and stared nervously.

Iggy turned around and smiled, "Don't worry, most of the crew are harmless and the few you do need to worry about I can keep them clear of you." He laughed, bitterly? Ari heard another emotion hidden behind his words, but the man waved him forward and Ari followed.

Your words are not reassuring. Ari grumbled, he stepped forward into the sun. The cold hit him first and hit him hard, shivering. Even with this beautiful sunny day, the winter sea wind nipped harshly at his face, the sounds of a crew keeping busy filled his ears.

It was as if time froze when the two walked out into the view. Everyone turned and stared at the stranger, mostly in surprise the Captain had released him from the brig so early on.

Ari could feel his heart pounding in his chest. He wanted to run back to the brig and seal himself shut in his cell. He didn't want to face these strangers, these pirates. He could feel their judging, untrusting eyes all over him.

Iggy spoke quietly, he turned to walk up the stairs leading to the helm of the ship, "Pirates are never the most trusting, but if Captain Far'mel finds you trustworthy, they will slowly accept you."

Ari swallowed uneasily, *how trusting is the Captain?* He had to fight the urge to attempt to speak allowed, as with every attempt to force sound, the burning sensation would increase in his throat, the pain was constantly lingering.

Aloud whistle broke the silence as the Captain called out to her crew, "Get back t' work!" Iggy and Ari looked up and spotted the Captain, her striking dark emerald eyes locked on Ari. She leaned her entire body against the helm. Her thick curls tossed around her face as the wind blew wildly. "Get up here already," she ordered with a small grin.

"Aye, Captain," Iggy called back, pulling Ari into motion as the two of them climbed the stairs towards the helm stopping a good foot away from the woman.

Her eyes traced up and down him once again before speaking, "So, my little stranger. Any memories returned to you? Or a voice perhaps?" Captain Far'mel asked, she tapped her long nails against the smooth wood.

Ari shook his head no, oddly enough he wasn't as intimidated by the beautiful, powerful Captain's stare compared to the rest of the crew. There was something about this woman that made him want to trust her.

"Captain?" Iggy spoke, questioning if he was allowed to continue, the Captain nodded as he continued, "I thought it would be best if we stopped calling him, Stranger, and give him a name until the time comes that he remembers his own."

"Aye, that is a good idea." She readjusted herself on the helm, she gave Iggy, and Ari a playful smile, "What have you come up with?"

"Ari," Iggy fought back his own laugh.

She laughed a loud, "Took my joke to heart?" But she thought about it for a second and it grew on her, "I doubt any pirate is going to respect someone with the name Ari. Do you like the name?" She asked the stranger.

Ari shrugged his shoulders, giving an 'it's alright' expression.

She adjusted the ship slightly, standing up straight, "Ari is as good as any name for now. I only hope you remember your real name before your journey with us ends."

How long do I have till the journey ends? Ari asked himself as he attempted to gulp out loud. He wasn't entirely sure that her words weren't meant to be threatening.

She could see his discomfort. Captain Far'mel stuck

her hand out, with a very small smile on the corner of her mouth, "Welcome aboard the Shadow's Blade, Ari." Ari looked up at her and took it, she had an incredibly strong handshake as he met her small smile with his own.

"As you can see, I am a very busy woman, so I am leaving you in Iggy's capable hands. That means where ever Iggy goes, you go. At night until you've gained the trust of the rest of the crew or you decide to part ways with us, you will remain below decks in the brig. It might not seem like it, but it's more for your safety than my crews." She grinned and turned to address Iggy, "Report to Victor, he knows what needs to be done today."

"Aye, aye Captain," Iggy replied, he turned away from the Captain. Ari understanding that he was to follow.

Once they were halfway down the stairs Iggy spoke again quietly towards Ari, "You should have no issues with Victor. He is a man of very few words, the more someone talks, the less likely he is to like you. So, who knows you could be his best friend by the end of the day," Iggy chuckled at his own joke as he patted Ari on the shoulder supportively.

Victor was an easy man to find. He was the tallest

man on the ship; extremely fit, clean-shaven head, dark chocolate coloured skin, thick dark brows and all-knowing eyes as he stared into you. He must have had a thing against shirts, he only wore an ash coloured vest, along with slightly lighter coloured trousers. Ari's eyes focused on the two curved swords on the man's belt, Victor seeing where his gaze was drawn, rested both his hands on their hilts for easy drawing.

"This is Ari, at least that is the name we are going with for now. He's sticking with me today."

"Ari?" he questioned, he took a long moment of silence, grumbling something under his breath before speaking towards the two, "Ye're t' swab th' deck, 'n th' hold cabin if ye complete that return t' me 'n I shall find more fer ye t' complete."

"Aye, Victor," Iggy spoke as he turned to go.

Ari went to follow Iggy when Victor's hand clasped around Ari's wrist, turning him back around their eyes met. He whispered his threat in Ari's ear, "Any funny business 'n I shall be th' one who gets t' skin ye alive."

Victor released him and Ari rushed to Iggy's side, his heart pounding rapidly in his chest. He tried to keep up with Iggy's pace.

Iggy grabbed a broom, bucket and cloth as he

attached the bucket to a pully system and tossed it over the side of the ship. "I think Victor likes you," He mocked, even though he was oblivious to Victor's threat, he saw the look the large man was giving the stranger.

Ari crossed his arms over his chest, Iggy's cheerful composer was back, "Victor will be one of the harder ones to win over. He means well, in the past Captain Far'mel hasn't always had the best luck with newcomers aboard her ship. She is a feared pirate Captain, but she sometimes isn't the best judge of character. Victor and Daric are her protectors from that personal flaw of hers." He smiled, pulling the bucket back up, handing Ari the cloth, he untied a bandana that was tied around his ankle and they went to work.

The sea was calm that day, as the sun and the chill beat down on the crew of the Shadow's Blade; Captain Far'mel kept a good eye on her crew making her way around her ship. Daric stuck to her side as he watched Iggy and Ari closely, but to be fair, every crew member kept a good eye on Ari that day. The hair on the back of his neck would rise every now and then when someone would walk near the two of them working.

Iggy was a talker; Ari got the impression that he

didn't get to talk too much usually. So, he talked about every member of the crew as they crossed paths. Warning Ari of the do's and don'ts of every different crew member, such as the less words you use when speaking to Victor the more likely he is to like you, or Jorgen likes a good long tale, if he starts there is no stopping him from talking old folk tales and lore for hours, or that Karlic get very emotional when he has one too many pints of ale. As well as not to bother Vendell, for anything, he gets testy very quickly, or don't stand in the way of Reefer and alcohol. There were sixteen crew currently as they had recently dropped off many of their usual crew at the last port after a long two-year voyage from Klemm to Tasyrn and back. Ari had put a face to every name, except one.

Ari scrubbed the railings listening carefully to Iggy's stories, his first sincere smile was stuck on his face. Something about listening to Iggy speak, telling tales, there was a sense of familiarity? That didn't seem like the right word, Ari thought, but whatever it was, he was happy to listen to the man speak.

"Captain one took on an entire bar filled of drunken sailors, while very drunk herself. She was far passed the point of slurring her words and stumbling around. I do have to note that she technically started the fight," Iggy continued, "One of the sailors at the bar made a remark about her figure and what he wanted to do with, said figure. Daric went to jump in to defend the Captain, but no, she wouldn't have it. She cracked the man in the jaw with her mug, ale flew everywhere. It was apparently chaos and even after the fight was over, Captain helped dragged a couple crew members back to the ship because they were in too bad of shape to get there themselves."

Ari tried to laugh, but no sound would produce, and instead pain tore through the muscles of his neck. He slouched over, placing his hand on his throat as the presser slightly soothed the ache. He closed his eyes and took a moment to recover himself.

Iggy stopped and studied Ari closely, "Are you alright?" He asked.

Ari, nodded that he was alright and reopened his eyes smiling trying to ease the concern on the man's face.

"Why don't you just take a break, I can finish this up and we can go to the mess with the rest of the crew?" Ari shook his head no and went to continue cleaning the spot, but Iggy grabbed the stranger's hand and took the cloth away, "Just go sit over there, take a break. You aren't very good at cleaning, and I usually do this by myself anyways so its not a problem." He smiled again, shooing Ari away.

Ari finally did as he was told, taking a seat in an area that had already been cleaned and dried. Resting his head and back against the railings.

"If I've been talking too much, you just signal for me to be quiet. Even Daric who has the most patients for me would have asked me to shut my yap well before now." Iggy laughed at himself, he turned to look at Ari.

Ari just smiled and shook his head no.

He didn't realize it, but that meant something to Iggy, he smiled and he continued to work, "I think we will be good friends, Ari."

The stories which mostly focused on Daric and the Captain continued while Iggy worked.

A few short hours had passed and finally, the crew was heading to the mess hall. Iggy stretched and offered Ari his hand, helping him off the deck as they made their way behind the rest of the crew. The two of them being the last to leave, besides the few staying to control the ship.

Iggy lead them to the back of the hall, far away from the rest of the crew while everyone else seemed to all pile into two large tables.

This seemed strange to Ari, seeing the rest of the crew sitting together, enjoying each others company as they got rowdy and loud. Iggy placed two portions of food down as well as two mugs of ale on the table before sitting down quietly with his back to the wall. This was the first time all day that Iggy didn't have something to talk about. His mood seemed completely shifted. He just ate, with his head slightly down.

Ari took the mug of ale in both hands, downing half the glass unknowing what he was really drinking, but the cool liquid felt great on his sore throat. He hiccupped and felt a strange warm sensation in his stomach.

The silence was causing Ari to become uncomfortable. He tapped Iggy on the shoulder.

Iggy looked up as Ari motioned towards him and then to the empty seats around them.

Iggy placed an elbow on the table, resting his head on his hand, "Asking why I don't sit with the rest of the crew? And vice versa?"

Ari nodded.

Iggy took a moment; he was considering his words very carefully. He sighed sadly trying to put on a smile, to Ari's untrained eye it seemed genuine. "A good chunk of it is because most of them don't see me as part of the crew. I'm more of a pet project for Daric and the Captain. I'm," he paused and smiled,

"I'm different. I was never was a trained sailor. Never planned to be a pirate. When I was younger, I dreamed of running far away from the sea as my legs would take me. There are reasons, but it's a very long story. Maybe a story for another night." He took a long drink before continuing, "If Daric was here, he'd sit with us, he always sits with me, and if it was late enough the Captain sometimes joins me." Suddenly Iggy tensed up, the air around the two of them changed as Iggy focused his head down at his tray of food.

Ari looked up as he spotted a large man entering the mess hall. His head was shaven, revealing a large snake tattoo wrapping around his skull and neck, he was the only crew member who even came close to Victor in size. There was something about the man that gave Ari a deeper chill, rather than just unease from the rest of the crew, and Ari wasn't the only one to feel it as Iggy and even the rest of the crew seemed uneased by the man. Iggy didn't look up from his tray as he swallowed a mouthful of food quietly, before asking Ari's obvious question, as Ari's eyes were focused on the man who sat down at the table with the other crew members, but his eyes were locked on the two of them.

Iggy went to take a sip of ale from his mug as he

spoke just loud enough for Ari to hear and his words to be hidden by his drink, "That man, is Gibson Ungar. He's the cook. Do not take this warning lightly, do not cross that man. If you find yourself alone with him, run away and avoid him at all costs. He is not someone you want to be close to."

How scary can one man really be? Ari asked himself as he unconsciously continued to stare at the strange man. The way the bald man stared at young Iggy made Ari's skin crawl. It wasn't as if the man was looking at another person, it was more like a starving animal would look at its prey.

Iggy pounded down his drink and spoke, "Guess you should hurry up and finish eating. I have night watch and I'm more then positive you are not joining me for that." He was unemotional, a huge change from his usually chipper attitude as he downed his last few bites of dinner.

Ari followed Iggy lead as the two then make their way from the mess hall back to the main deck. Iggy's smile returned to his face once they were clear of the mess hall and stepped out on the main deck, the cold air filled his nose as he took the moment in.

Daric approached, he was waiting for them, but he didn't make it obvious that he was doing so. "Head up and dismiss Matthias, I'll take Ari to his quarters."

"Aye," Iggy replied trying to sell it with just as much enthusiasm as he had earlier in the day, only fall just shy of it before walking away.

Ari watched Iggy swiftly climbed up the crow's nest as Daric started to lead the way back into the ship. "Come on lad," Daric called back after he didn't hear Ari trailing behind him, Ari snapped out of it and rushed to catch up. Daric looked over him once before turning his head back to where they were going, "'ave any o' yer memories recovered?" Ari shook his head no, "'n still, no voice I see?" Again, he shook his head no. Daric slapped Ari on the back, in a rough, but friendly manner, shocking him slightly, "Well, I 'ave no doubts 'twill return t' ye in time. Now, th' real riddle be wha' are yer plans? On advisement, th' Captain hasn't given ye much choice in th' matter. We spoke today about it in depth. Be yer plan t' remain on our ship 'til ye regain yer memory? Or we can drop ye off at th' next port."

Ari stopped in his tracks, he thought for a long moment. *I haven't even had a moment to process everything, do I really have a choice to leave? If I did, where would I go?*

Daric looked over his shoulder, Ari started walking again, "Ye don't needs t' decide anythin' right away. 'twill be a short while afore we hit th' next port,

Captain even offered t' take ye back t' our previous port as 'tis closer t' where we found ye if ye wished."

This Captain Far'mel seemed strangely accommodating for a feared pirate captain. Ari shrugged his shoulders, unable to explain what was really rushing through his mind.

Daric nodded as he understood, "If ye find any o' th' crew are harassin' ye at any point, come directly t' me. I know some o' th' crew are hard on newcomers aboard our ship."

Ari nodded.

They finally reached the brig, Daric sent Ari in alone, not bothering locking the cell door but locking the main door to the brig behind him. Ari dropped down on the cot and stared up at the ceiling processing the loaded question Daric had left in his head. *What is going to happen to me if I don't ever regain my memory? What is my plan...* The thought of having a plan made him want to laugh, he couldn't remember how he got on this ship, where he was found, how he was found, or why he was covered in cuts and bruises. He placed his hand on the back of his head, the welt still healing, he caught a glimpse of his bruised wrists, it did look as if he had been bound at some point, but why? Then again it could be from anything... Ari understood that the memory loss was likely from however he hit his head, but the lack of his voice troubled him the most. He had this deep desire to hear the sound of his own voice, he felt that he was missing something. He fought to bring sound to his lips. Something in him told him that if he could hear the sound of his own voice that it would bring back something to remind him of who he really was, that it was a clue? Right now, all Ari wanted was his voice back, he could manage without his memories for a while, but being so defenceless, unable to call out, explain himself, scream. He just felt empty and depressed. Ari rubbed his eyes and yawned, pulling the ragged quilts over himself. He fell into a deep sleep.

Chapter 3

The next few days were very uneventful for Ari. No memories, no dreams. His throat ached with every unintentional and intentional attempt at trying to make an audible sound, he wasn't improving to his own disappointment.

Every morning Iggy would come to retrieve Ari, and they could spend the day doing the chores around the ship. The only difference in the start of this day was Iggy looked more tired than he usually did, or distracted? Ari couldn't be sure what it was, but there was something different about him that morning. Blue bags had formed under his eyes as the young man tried to play it off as normal.

Daric stopped the two of them just as they reached the main deck. Iggy spoke with his usual cheerful tone and a soft smile, "Morning, Daric."

Daric looked at Ari who was standing at attention, waiting for him to speak, "Mornin', Iggy ye be t' go start inventory alone this mornin', we hit port in three days. Captain 'n I require Ari fer a wee while, then I shall send 'im down t' assist ye once we be finished wit' 'im."

There was a small twitch in Iggy's smile, something so small that Daric missed it due to the fact he was still focused on Ari, but Ari caught it. He wondered what it was about.

Iggy seemingly brushed it off, he nodded, "Aye, I guess I will see you later Ari. Don't talk the poor Captain's ear off, yah hear me." Iggy said once again in his usual playful tone. He placed his hand comfortingly on Ari's shoulder.

Ari smiled at Iggy's sarcasm and watched Iggy head back into the belly of the ship.

"Come with me, lad." Daric waved Ari to follow.

They walked up the stairway towards the helm where the stern of the ship where the Captain was standing tall with her back to them. She watched the trail her ship made in the ocean as she cut through the waves.

Ari couldn't help but note to the fact, the Captain was breathtaking. Her thick hair tossed wildly; her green eyes sparkled against the sea. She was wearing a deep purple blouse, the top buttoned showing off her tanned smooth collarbone, she had rolled up the flared-out sleeves that now revealed a strange, scar? Ari found his eyes now drawn and focused on the scar, but it wasn't just a scar. It looked like the skin had been burned by something as well as cut by a sharp knife to distort whatever the symbol was, like a brand mark.

Daric elbowed Ari in the side.

Ari's eyes jumped back up to the Captains face, she was oblivious to his insensitive staring.

She smiled finally turning to face the two of them, "Daric, you can leave us now." It didn't sound like an order, but it clearly was. She waved Ari over, "Come, lean with me."

Am I in trouble? Ari asked himself, standing next to her looking over the side of the large ship.

She looked him up and down, letting out a small laugh, "Do I make ye nervous?"

Ari nodded, *wouldn't that be expected?*

"Take a deep breath, you aren't in trouble if that is what you are worried about."

Ari did as was asked of him, leaning against the railing as the Captain was.

"So, having a conversation with ye will prove to be a challenge, but I have a few things to touch up on, so a nod, for now, will do." She looked over at him ensuring that Ari understood what she was saying.

So, he nodded simply at the Captain and she continued, "First off, are you enjoying my ship? She is a beauty." The Captain was clearly proud of her vessel, and she had every reason to be.

Ari nodded to her question with a small smile. "Good, it seems like you and Iggy are getting along well, right?" This time without even a second to think he nodded yes, she smiled and nodded happily, looking back out to sea. "Anything spark any memories?" She tossed her hair over one shoulder, holding it in place with a firm hand. Ari shook his head no but was stuck looking at her strong jawline. She sighed, "That's unfortunate." He snapped out of his trance when she smirked back at him, "Well, you've been on my ship for a few days and it's been a good few days. Daric seems to agree with me in the fact that we should take you out of the brig. Give you a little bit more freedom. Iggy seems to trust you and Daric agrees with that assessment. Though we are giving you free roam of the place, Daric and I will be keeping a close eye on you still, seem far?"

Ari was shocked but nodded.

She smiled and waved him off, "Good, Iggy could use some help down in the storage bunker, we have a lot of junk to go through since this is our first big stop after our long sail, and you'll be less in our way below decks." She meant in a nice way.

Ari nodded and saluted the Captain, that being the only way he could think of to show the woman respect.

The Captain gave him directions on how to get down to the storage bunk and left him to figure it out as she walked over to the helm taking over for Stephen.

It took Ari a while to find his way down towards the storage bunker. He got lost twice as the Captain's instructions didn't stick well in his still messed up mind. But after finding many seemingly dead ends, he finally found the right room, not bothering knocking as he entered. Making his way down the steps silently, he looked around the stuffy, dark, dry room. Boxes of mostly empty food, weaponry, loads of barrels, containing wine, rum and ale were scattered among high selves throughout the room. There was a large wooden table with parchment scattered along it. Iggy bent down his back to the door, focused on what he was scribbling in ink.

Ari walked up to Iggy and placed his hand on his shoulder, unintendedly scaring Iggy. he spun, knocking the ink bottle over, stumbling away from the table now a few feet away from Ari. There was genuine fear in his eyes as his chest moved up and down rapidly. Ari had also jumped back, placing his hands in the air, his apology was written all over his face as he didn't mean to scare him.

Iggy smiled uneasily, placing his hand on the back of his head. "Sorry, I didn't hear you come in." He took a deep breath, his eyes shifting around the room. He ran his fingers through his hair, tussling it around, something he did quite often Ari noted in that moment.

Iggy saw the unturned bottle of ink and flipped it up right, cleaning up the small mess while explaining, "Um, so we count all the stock we have left, and we calculate our usage compared to when we last stocked up at port." Iggy took a deep breath showing Ari what he was doing, explaining the process in more detail.

Ari took the quill and rolled up his sleeve as he wrote on his forearm, *are you alright?* He held out his arm and stared at Iggy with concern.

Iggy smiled and adjusted the bandana holding his hair in place, "Yeah, I'm great." He said overly excitedly. But his body language told Ari that he was telling a lie. His face was pale, his forehead slightly sweaty and Iggy couldn't push aside that uneased expression. Ari couldn't argue or even prove that he was lying, so he left it at that.

But Iggy felt the need to make an excuse for himself, "Inventory always stresses me out, just long days and nights, in here. Alone." Iggy smiled, unable to look Ari in the eye, "Now that I know you can write, you should probably just walk around with a quill and parchment at all times, don't you think?" Ari nodded, and finally, Iggy's warm and innocent smiled filled his face again.

It took a while, but surely enough he settled back down to his normal, enthusiastic self with Ari at his side. Iggy wouldn't admit it to anyone who asked, but they were slacking off more than he usually would while working stock. They laid in the back of the room, hidden by the shelves, with their feet up on the wall. Iggy placed the ledger down as he scratched at one of his leather arm bracers. He spoke, not bothering looking over at Ari while he did, "I find it kind of funny," Ari looked at the seriousness that washed over his face, replacing his smile, "I know so many people who would kill to forget their past. Start anew."

Ari thought for a moment, *but if you forget that you didn't want to remember, you'll just end up lost looking for something you wanted to forget anyway.*

But of course, Ari's words were just thoughts stuck inside his head as he nodded sadly.

Iggy laughed turning to finally face Ari, "Do you have conversations in your head? Like as I keep talking about nonsense, you are replying to me in your own head?" With a nod from Ari, Iggy continued, "I can see it in your eyes, I can see you thinking. I hope your voice comes back, and your memory. I imagine you have a killer story to share."

Ari tried to clear his throat, but the burning sensation flared up once again, *I hope so as well.* With a sad inaudible sigh Ari looked away from his... His *friend.* The thought brought a smile to his face.

Iggy scratched his head, tussling his hair, he jumped to his feet, "Let's get something to eat, I'm starving."

Ari could hear Iggy's shoulders crack, stretching before returning back to scratching at his wrist guards once again. He found himself curious about them, he hadn't seen them off of Iggy since they met. Yet they clearly bothered them, he continuously scratched at the leather. He wanted to question the reason for them, but Iggy pushed the thought out of Ari's mind as he pulled him to his feet pushing him towards the stairs.

Iggy complained playfully, "Hurry up."

They reached the mess hall and well before they opened the door, they could hear the roaring laughter of the rowdy crew inside. Iggy smiled, "The Captain has graced us with her presence tonight, this might be a very interesting night for you."

Ari hesitated, *do I really want to go in there?* But he did follow Iggy, even though he wasn't sure what to expect. The sight of the crew made him want to turn himself around and run back to the brig to hide.

The Captain was arm wrestling with one of her crew; a man by the name of Dorian while the rest of the crew cheered the two on. Jane looked up from her match and gave a crooked grin towards Iggy and Ari before slamming Dorian's hand down against the table with a loud, bang. The Captain won, standing up from her seat beckoning them forward with open arms, "Come, join us, lads!" She came over and placed her arms over both of their shoulders and led them along towards the table. Ari could smell the hard liquor on her breath, "Gibson, bring more rum and come, join us!"

Gibson grumbled, but not loud enough for the Captain in her drunken state to take notice of it.

Ari just let the woman lead them to the table as the Captain sat between Iggy and Ari.

Iggy stiffened and grew uneasy as Gibson placed three more bottles of rum on the table. Placing a firm hand on Iggy's shoulder, his nails dug in while Ari looked at the creepy man. Gibson turned his gaze towards Ari, which caused his skin to crawl as he turned away instantly from the man. Iggy's warning ringing in his head. There was clearly something going on, but what was still a mystery.

Jane grabbed the bottle of rum and filled her glass to the rim before pouring some for Iggy and Ari.

Now that Ari wasn't completely flustered by the skin the Captain was showing off, proudly, nor solely focused on the burn mark. He saw that her arms and chest were also decorated in tattoos. Ari found himself studying her, less discreetly than he assumed.

Jane turned her gaze towards him, it was obvious that he was staring. The crew let out a laugh as she elbowed the newest guest of her ship, "Oh dear, Ari are you awestruck by my beauty?" She bit her finger, seductively as she fluttered her eyelashes at the now blushing man while the rest of the crew tried their hardest not to bust a gut laughing.

Iggy placed his hand over his mouth trying to contain his laughter as the red-faced Ari tried to figure a way out of this, shaking his head no and waving his hands out in front.

She placed her hand on her chest, looking sarcastically offended as she pouted, "What? You don't find me absolutely stunning?" Ari shook his head no still waving his arms trying his best to rectify his actions, before burying his face in his hands.

The Captain finally broke into laugher placing a warm hand on his shoulder, "I'm only bugging ye', obviously you think I am attractive," She winked playfully, "I am stunning, if you have eyes, you can see that. ye 'ave th' wrong equipment if ye know wha' I mean."

Ari, of course, did not know what she meant.

Daric spoke up from the other end of the table, clearing up poor Ari's confusion. "She be into poppets, lad."

Finally, it clicked in as he blushed even redder placing his head on the table as the crew laughed at his expense.

Jane placed her arm over Ari's shoulder pulling him into her, "Sorry for you playing ye' like that," She laughed as she took another drink, "Guess it's not fair of me to bug you like that, being that you can't really defend yourself." She laughed again, handing Ari his cup, "Drink, loosen yourself up a little." She nudged him. Ari took the drink and pounded it back. The crowd cheers, Ari held down the bitter liquid as it burned going down and settling in his stomach with a full body warming sensation. Everyone celebrated taking a drink together.

Jane finally turned her head in the direction of Iggy, nudging her with her elbow as he was just looking down at his drink, quiet. "Have you told our friend all the good stories, yet?"

Iggy cheered up, but there was a falseness hidden behind his eyes, no one else took note of it, because no one was looking, expect Ari. If Daric had been sitting closer, he would have also seen it. "Not all, Captain. I saved all your favourites for you to tell."

"So, nothing of how Daric and I met?" Iggy smiled again and shook his head no. Jane smiled rubbing her hands together as the crew cheered, excitedly, "Good, it is my favourite to tell." She smiled over to Daric who put his hat over his eyes. Leaning back in his chair as she began to weave her adventurous tale of how they met.

It was late in the evening when the teenage Jane Far'mel was dragged, kicking and screaming into the prison in the Capital of Borvil. Her crime? Murdering a literal boatload of men, slave owners to be more specific. She had been surprisingly lucky until that day. Jane managed to evade capture for just over a week, and still, the young girl did not go down without a fight. Therefore, the reason of her broken nose, black eye, and bruised, bloodied knuckles.

She was barefooted and wearing a bloodstained beige dress, her hands were shackled, she had fought the guards every step of the way towards the cells. Screaming profanities and threatening to murder them as they unlocked a cell and tossed her in. She hit the floor, bouncing back up to throw herself at the bars. The two guards jumped back after locking the door behind them, afraid of the feisty child. She cursed at them again, shaking the bars like an animal. The two soldiers ran away from the cells.

"I'd sit down, poppet. No one besides me can hear yer screams." A dusty voice came from behind the girl, in her fury she hadn't even noticed the middle-aged man, with his ankle chained to the bars in the cell alongside her.

He had a dark coloured beard and dark eyes that were hidden by his overly bushy eyebrows. He was wearing no shirt, ripped tan trousers that were covered in blood, he was covered in dry blood and bruises. The guards weren't kind to prisoners on death row. Two black bandanas' were around his bicep while the other was around the opposite wrist. He had many tattoos all over him, covering him; a map with an 'X' marked on it just above his heart, skull and cross and a large pirate ship on his arm.

The young girl smiled twistedly as she stepped towards the man, curious and unafraid, "Are you a pirate?" She paused where she stood, not even giving the man a chance to answer, "You are, aren't you?!"

The man looked up at the young child and rolled his eyes readjusting himself as his bones cracked, "Wha' be it t' ye if I was?"

She continued to smile, turning away inspecting the lock to their cell, "Maybe I'll be a pirate one day."

The man scoffed at the young girl, she snapped her head back and glared coldly at him, "A pretty wee thin' like ye, become a pirate? That be laughable,"

She growled, "Don't call me pretty."

He raised a brow and set that comment aside, "We be both headin' t' th' gallows pretty soon, so all that be wishful thinkin' on yer part."

Smugly and sure of herself she spoke, puffing up her chest. "It may be your plan to stay here and be hung like last weeks laundry, but I am getting out of here."

He laughed, "Good luck wit' that wee lass." He leaned back, with his large arms over his chest, closing his eyes trying to ignore the little girl.

She looked around the cell before planting down in some damp hay that was piled up on the floor and stared at the man as she spoke, mocking the man's accent, "Wha''s yer name, pirate?"

He opened one eye and sighed with a dry cough, "Daric Greymorn."

"I am Jane Far'mel, you will want to remember my name pirate, because mark my words. I am going to do great things."

"Whatever ye say, Miss Far'mel," Daric grumbled again, closing his eyes.

When morning broke Jane hadn't slept as she was calculating and plotting her escape, while the uncaring pirate slumbered, very lightly.
The young girl knew that even though his eyes were closed, and he was softly snoring that he was watching her. Watching her every move.

That thought proved true as when the guards entered the cell, he squinted with one eye, watching.

They were different guards from those who had brought Jane in as they stepped up to the cell and barked ordered towards the two, "Both of you up, your trial start soon."

Daric laughed at the word trial, but he stood as instructed.

Jane, on the other hand, fell to her knees, tears

streaming down her face. "But, I didn't do it sir! You have to believe me. I'm innocent, I'm just a little girl? How could I do what they are accusing me of?" Her lips trembled as she looked up at the two guards who were thrown back by the hysterical girl. Daric knew her bluff, but the poor unexpecting guards couldn't see through it. Daric had to fight hard to hid how impressed he was with the girls thinking and acting.

The first guard bent down and placed a soft hand on the pretty, crying girl's shoulder, "If you are innocent, as you say. I'm sure the king will see it and find you innocent of all charges."

"You really think so, Mr?" She smiled, patting away her tears.

He nodded, "Yes," he turned to the over the guard and spoke, "You deal with the pirate scum, I got the young lady." He placed his hand on the very, lower end of her back as he led her out of the cell. His partner shackled Daric's wrists together before unchaining him from the bars of the cell.

Once the guards weren't paying attention she gave the pirate a quick wink, indicating that she had her plan all laid out. They were escorted through the prison, towards the gallows where the king waited to find them guilty of their crimes, towards Jane's freedom.

Jane knew the layout of this town well; the prison was located very close to the docks, which made for a perfect getaway.

They stepped out the prison doors onto an empty street when she continued to put her plan into motion. She stumbled to the ground, intentionally riding the skirt of her dress up, revealing plenty of thighs, her eyes again filled with tears, "I'm so scared," she placed her hands over her face as she continued to sob.

The guard, naïve to the cunning of this little girl knelt down and placed his hands on her shoulders. She looked up at him and bit her lip, leaning in as if she was going to kiss him, but instead of pressing her lips against his, she wrapped the chain to her shackles around his throat and spun around him, strangling him as she locked her arms. Knocking him to the ground, Jane placed her foot on the mid of his back.

He clawed at his throat as she twisted the chain, tightening it, grabbing the keys to her shackles and taking the guards knife, placing that in her mouth as she quickly freeing herself as she ran down the street towards the dock.

Jane dove off into the cold water. That girl was right, Jane Far'mel was a name Daric would never forget.

She swam under the dock, finding a small air pocket, just big enough for her to fit as she trod the water silently listening to the scene above her.

She could hear the guard who she had strangled into submission, pant as he rushed to the edge of the dock and searched the water shortly before returning to his fellow guard and Daric.

"When asked, she wasn't in the cell this morning, we say the cell door was unlocked. This didn't happen."

Daric Greymorn laughed loudly as the guards continued to take their now solo prisoner to his trial. Clearly embarrassed of their epic failure.

Now, Jane did something everyone agreed was stupid of her to do. She waited as long as she could, wanting to ensure that they were long out of sight before she swam back to the edge of the dock and pulled herself back up and over.

Borvil was a small capital, and there were no other prisoners in the prison, she knew that it would be stupidly unmanned. So, she made her way back into the prison as she searched for the storage room, this was where they kept their prisoner's possessions. First, she found some clothes, they were way too big, so she tore and tied them to fit her curvy frame before rummaging through the weapons grabbing a few smaller knives, something she could handle easily, and hide if needed. She turned to leave when she saw a dusty old pirate hat hanging on a hook, with a leather belt and a long cutlass hanging from the loop. She smiled wide and put the hat on her head and tied the belt around her waist. The blade was bulky and heavy; she knew well enough that she couldn't handle this weapon herself, as another plan filled her head.

Jane yawned loudly and stretched her shoulders, arms high in the air, "How I rescued Daric from the gallows will be for another night, but as a reward for saving his life, I kept his hat." She smiled as she placed the old hat back on her head and smiled towards her old, dear friend.

Daric grumbled, even though he was pretending not to hear the story, "That was me favourite hat."

She blew him a kiss and stood up from her seat, "I am off to bed, mates, good night."

The crew awed and groaned in protest, but they all knew how the story went, Ari was left without an ending! He had found himself so emerged into her story that he saw everything she spoke of as if he was standing next to that small little girl that once was the Captain before him. He had lost all track of time and only found himself realizing where he was once she had stopped talking.

He shook his head trying to shake the confusion. Daric brought him back completely as he smacked Ari on the back, "I'll tell ye th' rest o' th' tale if ye'd like, th' rest o' th' crew has heard this tale many times, but I can still see th' curiosity in yer eyes." Ari nodded quickly without hesitation as the old pirate smiled, looking to Iggy with a smile, "Headin' t' yer cabin?"

Iggy nodded with a weak smile. He brushed his hair back, "Yeah, going to try to catch some sleep before heading back early to get the inventory done."

"Alright, I'll come t' see ye in th' mornin'. Goodnight," Daric waved, stepping away from the table, beckoning Ari to follow.

Ari looked back at Iggy as he followed Daric.

Iggy was still sitting, now alone at the table while he slowly finished off the last of his drink.

Ari felt uneasy about leaving him this night, but he shook that feeling aside and continued to walk beside Daric.

Once they stepped out on the main deck, their silence was broken. "Th' Cap'n be good at tellin' that tale 'cause that's th' only way they know her. Cunnin', fearless 'n definitely nah th' type o' scallywag ye'd want t' mess wit'. But she does 'ave other sides t' her, sides she doesn't share wit' most." Daric studied Ari's face as he spoke. The stranger always intently listened to the people around him, to the stories they told, it was strange, he never seemed to get bored of these long tales. There was something bazar about him, but so far Daric couldn't put his finger on it.

Daric began to climb up to the crows nest, Ari climbed up just behind him. Resting against the sides, Daric scanned the seas around them. It was a calm dark night as the sky lit up with a million stars as the waves rocked the sea softly, the moon-pale, in it's waxing crescent state. Daric continued the tale.

Being led to the hanging noose for most would be terrifying, nerve weakening, but for Daric Greymorn, he was ready to meet his maker that day.

Daric was almost disappointed in the turnout as the king sat at the other end of the relatively small crowd, facing the execution stand.

Daric was placed on the trap door, and the noose was placed over his head. He and the king's eyes met, as the over weight man adjusted in his seat, before repositioning his crown.

The guards tightened the noose, stepping away from the podium. They quickly made their way to the king's side and told him of "why" the girl was absent from this trial.

The executioner; a large man in a black leather mask, held tightly to Daric's shoulder, keeping his prisoner correctly placed over the trap door. The door that would open and kill him a few minutes from now. The question Daric wondered, was it going to be a quick snap of the neck, or was he going to slowly suffocate as he swung there before the crowd?

Daric could see that the guards were done explaining what happened to Jane as for how red and angry the king's face went, putting his burgundy blouse to shame.

Angry, Daric knew this was really going to be a short trial. The king stood up from his seat as the guards hushed the crowd to silence. Their "king" spoke, "On this day, you Daric Greymorn, are accused of piracy and murder, how do you plead?

Daric shrugged and gave a smug smile, "No matter wha' says I, ye be goin' t' hang me."

The king grumbled to himself before speaking, "So, you do not deny the accusation?" Daric shrugged as the king sat back down in his seat, a smile beginning to form back on his pudgy face. "Than by my authority as King, I find you Daric Greymorn guilty of piracy and murder, and sentence you to death, by hanging."

The crowd went wild, but Daric found himself distracted as through the cheers and the king's verdict of his guilt, his eyes were focused on a small figure, making their way easily through the crowd.

It was a young child? In clothes that clearly did not fit them, but that meant nothing to Daric. What did catch his eye was the fact that this child who somehow had made there a way to the front of the crowd was hiding their face with his hat! With his cutlass tied to their tiny waist.

The child lifted the hat, revealing her face to Daric. Jane Far'mel, *that wee cur pilfered me hat.* That was the last thought he had before the hangman pulled the lever that held the trapdoor closed. But Daric's feet didn't leave the wood. Jane tossed a knife towards Daric as she rushed under the stage, he had good enough reflexes and managed to catch the blade with barely an inch before his chest. He had a decision to make. He quickly cut the rope around his neck in just enough time as the trap door unstuck itself and he fell through, landing painfully on his ass.

The crowd screamed in terror as Jane stood next to the pirate with a smile. She handed him his sword, keeping one hand firmly on his hat.

There was no time for words between the two as

she unchained his binds before the two made their way through the panicked crowd.

Again, she led towards the docks, they dodged arrows and only just barely lost their trails as Daric took a breath as he looked behind them. "Did ye reckon o' a plan fer aft yer ridiculous stunt?"

She shrugged her shoulders with a smile, "You're a pirate, you know how to swim."

Daric took a deep breath of salt air as he finished, "Th' true endin' t' th' tale was I convinced her hidin' under th' dock till nightfall or 'til a pirate ship pulled into port 'n sneakin' on board was squiffy 'n wouldna work. As we actually went down through th' sewers 'til we were safe out o' th' city limits. She was persistent in becomin' a pirate, 'n she held me hat ransom 'til I did as she asked. I knew we couldn't pass her off as a lad, fer obvious reasons. It took us a while t' find a Captain that would take a lass on, once we did, she struggled, but she worked hard, surpassed everyone's expectations o' her. She got herself her owns ship 'n her owns crew in no time."

Ari smiled, still thinking of the tale he was just told, he had so many more questions he wanted to be answered!

Daric could still see the curiosity in the stranger's

eyes and laughed, "Aye, thar be still a lot t' learn about th' Captain, maybe in time, 'twill come clear fer ye."

Ari stayed up in the crows nest with Daric for a while. He sat down, curling up and eventually falling asleep. Daric had let him sleep for a while before waking him and sending him off to his sleeping quarters while Daric enjoyed the rest of his night in peace.

Chapter 4

That morning, Ari wasn't woken by Iggy. When he finally woke it was early afternoon, realizing how late in the day it already had become Ari quickly got up and headed down to the storage room to assist his friend.

He had overslept and was groggy. He rubbed his tired eyes and yawned.

Ari reached the door and knocked loudly, remembering how uneasy he had made Iggy last time, when he entered unannounced. Peeking in as Iggy turned and gave him an uncomfortable wave and a bright smile. "Did Daric keep you up all night with his tales of his many adventures with the Captain?" He laughed softly.

Ari shook his head, no, as he made his way down the stairs, even from that distance, Ari noticed something was off as Iggy shifted uneasily turning his back towards him. Once Ari was standing next to him, he tapped Iggy on the shoulder.

Iggy gave Ari an overly cheery, fake smile, before turning away once again. He was focused on the ledger he had open on the table.

Ari rolled up his sleeve revealing his question, *Are you alright?* That was slightly smudged but still readable on his arm. He placed it out in front of Iggy's view.

Iggy nodded, "Yeah, I'm great." But when he lifted his head to smile, that was when Ari noticed the small bruise around Iggy's left eye.

Ari couldn't hide his concern as he stepped around the table pointing to it.

He covered it up with his hand and smiled widely, "Yeah, I dropped a box while trying to put it up this morning, my face caught its fall." His words weren't very convincing, but Ari knew that it was the only explanation he was going to get. Iggy nudged him with another sincerer smile, "I got a lot to get done, so no fooling around today."

Iggy gave Ari instructions and sent him off to the other side of the room as he continued what he was doing.

The two of them lost track of time as they worked together. Ari was putting some boxes back up on the shelves as Iggy stood over the desk calculating the numbers for a final count.

The door slammed open, causing Ari to jump as he peeked around the corner. Iggy and his eyes met as Iggy sadly placed a finger to his lips telling Ari to keep quiet. Ari peered around the other side of the shelving unit he saw Gibson close and lock the door behind him before stumbling down the steps with a bottle of rum in hand. Turning back, he looked at Iggy who backed up from the man as he slammed his alcohol bottle down on the desk. Stepping up to Iggy stroking Iggy's chin with the back of his hand, leaning in, inhaling in his scent.

Iggy trembled under the man's touch as he tried to push the large man away. There was genuine distress and fear in his voice that made Ari's skin crawl, "No, I'm not doing this, you had your fun last night," He went to argue more, when Gibson placed a firm hand around Iggy's throat slamming him back against the shelves. Iggy clawed at his hands, as he pleaded, his voice shaky, afraid, "Please stop," But before Iggy could say anything else Gibson clamped his hand over Iggy's mouth.

Gibson's breath stunk as he smiled and spoke quietly, "Shut yer mouth, wench. I know ye like th' attention." He turned Iggy around, twisting his arm with a great deal of force. Ari could hear the pop of Iggy's elbow, as the large man pushed Iggy over the desk. He moved his hand from Iggy's mouth to the back of his throat as he held Iggy' down over the table, and untied Iggy's trousers, before dropping his own. Tears filled his Iggy's eyes as he met Ari's.

Ari stood up ready to step in, ready to intervene and stop this, but Iggy shook his head just slightly no, his lips trembled. He closed his eyes tightly and looked away. Giving in to the man's wants.

Ari froze, unsure what to do. Iggy didn't want him to help, so sadly, Ari did what Iggy wished and sat down out of view of the assault as he tried to deafen the sounds of the man grunting as he took advantage of his crying friend.

Time seemed to stand still. It seemed that Gibson took forever to finish, when in truth it wasn't that long, but try to tell that to Iggy as Gibson smacked him lightly on the cheek. He retied his trousers. "See? I told ye, ye'd like it, Ignatius." He licked his lips with a proud smile.

Iggy slumped off the desk, too afraid to say anything back or even look at the man who sauntered away, ever so satisfied with himself, closing the door quietly behind him.

Quietly without a word or a sound, Iggy redressed himself before pulling his knees into his chest. He was in a state of shock, and unable to pull himself off the floor. Iggy untied two of his bandana's, fanning them out before retying them around his neck, hiding the red, soon to be bruises of Gibson's hand, and the cuts his nails had made in the soft of his skin. Iggy's elbow had been pulled out of his socket. He tucked it into himself, the pain finally hit him as the adrenaline of the assault had began to dissipate.

His whole body shook as he fought back his tears. Ari finally having the courage to come out of hiding; his face written with guilt and pity as he knelt down next to Iggy, unsure what to do to help his friend.

Iggy looked away unable to meet Ari's stare, "Please, don't look at me like that. It's really not a big deal," Iggy swallowed hard as if trying to take down a bitter pill. That pill was the lies he was telling himself.

Ari tried hard, he really did, but the expression of guilt and sorry was glued on him.

Removing one of his leather arm guards he held his arm out for Ari to inspect it, it was a burn mark, the shape was extremely similar to the one the Captain had on her forearm. But with Iggy's, it was cleaner, clearer, no scars trying to hinder its appearance. It was a snake, twisted into an 'S', as the tip of the snake's tail curled into a small, spiked 'P'. Iggy took a breath, "This is the Slave Company's brand. The snake indicates that I have been bought and sold as a

slave, " He took a long breath, "The small 'P',
indicates the profession on which you've been forced
into, 'L' for labour, 'S' for soldier, and 'P' stands for,"
he really didn't want to say it, he didn't have to say it
for Ari to understand what he was going to say, but
he felt he had too. "I was a prostitute." Ari pulled his
knees up and hugged his legs, he listened to Iggy's
story, "Daric and the Captain rescued me from that
life, just over two years ago." He rubbed his eyes as
tears were now beginning to force their way down his
face, "I don't want to be this anymore, but every time
I fight, he just gets more abusive. If I don't want to
deal with the pain, I just have to put up with it."

The idea of the whole thing gave Ari chills, as he
thought of the obvious answer to his problem as Iggy
sensed what he was thinking, "You must not try to
bring this issue up with the Captain, and especially
not Daric."

Ari's face showed his distaste for Iggy's words.

"Please don't make a big deal about this," There was
desperation in his eyes, "swear to me that you will
not try to inform either of them? Please, Ari, I can
handle it."

Reluctantly, and even thought it made him sick to
his stomach to do so, Ari nodded to his request.

"Thanks," turned away from Ari as he stood up

before speaking, "We should call it quits for the night." And with that, Iggy walked out in silent shame.

Iggy, Ari wanted to call out to his friend, to comfort him, but he was also in shock. He stood up and watched him go; standing there in the silent room for longer then he realized. He couldn't process the emotions that were running through his head, as much as Iggy was telling him to leave it alone, he felt obligated to do something, anything! He wondered if Iggy was saying one thing out of shame, but really just begging someone to go out and actually say something? To help him! Though what if intervening made things worse for him, Ari feared. He couldn't physically tell anyone what happened, he couldn't call out, and even if he did who would believe him? He was just the new comer... Maybe he should have stepped in between Gibson and Iggy, but he wondered what that would have done? Gibson could have just said that Ari was overreacting. It would be Gibson's word, a well-liked, respected man, vs a Stranger, a no-body...

Next thing he realized he was laying on his cot, honestly, he didn't remember getting up and leaving the storage room.

The feeling of being sick filled in his stomach as he

threw up. The image of Gibson over top of Iggy flash through his mind. He rolled back over in his cot and stared through the porthole as the clouds covered the night sky, leaving it black and endless. *How long has he suffered like that by that man's hands? How many others have taken advantage of him?* Ari didn't get a second of sleep as all he could do was think about Iggy and if he was really going to be alright...

Iggy was quiet that following morning, Ari didn't dare try and push for more answers, or even ask him if he was alright this morning as by the expression on his face it was clear that he wasn't. He knew that Iggy's arm had to be swollen and had to be causing him great pain, but he hid it entirely too well. The thought of it all made Ari sick to his stomach, this also being the first time since Ari had seen Iggy in a shirt with sleeves to hide the bruises caused by his attacker. Iggy's bandanas were still tied around his neck, but if you knew what you were looking for you could see the purple bruises peeking out from behind the fabric. Every time Iggy caught Ari staring, he would adjust his bandana's and look away in shame.

Iggy reached up trying to pull a box off the top shelf, only for the box to tumble. Hitting his elbow hard as the box shattered into pieces. Iggy cursed as he grabbed his arm and pulled it into his chest, trying to focus out the pain.

Ari rushed around the corner the second he heard the crash, his heart pounding.

Iggy just dropped to the ground his back leaning against the shelf as he kicked the broken pieces of the box in defeat. "I'm fine," he snapped bitterly as he stared emotionlessly ahead of him.

Ari slowly walked up and sat down near him, being careful not to sit to close as right now Iggy just needed space.

Iggy turned his gaze away from Ari as he spoke quietly, disgusted by his own words, "If I told you that he didn't get like that often, I'd just be lying to you." Ari crossed his legs and looked down at his feet as Iggy continued, "He gets really pushy through the closer we get to port, sometimes after we've just sailed off. He knows I'm down here for days and I can hide the bruises." Iggy neared his throat, "He likes roughing me up, and this is probably the only time Daric doesn't have eyes on me most days," Iggy let out a small chuckle, "Daric gets mad, and flustered while thinking or even looking at all these numbers, so he doesn't even like coming down here unless he needs too."

Ari took a scrap piece of parchment and began to

write, *why hide your bruises? Why hide the truth?*

Iggy took a long, disappointed breath, trying to smile, "Gibson may be a disgusting monster, but he is liked on this ship. Daric and the Captain got a lot of hate for keeping me aboard, many of the crew believed I didn't belong, I'm not a pirate nor a sailor, so I had no reason to stay. Quite a few men even left in protest. If the Captain even caught a whiff of half of what Gibson had done he'd be off this ship before he could protest. I'm worried the crew would hate me even more then they already do." Ari wasn't believing what Iggy was telling him, "Just go around the ship and pay attention to who calls me Iggy, and who still calls me by my given name, Ignatius." Iggy stretched his arm, trying to push the limits of his pain threshold. "To the crew, I am just a pet for the Captain and Daric. Someone she pities because she feels like she understands where I came from." he paused, "I'm just a weak, scared, laughable," He paused again wetting his lips before continuing with a fake, broken-hearted smile, "slave, a little man whore, a toy for everyone else's amusement." He swallowed hard, chewing on his lower lip.

Ari's expression changed from sympathy to disappointment as he pushed Iggy angerly, his eyebrows scrunched as his final words didn't sit well.

"Sorry," Iggy scratched at his wrist guards, looking away once again ashamed, "You've probably noticed that Daric treats me differently from the rest of the crew. If he knew what was going on, he'd only blame himself. He'd think he failed to protect me like it's his job to do that. He taught me how to defend myself, he taught me to stand up for myself, to be tough and not let what I am," Ari pushed Iggy again forcing him to change his words, "What I WAS effect who I can be. The Captain and I share one thing, this brand on our arm." He stopped scratching at the leather bracer and placed his hand over it, "But, she fought her way out, she earned her freedom." Iggy was on the brink of tears as he held his breath to compose himself, "I had many opportunities to fight back, but that was my life for eighteen years. It was all I knew. I was always told I was born there, but I can't know for sure. All I do know is the oldest memory I have," It took him a few solid minutes to force the words out of his mouth, it was a story he had never told a living soul. "My first memory is of a man, a story I've dared not to tell aloud before." Iggy continued to explain his previous life, in painfilled detail.

Ari didn't know when it started, but tears were streaming down his face. *Eighteen years?* The urge to be sick flooded him again as he placed his hand over his mouth, fighting back his urge to vomit.

Iggy wanted to stop talking but he couldn't as he took another breath and continued, "I was well sought after by very, exclusive clients; mostly kings. Sometimes they would dress me up as a woman to get me in and out of their castles, to hide suspicion that they were bedding a boy, much less a man. The more money in the king's pocket, the more abusive they could get with me. Since, I was in very high demand they would be required to pay a premium for recovery time. As long as they didn't mess up my, pretty face," His words were bitter and sore, "anything was allowed." Iggy wrapped his arms around his knees still unable to meet Ari's horrified, tearfilled expression, "There was one king, I can't remember his name, or what city we were even in because he beat me so bad, I was black and blue for a month, and I couldn't stand or move for three days after the fact. They had to carry me to a cart through the slave tunnels."

The person who belonged to these stories couldn't be the man he was sitting next too, he couldn't be the man with the overly cheery composer he had just gotten to know over these few days. *How can you wake up every day and want to keep moving forward? After all the terrible things that have happened too you, after all the terrible things that are still happening to you, how can you keep going?* Ari was sickened. Iggy's retelling of his horrors was so detailed in Ari's mind that he felt like he was there with him, every touch, every, disgustingly invasive touch, Ari could feel as it sent chills through his own body. Every broken bone he felt the lingering pain. He felt the fear, the desire for everything to end, the disgust of himself, the same disgust Iggy tried to hide from the world on a daily basis. Iggy had no one, he had no one to defend him when he was too young to do so, or when he had been beaten down, no one protected him when he needed someone.

Iggy started to laugh. Which confused Ari, shaking him out of his head, as he now attempted to stop his tears as Iggy wiped his mostly dried eyes. "Now look at us, we are clearly the most fearless pirates aboard this ship."

Ari tried to bitterly laugh with him, but the pain in his throat just made him want to cry more.

"It was a very tough life. So, if being here on this ship means every now and then I have to put up with Gibson's abuse. I am willing to do that, to feel safe for a little while."

Ari shook his head, *you shouldn't have to deal with*

any of that anymore! He wanted to yell these words to force them into his seemingly thick skull, *the Captain and Daric saved you from that life, not in the hopes that you'd be forced into that life by a sick twisted bastard like Gibson.*

The door opened and they both turned their heads to Daric stepping down towards them with one hand in his pocket and the other scratching at his face. "Ye lad's slackin' down here?" He said lightheartedly. They stood and smiled, Ari wiping his eyes dry as Daric could tell at least that Ari had been crying, "Ye both alright? Iggy?" Daric's professional composer broke as he stepped forward with fatherly concern.

Ari looked to Iggy for the answer to his question, while Iggy put on his usual smile and nodded, "Yeah, I dropped something and managed to twist my arm funny, so we took a short break."

"Needs me t' check that arm fer ye?"

"No," He rushed to answer before calming down slightly, "No, really it's fine." He worked his arm showing off that everything was alright, Ari being next to him could hear the elbow popping uncomfortably as Iggy somehow managed to keep a straight face.

Daric looked between the two, if it had just been Iggy trying to convince him everything was fine he wouldn't have suspected anything, but Ari wasn't as proficient at lying as of yet. "Alright," he crossed his arms over his chest looking over the room, "Captain wants this done by tomorrow afternoon, be that doable? Or do ye needs some more help?"

Iggy looked down at the ledger counting things quickly as he answered honestly, "I bet Ari and I can get it done by morning,"

Daric was hesitant, "Are ye sure? I don't mind stayin' back 'n helpin' ye two."

Iggy jumped to answer with a bit of a laugh, "You would make it take a bit longer, dear friend. You have more important things to be doing, Daric."

Daric paused again, now staring at Ari who wouldn't meet his gaze, "If ye say so," He looked as if he was going to turn away but didn't yet, "Ye know where t' find me if ye needs me. I'll come 'n get ye scallywags later, maybe we can enjoy a meal together? I've been so busy these few days I feel like I haven't gotten t' sit down wit' th' two o' ye."

Iggy and Ari gave Daric a nod, "Sounds great, Daric." That was genuine.

Still, he didn't want to turn to leave as he spoke one last time, "Are ye sure everythin' be alright?" Iggy nodded. Daric knew there was something odd going on, but he took a step back and waved as he headed up the stairs.

A few quick passing hours went by as Iggy and Ari could see the finish line, a lot quicker then Iggy had expected them too. Iggy was back to his normal smiling self, as he was even able to grace Ari with some more of the lighthearted tales he could think of.

Iggy was placing a few boxes back of the shelves when they both heard the door open; this time Iggy didn't jump uneasily as he was expecting it to be Daric. He didn't even turn around to face the man as he approached, Ari, on the other hand, saw the intoxicated Gibson the moment he stepped off the staircase.

Ari knocked on one of the shelves as he stepped up, this time to intervene.

Iggy turned around as Gibson was nearly on him, he jumped back, his heart pounding heavily in his chest as he was now backed into a corner. Gibson now knew that Ari was there, witnessing the entire thing, but he didn't care.

Iggy spoke, his voice shaking as he tried to be stern with the man, "No, enough of this Gibson. I'm saying no more."

Gibson laughed angerly as pushed forward pinning

Iggy against the wall by pressing his forearm against his throat, "Shut yer mouth," he grabbed Iggy by the arm and spun him around, now pushing Iggy's face against the wall.

Iggy pushed back, trying to squirm out of Gibson's grasp with no prevail. Though this time Ari wasn't going to sit back and hide. He stepped up behind Gibson and grabbed him by the arm, forcing the man to turn around and face him.

Iggy's stomach dropped as he looked back and faced the scene that was beginning to unfold.

Gibson growled at the stranger clenching his fists, "Get out o' here, stranger, this doesn't concern ye," he warned as he took another step towards Ari, but to Iggy's surprise he didn't back down to the threat. Ari stood tall and met Gibson's angry, fearless gaze.

Gibson shrugged and smiled as he went to take a swing, Iggy tried to grab him by the arm and hold him back, but the force of the punch was too strong for him to stop as Gibson's fist connected with Ari's jaw, sending him into the shelf as he toppled to the ground.

Ari found it strange, but after the initial connection, the pain seemed non existent as he quickly recovered jumping back to his feet.

Gibson stepped forward to take another swing at

Ari, but this time Iggy grabbed hold of his arm and held him back for just a moment, "Stop!" he begged, only for Gibson to shove him off easily enough.

Iggy caught himself at the last minute, Gibson stepped towards Ari, who was ready to meet the next attack.

Ari held his breath, puffed his chest and waited for Gibson to make his move, but instead, the man unclenched his fist and took a step back from the stranger.

The three of them heard the door creak open and hear the hastened footsteps approaching.

"Wha''s goin' on down here?" Daric commanded as he stepped up towards Gibson.

Iggy's heart skipped a beat, he turned to Gibson and Ari, watching them closing.

Gibson smiled coyly, "I came down fer more wine, I ran out in th' galley." He shrugged.

Daric looked to Iggy for an answer to his question, but Iggy just smiled trying to hide his discomfort. He wasn't believing a word that was coming out of Gibson's mouth, "Then get yer wine, 'n get out o' here. Iggy, Ari hurry up. Th' Captain be waitin' fer us in th' mess hall."

Iggy and Ari jumped at the opportunity as Gibson had to fight the urge to shoot a glare towards them, but Daric's eyes were locked on him.

Air and Iggy rushed up the stairs as Daric took his time. His eyes not leaving Gibson until he was out the door, catching up with as they made their way to the mess hall.

Ari then realized it was just going to be the four of them eating together.

The Captain had her boots up on the table, leaning back as far as she could in her chair, her stolen hat was tipped forward hiding most of her face as she yawned. Lifting the rim of her hat to the sound of them approaching she smiled as she waved them over, finally throwing her boots off the table. She beckoned Ari to sit down next to her, as Iggy took across from him and Daric next to Iggy. They all tucked in at the table, serving themselves some lukewarm stew and stale scones.

Iggy played as if nothing was wrong, jumping into conversations with the Captain and Daric with ease. Ari, on the other hand, listened as he stared down at the strange, salty liquid in his bowl.

Chapter 5

The following morning when Ari was awoken, he rolled off the edge of the cot, rubbing his face before looking up in confusion at the grey-bearded Daric who looked down at him with his arms crossed over his chest.

Ari nodded a good morning to Daric as the man responded to Ari's confusion of why he was there, "Iggy finished up th' last o' th' stockwork last night, he's sleepin' in till we prepare t' dock later today. So, today ye get t' be at th' helm wit' th' Captain 'n me. She had a few thin's t' discuss wit' ye afore we hit port."

Ari nodded and stood up to follow Daric when the thought crossed his mind, *I hope Iggy is alright after last night...*

Instead of leaving, Daric took a step towards Ari. Getting face to face with the stranger as he asked, "Did somethin' happen last night? Somethin' ye two are keepin' from me?" He didn't look angry, as much as he was trying to strike fear in Ari. In hopes he would speak the truth, he just seemed upset, and genuinely concerned for Iggy.

Ari held his breath; all he really wanted to do was nod, get Daric investigating the situation, put a stop to Gibson's abuse, but the thought, *this isn't my story to tell,* crossed his mind. He held his breath and shook his head no to Daric's question. A knot formed in his stomach as he did so. His heart pounded, he was afraid, and guilty to be lying to the man who was clearly just concerned for his friend.

Daric mostly believed him, leaving the conversation, sadly it at that. "We better nah keep th' Captain waitin'."

Ari nodded. Daric lead them down the hall without another word spoken by him.

The Captain rubbed the sleep from her eyes as she leaned against the helm only to perk up as Daric and Ari stepped towards her. This morning she was wearing a long black overcoat with the sleeves down, covering her tattoos for once, her hair was pulled to one side, Daric's old hat holding it partially in place as the wind threatened to ruin her hard work. A white blouse mostly unbuttoned as she usually did, and her black heeled boots were washed and shinning in the morning light.

She strutted over towards Daric and Ari and placed her arms over her guest's shoulders as she turned to her second in command, "Take the helm for me, Daric. Our friend and I are going for a chat." Daric nodded, doing as she asked, "We have something's to chat about," She paused and thought about it again, "Well somethings for me to chat about and you just smile and nod," She winked with a playful smile.

She was trying to make him feel comfortable around her, but so far it was doing the opposite as he stiffened up and nodded with a sly smile. He wanted to focus on what the Captain had to say to him, but really all he could think about was Iggy and if he was really alright.

The Captain lead Ari around the ship as she inspected her crew and her ship while she talked, "The first question, it's a big one," She smiled waiting to make sure that Ari had his full attention on her, which he now did, "We are pulling into port today, are you planning on staying aboard when we take off again?"

Ari stopped in his tracks and thought for a moment, Jane stopping also and turning her head to study his facial expressions. She watched him as he thought, *I feel like I need to stay aboard. I have no reason to leave, no memories telling me to go.* Thought he didn't admit it to himself, he didn't want to leave. He finally took note of the ever-growing impatient Captain as he nodded a yes to her question.

"You're actually going to stay?" She questioned just to confirm as Ari nodded with a smile, "As surprised as I am, I am happy to hear that." She waved Ari to continue walking with her as he caught back up, "Now, I realize if something triggers your memory or if someone at port knows who you are, that of course will change things. Next question," She paused, "Any memories returned? Anything trigger even the faintest of thing?" Ari shook his head disappointedly no, "It's alright, give it time. Clearly no voice still, but I do know an herbalist in town, I'll see if I can find something today that may help you with that and maybe she has something that could help with your memory loss as well."

Ari nodded with a thankful smile as he gave her a small bow of his head, that being the only way he could think of thanking her.

She smiled knowing what he was trying to say, "You're welcome. It is selfish of me to say this, but I hope you plan on staying with a while. I think its good for Iggy to have someone to chat with. Someone who's on the same level with him." She spoke a bit softer as she kept her eyes on her working shipmates, "He's been with us for a while now, and I'd like to think he's grown to trust Daric and me as at least friends, if not family, but I also understand that it's hard to approach us, we are his superiors, it's hard for him to relax sometimes. You though, you are just a regular, temporary crew member. Someone he can open up too."

You can say that again.

Jane rolled up her sleeve and revealed her brand mark. "Daric said that you and Iggy were having a tough to swallow conversation, about this?" it was identical to Iggy's, the only difference was hers had healed well and faded, but there were deep scars throughout her arm. "I cut my arm a few times trying to hide the brand, until I came to understand that I didn't have to be ashamed of my battle scars." She hooked her thumbs in her trousers and continued to talk, "Iggy and I share this brand, but I was in that life for such a short amount of time in comparison to him. I can't imagine the horrors he had to face, even more so being a young male in that world. The daily struggle to push on. My crew," She looked out towards the sea as her expression changed to deep contemplation, "they will never understand Iggy. Most of them look at him and see a joke." She swallowed hard thinking about it, "A man being forced to do all those things is humorous to them. It makes me furious; I've dealt with people judging me for this brand. Thinking they can take advantage of my past but, I am still just a girl to them, they can forgive my past. They can admire the fact that I fought and killed to escape that life. I was only in that world for a little more then a year. I had a family before that life, I had people who loved me, a mother, a father and a sister. I knew what freedom was. I knew what had been taken away from me. Iggy never knew anything else but that pain and torment. It's ridiculous that some members of my crew see Iggy as this weakling, but he's probably the strongest person on this ship today, including myself." The Captain stopped for a second looking out to sea, "He's grown so much from who he was the day we met him, but he still has so far to go, maybe you can help him get where he needs to be."

She turned to Ari who nodded with a weak, and sad smile.

She lightened the mood, patting Ari hard on the back pulling him into her. She placed her arm over his shoulder leading him back up the steps towards the helm, her tone changing on the flip of a coin, "Well, Ari, my strange, stranger friend. I sincerely and officially welcome you to the crew of the Shadow's Blade." She smiled excitedly as Ari smiled and nodded. "We need to find you a new way to communicate, the nodding will get tiresome." She laughed as they reached Daric once again. She released Ari and took her position at the helm.

The Captain traced her fingers against the warn wood of the helm before grabbing a strong hold, "We will need to find some official jobs for Ari. He is planning on staying aboard with us for a while more."

Daric nodded with a subtle smile threatened to appear on the corner of his mouth, "Good t' hear ye be wantin' t' stay wit' us." Ari smiled with a nod, "Why don't we leave 'im in Iggy's trustin' hands? He's done wonders keepin' 'im out o' trouble so far, 'n he could always use t' help. He can teach Ari th' ways o' th' ship."

The Captain thought about it for a good minute before nodding as she turned towards Ari, "You good being a cabin boy? It's a lot of hard work,"

Ari nodded, *it would possibly be the only place I could be useful.* And even that was debatable.

The sun was at its highest point and the port was in sight. Ari had been standing behind Daric and the

Captain, studying the crew as they worked in sync with one another. He felt lost and out of place. Everyone had a purpose, while he was just in the way.

Captain turned her head and smiled at Ari, "Can you go wake, Iggy?" She gave Daric the wheel and walked down the stairs calling out to her crew, "All hands-on deck! Prepare her for dropping anchor, land ahead, lads!"

"Aye, aye Captain!" Her crew called back as she watched them work, jumping in to assist where needed.

Ari slipped behind her and made his way down the hall to Iggy's cabin. He stopped at the door and knocked softly as he wanted for a response. Silence. He knocked again, this time a little louder, still silence, his heart pounded, *Iggy?!* Ari opened the door and peeked his head through.

Iggy was sitting up on the corner of his hammock, rubbing his bruised elbow while he tucked it in, resting on his lap. He was mostly nude as all he wore currently were beige undershorts, his hair wasn't up in his usual bandana as it hung limply covering his eyes. Iggy looked up and beckoned Ari into the room, "Close the door behind you, please."

Ari found his eyes focused on the dark purple and

green bruises that enveloped his throat and elbow. Iggy smiled weakly as he brushed his hair back with his fingers, "I knew it couldn't have been Daric or anyone else coming to wake me, you are the only person on his ship that feather-footed."

With an inaudible sigh, Ari placed his hand over his own throat and elbow.

Iggy looked down at his bruises and smiled knowing the obvious question he was asking, "It actually doesn't hurt that bad, anymore." He could see Ari's disbelief as he crossed his fingers and held them up, "Promise."

Ari didn't accept his answer, he tried to look away.

Iggy began to dress himself, starting with his wrist guards. He tied them, pulling them tight before throwing on a pair of dark coloured pants, a loose dirt coloured blouse before retying his bandana's around his neck, hiding the bruises with finesse, this time even as Ari was looking for them, he couldn't tell he was hiding anything.

Iggy pulled on his boots as Ari went to turn around and leave the room. Only to have Iggy grab him by the arm, turning him around to face him with a sincere smile, but Iggy didn't make eye contact as he looked at the floor, "I know I didn't seem to appreciate what you tried to do for me last night, but

I did, so thank you for trying to stand up for me, even if it makes you stupid for doing so." He smiled, finally looking up.

Ari smiled uneasily. *It was what I should have done the night before.*

"Next time," Iggy stepped in front of Ari, "let me handle things. No reason for the two of us to get banged around for nothing." He punched Ari in the shoulder weakly.

As much as the dark tone of their conversation was still kicking around, Iggy was back to his normal cheery self as if nothing had happened. It made Ari more depressed, and guilt ridden. Questioning if Iggy was always just hiding his real pain behind his smiles? Were all his smiles faked?

Iggy could see the seriousness behind Ari's eyes as he messed up his hair trying to brighten his mood, "Come on, all hands-on deck."

Ari grabbed Iggy's arm as he tried to head down the hall, their eyes met and they both froze for a minute. Iggy softened to a more realistic smile, taking Ari's hand in his, "I really am okay."

Finally accepting that he nodded, following slightly behind Iggy.

They docked and all but three stepped off the

Shadow's Blade heading into the Pirate town of Orvos.

Iggy and Ari stood together just at the end of the dock as they waited for Daric to finish business with dockworker. The Captain had already disappeared into the crowd of towns folk, along with the rest of her crew when Daric finally caught up to the two.

He seemed annoyed as he spoke with a grumble, "Captain ordered shore leave, so, I suggest that we use our time wisely 'n natter t' some locals, maybe someone be missin' ye around here?"

Ari looked at Iggy who straighten his back and smiled, "That's a great idea, I want to look for something in the market anyways."

Daric and Ari both shared a curious glace at each other as Daric asked seeing the stiffness in Iggy's arm, "How's yer arm? Still, don't wants me t' look at it fer ye?"

"Good as new," Iggy lied convincingly as he stretched it out to prove his lie with a smile.

Daric nodded and turned around walking ahead, he didn't bother keeping a good eye on the two of them as he was confident that they were following close enough.

Iggy walked with his arms crossed over his chest. That way he could keep his elbow bend with presser against it, without drawing attention to Daric that it was bothering him, but Ari knew. Guilt buzzed through his head. *This would be the perfect time to do something. I could show Daric and Iggy wouldn't be able to do or say anything to stop me.* But sadly no, he turned his gaze away from Iggy, keeping his head down as he followed closely behind Daric.

Iggy saw his reaction and placed his arm over Ari's shoulder, giving him another reassuring, innocent smile while they walked together. Ari tried to keep his sombre mood, but it was nearly impossible as Iggy pushed him around playfully.

The town market was hectic and confusing for poor Ari. He held on tightly to Iggy's good arm, so he didn't get lost in the mass amount of strange people going about their daily business. Something seemed off with him. Ari hadn't felt like this before as a throbbing pain began to build in the corner of his forehead. He placed his hand over it, trying to focus with dizzying eyes. All their voices melted into one inaudible conversation as Iggy and Daric wondered around asking vendors questions. Pointing to Ari who was now standing alone, circling as he studied the peoples around him. He managed to smile as one lady looked between Daric and Iggy's shoulder before shaking her head no. Ari watched the two pirates thank the lady for her time before turning around and walking back towards Ari.

Iggy and Daric studied Ari. Iggy reaching out and placing his hand on his friend's shoulder. Ari followed Iggy's lips as his words didn't make it to Ari's ears, *are you okay?*

Ari nodded and placed his hand back to his side with a smile, but Ari didn't have the art of deception as Iggy did.

Daric and Iggy looked at each other and continued their questioning, but now keeping a closer eye on him. They continued, making their way throughout the town, they had been extremely unsuccessful in finding any information on Ari's real identity, which was expected, but still a hard pill to swallow.

Nearly deflated, Iggy suddenly perked up and rushed away from the group without a word as he stopped at a stall.

Daric grumbled, he and Ari followed Iggy's lead. Leather bound books laid neatly placed on a wooden table, as a tall elven woman watched as Iggy's eye caught a dark red, stained book with elven script carved into the cover. A soft, reminiscent smile formed on his face as he opened it and scrolled through the thick, blank pages. The subtle musty dirt smell of fresh paper filled his nose.

The elven women, with long tanned features, smiled as her emerald eyes sparkled, "It's ancient elvish, the translation into common would be-"

"Life," Iggy answered closing the book as he looked up at the woman with a smile, "It's translated into life."

Seer shock filled her face as she managed to break back into a smile with a nod, "Very good, sir."

"I'll take it, this as well." He said as he grabbed a charcoal quill made out of the tailfeather of a bluebird as he dropped some coin on the table, she thanked him with a small nod of her head.

Iggy turned around rejuvenated with excitement as he offered Ari the book with a smile. "For when you have a little more than a yes or no to say."

Ari took the book in both hands and smiled as he ran his fingers over the engraving, *life.*

"You are welcome!" he said loudly, he turned around not waiting for Ari to actually make an attempt to think of a thank you for the gift, "Now, let's actually enjoy our shore leave. No more questions, no more disappointing answers to our questions!"

"Shore leave be ne'er fun," Daric replied cynically.

Iggy made a face sticking his tongue out, "That's because you are old and grumpy," Iggy winked as Ari attempted to laugh.

Daric scolded the two, as they fought hard to hold back their smiled, until Daric finally broke and smiled at the fool, "Aye, I may be grumpy, but ole! Ne'er, I 'ave plenty o' years left in these bones."

Iggy placed his hand on his old friend's shoulder before stepping out into the crowd with a smile plastered to him, "Aye, of course, you will probably out live all of us."

Daric grumbled again as he tried to hide his smile as he and Ari caught up with Iggy.

Jane adjusted her hat, tossing her hair behind her as she strutted through the streets of Orvos, confident, head held high, and with every strong step, her cleavage threatened to topple out of her blouse. On purpose of course. She enjoyed the onlookers; she wanted to watch and laugh as men and straight women turned their heads in awe and in a sinner's desire. She would wink and bit her thin lips as women, shamed as they fanned themselves, batting their lashes at the strikingly beautiful, strong woman. Jane was good at playing the role of a tease.

But she had no time to actually fraternize with the beautiful ladies, as she had her own lovely lady to seduce.

Lilianna Tremont; the owner of the herbalist shop, located just slightly out of the main market area. It was a small stone cabin, ivy wines and flowers encased the walls, and snuck into each and every crack, the entire area around the house was an herb garden which she allowed to grow mostly wild.

Jane stepped up to the large cheer oak door, her knuckles didn't even have a chance to touch the door as it swung open.

Lilianna smiled lustfully, looking Jane up and down. She had a snow-white complexion, large cloudy grey eyes, and her pointed pierced ears stuck out in front of her tight ponytail, her silver hair even being tied in a high pony trailed down to her mid-back. She was dressed in a sleek, green dress, her stomach nearly completely revealed. "Oh, why Captain. What a surprise to see you," She winked, as she leaned in, "Come in,"

"Lillianna, you know better then to call me Captain," She winked, stepping inside placing her hand against the woman's cheek, teasing to kiss her lips only to pull away at the last second.

"Oh, right," she sighed, "No bedroom talk before business." She closed the door behind Jane. "So, did you find anything on the stores, like I said?"

Jane sat down at a small table with a thick purple

cloth draped over it and a large ivory coloured crystal ball stood on a golden vined stand. "We found a man."

Lilianna's face wrinkled in confusion as she finished lighting a few incents before sitting down across from Jane at the small table, "A man?" She twirled her finger over the top of her crystal, "When I sent you there, I was sure it was a something you were looking for, not a someone." The Crystal smoked black as a white form appeared walking through the darkness. It was now clearly a man to Lilianna's eyes, "You found what you were supposed too." She seemed puzzled as she scratched the side of her face. "He claims to have no memory, and he is a mute."

Lilianna shook her head, still puzzled, barely realizing Jane had spoken, "Strange." She breathed as she focused, placing both hands on the crystal, "Your stranger has nothing, no threads of time to tell me his story. I've never seen this before, there must be some dark magic's blocking his past from my view. Maybe a curse blocking his memories?" She stood up and tore through a box coming back to the table with a bundle of herbs and a cast iron plate, she hit it ablaze and studied the smoke as Jane watched her in silence, "Stories," She whispered, zoning out Jane who stared curiously. "He has so many stories locked away, yet neither I nor he can access them." She zoned back in, smiling at Jane, "This stranger, he is the key to a great adventure, I feel it, even if I can't see it." Lilianna scratched her chin. Standing up, she walked over to Jane, sitting down on the confused woman's lap, pressing a kiss to her lips. She removed Jane's hat only to brush the tangled hair from Jane's face. "Promise me you will tell me all about this great adventure when it has been completed?" Jane nodding closing her eyes and coming back in for another kiss, but Lilianna had already stood back up as a dizziness washed over her. Once she recovered, she rushed over to one of her dressers and began rummaging through bottles and herbs. "Your Stranger will have a few terrible days ahead of him after taking these. Get him to drink this," Handing her a large green bottle, "Twice a day, and this before he falls asleep. It will likely be a rollercoaster of symptoms, vomiting, strange recurring dreams, pains, body aches are all normal, just let him rest for the first few days as his body readjusts. Tell him he will live and to push through the discomfort." She pulled Jane from her seat kissing her once again, "But you need to leave. Your adventure has already begun as Daric and Iggy need some help with your Stranger."

Jane pulled Lilianna into her as she pressed a passionate kiss to her lips, their mouths parted as they tongues' twirled around their mouths.

Lilianna pushed her away, turning her around and forcing Jane towards the door, "You will find them at the old pier, go, quickly now my love!"

Jane stood now outside the door with a pout, "That's all I get?"

Lilianna smiled sadly and kissed her one last time, "I am sorry dear, but you need to go help your family."

Jane smiled with a sign, "Thank you, I adore your face. May I see you later?"

Lilianna smiled, "You will not leave their side once you find your friends. I know they mean more to you than a little fun with me." She winked.

Jane nodded and turned away following Lilianna's instructions.

There was a strange chill that took the breath from Ari, he was frozen. He tried to reach his hand out for Iggy and Daric, but they were just out of reach, and as if in a trance he walked away from them. He didn't even feel himself moving his legs, he was just gliding. Away from the crowd of people and away from his friends. The voices, the noise that had been ringing in his head finally began to dull as now a single voice appeared in Ari's head. A song. A child's good night lullaby, a motherly voice singing and a fading, pounding noise.

Ari couldn't tell you which way he went, only that he found himself at a small dock, and sitting over the edge sat a woman, alone. Holding something, cradled, wrapped tightly in her arms. Now the singing wasn't just in Ari's head. He couldn't help but approach the weeping woman.

Now he looked down at the bundle in her arms as it was revealed to be a small, baby, wrapped in an old wool blanket. The woman didn't stop singing, she didn't even register Ari's presence as she kissed her child's forehead, tears streaming down her face. The beating sound slowed and slowed. Boom... one, two, three. Boom, one, two, three, four, five. Boom, one, two, three, four, five, six, seven, eight, boom. The beating stopped.

Ari still tranced and having no control over his actions knelt down beside the woman. She finally turned to face him, staring blankly through him, as if he was a ghost of a person, rather then a physical form next to her. Ari placed his hand on the baby's forehead, *rest now little one, a new world awaits you.*

"Ari!" Iggy yelled, as him and Daric caught up.

Jane could be seen walking down the way as she

waved towards them, confused on what was going on.

The air changed again, whistling loudly in Ari's ears. He turned away from the grieving mother, out of his trance he stepped towards them, his legs grew weak and his body swayed. Forcing him down to his knees, the ringing came back stronger than before. Ari placed his hands over his ears, trying to block out the sound, only for his eyes to roll to the back of his head, he blacked out. Ari's head hit the wooden deck hard as Daric, Iggy and Jane all raced to his side.

Chapter 6

When Ari woke it nearing dark. He was light headed
and confused about where he was as he looked
around, realizing that he was back on the ship.
Daric, Iggy and the Captain were all sitting around
him, focused on him. Daric and the Captain's arms
were crossed over their chests.

Iggy spoke leaning in, his concern was written on
the wrinkles in his forehead and the black bags
around his eyes. "Are you okay? What happened? You
just disappeared on us!"

Ari pulled himself to a seated position as he placed
his hand on his throbbing forehead, the spot his head
hit the ground. The ache from the impact had
replaced that strange pounding, it was all he could
remember what happened.

Iggy placed the leather-bound book and the quill on
Ari's lap. The three of them were looking for answers
from Ari, but he couldn't even begin to wrap his head
around what happened. "There was a beating, a

pounding in my head, but I think I'm okay." He wrote as he tried to find more pieces to the puzzle, but his memory was foggy.

Daric spoke, "Ye be lucky someone in th' square saw which way ye went. That poor lass jus' lost her sprog, she didn' needs t' be concerned wit' a stranger passin' out at her feet as well."

The baby died? He thought to himself, suddenly he remembered speaking to the child, *why did I do that? Why did I say that...* Ari wondered if he should tell them what he now remembered, but decided against it. He wasn't sure what really happened. He knew that Iggy, Daric and the Captain wouldn't be able to figure the mystery out either.

The Captain uncrossed her arms and grabbed something from behind her, pushing Iggy out of her way and taking a seat next to Ari, she gave him a sweet smile and stuffed an unknown item in his mouth. Shocked as their eyes met, her stern voiced ordered, "Swallow," he did as his Captain ordered and swallowed the strange, bitter, grainy herb mixture. Her toughness melted away slightly as she warmly placed the back of her hand on Ari's forehead, checking his temperature, "Lilianna, my beautiful fate whisperer, you made me run out on, said this and this," putting out another bottle from behind her, "Should help with your memory and your voice. She said it will suck, but you will live." She inspected the pale Ari, "Maybe I should have gotten something for your fainting spells." She said with only a hint of sarcasm. She smiled as Ari struggled to keep down as the aftertaste stuck to his tongue. "Are you sure you are okay?" There was genuine concern in her voice, "Are you telling me you made me miss out on the company of my lady friend for nothing?" She fought her emotions with her sarcasm as she stood tall and waited for a reply.

Ari smiled and nodded, she glared down at him, and he gave her another small nod to force the fact that he was alright.

The Captain pressed her lips together and turned away, her heels clicked loudly against the floor with every step. She sighed angerly, "I have a ship to run! I don't have time for this, Daric, Iggy he is your problem now." She tossed her arms in the air and disappeared even before Daric and Iggy could respond to her.

The two of them didn't turn their gaze from Ari, he grew more uncomfortable, as he wrote, *I'm alright.* In large letters hoping to get the point across.

Daric grumbled leaning back in his seat, "Somethin' be off about ye, somethin' I can nah put me finger on, jus' yet."

You and me both. Ari nodded and laid back down in his cot, his hands covering his eyes. His head continued to throb and the bitter taste still overwhelmed his palate.

Iggy leaned his head against the wall, "Another weird thing about all of that, that woman. She just walked past you like you weren't even there."

Daric sighed, "She jus' held her sprog as he took its last breath. She was grievin'. 'til ye lose a sprog ye will ne'er know that pain." Iggy didn't rebut, as Daric shifted uneasily, rolling his eyes restlessly, "I 'ave better thin's t' do than babysit th' two o' ye! But bound by th' Captain's orders, I be."

Ari quickly wrote, turning the paper over, "My apologises."

Daric sighed and fought back the urge to grumble again as Iggy chuckled, "Ye best be sorry."

There was a smile on Ari's face, but as he suddenly shot up as there was a rumbling pain in his stomach, he heaved over the side of the bed as Iggy placed his hand on Ari's back and Daric kicked a bucket out in front of him, right as Ari proceeded to vomit.

Iggy looked away as he fought his own urge at the sound, while Daric leaned back, tipping his hat down over his face. "Th' gypsy's potions 'ave that effect on most scallywags, jus' wait fer later when ye take her memory mixture."

Ari glared up from the bucket, Daric didn't take notice as Ari bent back down continuing to throw up. Daric finally reached his limit as he stood up with his hands out, "Once he stops emptyin' his stomach give 'im this, 'n both o' ye get some sleep."

Ari gagged again, there hadn't been anything in his stomach for a few hours now. His face was pale, and he was coated in a thick sweat.

Iggy rubbed his back and looked up at Daric taking the bottle, "Should I stay with him tonight?"

"Aye, that may be best. Needs me t' brin' ye anythin' from yer cabin?"

"Nah, I'll grab stuff later."

Daric nodded and left the room, Ari dry heaved again as spit drooled from his lips.

Iggy continued to rub Ari's back as he spoke, hoping to distract him from the discomfort, "I'm surprised that Daric managed to sit here all day like that. I swear he doesn't even sleep that long because staying still drives him insane."

Ari tried to put a smile on his face, but he couldn't. He took a deep breath, before running his fingers through his sweat, oiled hair. He rolled down on the cot and pulled the blankets to his face, waiting as another wave of dizziness took over.

"Maybe take a swing of this, and try to sleep this off?"

Ari wanted to protest but another wave of dizziness washed over him as he pulled his knees to his chest knowing he had nothing possibly left to vomit.

Iggy took a seat across from Ari and offered the bottle again, "Come on,"

Ari glared but took the bottle, pressing it to his lips as he hesitantly took a mouthful of the oddly, thick liquid.

"Don't vomit," Iggy ordered as Ari's face told him all he needed to know about the taste.

His eyes and nose scrunched, his lips pressed together as his body shook, the sour, bitter taste hitting the back of this throat. He swallowed hard passing the bottle back to Iggy who fought the urge to chuckle at him, before placing the cork back on the bottle and placing it in the chest he was sitting on. "Close your eyes and try to get some sleep." Iggy leaned back placing his arms behind his head watching over his friend.

Ari didn't have to be told twice as he pulled the blanket over his face and his eyes closed. He was asleep in seconds as Iggy turned down the oil in the lamp and got comfortable himself.

"Wake up, silly! It's not the time to be sleeping."
An older woman called out to Ari as her image
appeared from the darkness. Revealing an elegant
woman, with a warm, large smile that placed dimples
on her sun-kissed face. Her age showed behind the
wrinkles in her amber eyes, but it didn't deter from
her beauty. She reached her arm out and went to pull
Ari to his feet, "Come on, get up!" The woman
ordered as she lifted him off the warm, inviting grass
which he had been laying in. She cocked her head and
placed her finger on her lip tapping it a few times, "Is
something wrong? You are being quiet, even for your
usual self? Did something happen?"

Ari went to reply, but as out of the dream world, he
was unable to conjure up any words.
"I suppose it's a blessing from the gods!" She winked
with a playful, cute giggle as she entwined her hand
with his. She turned away, pulling him along behind
her as her long black hair, tossed softly in the wind.
She was in a pure white dress, the back of her dress
was slit wide, revealing the subtle muscle tones of
her shoulder blades and spine. The hem of the dress
hung just before her ankles, revealing her bare feet
and a small gold chain.

Ari looked down at himself he was only wearing

dark coloured trousers and a cloak. His feet were also bare and sunk into the grass. This dream felt so real, he could feel the grass in between his toes with every step, he could feel the wind kissing his face, he could feel the warmth emitting from the woman's touch. Who was this woman? He wondered as she led him through the large grass field, climbing up a small hill. The woman spoke turning her head to face him with a smile still glued to her face, "Don't worry, I won't tell Kitari that he was right about you. He said that I'd find you sleeping the day away, again, and you know how much your brother likes to be right." She giggled taking both of Ari's hands and bringing them to her chest, excitement filled her face, "Close your eyes, I have something beautiful to show you!"

He obeyed her command as he closed her eyes and she led him over the hill. She stopped and wrapped her arms around his, and rested her head on his shoulder, "Open your eyes." Again, Ari did as he was told as he looked down the hill, where a small pack of wolves were ripping a boar to shreds. The creature's body was still convulsing. Confusion filled his face as he watched the blood-soaked dogs cheerfully ate.

She stepped in front of Ari, sadness and confusion twinkled in her eyes, "What's wrong?"

The world fell into darkness as Ari found himself stuck in a crowd of screaming villagers, he tried to force his way through only to be tossed around as he tried to rather in bearings. *Where did the woman go?* He was confused as he followed the smell of fire burning, he reached the front of the crowd. The woman in white was now tied to a stake, her hands bound above her head. She stood silently, not fighting or trying to escape.

The words the people were chanting didn't make sense in Ari's ears. They grew louder and louder, the more muffled they seemed. He placed his hands over his ears and went to step forward towards the woman, but the crowd sucked him back in. He reached out, but she was unreachable, a man with a torch came and set the woman ablaze. She didn't scream, she didn't cry, she just smiled, accepting her fate. Ari lost track of her, as he was again tossed back into the darkness.

Iggy had grown very tired, he got up from the spare cot he had been resting in and walked down towards his cabin to get a fresh change of clothes and some extra blankets before returning to Ari's side, but as he reached the last set of stairs right before his cabin, he found Gibson waiting for him.

Iggy took a deep breath and tried to just walk by the clearly annoyed man. Gibson grabbed him and pushed him into the wall, holding him tightly by the forearm. "I don't like him,"

Iggy refused to look at the man.

Gibson grabbed his chin and yanked it, forcing their eyes to meet, "If he be goin' t' become a problem fer our arraignment I might 'ave t' do somethin' drastic."

Iggy straightened and puffed himself up slightly, trying to take a calming breath before speaking, "Ari isn't a problem because this isn't an arraignment, it's never been an arraignment."

"I owns ye," Gibson grabbed Iggy's throat and held him against the wall.

"No one owns me." Iggy growled, pushing Gibson away.

Gibson went to grab Iggy to turn him around to face him, "I be nah done wit' ye," he barked, only for Iggy to turn around and punch him once in the face.

They both froze. Gibson placed his hand over where Iggy's fist connected with his jaw and smiled, "Ye wants t' play tough?"

Iggy took a step back, he tried to put his hands up to defend himself, but Gibson's right hook was too fast for him to react. The force knocked him off balance as he tumbled down the stairs. His face hitting the floor hard and his shoulder on his bad side twisted, dislocating from the socket. Iggy pushed himself up on his elbows with great struggle, the pain intensified, blood pooled from his nose.

Gibson walked down the steps and picked Iggy up by his hair dragging him into his cabin. "Take a few days t' reckon about wha' I said," throwing him back down to the floor he left him laying in a small pool of his own blood. Iggy just curled himself up and stayed there, to tired and defeated to pull himself up off the floor.

Ari woke finally from the darkness, shooting right up in his bed, his heart pounded hard, his breathing heavy. The name *Kitari,* and the woman's face was still so fresh in his mind, he reached for the lantern, still slightly burning next to him. He gave more oil to the flame. Though to his surprise, he found himself alone. *Maybe Iggy got tired and decided his own cabin was best.* He thought to himself as he tried not to over think it. Grabbing the leather book, he first off wrote down the name, before sketching the strange, but beautiful, burning woman's face. There was something, so familiar about her, but he couldn't place her, or the name she said to him. *Brother...* He thought to himself.

A few more hours went by and Iggy still hadn't returned as it started to now make Ari question if it was the right thing to suspect that he had just wondered off to his cabin. His sketch was now completed as he looked out the porthole and saw it was a clear, calm afternoon.

A knock came at the door as his nerves eased, only to have his stomach drop once again. Daric was the one who entered looking at some parchment with a perplexed expression glued to his face, "Iggy, Captain needs-" He stopped as he looked up and realised that Ari was sitting alone in his cot, "Where be Iggy?"

Concern filled Ari's face as he shrugged his shoulder and went to stand. Daric quickly came to his side and offering his support as the light headedness washed over him once again. "Take it easy, lad. Maybe Iggy decided t' go t' his cabin?" Daric even felt uneasy.

Daric waited to ensure that Ari was settled on his feet before releasing him and making a charge for the door as Ari tried to keep pace.

"Has Iggy been lyin' t' me about wha' really happened t' his arm? Or how bad his arm actually be?" Daric looked back and he continued forward, watching Ari's facial expressions closely.

Ari looked down and shrugged his shoulders. Daric could sense the shame as he stopped and turned around corning Ari against the wall. "Are ye hidin' somethin' from me?"

Ari held his breath and looked the man in the eye as he forced himself to shake his head no. He didn't want to lie, he wanted to tell Daric the truth with every bone in his body, but he couldn't.

Daric dropped his tough guy demeanor and turned back continuing down the hall swiftly, walking down the last staircase that lead towards Iggy's cabin.

His door was open, which was very out of character for him. Something instantly didn't feel right, Ari's stomach dropped as they approached.

Daric went to knock on the already open door, only to push into the room at the sight of Iggy collapsed on the floor, laying in a small pool of his own blood, an open wound above his eye, his nose and mouth covered in dry blood.

Daric dropped to his knees, placing two fingers on Iggy's neck before shaking his softly, placing Iggy's head on his lap, "Wake up, Iggy. Iggy!"

Ari was frozen at the door as Iggy's eyes fluttered open, it took him a long second to realise who was looking down at him as he jolted awake, jumping to his feet. He felt instant regret as Daric then had to catch him. Iggy's legs gave way, and even before that the excuses began to come out of Iggy's mouth, slightly jumbled, "I," He groaned, "Uh, fell down the steps," He blinked, "last night." He placed one hand on his face. His other arm hung limp, tore completely from its socket. "Guess, I was so tired. Hit a wave at a bad time and down I went." He tried to laugh as he saw Ari's stare, he adjusted his bandana's that were around his neck.

Daric moved Iggy's hand and inspected the wound above his eye, before moving Iggy's shirt off his shoulder and inspecting his arm. "Ye must 'ave been really tired, 'twas calm waters last night."

Iggy laughed uncomfortably as he played with his hair, "Ari took a while to fall asleep, and I was keeping a good eye on him." Iggy smiled at Ari, looking for his support in his lie, "Right?"

Daric turned to Ari who did as Iggy wished and nodded a yes.

The old pirate grumbled, "ye both sit down 'n don't move." Sorrow was hidden in his voice as he spoke again, "Can nah leave ye two fer a minute, without ye goin' 'n gettin' yourselves injured."

Iggy bit his lip and turned his head away from his friend, he couldn't look Daric in the eye as he continued to lie.

Daric approached and placed both hands on his dislocated shoulder, "'tis goin' t' hurt."

"I know." Iggy said as he ground his teeth.

Daric rolled his shoulder around, trying to locate the socket, as he popped it back into place, Iggy fought hard not to cry out.

"Stay here, I'll go get somethin' t' swab 'n stitch ye up."

Once Iggy and Ari were both seated on the cot, Daric left the room. They looked guilty as they sat side by side, unable to look at each other.

Ari nudged Iggy once he knew that Daric was far enough away for Iggy to feel comfortable speaking the truth.

Iggy placed his hand on his shoulder, looking down at his feet, "I was telling the truth," He tried to lie, but Ari tugged at the bandana as Iggy slapped him off, readjusting it quickly hiding the new set of bruises around his neck he turned his head looking at the wall, "Maybe why I fell was a lie, but it's fine, I dealt with the problem." He was lying again, he was in a lot of pain, as much as he was good at hiding it, Ari could now tell.

Ari sat closer to Iggy and placed his hand on the back of Iggy's good shoulder. Iggy turned to him and smiled as the two of them waited in silence for Daric to return.

Daric and the Captain decided it would be best for both Ari and Iggy for them to bunk together, meaning Ari now didn't have to sleep in the closet they called a cabin, as they could keep a closer eye on each other. With Ari's last fainting spell and still getting use to Lilianna's mixtures as well as Iggy's arm wrapped in a sling, they were both stripped of duties and ordered to rest till farther notice from the Captain.

With his hands on the helm, Jane sighed loudly resting her arms on Daric's shoulder watching her crew work the sails as the wind picked up. "Do you believe him?"

"Nah even th' slightest." Daric admitted sadly.

She rested the side of her head against his, "I thought he got over his hiding the truth from us, do you think it could be our stranger this time?"

"Nah," Daric said as he kept the ship straight.

Jane stood up and replaced Daric's old hat on her head, "I don't like being in the dark about stuff on my ship."

"I know, Captain. I'll keep a closer eye on Iggy, 'n me suspect."

"Are you going to tell me who you do suspect?"

Daric didn't answer.

"Even if it's an order from your Captain?"

Daric didn't have to answer, as she turned away from him leaning against the railing over looking the main deck. "We can nah force Iggy t' natter, 'n ye nor I can go around accusin' scallywags o' somethin' we can nah prove. Nah unless ye wants mayhem on board." Jane looked back and grumbled at Daric's logic, "'n if I told ye who I did suspect, ye'd run them off this ship afore th' first riddle was asked, wit' a pail o' fish guts t' call th' sharks t' attention."

She sighed, "Aye, that is true." She couldn't even pretend that Daric's words were untrue as she tied her hair back loosely. "Is this because he still doesn't trust us completely?" Jane asked sadly as she turned around facing Daric with her arms crossed over her chest.

"I reckon 'tis fear o' appearin' weak,"

Jane laughed bitterly.

"I reckon our stranger will be good fer Iggy's situation. They seemed t' connect easily, they 'ave this bond ye, nor I can compete wit'."

"Does Ari worry you?" She asked, Daric locked the helm in place as they hit clear open water, he walked up to her. She continued to speak without waiting for him to reply, "Something about him bothers me. Lilianna had no insight on him, he's a white shadow in time, she said. Someone with many stories to tell,"

"A storyteller wit' no voice? Now that be a real curse." Daric went to laugh but held his smile as he could see the seriousness in her face, she scrunched her forehead thinking.

Jane licked her lips before chewing on the corner, still lost thought, "Somethings just weird. Everyone has a past, everyone has a story, but he was a mystery. I don't like mysteries, I don't like not knowing everything that is going on, especially on my ship." Her anger built, she clawed at the railing.

Daric patted her on the shoulder, she settled down, the tension in her muscles, melting with his touch. "Take a deep breath, Captain." She listened, "I be usually th' cynic in this situation, but I reckon our mysterious Stranger Ari be a blessin'. Nah all mysteries are bad, Captain. Remember once upon a time ye were a mystery, as was I."

Jane rolled her eyes and scrunched her nose, "I am an open book, always have been."

Daric could hold back his laugh, "Sure, Captain, sure."

"Men are difficult!" Jane grumbled.

Chapter 7

Two more weeks aboard the ship and come and gone. Ari's nights were filled with strangely cryptic dreams and nightmares. Every morning when he woke, he would fill the pages of his book with these stories, hoping that they would hold some key, but so far it just made him confused and the potions from Lilianna still made him sick.

Iggy's arm was healing well, and there had been no sign of Gibson coming around to bother him, which made Ari sleep just a little sounder. He couldn't be sure if it was because Ari was now Iggy's roommate or the fact that Daric seemed to be keeping an uncomfortably close eye on the two of them. Whichever the reason, it made Ari happy. Even while Iggy continued to act as if nothing even happened that night.

Iggy placed his arm back in its sling as he rolled over in his cot, tossing his feet over as his bare feet hit the floor. He looked over at Ari who was just finishing up writing down his latest dream. "Do you think they are memories?"

Ari shook his head no, he wrote, "Too strange to be memories, but maybe they mean something."

Iggy looked over Ari's shoulder reading part way down the page, he cocked his head to the side, "You dreamt these?"

Ari nodded, Iggy leaned in more, Ari handed him the book as he scrolled through a few of the pages. Thinking, he paused staring at the words, "A woman in white, burning at a stake. A child in a crib immune to the flames? Kitari." Iggy flipped through another page, "Kitari is the name of the god of Fire. It's a popular name in Tasyrn, commonly given to the sons of military men in the Volcanic Spires' Kingdom. Maybe if you actually know a Kitari, maybe you are from Tasryn? Maybe as your dream suggested you have a brother named Katari?"

His thought process was sound, but he instantly began to question that, "I wonder if you just studied lore, because a few of these dreams remind me of old fables. The woman in white could be referring to the mother of gods. It was said that she was lured to her death by a magic wielding barbarian tribe, they burned her in a pyre in defiance to the gods." But Iggy just shrugged and handed the book back to Ari, dismissing his own arguments. "Or they could just be dreams. I have odd dreams now and then, it's why I sleep down here away from everyone else. I used to have crazy night terrors." His smile was once again overly cheerful for the conversation.

Though the two of them didn't have time to continue their line of questioning on the possible truths hidden behind the message of Ari's dream, they could hear a commotion on the main deck arising. A bell sounded. Ari turned towards Iggy not understanding what it meant. Iggy rushed towards the wooden truck at the foot of his cot, pulling out a sheathed cutlass, "We are being attacked."
Something hit the side of the ship hard as it sent Iggy flying into the wall and Ari to the floor.
Iggy quickly recovered and went to leave the room, Ari grabbed him by his injured arm. Iggy smiled and tore the fabric from his arm and rolled his shoulders, "I'm fine, I need to do my part to protect the ship, you stay here. Be safe." He rushed out the door and up the stairs, he was gone in seconds.

Ari wasn't sure what to do as he stood in front of the open door, *do I even know how to fight?* It was a question that he decided he was going to find out the hard way. He dug into the truck only to disappointingly find a slightly rusted short sword. He took it, unsheathed the blade and rushed up the stairs after his friend.

Standing in the doorway he stepped out onto the main deck. Ari was shocked and unsure what his move was here as everyone was in a frenzy. The unmarked pirates had already boarded the ship.

Iggy had found Daric in the furry of battle and was fighting alongside him, keeping each other's backs guarded against attack. Ari's eyes darted across the battlefield as the question alerted him, *where is the Captain?*

A corpse of an unknown pirate fell from above. Ari came out from under the threshold and spotted the Captain fighting off three pirates on her own, Gibson fought two just a few feet away from her. Ari had to decide to run, or to fight, so he rushed up the stairway towards the Captain.

Jane gripped her cutlass tightly as she kicked the closest pirate in the chest, knocking him off balance. She pounced on him, diving her blade deep into his chest. She tore the blade free of bone as blood sprayed up her arm and across her face, her eyes locked on Ari when he finally reached the top of the stairs and froze again. His sword was at his side as he stared at her and the pirates in confusion. She grumbled, still focusing on the battle before her, "Ari, it would be best if you stayed below decks. Can you even wield that?" The Captain asked as she blocked the next attack, their blades locking together. She turned away from him as her and the pirate's faces were inches from each other. She smiled and with her free hand reached down in her blouse, pulled out a dagger and stabbed it into the man's throat. He fell limp as she casually wiped the blood from her face, turning back to Ari, "There is no shame in staying out of a fight."

The next pirate dove at her, this time getting a little too close for her comfort, nearly landing a blow as she jumped back, growling at her new attacker. She charged him, forcing him off balance as Gibson snuck up from behind and slit the man's throat.

She turned back to Ari whose knuckles were turning white as he gripped the handle of his blade too tightly, with determination. He decided he wasn't going to back down while everyone else fought for this ship, he was going to fight alongside them. Jane knew it was a hopeless fight to convince him otherwise, she sighed scanning the enemies. "Hold your blade like this and go for the kill. Keep close to me, and if you find yourself in trouble fall back, agreed?" He nodded as she rushed a new pirate who had wandered up the stairs to meet them. Ari was close behind, following her lead, watching her move trying to get an understanding of the workings of his blade.

A pirate charged Ari as he held up his blade to block, he was knocked off his feet by the force of the blow. The man grinned with his broken yellow teeth, he stepped forward, confident in his kill as he hovered over him.

Ari froze once again; his sword was just out of reach. The pirate raised his sword, going to plummet it deep into Ari's chest, only for a blade to pierce through the pirates back. The man dropped his sword and looked down at the blood-soaked blade, watching while it was retracted from him. The man's corpse limped forward as Ari just barely rolled out of the way.

Victor grumbled under his breath as he offered Ari a hand, lifting him off the ground, "Watch yer back." Ari nodded grabbing his blade, he was going to be ready for it this time, he told himself as another pirate came to face him. Ari took the first move as he swung his sword hard at the enemy pirate. The man easy blocked the attack with his own sword. Their blades clashed, hard, Ari's blade rattled painfully in his hand, forcing him to drop it. Ari quickly stumbled back from the crooked grinned man, only then did Ari realized it was a mistake for him to jump into this fight, he didn't know the first thing about wielding a sword! *I'm very stupid.* He said to himself, eyes wide.

Ari knew he had to think of another plan, quickly as the pirate charged forward; he drove for the man's feet, knocking him down. The shocked pirate went face first into the railing, luckily for Ari he was knocked out cold.

Jane raised her sword above her head, her blade was soaked with another slain victim. "Board the enemy vessel! Show these pirates no mercy!"

Her crew cheered in victory! They had finished the last of the invading pirates.

Jane walked over to Ari and placed her hand on his shoulder as she tried to not laugh, "You did, well." She lied, "At least you stood up and defended the ship." Her voice was filled with mockery as she paused trying to think of the words to use, in an attempt to not be mean, "We will train you for next time, or I'll have you locked up downstairs." She winked as they both turned away.

The pirate grumbled as he awoke, stumbling to find his cutlass, he charged, his eyes locked on the Captain. Ari saw the man out of the corner of his eye, but he was unable to react in time. Jane on the other hand turned around, diving her blade into the soft flesh under his chin. Dropping finally dead. She sighed and cleaned her blade on the dead pirate's shirt, before turning back to Ari with a calm and enthusiastic smile. Her lips curled, and her eyes sparkled, "Let's board our enemies ship." She bolted down the stairs and rushed across the planks onto the enemy's ship. Ari tried to keep up, nearly slipped as he walked crossed the planks nervously.

Iggy and Daric grabbed him and pulled him in, to Ari's relief they both seemed unharmed as the only blood on them seemed to be the drying blood of their enemies.

Daric placed a firm hand on Ari's back, "Good t' see ye made it through yer first battle on th' Shadow's Blade unharmed."

"Not over yet," Iggy said with a smile.

Jane called out, "Bring me the Captain's head! Take everything of worth!"

Everyone cheered as they began to ransack the ship. Ari followed Daric and Iggy into the hull as they made their way down deeper into the ship.

Daric seemingly knew exactly where he wanted to go, as he made his way towards where he expected their armoury to be kept.

They reached the door to the armoury as Iggy grabbed Daric's arm, causing them all to stop as him and Daric smelt the air around them. Daric noted, "Black powder, shouldn't be anythin' t' worry about." With that Daric kicked the door in as the three of them piled into the large room.

The three of them were in the center of the room before they realized they weren't alone. The Captain of the ship came out of the shadow's a lit pipe in hand as Daric drew his blade.

The captain was a man even older than Daric, his beard once a long time ago was black. You could still see it peppered in the grey, his long hair, was thinned and greasy under his large feathered hat, red in colour, matching his thick doublet with gold trimmings. The man sat on a large locked chest, eyeing the three men.

Daric continued to step forward. Iggy motioned Ari to flank Daric's right, he took the left.

The Captain smiled and shook his head, "I would step back if I were ye." He placed his hands on one of the barrels which were piled around the Captain and the right side of the room, with small red writing it read, BLACK POWER. "Take another step 'n I shall blast ye 'n yer fellow crewmates t' pieces."

Daric and Iggy took a step back, but Ari swallowed hard, realizing he was too far in. He could reach his hand out and touch one of the barrels of powder. He wouldn't have a chance to run away from the blast before it was too late.

Daric didn't see even the slightest hint of a bluff in the man's eyes. He motioned both Iggy and Ari to take another step back as he did also, Ari sadly was still frozen.

The next thing that happened sealed the fate of the crew of the Shadow's Blade. Fellow crew members charged into the armoury as the Captain dropped his lit pipe into an open barrel of black power as it easily ignited into flames.

Daric dove towards Iggy, wrapping his arms around him and pulling him into him, and dropping to the floor. Iggy tried to reach out for Ari, calling out his name, because that was all he could do as barrel after barrel combusted. The room began to collapse in on itself, flames engulfed the room.

Lucky for the majority of the crew, including Daric and Iggy, most of the barrels of black power were empty, meaning a far less devastating explosion than the Captain had led them to believe.

Ari and the ill-fated Captain being the only two really unlucky ones. Ari was thrown though a large gaping hole of the ship as he was sucked under the waves. The force knocked the wind from his chest, he sunk into the cold waters.

Disoriented, Ari unintendedly took a breath. He choked on the salty water that filled his lungs, Ari reached out for the surface only to sink deeper into the dark depths. All he could manage was watch as the burning ship became darker and blurry the farther, he sunk, he was losing consciousness. His brain was losing its oxygen as a soft voice beckoned him. Ari's eyes slowly blinked close and as he opened them again a figure of a woman appeared in the sea in front of him. Her arms reaching out for him openly as she spoke, seductively. Her face was a blue as a drowned corpse, her eyes a chilling shade of purple clouded over, her ruby red lips pressed together in a strange smile, as her long-clawed finger nails reached out and dug into the skin of Ari's face. Her hair tangled around her head, she giggled twistedly as she spoke, leaning in to whisper in his ear. Her teeth brushed his earlobe. "Oh, there you are, I had feared that I had lost you." Her voice gargled as she swam around him wrapping her arms over and around his neck and shoulders. The corpse like woman's pretty face turned twisted, and monstrous. She screeched inhumanly, fury placing her boney hands around Ari's throat, shaking him, "I'm not done with you," A weight seemed to wrap around his chest, dragging him deeper into the unforgiving ocean. "I won't lose you again," The voice laughed as the last of Ari's air bubble from his mouth.

But something warm grabbed hold of Ari's wrist, as the corpse like woman of the sea screamed, "No, wait!" The weight around Ari's chest slowly lost its power as a hand was pulling him back towards the surface. The person dragging him to the surface struggled. The corpse like woman tried to grab hold of Ari's other hand, trying to drag him down, but the warmth of the person trying to save his life woke Ari enough to fight as the weight that was dragging him down and the woman from his mind disappeared. The lights of the burning ship and the side of the Shadow's Blade became more and more clear.

They broke the surface of the water as the person holding Ari's wrist gasped for air, coughing up water, pulling Ari into her as she treaded water waving to her crew to throw down the ropes towards them. Relief filled their faces, as they tossed the rope towards their Captain and the rescued Ari.

The Captain wrapped the rope around Ari first as she waved them to pull him from the water, she then swam to the side of her ship and climbed a rope ladder unassisted.

Ari hit the deck hard as the force knocked the

water from his lungs he coughed painfully, air finally filling his lungs once again. Still fuzzy, Ari looked around at the blurry figures, slowly they started to make sense, as Daric and Iggy looked down at him.

Daric's shirt had been shredded, and he was bleeding from shrapnel being blown at him, while Iggy looked completely unharmed, Daric had shielded him from the impact.

Iggy's eyes filled with relief, "Holy Mother Madea, you're okay."

He was just as shocked as Ari was, just as shocked as everyone else aboard the ship.

Ari rolled onto his side as he coughed up the remaining salt water as Daric patted Ari's back forcefully. Ari took a deep breath.

Daric spoke in disbelief, "Ye be unbelievably lucky, Ari. We found pieces o' th' Pirate Captain, yet ye seem relatively unharmed." Besides most of Ari's clothes being torn and a few small cuts here and there he was unharmed, nothing even hurt.

Daric groaned, struggling to stand up straight. Ari pulled himself to a seated position, the Captain walked towards them twisting her hair, straining it. "You are like carrying an anchor," She rolled her shoulders, there was a subtle lingering ache from straining herself, "You okay?"

Ari wasn't entirely sure, but he nodded anyways as his face was still drained of colour. He tried to listen to everyone talk, but he was lost in his own mind. *How did I survive that? Who was that woman... Was it my mind playing tricks on me, or something else?* Ari recognized the woman's voice who had called to him, but he couldn't place a who or why. Ari knew that the person who the voice belonged to meant something to him. He could feel it in his heart, and he knew that she was going to be the key to his past, the question was, does he want to find who this mysterious voice belonged too?

Iggy spoke noticing that Ari was blanking out of focus, "Maybe you should go lay down?"

Ari broke from his trance as Jane offered him her hand, "Aye, go rest." He took it as she then turned him around pushing him in the right direction before barking to the rest of her crew, "I want this ship spotless and ready to sail, you hear! If I even find a single bloodstain no one is getting shore leave at the next port!"

"Aye, aye Captain!" her crew called out as they rushed off to work.

Daric shifted uneasily as he went to assist in the cleaning when Jane took his arm softly trying to avoid his lacerations.

"You need to sit and rest yourself, but we need to talk in private."

That was all that needed to be said. She turned on her heels and clicked her way inside the ship to her quarters, Daric followed, aching in silence.

Once inside her cabin, she closed the door behind Daric, locking it as she pushed him down in a seat as she removed the remains of his shirt, inspecting his back. She began to pick the large splinters from his skin, wiping the blood while she worked.

Jane took off her hat placing it down on her desk, "There is more to our stranger than I think we realize. Maybe even more than he realizes himself."

"Aye, I dunno how someone could 'ave survived that explosion unharmed like that," Daric grunted as she pulled another large splinter from his back.

She sighed grabbing her cloth and soaking it with strong liquor before pressing it against his skin, "So, what do we do about this? Do you suspect that he knows more than he is telling us?"

Daric leaned forward, resting his elbows on his knees and his chin on his folded hands. His mind wandered off. He tried to pinpoint the moments where Ari's story seemed inconsistent, where he could be keeping stuff from him, but nothing came.

"If he does know more then he be leadin' us t' believe, he's a pretty good liar. Do ye reckon Iggy might know more?"

"If anyone on the ship was going to know more about our friend it would be him. We need to find out more about Ari's past, there is something about him," She finished bandaging Daric's wounds before sitting on the corner of her desk. She continued to think it over in silence.

Daric stood up and eyed the woman, "Are ye afeared o' 'im?"

Jane raised her brow as if Daric had just slapped her across the face, "I am not afraid of a man who can barely wield a blade."

"Me apologies, Captain." As he raised his hands in defence, trying to hide his smirk.

"Ari, is just more and more mysteries piled in one petite, handsome package. Like I said there is something about him. I don't know if we should be afraid, but there is something to learn about him. Now if Ari knows about it or not, is the question."

Daric nodded as he rolled his aching shoulders, his back starting to seize up on him, he silently cursed old age. "I'll riddle Iggy, see if he has noticed anythin' that we haven't."

Jane nodded, "Thank you Daric, keep this quiet. I

don't need the rest of the crew suspecting that there might be something off with our friend."

"Might be a wee late fer that Captain, I've heard tales comin' around th' ship that Ari maybe a Demon, a Siren or a Witch. I cannot confirm who started these, but ye 'n I can both assume 'twas Jorgen, as always."

She laughed, "A siren? Didn't know Siren's came in the male figure. We will approach Jorgen and address him about these rumors," with that she began unbuttoning her still soaked blouse, while Daric took that as his cue to leave.

Jane hung her wet clothes and stood in her cabin naked for a few moments as she thought, *what is my next move here? Is it safe to keep Ari aboard my ship?...* She didn't know the answers to her questions and that was what bothered her the most, the unknown.

Finally she shook her head clear and dressed herself, before going to check on her crews progress.

Ari sat on the cot in his and Iggy's room trying to process what was going on with him. He dried his hair and changed his clothes, the voice still rang so loudly in his ears, a voice; a familiar voice, but *it had to all be a hallucination, right?* He questioned. Maybe a piece of his memory had been jogged into his head? Maybe the ocean is a key to learning who he is? All this seemed ludicrous to Ari, but it was the only thing that triggered something familiar. The idea was comforting, but the voice scared him. Even if he didn't know why, or even realize it as of yet, Ari knew the woman who belonged to this voice wasn't someone he wanted to mess with, but at the same time, she was the key to everything he was. This was just a small part of the puzzle that is the mysterious stranger. A small, crucial part of the puzzle that would begin the rippling effect of answering all the questions that they seek and more that they can not yet comprehend.

Ari jotted down in his book the words that were now burned into his mind, *'Oh, there you are, I had feared that I had lost you. I won't lose you again.'* Ari closed his eyes, to rest them for just a moment, but his dreams swept him away from reality. Leaving his book open to all who wish to peer into Ari's mind.

A woman stood in the sand, her bare feet sinking into the sands as the waves washed over her ankles. Holding her dress up to her knees so the water dared not to soak her white cotton dress. The early morning wind howled through her dark, multicoloured hair that had been threaded into nots resembling tentacles from the sea. Her ears were decorated with black and white pearls hung by strings, her skin christened in the old marking of an ancient language lost to most, the sun warmed her glowing skin. As she looked out into the sea with dusty, clouded eyes, circled with dark black liner. A smile curled onto her delicate face as she whistled a song, so softly into the nothingness before her. "Oh, very soon, very soon we will be together again." Her voice as seductive as a siren calling to her pray, chilling to the bone. As she began to whistle once again, she walked deeper into the ocean, her dress floating on the surface as the ocean accepted her.

Chapter 8

Night finally fell, and the crew of the Shadow's Blade were exhausted. Jane and Daric took the midnight shift, they couldn't sleep even if they wanted too after the days' events, even though Daric needed the rest. They knew something different was in the air, they could feel it in their bones and somehow, they knew that troubling events were on their horizon, even though neither of them noted it aloud.

Luck of the sea was not on their side.

A strange bitter wind cut through the sails as The Captain shivered, loosely gripping wheel. She let the ocean guide her ship along its moody waves. Jane bundled her jacket tighter around her, watching the waves around them storm angrily, taking a deep breath and called out to her second, "Daric, I'd reef the sails. It looks like we have a bumpy night ahead of us."

"Aye Captain," He called out, but the wind was too

loud and his voice to quiet for the Captain to hear, but she knew by the tip of his hat that he understood and went to work.

Daric had reefed the last sail when he climbed up to the crow's-nest and stood there. Staring out into the blackness that was the ocean, there was a smell in the air, it blew hard against him. One hand on the rope while the other planted firmly on his hat he turned to the Captain who was also seeing what Daric was seeing. She locked the steering wheel in place and quickly swung around and rang the bell viciously, calling the crew to the deck, a storm was hitting the shadows blade this night.

Within minutes the entire crew was on deck and rushing to stations. Victor came and took the helm from The Captain as she rushed towards the viewing deck and barked orders to her crew; her eyes locked onto Iggy and Ari. "Batten down, we got a bad storm coming our way! Everyone man stations, I don't want to see any damage to my ship by the end of this night, ye hear me!"

"Aye, aye, Captain!" They voiced together loudly as they rushed to work.

"Iggy, Ari come here!" She barked, and the two rushed up the stairs. "Iggy, keep Ari close. Go down stairs batten down what you can in storage, be quick. Come back up and jump on where ever is needed, this will be a long night, and I can't have anyone slacking." She eyed Ari alone as the words left her mouth.

The thunder and lightning now stormed, Ari jumped slightly and looked to the skies.

Ari stood in awe as he watched the lightning clouds. There was something about this storm that made him want to remember, it was right there, he could feel it in the back of his brain, but all he knew for sure if he was very worried for the entire crew of the Shadow's Blade. He swallowed hard as he prayed to himself, that they'd make it through the night unharmed.

The Captain looked out at the angry sea, there was no turning back tonight they fought the sea and they were either to win or die trying. She didn't plan on losing her ship this night as she began to bark orders, taking a firm grip on the helm as she steered the Shadow's Blade through the storm.

Iggy took Ari by the hand, holding it tightly, and keeping him close as he led them down the halls, quickly. The ship hit a hard wave and the two stumbled, Ari pulled Iggy into him, keeping them steady as he hit the wall. Their eyes met, but Iggy pushed away and grabbed Ari's hand again, not wanting to slow. "We just have to get down to storage, strap down as much as we can, then head to the kitchen to do the same."

Rushing down the stairs to the storage room and Iggy began to work quickly and efficiently. Ari studied what Iggy was doing for a moment, analyzing what all he had to do before jumping in. Together they pushed the shelves up against the walls and strapped them down securely, moving the more fragile supplies to the other side of the room, securing them separate from everything else.

Once Iggy was satisfied with their work, he did one last check on the ropes and the two moved on to the kitchen to do the same, before returning to the main deck.

The crew were chaotic, or so that's how Ari saw it, where Iggy saw the calculation and the understanding of the storm. They read the erratic waves that dared to try to sink, the mighty ship that was the Shadow's Blade.

Iggy turned to Ari and began to tie a rope around his waist with a smile. He could see the confusion written on his face, "You've never faced a storm, at least that we know of, and you don't got your sea legs. Best to tether you to the mast, or we might lose you by mornings light, and I really don't want that." He smiled uneasily.

That did not comfort Ari as he nodded, allowing Iggy to lead him through the chaos. He tried to keep his footing as rain poured down heavily, blurring his sight. He now grabbed onto Iggy's arm for balance, Iggy tied the rope tightly to the mast. "If needed, you can easily slip out of your binds. Ari, you don't have to worry. This crew knows how to navigate through a storm, even one as terrifying as this one might be. Help where you can, and stay out of the way if ordered to do so, understood?"
Ari nodded as Iggy placed his hand on his friend's shoulder before rushing away to assist where he was needed.

The rest of the night was a blur for Ari; the crew passed him rushing around with purpose and intent. No one asked for Ari's help, no one even acknowledged him, it was like he turned into a ghost as the ship was tossed around the ocean waves. Which was for the best, every time he tried to step away from the mast, he was tossed around stumbling to his hands and knees. He couldn't maintain his footing even for a minute.

The Shadow's Blade was hit hard throughout the night, thrashed around like a rag doll in a small child's arms. This storm was like no other, there was no clearing in distance, there was no turning back. The moment the ship entered its grasp they were stuck until the storm wished them to be free, something otherworldly about it.

The Captain and two others now manned the helm as the winds picked up the ship, forcing her in another direction, the Captain groaned, "Keep her steady! This storm must break just beyond our sight, keep it up! We will not lose this night!"

Aye! Her crew called out, the sound of their voices breaking through the storm.

The morning was now in sight! The sun's hue dared to show itself in the distance, breaking through the thick dark clouds, as if a sign that their curse had been lifted, the storm evaporated from sight. The sea calmed once again. Uncomfortably calm.

Jane was confused on what she was seeing. She rushed to the stern of her ship, forgetting the torturous storm they had just faced, shaking her head in confusion. Climbing up the crows' nest, Daric offering his hand as he pulled her up alongside him. He was in just as much confusion, and awe as she.

"Daric,"

"Aye,"

"Is that what I think it is?"

"If Port Coraline be wha' ye reckon ye be seein', then aye, 'tis wha' ye be seein'.'"

She couldn't hide her disbelief, "That shouldn't be possible, we were at least two weeks away.

"I may 'ave miscalculated wit' me charts, or th' wind was more in our favour then we realized last night."

"I've never seen you that far off with charting, Daric. Whatever the cause, strange as it may be, it is a welcomed surprise after the beating we just took." She let out an angry, tired sigh as she leaned over the edge of the crow's-nest calling to her crew, "Get ready for dockin'."

They climbed down together; Daric started handling the crew, ordering Victor to take the helm as he steered her steadily towards port.

Captain stepped towards Iggy and Ari, as he freed himself from his security lines, "Iggy, I'm sorry to ask this but I will need an update on inventory. No real rush, I am predicting a few extra nights at Port to recover from the storm and the attack, hell I need a week to process all of what we've gone through." She exclaimed as she rubbed her hands over her face.

"Aye, Captain. With Ari's help, we can get it done in no time."

"Good, thank you, Iggy." She placed her hand on Iggy's shoulder, "I can always rely on you." Jane tipped her hat as she clicked off to inspect the damage to her ship.

Even though they were ready to dock before night fell, the crew of the Shadow's Blade took their well deserved and needed rest aboard, most had just fallen exhausted at their post rather than wasting the energy to crawl to their bunks.

That following morning Ari found himself curled up next to a box of old maps and logs, with a blanket draped over him. He yawned, his back cracking as he stretched his arms above his head. Rubbing the tiredness from his eyes and pulling himself to his feet. Ari walked around the storage room, looking for Iggy. To his surprise found himself alone. Assuming the innocence of the situation, he thought Iggy was smart enough to drag himself to their cabin before falling asleep, unlike Ari. With that he pushed the thought to the side and wondered over to the table, Iggy had finished their paperwork without him.

Ari sighed silently as he began to sweep up the broken supplies.

The door swung open and Daric thumped down the steps, "Mornin', Ari. Be Iggy about?"

Ari shook his head no as he walked over to the table grabbing the papers for the Captain and handing them to Daric.

"Prolly still asleep." He looked over the numbers and nodded, "Captain wants ye t' join her fer shore leave. She says she knows exactly where t' search fer answers, Captain be strangely optimistic about this stop."

Ari pulled some scribbled-on parchment from his trousers and with his coal pen wrote a single word, "Where?"

"We be in th' port o' Coraline. It's a true pirate port, its main export are stolen goods, strumpets, folktales 'n fish. When yer feet hit that dock, ye will smell all o' that, 'n more. In its full glory." There was a strange tone in Daric's voice, something that Ari had never heard from him before, he couldn't pinpoint the emotion, bitter seemed to almost fit. There was something more to this place than Daric was leading on.

Ari nodded as Daric handed him the inventory list back, "Take that t' th' Captain, she's waitin' on th' main deck. I'll go get Iggy 'n meet ye both up thar." Ari nodded, grabbing the list and following Daric out the room before parting in the hallway and heading towards the Captain.

Iggy didn't get any sleep that night and it showed on his pale face in the form of blue bags under his eyes. After Ari fell asleep, he finished the last of the paperwork, before placing a blanket over his friend and heading to their cabin, only to find his cabin wasn't empty. Gibson was waiting for him at the end of the hall, once again.

Now, he sat on the floor looking at a small shard of a mirror inspecting the inch thick bruise that wrapped cleanly around his throat, and the swollen cut lip, Gibson gave him after he tried to push the man off of him. Iggy placed his hand over his throat, he could still feel the leather belt strap tightening around it, remembering as he struggled to take a breath. Remembering as he tried to call out, beg him to stop, but he couldn't... He couldn't see it, but there was even a mark at the back of his neck, where the belt buckle had dug into him, cutting him.

Iggy tried to get past the image of Gibson pushing him down on the bed, forcing himself upon him. He shivered; he could still feel Gibson's hands all over him. Iggy tied two bandanas around his neck, carefully hiding the evidence of the assault, before tying his leather wrist guards looser than normal. Gibson had dug his nails so deeply into his wrists while holding Iggy's hands above his head. They still stung as if his nails were still embedded in his skin.

Iggy sat on the floor a while, looking at his reflection in that mirror, all he could see was the scared boy he had always been, nothing really had changed. As much as Daric and the Captain tried to drill it in his head over these years that he didn't deserve this abuse, that he could escape from it, he never believed it, as much as he led on with his happy smiles. He thought that even if Gibson was dealt with, that once again he'd find himself trapped in this situation, it was a vicious and terrifying cycle he couldn't escape. Maybe it was just the life he was born to live, he questioned as he combed his hair back with his fingers. Spiking it up just slightly before tying one last bandana around his forehead keeping his hair in place.

He placed the mirror in his supply chest and sat back up in his cot, he was numb to the world as he tried to think of an excuse for his swollen cut lip, wondering why he even bothered with lying at this point, did he really think Daric and everyone were that stupid? He wondered if anyone would care if he just told them the truth; Iggy knew deep down it was just the self-loathing talking, but at the time he took his own words to heart.

Footsteps approached; by the loud thump of the person's boot, Iggy knew who to expect even before they appeared in his doorway.

"Good morning, Daric," Iggy said with a weak smile as Daric stared at him.

Daric's eyes, of course, were glued to Iggy's swollen lip as he stepped forward reaching out to inspect it, "Wha' happened?"

Iggy pulled away, "I hit myself in the face with a box that I was trying to put back, last night." Iggy answered almost instantly.

Daric took a step back and asked, "Ye sure? Ye know ye can natter t' me.

"There isn't anything to talk about. What do you need?" Iggy snap back with an irritated tone.

Daric straightened and took a step back, turning away from him, "Captain, Ari 'n I are headed t' shore, she did request fer ye t' join us, but I be sure she will understand if ye aren't feelin' up fer th' trip."

"No, I'm good. Let's go."

"Needs me t' stitch that up afore we go?"

"No," He pushed past Daric, "The scar might make me look more like a Pirate," *and less like a prostitute.* Iggy managed a more believable smile as he headed up the hall.

Daric sauntered behind, he was wanting answers to

what was going on with Iggy, as well as some personal feelings were brewing in his mind, he struggled to seem unaffected by this own thoughts.

They reached the main deck as Jane was talking to Reefer, Echo and Jayson giving them some tasks while in the city, that's when Iggy realized where they had docked. It shook him from his mood, he turned around and concern for Daric filled his eyes, "Are we?"

He was cut off by Daric before he could finish his question, the older man knew what he was going to ask, "Aye, we be in Coraline." He refused to meet his gaze.

Iggy held his breath for a second as he now studied Daric, "Are you okay, Daric?"

"Remember thar be naught t' natter about," Daric shut down Iggy's questioning. It crushed Iggy as he now realized his mistake in words earlier. Daric walked towards Jane, "We be ready, Captain."

She turned with a smile, only for it to die as she saw Iggy's lip. She looked to Daric who gave her a low-key shake of his head, not to bother asking the obvious question.

The Captain was dressed to attract, as always, in a dark burgundy blouse, only mostly done up, and dark trousers, she clearly spent time on her hair as it's usual untamed mess was curled to perfection, framing her tan face perfectly. She smiled, "Okay, let's get going. We have daylight to burn." Turning away walking down the platform onto the dock of Coraline Port.

Daric followed second behind, Iggy just behind him while Ari stepped up next to Iggy.

Everyone saw the fat lip, Ari just wondered if Iggy was going to admit to the truth of how it happened. Even though Iggy hadn't told him an excuse for the lip yet, seeing just a peek of purple through the bandana's he knew well enough.

The four of them found themselves walking through a lively, yet smelly town. Tt was still early morning, but it seemed that everyone was already about. Ari struggled to keep up with Jane, Daric and Iggy through the never-ending crowd as he grew more and more distracted by sea of faces flashing before his eyes.

At one point Iggy took Ari's hand in his, with a soft smile, "It's a lot to take in,"
Ari nodded, paying slightly more attention to where everyone was going.

Finally, they reached a clearing big enough for the four of them to regroup.

Captain, of course, was the first to speak, directing it towards, "Every ship that sails around these islands stops here, there is a good chance you were once on a ship, so it's more than likely you've crossed through here. There is something inside me saying that this is where we are supposed to be. The Fates have led us here, somehow." The Captain could see Daric's disapproval, he wasn't one to believe in the hocus pocus of life, but she continued with a twisted smile, "I have a lady friend who lives here, she generally quite busy so I will go see her myself and see if we can fit you in tomorrow. After that, I have some repairs to attend to, so while I do that, you three can go inquire if anyone recognizes you, or knows a ship that would have passed by here around two months ago heading towards Orvos. Sound like a plan?"

Daric turned to Iggy and Ari, before answering for the two of them, "Aye, regroup back at th' ship tonight?"

She shook her head no, "Nah, I'm paying for lodging at the inn. When you are all finished meet there, the rest of the crew will be there harassing the women and drinking their weight in ale."

"Aye, Captain." Daric flashed a sly smile and winked towards the Captain as she was about to turn away, "Enjoy yer time wit' Miss Nightingale."

She flashed a wink before disappearing into the crowd.

Once the three of them could no longer see her burgundy blouse between the crowd Daric turned towards Iggy and Ari, crossing his arms over his chest. "Let's get t' work."

Chapter 9

Ari felt lost and out of place as he walked behind Daric and Iggy. His stomach turned, and he couldn't express or explain his discomfort. It was different from last time they were at port, but also that light headedness had returned, just not as strong.

Daric was also feeling lost as they made their way through the town, but for an entirely different reason. He knew this place like the back of his hand, even if it had been a very long time since he had wondered it so, freely. Everywhere he turned, he recognized someone, something. He realized that he had to put his own feelings aside and do his job. Something he was exceptional at.

Daric would walk up to fellow sailors, asking if they had news of missing persons, or of Captains looking for a replacement crew member, while Iggy dragged the already uncomfortable Ari around to talk with the locals, placing him awkwardly on silent display.

Everyone seemed to say roughly the same thing, "Sorry, yer friend doesn't rin' any bells."

It seemed hopeless, but Iggy wasn't ready to give up.

Ari and Iggy weren't sure if Daric was getting lucky with his line of questioning or if he was just catching up with some old mates, his conversations tended to be a lot longer than Iggy's.

Daric stepped up to three pirates who were sitting on some wooden rum barrels chatting away.

Before Daric even spoke up to the three one of the men; a shorter man, with a thinning dark coloured beard, fading eyes and a thick old tan that you couldn't be certain that it wasn't just caked on dirt, wearing old well-kept trousers and a dark blouse. "Daric ole scallywag, how are ye? Home fer a while?"

"All work, no fun, as always. How about ye lads? Still on th' Stray Cat?" Daric said uncomfortably.

The three men sitting before him; were Darek Jolken, Mendez Bradley and Raymond Shaw.

Darek spoke up again adjusting in his seat, "No, we retired. We jus' charter an ole fishin' boat now. Are ye still sailin' wit' that pretty beauty Captain?"

"Aye, Captain Jane Far'mel. She's th' best Captain I've had."

Mendez spoke up, he was a dark-skinned man, dressing in lighter colours, "I knew yer previous Captains, that doesn't say much." He chuckled bitterly.

Daric shifted uneasily again, "Aye, that be true." He crossed his arms over his chest, trying to keep himself seemingly unaffected by the thoughts filling his mind again, "As much as its great t' catch up, I be here on business. Has a ship come through here lookin' fer add a new hand t' thar crew? Or that anyone claimin' they lookin' fer a missin' person? A young lad, average height, dark hair, skinny?"

The three of them looked at each other, clearly trying to think back, which was harder for the old sailors.

Raymond finally spoke up, he was another tall man. Tanned, with light coloured hair and large light-coloured eyes. "Cant say I've seen a crew speakin' o' a missin' scallywag, but thar was a beauty here yesterday. Weird-lookin' beauty, cryin' how her brother was missin'."

"Be she here today?"

"Nah, shes a beauty ye can spot nigh-on half a league away. She has dark, coloured dreadlocks, pale skin. She showed up a few days ago."

"Oh, I remember her now," Mendez spoke up. "Any idea where she be stayin'?"

"No, didnt see her in th' inn at any point, maybe she has a matey jus' out o' town." Raymond finished, "She was here early in th' mornin', maybe if ye aren't lucky enough t' see her today, tomorrow may be in more yer favour."

Daric patted Raymond on the back, "Thank ye, heartie, that be a lot o' help."

"No worries heartie, 'ave ye been by t' th' beauty 'n sprogs grave yet?" Darek insensitively added.

Daric took a calming breath as he pushed back his emotions with the shake of his head.

"Well, ye should. We maintained it fer her, she was a good wee beauty. Maybe we shall catch up a bit afore ye weigh anchor."

"Aye, sounds good," was all Daric managed to say as he toughened his composer. He shook the emotion back to the darkness where he kept it locked away, walking to catch up with Iggy and Air to inform them of his promising lead.

They continued to make their way through the town, looking for the woman and continuing to ask more questions. Now adding the question if people had seen this strange woman around town. They reached the outskirts of town. Daric grew even more silent as they reached an old, should be condemned house. If anyone was living there, they hadn't been taking care of the place, the garden was all dead, the wooden door rotting away, the stone structure was riddled with holes and weeds running amuck. He placed his hands in his pocket and took in the sight, he could remember this home in it's prime, but not as well as he could imagine the last time he stepped through that door.

Iggy understood the sentiment as he took Ari by the arm and held them back a few feet away from Daric, letting him have his moment. Ari didn't understand what they were looking at but could understand that now wasn't the time to question anything as Iggy whispered with a smile, "I'll explain later."

There wasn't a smile on Iggy's face as Daric finally turned around, he shook his unease as he glared at Iggy and Ari, "Stop yer mopin', let's end our search fer now."

They nodded and headed towards the inn to meet up with the rest of the crew and the Captain. To little surprise the majority of the crew were already well into the alcohol as they staggered around the pub. Daric rolled his eyes as he pushed their way through the crowd, clearing a table at the back before sitting down.

Iggy looked over the sea of singing sailors and smiled as Jorgen stood atop a table leading a song about the ocean.

"Doesn't look like the Captain is back." Iggy noted.

Daric adjusted his hat and leaned back in his chair, "Miss Nightingale be known fer keepin' th' Captain occupied fer quite awhile."

The bar maid walked over with three empty mugs as she placed them down in front of the three new customers. She was a long, thin blonde girl, with big blue eyes that sparkled even in the poor, dim lighting. Wearing red lipstick along with a white blouse with short sleeves, a tightened black corset with a dark green ruffled skirt, that she tied up, revealing her long-toned legs and black shoes. "Whats yer poison fer th' night lads?"

"Ale fer th' table, Ma'am" Daric tipped his hat to her, as Iggy and Ari nodded politely.

The young woman smiled and turned away, only to return a moment later with a large jug, topping off the three of their mugs before setting it down on the table and attending to the rowdier customers.

The mood in the air at the table was still down as Daric stared down at the amber coloured liquid, still thinking to himself. Iggy pulled into his seat more resting his arms on the table. "Do you want to talk about it?"

"Remember we 'ave naught t' natter about. Maybe if we natter more truthfully about ycr lip, I'd be more inclined t' speak about what's on me mind."

That shut Iggy up as he drank quietly, Daric doing the same, a chill went through the three of them. Daric down his drink and dropped a few coins on the table, "I got somethin' t' do, I'll see ye two later."

"Okay," Iggy nodded looking down at his drink, unable to look at Daric walk away.

Jorgen strutted over mid-song as he placed his arm over Iggy and Ari's shoulders, "Ignatius, Stranger come, enjoy th' tale I be about t' tell."

Iggy was visibly uncomfortable to Jorgen's touch but agreed. Iggy and Ari filled their glasses before moving towards the bulk of the crowd.

Jorgen jumped up on the table at the center, ale in hand, raised above his head, he began to weave his tale.

He told them of the creation, the beginning that brought life and everything they know and love now. First there was Darkness, Huzoe; the nothingness for thousands of years it was just that, nothing but boredom arose and Huzoe wondered what could be, that first thought spawned a light, a small little star that he held in his black hands, a small piece of hope that grew and grew until she became Lula; light, hope.

Together they became the creation; everything was

born from their love, from their design. Mandela was the first born of Huzoe and Lula, she became the world we see and live on to this day. She became the grandmother of all life, and the mother of gods, she birthed the elements. Kitari, the god of fire, Toma the Goddess of Air and Kali the Goddess of water. Her three children wanted to make something beautiful for this world, something their own, as together they began to form the seeds of life, the first animals and living mortal creatures that would inhabit the world.

Mandela seeing these creatures walk for the first time knew they needed something else, so she created the Sun and the Moon. Tiki and Moki, but as she formed them and they came to life from the stars something, strange happened. Something she never expected and something that scared the other gods and goddesses, her other children. Because as Tiki and Moki formed, they looked down at something else. It was small, but there was something terrifyingly, powerful about it. Mandela scooped the small god in her hand as he stood in her palm, the other gods and goddess appeared around her, studying the near naked god who more resembled the mortals they were still creating than any god before. He stood there silent, with six thick threads wrapped around his wrists. Those threads were the threads of life; the gods lives. This creature was death and time itself and as everything was born and created, threads would form around this god, threads that told a story of every things' death, their lives. If you had a thread, it meant your existence was limited. It told the gods that they were not purely immortal.

Mandela accepted the unplanned god as her son, while the other gods took awhile to accept the oddity, it is unsure if they ever did accept him. It is said he lives in his own world, unchallenged by the laws of time that he himself created.

The Captain had sauntered in sometime around the end of Jorgen's story, taking a seat next to Iggy and Ari. Her blouse was buttoned incorrectly, untucked, her hair that was previously curled nicely for her visit with Miss Nightingale was tossed and tangled. Her morning lipstick was no more. She yawned as she took a drink from Iggy's cup, finally speaking up and making her presence known, "I always question the creation stories. Don't you think there is more to what was needed for mortals to come into existence?" She looked around the bar, "Where is Daric?"

Iggy turned around in his chair to address her, "He

said he had something to do,"

"Oh, I see." She instantly understood.

The barmaid approached the Captain with a full mug of ale, as she handed it to the woman, "Need anything else Captain?" The woman smiled and batted her long lashes at the Captain.
Jane looked the lady up and down before smiling coyly, "I am good fer now beautiful, thank you."

The barmaid smiled and turned away with just a subtle nod.

"Might have some company to keep you busy tonight as well Captain?"

"Angela tired me out, no way I could indulge another, at least not tonight." She laughed; Ari finally understood what she had been doing the whole day. "Well I can't be playing favorites tonight. I'll see you in the morning Ari, as you and I have a date with Angela." She smiled, patting Ari on the back, getting up from her seat joining the rest of her men in a song.

Iggy stretched, "I'm off to get some rest, are you coming?"

Ari nodded.

They were led to separate rooms by the innkeeper. Ari slumped down into the incredibly comfortable bed. He found himself filled with dread, unsure if he wanted to solve the mysteries of his past, but no amount of will power could have kept Ari awake that night, his dreams wanted to take him to another place once again.

Ari found himself in a sea of darkness, he wasn't entirely sure if he was even standing on solid ground, or if he was just floating in the black abyss. As much as this place might scare the average person, for the first time that Ari could remember, he felt as if he was home. This darkness and him were connected, this was where he belonged somehow. He looked down at himself to find himself naked, but he pushed that thought aside, brushing the hair from his eyes, he wondered. Even though the world around him was a sea of black he knew he was walking towards something, even if he didn't know what exactly that was. He was on auto pilot, his body remembered, even if his mind was blocked from the truth.

He was alone in the world, but voices echoed ever so softly in his ears, calling to something. To him? Were these the voices of his past? Were his memories trying to rebuild themselves, putting the pieces together? Something again told him that was the wrong answer, but maybe, this was still the key to who he was. He didn't want to leave. He could feel his mortal body waking but he hung on to the darkness as long as it would allow him.

Moments before the morning sun woke him, there was a person who appeared in the darkness. Ari froze and held his breath, the young man raised his hand and waved, running towards him.
Still frozen Ari looked down at the boy who now stood before him, with a beaming smile across his face.

"Where have you been? I've been looking everywhere for you!" The boy was waiting for a respond, but of course Ari couldn't provide one for him. "You okay? Where is your-"

Ari was shot awake. His heart raced and his head rang with fury, why couldn't he stay asleep a little while longer? What was the boy going to say, who was he? So many more questions and no answers to settle his buzzing mind. He rubbed his eyes awake and only then did he hear the knock at the door.

"You awake in there Ari?" The Captain called out to him, knocking again, louder.
Quickly throwing on a brown tunic, and dusty grey trousers, he rushed to the door to answer her. The Captain smiled at his messy, still groggy appearance. She ran her fingers through his hair, taming some of

the strays. "I wasn't sure if you were going to wake up, I've been knocking for a while now." Ari went to pull out his note book, to jot down an apology to the Captain but she waved him off. "I must have woken you from a very good dream." She smiled, "Hurry and finish getting ready, I recommend a cloak as today is rather chilly. They have a breakfast feast down stairs than we are off to see Miss Nightingale."

Ari nodded, turning away from the Captain as he made himself presentable, he lastly grabbed a dark cloak. He tied it around his neck and looked at himself in the reflection of the vanity. He paused cocking his head as he stepped closer to the mirror, flipping the hood of the cloak over his head. His heart slightly raced, he was trying to remember something, but it was just on the tip of his tongue. Sadly, the moment disappeared, and he removed the hood of his cloak hesitantly before heading out of the room and down the stairs to meet up with the Captain, who of course was not alone.

Chapter 10

Daric and Iggy sat at one end of the long table the staff had laid out for the crew. The Captain sat dead center so that she would be able to hear and keep an eye on her entire crew. A large bounty of food and drinks had been placed before them.

Ari walked over to Iggy and Daric who saved him a seat.

Both of Ari's friends seemed to be in a better mood this morning, Daric even managed a subtle smile as Ari took a seat beside them. Daric enjoyed a hot sip of black coffee. "Good morning," he mumbled between drinks.

Ari smiled with a nod, happy to see that the tension from yesterday had mostly subsided between Iggy and Daric.

Iggy spoke with a mouth full as he continued to down more and more food, "I'd eat up if I were you, you have a long day with the Captain and Miss Nightingale.

Half the crew laughed aloud to Iggy's comment. "Oh she isn't that bad," The Captain laughed, "Miss Nightingale is sometimes a handful, that is all that my crew is insinuating." The Captain gave everyone a playful glare. "You'll be fine, the worst she will do to you is make you drink and smell some disgusting concoctions."

"And other times she makes you hallucinate!" One of the crew chipped in and everyone again laughed. The Captain even joined in, "Yeah, sometimes what she brews up has some weird side effects, but it's all for a reason, remember."

Ari swallowed hard.

"Eat up," The Captain beckoned with a smile, "The side effects are a lot less daunting on a full stomach." She winked.

Ari stiffened up, only to have the crew laugh again, causing him to loosen up once again, he began to eat.

Once Ari and the rest of the crew finished their feast, the Captain beckoned him away. Daric and Iggy were off to see if they could find the woman they were told about the day before.

Ari kept his hood down, even as it began to rain down on the two. They made it through the heart of town. The crowd was measurably smaller then yesterday, most likely due to the weather.

They reached the city limits and ended up on an unkept dirt path. "Angela doesn't like the sound of the city around her. She moved here many years ago in hopes that a smaller town would quiet the voices, but still so many thoughts running through everyone's heads filling her mind with their hopes and dreams. So, she built away from the crowd, now the voices are clearer, not so cluttered." The Captain turned and looked at Ari, seeing that oddly she had his full attention, "I am unaware if you believe in these mystic's you are about to be the subject to, but Angela is one of the best. Some of the ladies I go to, I question them from time to time, but Angela Nightingale has never once failed me."

Do I believe in this stuff? Ari asked himself. *I have no reason not to.* Was his final consensus as the two reached Angela Nightingale's home.

It was a small stone cabin with a windy stone path leading to the unkept wooden door, vines climbed up the walls freely, the whole area around the home was an herb garden, with strange plants growing in abundance.

They didn't even reach the door yet when a tan, foreign woman opened the door. She was a very petite woman, with long dark hair that was braided loosely kept together with a thick piece of cloth. She was in a purple dress, with a gold shawl with silver beads and bells. "Welcome," She greeted, already her wide eyes were fixated on Ari, she almost forgot that Jane was even there.

A thought ran through Ari's head, *she must be good, she knew we were here before we knocked.* He chuckled in his own head.

Angela smiled, "I've been waiting for you, so I was listening. But thank you for thinking I am that amazing." She winked as she opened the door move out of the way, finally out of her trance she smiled towards the Captain. "You didn't tell me that his aura would be this, intoxicating." She purred, gleefully, brushing the side of Ari's face with the back of her hand.

"I'm not in tune with that like you are."

Angela smiled and welcomed Ari and Jane into her home.

It was cluttered with books, bottles, flowers and herbs. There was a medium size round table with three chairs and a crystal orb on a gold stand in the center. She stepped over to the table, beckoning Jane into the chair next to her, and Ari to the one across from her.

Once Ari and the Captain were sat at the table, she walked over to her stove. Spooning two tablespoons of herbs into three cups she poured hot water over them. Taking in the aromas before walking back over to Ari and Jane, taking a seat next to the Captain.

Handing everyone a cup she took a sip from her own, the Captain did the same. Angela looked deep into Ari's eyes who looked at the darkening liquid and hesitated to take a sip, once he finally did Angela began to speak again, "So, as your Captain has told me you have no voice, as well as no memory. Am I correct?" Ari just nodded and she stared into him more, "You've been having strange dreams?"

Ari's face scrunched with confusion, before nodding again.

"Dreams can unlock truths that our brain is sometimes forced to forget, either from our own choice to protect ourselves, injuries, horrors of trauma, or even black magic. I feel there is black magic in your past, but I do not feel as if that is why you cannot remember."

"He had clearly suffered a head injury when we had found him."

She hummed, reaching out her hands, palms up, "Place your hands-on mine, palms toward the sky." Ari did as she asked, the moment their hands touched the room went cold and every candle and incent in the room fluttered, threatening to blow out.

Angela smiled as her eyes traveled across her room, her eyes were following, or seeing something that neither Ari, nor the Captain could see.

The Captain's eyes shot around the room; she had never seen a reaction like that before.

Angela laughed slightly, "Wow, there is something more then meets the eye here with you, handsome." She flirted with a toothy grin, biting the tip of her tongue. Angela looked down at his palms, following the lines of his hands, confusion filled with her face, before empathy took over. "You're a telltale or sorts, I feel it. Someone whose soul purpose is to preserve the stories of old and new."

Ari looked at her, he wanted to feel confused about her words, but something rang to close to home that he couldn't deny her observation.

"How tragic and ironic for a telltale to lose their voice, as well as their memory." She closed her eyes and tried to focus on his energy in the room, which was filling the air. "You lost something," Her brows scrunched together. Ari and Jane could see her eyes rolling around behind her eyelids as she tried to make sense of everything that was going through her mind. "Someone took something very important to you, something that holds the key to who you are, but I must warn you." Her eyes opened as she locked onto Ari's face, "There is someone who holds the key that could unlock your mind, but there is a dark aura around this information, this person. Giving me the idea that who ever this person might be, they do not wish well upon you. They are likely the cause of your condition." Angela stood up and Ari looked down at his hands, he brought them back into him. The Captains eyes were also locked on Ari now, making him uncomfortable. "Drink your tea and pass me the cup." She ordered. Ari did as she asked and chugged the bitter sweet drink before handing her the empty mug. Angela looked at the tea leaves that were formed at the bottom, walking over to the candle for a better view. "I see." Studying the cup closely, "The answers to your questions will be revealed very soon. Some or most of these answers will be to the questions you are fearful of having answered." Angela placed the cup down and turned to Jane, "You have a role in this tale my dear, Jane. This man will bring on change, for the better or the worse it is yet to be determined. His fate, his story is not his own."

"What does that even mean?"

Angela shrugged, "I don't even know, I have never seen someone like him before." She whispered this last thing just to Jane, "You need to protect him, Jane."

Ari looked back and forth between the two women, there were so many things running through his head, he didn't know how to process any of this information.

"Take a moment and collect yourself, this is a lot to take in. I can't imagine what you've gone through." Angela said as she stepped over to Ari and placed a comforting hand on the side of his face. "You have an important role in this world, you just have to find it again."

"Are we done here?" The Captain asked, her eyes still locked on Ari as she was unsure if the information, she learned today was good or bad, for her and her crew's safety.

"Not just yet," she took the Captain's hand and whispered again, "Leave tonight, and don't trust the woman's allure. The sirens call will only bring death to sailors in her grasp." Angela's eyes were locked on the Captain's.

Her words at the time seemed so cryptic, but Jane knew to take Angela's warnings to heart. They quickly said their goodbyes as Ari and the Captain walked away from the cottage.

Ari hadn't heard Angela's warnings to the Captain, so he was oblivious to the Captain's unease as they continued in silence, Jane also processing all the information she was just given.

While the Captain and Ari were busy with Miss Nightingale, Daric and Iggy were off in search of the woman they were informed about the day before.

"It's almost odd just being the two of us again." Iggy noted walking beside Daric.

Daric grumbled, pretending to be insulted, "Well if we find this wench, 'n all goes well fer Ari ye be jus' goin' t' 'ave t' get used t' jus' ole me again."

"I didn't mean it like that!" Iggy nudged Daric, the somber realization washed over them. They both wanted Ari to remember his past. Finding someone who knew and cared about him would make them happy for him, but the thought that he'd be no longer a part of the crew, did put a damper on things.

"I'm nah hopeful about this lead." Daric crossed his arms over his chest as he stopped, looking around, "We be pretty far whence we found 'im, no one else recognizes 'im. Its mighty unlikely he came from these parts."

Iggy began to feel better about their search, there was guilt in his chest as he hoped no good would come from this lead.

The two of them spotted Raymond sitting alone at one of the fish stands as he waved them over. "We went t' th' pub last night 'n didnt find ye."

"I took yer advice 'n went t' see th' beauty 'n son."

"Good," The man nodded taking a drag from his pipe.

"'ave ye spotted our mystery strumpet today?"

"Aye, ye jus' missed her, she was headin' fer th' docks."

Daric nodded motion Iggy to move, "Thanks, ole heartie, maybe see ye tonight at th' inn?"

"Sounds like a plan ole timer,"

"Ye be older than me, remember." Daric grumbled as he waved. They turned away heading towards the docks, hoping the woman hadn't left to continue her search somewhere else.

When they reached the docks Iggy opened his mouth as he was about to ask how they planned to spot one woman in a sea of people, but as the words were forming on his lips the question seemed silly. A stunningly beautiful, woman appeared like a beacon in the crowd. Time stood still as their eyes locked on her, she turned her gaze as their eyes met.

Daric and Iggy both lost the brain capacity to breathe for a moment as they stood there, stunned by her beauty, Raymond had gravely understated.

Two shades of blue, green and white coloured hair trickled down the back of her revealing, white dress that framed her toned body, leaving her arms uncovered. Even from this distance the two could clearly see her glistening turquoise eyes that melted their souls. Her skin was flawless and pale, almost like a painting rather then a real woman. With long, thick black lashes, she blinked slowly, and she fanned herself with her hand, before wrapping a black slaw around her nearly bare shoulders.

Her eyes left the two as she spoke to the closest sailor, asking him questions, only to have the man shake his head and move along. Her face filled with disappointment, picking up her skirt she continued on.

"She's stunning." Iggy spoke breaking their silence as they stared at the woman, nearly drooling at her appearance.

Daric shook his head clear, "Might as well do wha' we came here fer," Stepping a head of Iggy he approached the woman, tipping his hat to her. "Ahoy Ma'am, I heard from a fellow that ye be searchin' fer someone?"

She brushed a tear from the corner of her glassy eyes with a piece of black cloth as she spoke in a strange intoxicating, accent that even Iggy couldn't place, "Why yes I am," She hugged her self, "My younger brother, him and I look nothing alike, he has dark brown hair, and matching dark eyes, probably a little bit taller then you, Pretty eyes." She batted her lashes at Iggy. Ahe placed her hand on his bicep, biting her lower lip. "I've been every so worried about him, a slave trip came and kidnapped him, I tried to follow, but the ship I was on lost track of them in a storm and I haven't seen him since." She placed her hands over her eyes as she began to sob quietly.

Daric and Iggy looked at each other before Iggy responded placing a comforting hand on her shoulder, "Almost two months back, we found a man on the shores of Orvos, he does fit the generic description you gave us."

Her face brightened up as she clasped her hands together, "Could it be true? Could you have found my brother! If there are any gods left in this world, I pray that this man you speak of is," She kissed both Iggy and Daric on the cheek as she continued to speak ecstatically, "Is he well? Is he with you? When can I see him? I have so many questions."

Both Daric and Iggy couldn't control their pounding hearts, they blushed red. Daric cleared his throat before managing to speak back to the woman, "If our matey be yer brother, then aye he be safe 'n aye he be wit' us."

"Matey? Friend?" She seemed confused.

"Aye," Daric looked at her confused. "If ye join us, we can take ye t' 'im."

"Oh, thank you." She entangled her arms around both Iggy and Daric's arms, "Please, take me to him." She rested her head on Daric's shoulder. Looking up at him, their eyes met, she blinked so slowly, Daric's heart continued to race in his chest.

Never before had a woman had this effect on Daric, not even his late wife gave him this feeling, but then again, he had never met a woman like her before. He managed to pull away from her as she wrapped herself tighter around Iggy's arm looking up at him as he was completely entranced by the beautiful stranger.

"So, what are your guys' names?" She asked innocently.

"I'm Iggy Dawning and my Friend here is Daric Greymorn.

She bit her bottom lip as she asked, "Are you, pirates?" She giggled as Iggy seemed surprised by her question. He stared slightly opened mouthed at her perfect face.

"Yes," he finally managed to say, "Our ship is the Shadow's Blade, Captained by the Great Jane Far'mel."

"Jane?" The woman shook her head in shock, "A

woman Captain's the ship you serve on?" She tried to hide her displeasure of this information, but Daric caught it in the corner of her eye as Iggy was oblivious to the fact.

"Aye, she does," Daric spoke coldly, questioning this woman's intentions.

She smiled sweetly pressing her lips together in a pout as she batted her eye lashes again. She turned back to Iggy, "In my country, it's unheard of to have a woman Captain a ship. So many strange customs here, I suppose." She smiled innocently.

"Where are ye originally from?" Daric pressed as red flags were being raised.

"Tasyrn," She answered in a rehearsed tone.

"That's great news, that's where the Captain is from, and we just sailed from there." Iggy added.

Her eyes went wide as she continued to smile, "Tasyrn is such a big place, it would be interesting if she use to live near were I am from."

"We'll see," Daric said in a sceptic tone.

The woman nodded it as she smiled again, wrapping her arms tighter around Iggy once again, resting her head against him. "I've been so lonely without my brother. You see, my husband died a few years back and my brother was the sweetest and never left my side." She sniffled.

"Wha"s yer brother's name, if I may ask?" Daric butted in again.

"Axel,"

"And yours?"

She paused to answer, "Kali." Seeing the suspicion in his eyes. She smiled, Daric's unease towards her melted away, he tried to shake the trance her beauty had on him, but he was snared again.

Once they reached the inn, Daric opened the door for the woman as she released her grip on Iggy and strutted into the pub. Her aura filled and suffocated all conversation in the room as every man turned their gaze and paused; taking a second to catch their breath.

She smiled innocently, biting her lip and tossing her hair behind her, acting as if she was intimidated by the attention.

Her eyes were locked on the back of Ari's head, he was sitting with his back to her at the end of the bar, facing the Captain who was also entranced by the woman's beauty.

The Captain tapped Ari on the shoulder as Kali, Iggy and Daric approached.

Ari turned.

Kali and his eyes met. Unlike everyone else, whose

hearts fluttered, his stomach dropped. The feeling of terror filled him as his mouth went dry and he lost all breath, she marched right for him. Her face read innocence, but Ari could see the dark intentions in the glitter of her turquoise eyes.

"Axel!" She smiled twistedly, arms out stretched to embrace him, "My dear brother." No one heard the dark tone in her voice, no one else saw her twisted smile as they all were enchanted by her beautiful spell.

Ari stumbled, he got up from the stool and stepped away from her. She reached out and grabbed his hand, her nails digging in, grabbing hold of him. Again, his breath was stolen. He was frozen, their eyes locked on each other. He knew her, as her name flashed in his mind. *Kali?!* And in that moment, he knew real fear.

Chapter 11

Ari; no, my apologise, Axel. Was more confused
than ever. He knew to fear this woman before him,
his sister. He knew that she was indeed his sister, but
that was all he knew. No memories of why, just the
initial gut reaction to run. He tried to pull away, but
her grip drained the colour from Axel's hand, blood
now dripped down his wrists. He nails dug deeper
into his flesh.

"Axel, I've been so worried about you. I've been
looking everywhere. I am so happy to see that you
are safe now." There was a twisted, bitter smile on
her face, she emotionlessly spoke towards her
brother. Actual pain forced through his arm.

Axel's instincts were the only thing driving this fear,
his body knew to be afraid of her, his body knew he
had to get himself and the rest of the crew as far
away from this woman. But as much as his body
knew this, he was frozen in fear and the crew seemed
frozen in time.

Honestly, only seconds had passed, but it felt like

an eternity for Axel as he struggled to pull his arm away

Iggy somehow snapped out of his trance; seeing the blood dripping down his friend's wrist, and the distress on his face, "Hey, back off," He ordered Kali, stepping between the two of them, forcing Kali to release Axel. "Are you okay?" He asked offering Axel his hand.

Kali stepped toward placing her hand softly on Iggy's shoulders, she looked deep into his eyes, "He's just confused when I get him home everything will become clear once again." She batted her eye lashes, trying to lure him back into her.

Before Iggy could even think, Axel pulled him away from Kali shaking his head no, begging him not to trust her.

Kali fought hard to hide her anger and frustration as Daric and Jane had also awoken from their trance. They also stepped between her and her brother, she clenched her fist as her face twisted angerly.

Jane spoke crossing her arms over her chest, "I think you should leave, now." She threatened.

"He is my brother." She practically screamed, "You have no right to keep family from each other." She took a step forward, expecting them to move aside but they all stood their ground.

"It seems like yer brother doesn't wish t' leave wit' ye."

"He's confused! He doesn't know what he needs, he will remember where he belongs in time, mark my words." She growled as Jane and Daric stared the beautiful woman down.

Kali, in that moment, realised she had lost. She pulled out her black piece of cloth she had used as a handkerchief and tossed it on the ground at their feet, "He will remember, and he will know it was a mistake to refuse to join me this day, Captain Far'mel. A grave mistake." He eyes turned a slightly red. With that she turned and walked away, the clicking of her heels on the old wooden floors echoed through the silenced pub and the moment the doors closed around her, the rest of the customers returned to their normal activities as if that encounter hadn't occurred.

The three of them turned to face Axel whose back was against the wall, his heart thumping in his chest. He held his breath hoping to slow down the erratic beating in his chest.

Iggy placed his hand on Axel's shoulder, "Are you okay?"

Axel was shaking uncontrollably. He didn't know why he was afraid of her, but he knew that the crew and himself needed to get as far away from Kali as possible. Though something inside him knew that this wasn't the last they were going to see of her, he knew that she would come for him again.

Jane turned away from Axel and bent down picking up the piece of fabric Kali tossed towards them. She felt it between her fingers; there was nothing seemingly special about thick dark cloth. It seemed old, yet well sewn and held together well.

The Captain turned back and offered the cloth to Axel, "Does this somehow mean something to you?"

Axel locked eyes on the cloth and initially shook his head no as he reached out and went to take the fabric from her, but the second his fingers brushed up against it Axel found himself lost in to many memories, so many voices. This didn't begin to clear anything in Axel's mind; these memories were not from one person alone, but dozens of other peoples' memories, their stories flooded through Axel's brain. Axel's didn't recognize any of these memories and he knew for sure that these were not his own. He was a bystander, an unmoving, unnoticed person in the darkness. Something in Axel knew that he had never witnessed these memories, but yet here he was, watching from the sidelines.

The second Axel's fingers touched the fabric his eyes rolled to the back of his head and he collapsed. Iggy attempted to catch him, but he slipped through his fingers crumbling to the ground at their feet. All three of them knelt down trying to wake him.

All eyes were on them, the Captain spoke, "Let's get him up to his room. Now," She wanted to know what was going on, she wanted answers.

Daric alone picked Axel up in his arms and carried him carefully from the bar, up the stairs and into his room, placing him on the bed.

Jane closed and locked the door behind them all, the black piece of cloth held tightly in her hand. Unclenching her fist, she studied the fabric closer, there was something more to this then met the eye, she could feel it. And if only she knew the truth.

Iggy sat at the edge of the bed next to Axel, inspecting his every move, while Daric crossed his arms and turned his gaze towards the Captain. "Do ye believe her, Captain?"

Jane thought about it, "Clearly our friend recognized her, so they have a past. At this point, I'm going to assume she is speaking the truth about how they know each other.

Iggy chimed in, "This doesn't answer any questions, it raises more in my head."

Jane leaned her back against the wall and crossed her arms over her chest, "I second that. It also brings into question if it's safe for the rest of the crew to even have him aboard. This is reminding me that we know nothing about him, still. This woman, Kali, she seems very dangerous to me. How do I know Axel himself isn't also?"

Iggy perked up and replied to the Captain's comment. "I don't think this should change anything, he is still the person who has fought beside us, stood up for us." He paused as he thought Gibson and Ari/Axel standing up for him. He had the urge to tell them everything in that moment, but it wasn't the time, "He stood up for all of us, he fought alongside us. What that crazy woman said shouldn't change anything about our feelings towards him. He's our ally, our friend."

"We aren't sayin' we don't trust 'im, 'tis true he has been through a lot wit' us, but thar be a lot o' other peoples' safety we 'ave t' reckon about. 'n so far thar are more riddles leadin' t' 'im nah bein' a safe bet on board," Daric answered for the Captain, only for her to wave him off.

"Iggy, you are right. Axel, if that's his real name has done a lot for us, but what if this woman triggers his old memories and he becomes someone else?

Someone dangerous? I have a duty to my crew to ask these hard questions and protect them."

Iggy looked down as Daric stared down at Axel, "Wha''s th' plan, Captain?"

She thought quietly for a moment before walking over to the side table and placing the fabric folded neatly down. "For now we should trust that when he wakes he will be the same person we have grown so fond of over these months. Miss Nightingale warned me to not trust that woman and to leave tonight, saying that we need to protect him." She paused, her hands on her waist, "Let's get him to the ship, let him rest in his bunk. We can figure stuff out while we are out at sea and away from this godforsaken port."

"I'll help Iggy brin' Axel aboard, afore grabbin' a few crew hands t' get th' ship ready t' sail?" Daric asked in more of a statement then a question.

"Aye," Jane turned away and left the room.

Daric waited until he could no longer hear her footsteps before speaking again, "Dont take th' Captains words as bein' harsh. She has a crew t' also worry about it. If thar was another crew hand who may be a threat t' th' safety o' th' rest o' her crew, or one o' her crew, she would be questionin' them th' same. Ye know that, right?"

Iggy knew that he wasn't just talking about Axel

there as he looked down ashamed with himself, knowing that Daric was correct, as always. "Aye, I know. I spoke out of line."

Daric messed Iggy's hair and smiled slightly, "Ye're lucky th' Captain 'n I are fond o' ye. Ye're trouble," Iggy nudged him with a smile as they both took Axel's arms, swinging them over their shoulders as they carried him towards the docks and back on the Shadow's Blade.

Axel found himself in the darkness again, but this time as he looked down at himself he was thankfully in trousers as the young boy who approached him last time he was here, was sitting down as if waiting for him. *How long has he been waiting here?* Axel asked.

"Didn't feel like that long really."

Axel jumped back, confused. *You can hear me?*

The boy cocked his head to the side and nodded, "Of course, why wouldn't I be able too?"

It's so nice to be understood! Axel gave out a sigh of relief, even if it was a subtle relief being that this was a dream and all.

"You are acting really weird, Uncle."

Uncle?

"What happened to your cloak? Is that why I haven't

been able to find you, did Kali took your cloak?" Worry filled his face as he continued to go on, "I couldn't even count how many years went by, I've been doing all the work myself!" He placed both hands on his face, dragging his skin down in frustration, "I clearly am not ready to do this alone, I really should have listened to your teachings better." He laughed as he stood up and wrapped his arms around Axel's stomach, embracing him in a tight hug. "I missed you and I was really worried something bad happened to you."

This is a strange dream.

The boy backed up and laughed, "Dream?" Only when he saw Axel's seriousness on his face did he realize it wasn't a joke, "What happened to you?" He backed away more looking over Axel, "Did Kali mess with your head?" Axel shrugged, "Do you even know who I am?" Axel just shook his head and placed his hands in his pocket at the boy started to think with a frown glued to his face, "I'm Kai, your apprentice?"

Apprentice for what?

Kai laughed dropping down to a seated position, "Oh dear, I shouldn't be laughing because Kali must have done some crazy shit to you to forget this face. I'd take a seat, Axel." Axel did as he was told as Kai cracked his fingers, "I have a lot to tell you."

Hours had gone by, Kai continued to explain everything at least everything he knew as even he had gaps.

The sun had set over the sea and the waves tossed the Shadow's blade softly in the night. Axel was thrown awake from the darkness, only to find himself in his and Iggy's bunk, a lantern was still burning dim as Iggy was asleep in his cot next to Axel.

Panic filled him, he panted silently, cold sweat poured down his face as Axel looked around the room. That was when true terror hit him as the realization of where he was finally seeped in, they were already out to sea. His stomach dropped and his heart sank, he now knew everything he needed to know. He knew who he was and seemingly, more importantly, he knew who Kali really was, what Kali really was. Which meant terrible danger for every soul on the Shadow's Blade. As a pirate, you never want to be the enemy to the goddess of the sea.

Even if you have Time, Death on your side.

Chapter 12

Axel... No, I guess I had a choice to make. Do I tell the Captain, Daric and Iggy the truth about me? Or do I keep my identity a secret? I am a powerless god, who has an all-powerful Goddess after me. A Goddess who has my powers trapped away. I am completely defenceless against her, meaning that every member of this crew was in danger because of me. There is nothing I can do to protect them from her might. I'm fearful for all of them. I question if telling them the truth help with in the situation or hinder them more?

If they knew the truth, they might just toss me over board, but Kali has their sent, she wasn't going to let them get away with denying her, her prize. At least with me aboard they had something to bargain her with. *For now, it's safer for them to be in the dark.* I told myself. But was I just lying to myself? I couldn't be sure.

Iggy rolled over in his cot, still asleep; I stood up

and decided to take a walk, clear my head and let Iggy rest in peace. Maybe I was also trying to distance myself from him.

I made my way to the main deck, as to no surprise at all, I found the Captain at the wheel, she was in deep thought. She must have spotted me watching her, she waved for me to approach.

Once up the stairs, she gave me a small, tired smile. "You must have some neurological issues, or a powerful curse placed upon you with of all these fainting spells you get."

I smiled uneasily as I scratched the back of my head.

"You feeling okay? Something seems off... Was it what happened between your sister?" See seemed unsure if Kali was indeed my sister.

She was far more perceptive then I ever gave her credit for. She could sense that something was off, but I shrugged as it was the best I could do.

She nodded, understanding that I didn't seem up to a real conversation about it. She leaned her body against the helm, her arms hanging through the gaps as she looked away, "You might not get what I mean by this, but do you ever feel as if you aren't living the life you were supposed too?"

I just smiled, knowing that she had a story to tell.

"I doubt you'd know this, its not a tale the crew are privileged too, but I was never supposed to be on that slave ship. That one step that led me towards a pirate life was never meant to happen." She took a long pause as she sighed, "I have, maybe had a sister. I don't know what happened to her in the end. Our father died or left. Our mother refused us the details, but she could no longer afford to care for my sister and I, so she sold one of us, to pay for her expenses and sent the other to a sanctuary for protection. I was supposed to go become a priestess or something stupid. Where my little sister, Castriel was supposed to be sold off into slavery. For kids, they like them very young, because they can train them. Sell them for a premium. But she wasn't tough," I could see she was uncomfortable telling me this story, "Cass wasn't brave, she was soft, she would have been eaten alive on that ship, and I knew that. I knew I could fight my way through it. I switched places with her, pretending to be her when they came to take Cass away. She cried; she was such a baby." She laughed bitterly as a smile forced itself to her beautiful, strong face, "I've never stopped thinking about her. I still wonder to this day where she ended up. I could have tried to search for that sanctuary but as much as I am a brave, fearless Captain, I was always too afraid to.

Just by having it a mystery I could imagine her happy, alive, maybe a great priestess or maybe she left that life and had a family, kids running around. She was too young to even think of that stuff, so who knows if she ever even wanted kids."

If I ever get the chance, I'd like to tell you about her. I thought, listening to her tell her tale, seeing the affection she had for her sister. It was depressing. All the time they lost, how different their lives would have been.

"Do you know why I am telling you this story, Axel?" The sentiment left her face as she turned and looked at me. Hearing my real name on her lips seemed odd. I could feel her eyes on my face, but I did not turn to meet her gaze. The guilt in my soul would clearly show in my eyes as I just stared out over the ship I nodded.

"Good. If there is anything you wish to tell me, or Iggy or Daric, you can trust us. We are allies now."

I know... Could she read my mind? Or was it just so clearly written on my face? I began to wonder if there was sweat on my brow. I could feel chills running down my spine. There was no way she could have guessed the secret that I was hiding, but had she already guessed that I was hiding something?

Captain turned the ship slightly, with another long

sigh, she pushed all thoughts of her passed from the front of her mind, "Something about you makes me think of my past, it's rather aggravating." She glared playfully, "I don't usually dwell on that anymore. Maybe Angela is right, you are a telltale, so maybe you're just meant to listen in." She chuckled.

I looked over the deck of the ship and caught Daric who was staring up at the two of us, he couldn't hear what the Captain had been speaking of, but I knew he knew this tale well.

As much as it seemed the Captain was trusting me more and completely, Daric's distrust was building. I could see it even from where I stood beside the Captain.

"Do you wish to still stay with us, Axel?" The Captain finally asked.

I took a small breath and thought about my answer, truthfully I didn't want to leave, but I didn't want to risk their safety.

She saw my inner conflict as she smiled and placed her hand on my shoulder, squeezing it lightly, "You'll have a while to come to a decision, it will be a month or more until we hit port again. Think hard about it." She paused making sure I understood what she was asking before ending the conversation, "But you should be resting, a lot has happened, a lot to process."

That was her nicely telling me to leave, so I tipped my head to her and walked away. Daric and my eyes met at the end of the staircase. I turned, heading into the ship. I debated going back to the bunk, but instead, I walked down to the storage room. Iggy's check book was open on the desk, he hadn't finished going through the new inventory by the looks of it, so it took it upon myself to work away.

The door creaked open, and my heart began to pound as an image of Iggy's fear flooded my mind. Though, to my relief, Daric walked down the stairs. "Everythin' alright, kid?"

Kid? I was a million times his age, but I nodded as I put the book back down on the table.

He was soul searching as he pondered up and down me. "Iggy trusts ye, wholeheartedly. If he gets hurt 'cause o' whatever be goin' on around ye, I shall risk everythin' t' protect 'im, 'n th' Captain. I hope ye realize that."

I did. Even before he spoke the words. Getting anyone hurt was the last thing I wanted, especially Iggy, or Daric and the Captain. I wished that I could vocalize that to him. But there must have been something, a small flicker in my eye? Cause he smiled softly with a sigh.

"I don't mean t' sound so cold, jus' Iggy 'n th' Captain are me, family. They 'ave been through a lot, 'n I want t' try 'n make thar lives easier. I hope ye understand, Axel."

I nodded firmly. I didn't blame him for his warranted distrust in me. My sister is a powerful goddess, and even if he didn't know it, he felt it, he felt something when she was in the pub, he had felt it even before they reached the pub. He had been so trusting, needlessly trusting, when it is his job to protect those around him, those he cares about. The same people I have grown to care about.

After a long moment of silence, Daric spoke again, adjusting himself, "I be nah as naive as th' Captain, I know ye now remember somethin'. I can see th' difference in yer eyes, th' thoughts reprocessin' themselves, yer sister jogged some, if nah all yer memories. Maybe ye're afeared o' wha' ye remember, maybe nah, but we can nah help whatever ye be runnin' from if we dunno why we be runnin'."

I looked down at the book, unable to meet his gaze. "That's all I needed t' say, Goodnight, Axel." With that he turned around and walked back up the stairs leaving me to my thoughts.

I sat down at the desk and opened up my book as I

started to write. *I am the god of death, the god of time. The god all mortals' fear, all mortals' hate.* I started to just write my story on the blank pages. A story I've never written before. I was so focused as the words unfolding on the pages that nothing else mattered. Not even the fact that I was no longer alone in the room.

Iggy tried to get my attention, only to fall behind me as he read the words I was writing over my shoulder.

I imagine when he first read these words he laughed aloud. They seemed to be the ramblings of either a crazy person, or just a very imaginative dreamer. But there was a turning point for him, something caught his eye that seemed so crazy, that it had to be possible, it had to be true.

"You're a god?"

This time his words broke through my trance and I dropped the quill turning my head around so fast it caused poor Iggy to jump back, terrified for a moment. Terrified of me...

I swallowed hard and nodded slowly, *yes.*

Iggy studied me. He was trying to search for the stranger he had befriended in my face. He smiled?

"I don't think all mortals' fear or hate death," he bit his lip as he wasn't sure what to do or say. His mind was trying to process everything, and he was trying to push away this small sense of fear, he clearly didn't want to be afraid.

I took a deep breath and stood up from the chair stepping away from Iggy, not wishing to make him more afraid of me. Understanding that the truth of what I was had to be intimidating, but he did something that I never in my years would have expected. He approached, reaching out and taking my hands in his. Iggy was nervous his hand slightly shook, and his palms were sweaty.

I looked down at his hands in confusion before I traced my way back to his face.

"You don't need to worry about me, knowing the truth. It will be another secret, just between you and me."

I refused to pull my hand away but managed a small smile.

He finally took his hands back and brushed his hair with his fingers with an uneasy laugh, "Did you really forget everything?"

I nodded, knowing this was the beginning of the swarm of questions.

I explained everything he asked as I wrote out everything he needed and wanted to know. Well most of everything as he asked some questions that I couldn't answer for him. With every answer he became more and more comfortable with me once again, pretty soon it was as if nothing changed. To him I wasn't this dangerous, powerful monster of a god. I was still the stranger that he grew to love.

He could see me getting tired as my hand started to cramp, he was uncomfortable with it, but he ordered me off to bed. I didn't dare argue as he now had something to hold over my head. Just as I reached the last step before leaving the room Iggy called out with a smile, "Don't tell the Captain and Daric, not yet."

I nodded.

Chapter 13

Kai was waiting in the darkness for me. *Don't you have things to do?* I asked with a small smile as I took a seat in front of him.

He smiled, leaning back, straightening his legs, "I have been searching for you, for a very long time, not going to lose my place in time. I don't move as swiftly as you do."

I suppose that is true.

"I know this doesn't seem like the time, but since there isn't anything that I can actually do to help you, yet... I want to ask you something."

What about?

"My mother." I just looked at him slightly puzzled as he took it as a que to begin his questioning, "Why did you bring me to her?"

So, you know now?

"Yeah," he scratched the back of his head and smiled softly, "I had some free time while you were absent," He laughed uncomfortably, "I went back and saw how you found me, how you brought me to

Nora."

I'm sorry I never told you,

He waved that off, "I'm not mad. I just want to know why you picked her to be my mom?"

I leaned back and thought about it, thinking back in my still slightly fuzzy memory. *I met her, a few years before I found you, after the loss of her own son. I knew she'd love you and I knew she needed you.*

"Did you know that she'd..."

He was unable to say it as I shook my head, *no, I didn't know about that.*

Kai smiled through the dark conversation, "I'm thankful that you picked her, out of everyone else, even if our time was short together, she was the best mom I could have ever asked for."

She really was.

Iggy yawned, rubbing his tired eyes as he checked the last box on his list. If it wasn't for my help earlier, he'd still have the rest of the night of work left to do. "I'll have to thank Ari in the morning," He noted to himself as he started to do one last run through of his list, before heading off to bed himself.

If only he had ended his evening there, if only he waited to do the last run through for morning none of this would have happened.

Somehow, he missed the door creak open, but he didn't miss the click of the lock. Turning his head from his list, his mouth went dry and a shiver ran down his back. Gibson walked down the steps.

Iggy put the book down on the desk and stepped back from Gibson.

The man's shirt was already open, his pants untied as he placed his mostly finished liquor bottle down on the desk. "Ignatius," the man slurred as he began to close the gap between the two of them. "Ye know how this ends," He rubbed his forehead, "I be nah in th' mood fer ye t' play hard t' get wit' me." His voice growled with annoyance.

"No, I am not putting up with this anymore. I told you last time I'm done," Iggy's heart was pounding in his throat, Gibson could hear the fear.

A smile creeped on his face as he leaned back against the desk. "Remember how well last time ended fer ye?" Iggy looked away taking another step from Gibson. "'twill ne'er be done 'til says I so. Understood?" Iggy swallowed hard and remained silent as Gibson turned his head and reached for his liquor.

Iggy took that as the opportunity to rush up the stairs. He reached the door and tried to unlock it, but Gibson was already on him, grabbing him by his elbow, he tossed Iggy down the stairs.

He tucked himself as he tumbled, but it didn't help as much as he hoped. The back of Iggy's head cracked fiercely against the floor, disorienting him, his shoulder twisting painfully. He groaned in pain, biting his lips, and rolling over onto his stomach, trying to lift himself up by his forearms.

Gibson was surprisingly quick in his drunken state as he pushed his body down against Iggy's, his arm around his throat, his mouth against Iggy's ear, the lingering stench of his breath filled Iggy's nose.

"Get off me!" Iggy tried to yell out as he clawed at Gibson's arm, but the more he fought the tighter Gibson would squeeze.

"Submit." He whispered in Iggy's ear as he clamped his free hand over Iggy's mouth and nose.

Iggy ground his teeth as he continued to fight, trying to call him off of him as Gibson continued to slowly suffocate him.

I woke to the smell of death in the air. The halls were dark and the lantern next to my bed had been left unlit for hours. I placed my hands where I was expecting Iggy to be sleeping soundly to find an empty cot.

I didn't think as I threw myself up and ran down the

halls, down towards storage.

I reached the door only to find it locked from the inside, I placed my ear against the door; I could her muffled voices. I banged on the door trying to break it open. After three strong heaves at the door, it caved under my weight and I tumbled into the storage room.

Gibson was hiding behind one of the shelves taking a large swig of his liquor. Iggy was kneeling on his hands and knees, one hand over his red neck, gasping and coughing as air forced its way back into his lungs, his lips were slowly regaining colour once again. If I had been a few minutes longer, this would have been a different end to this story.

Gibson grumbled as he looked up at me coming out from 'hiding', "Oh, 'tis jus' ye," He reached for Iggy grabbing a tuff of his hair, "Guess I didn't 'ave t' stop me fun."

Iggy grabbed Gibson's wrist, trying to pull the man off of him, but he was already tried of fighting and defeated.

Something triggered in me, I marched down the steps walking straight up to Gibson, who eyed me, daring me to act.

"Axel," Iggy tried to ask me to back down, but he barley wheezed out my name. His train of thought dissipated as my fist connected with Gibson's face, "Axel?" He coughed in shock.

Gibson wasn't going down without a fight, he released Iggy and took a swing at me, he hit me good in the jaw. I stumbled backwards, he grabbed me by the shirt and tossed me towards the stairs. I stumbled just enough for him to catch me with another blow to the face. I hit the floor and Gibson climbed over me; grabbing my shirt again, tearing it slightly with one hand. He went to give me another right hook. I grabbed his fist with one hand and swung the other hand, connecting with the corner of his eye. Blood. His blood dripped down his face, as rage built in the man large. Elbowing me in the mouth. I could now taste my own blood.

Iggy got up and rushed over to the two of us, grabbing Gibson by the arm trying to pull us apart. Gibson took his free arm and elbowed Iggy in the ribcage.

Crack, was all I heard as I turned my gaze from Gibson to Iggy, who had dropped to his knees, gasping for more air, as tears pooled down his face, arms over his broken rib.

Rage was restored in me. I rolled Gibson, over powering him I grabbed him by his throat and just continued to pound my fist into his face without holding back.

Blood coated my fist. I had been in such a frenzy that I didn't even hear someone rushing down the stairs. I only realized someone else had joined us when Daric grabbed me from under my arms, locking his fingers together, dragging me off Gibson.

"Wha' th' Davy Jones' locker be goin' on in here?" He barked, still holding me back, even as I began to calm down looking at the damage I had done to Gibson's face.

Gibson answered as he used his shirt to wipe the blood from his eyes. "I heard a commotion; Ignatius had fallen down th' steps. I came t' help 'im when this bastard attacked me like a rabid cur. Maybe we should put yer new pet down afore it gets someone killed!"

Some how I managed a slight, small audible growl to escape from my lips.

"Shut yer mouth!" Daric ordered Gibson, he did as he was told.

Gibson wasn't worried though, I could see it written on his disgusting, smug face. He knew Iggy wouldn't protest his lie, either out of fear or the fact he was in no condition to refute at the moment as he tried to catch his breath still gasping on the floor.

Daric wasn't convinced, clearly, "I be goin' t' let ye

go, Axel, 'n ye be calmly goin' t' step back, right?" I did as I was told as he slowly released my arms, "Gibson, get out o' here, I'll deal wit' ye later."

Daric ignored me and rushed to Iggy's side, kneeling down next to him, placing one hand on his back. Iggy fell into Daric's arms. He let out a slight sigh of relief as Daric wrapped his arms around him. Iggy wanted to speak, but no words came out, only a breathless, painful groan.

"Come on," Daric inspected Iggy, lifting him up by his good arm being swung over his shoulders, supporting him with a soft hand on Iggy's hip.

Iggy and Daric stumbled as I stepped forward to lend a hand. Daric snapped coldly at me, "Stay where ye be," His glare cut right thought me, and killed all the lingering rage I had pent up inside me. "I be goin' t' take 'im t' th' infirmary then come back 'n take ye t' th' Captain. She can deal wit' ye,"

There was so much anger in his voice, that it petrified me. I managed to nod and dared not to move another inch as I watched Daric support Iggy away.

Ten minutes had passed when Daric finally walked through the door again, he didn't bother coming down the stairs. "Come," He ordered, yet again I did as I was told.

This wasn't going to end well, I thought. I kept my gaze down as Daric and I waited for the Captain to answer our knock.

She finally came; her hair was bunched up in a bun and red robe wrapped around her loosely. She rubbed her eyes to wipe the sleep away, but once she caught a glimpse of my bloody scratched face that was unnecessary. She was wide awake with curiosity. "What is the meaning of this?" She was asking Daric, but looking straight at me, she reached forward and placed her hand on my face inspecting my swelling lip. "Does it hurt?"

I shook my head no.

The Captain beckoned Daric and me into her chambers as she took a seat on her desk waiting for a reply from Daric. "I was doin' rounds when I heard a crash, found th' hold cabin door busted in. Gibson 'n Axel were fightin' downstairs."

The Captain raised her brow at me, it was completely out of character for the person she had grown to know in our time together. She ran her hands over her desk, clearing it of old parchment as she finally found a clean piece, offering it and a quill to me. "And what for what reason were you two in a scuffle?"

It wasn't my place to say. I promised Iggy that I'd keep the secret of what Gibson was doing to him, so I did not reach for the parchment and I looked down at the floor in shame for my defiance.

"No answer? I'm ordering you to tell me what that fight was about." There was a sternness in her face that I had never seen directed to me before, it sent chills down my back. But I did not waver from my stance.

"Gibson said Iggy had taken a fall down th' stairs," "Is Iggy alright?" Her concern took over.

"He best be, but Gibson seemed t' paint a picture o' 'im helpin' Iggy 'n Axel chargin' in attackin' 'im out o' nowhere."

She pressed her lips together, her brow still raised. The story was a joke, she and Daric both knew there was little if no truth about it and I could see their anger building out of frustration. She reached the parchment out again, slightly waving it in my face, "You have one more chance to tell me your side of this story. I do not, take fighting or harassment of ANY kind, lightly on my ship."

I swallowed hard but stood unmoving, I could feel tears threatening to form in my eyes.

"Does that mean Gibson speaks the truth?"

Daric slammed his fist hard against the Captain's

desk as the force caused everything to shake for a second, "Jus' tell us th' truth, I be tired o' bein' lied too!"

Still, I stood unmoving, hoping they would somehow see the answer in my eyes, but they had already known the answer, they just needed the confession.

"You're leaving me no choice. You need to be removed for my ship, I can't have people fighting for no reason."

The door to the Captain's chambers opened, the three of us turned to look at Iggy who had entered uninvited.

Chapter 14

Daric spoke, his face was drained of all his anger, concern was replaced. He looked at the barely standing Iggy, "Ye best be in th' infirmary."

Iggy wheezed one arm over his ribcage as he struggled to stepped closer to me, eyes on the Captain. I reached out a hand to support him, which he took gladly, "Gibson, isn't telling you the truth."

"Why would he lie when ye witnessed th' whole thin', 'n could easy discredit his tale?" There was bitterness in her voice. She had put all the pieces together.

Iggy swallowed hard as he tried to check his emotions before he spoke. Shame caused him to be unable to look anyone in the eye, "Because I haven't come forth about it before."

Daric and the Captain already knew what he was going to tell them, but they didn't understand the extent and it did not make it any easier for them to hear.

Iggy unbuttoned his shirt and pulled off his

bandana's revealing the thick bruises and his re dislocated shoulder.

Jane bit her tongue as she wanted to lash out angerly at him, "How long has this been going on behind our back?"

He finally looked up at the Captain and spoke honestly, "It never stopped." Tears were forming in his eyes, he struggled to say this all aloud. He swallowed hard, "Daric had ensured that the rest of the crew wouldn't take advantage of me after he caught them that one night, but Gibson continued shortly after. At first, I'd try and fight back every now and then, but he's just hurt me more. So, I'd give in. With Axel around I started standing up for myself, again." He paused, rubbing his still sore throat, he wouldn't have been able to hide this bruise with a few bandannas. "He may have killed me tonight if it wasn't for Axel," He held his breath, "he was just trying to protect me."

"Why couldn't you just tell us that, Axel?" She demanded, unable to hide her anger anymore as she snapped.

Iggy stepped in to defend me, "It wasn't his place to say, I made him promise not too."

Daric finally spoke, we could hear the hurt in his voice. "Why didn' ye tell us, me about this?"

Iggy failed to fight back his tears, his voice croaked, "I," he bit his lips, "I didn't want to disappoint you. I wasn't able to defend myself, wasn't able to fight back like you taught me."

Daric grabbed Iggy and softly pulling him in for an embrace, placing a fatherly kiss on the top of his head, "I shall ne'er be disappointed in ye, I jus' wished ye knew that." He released him, placing him slightly to the side and stormed out of the room.

"Daric?" Iggy called out, "What are you doing!" The Captain followed Daric on his witch-hunt. Iggy followed, every step more painful then the last, as I followed closely behind him, helping him when needed.

"Daric, Captain don't you anything rash! Please!" He already began regretting telling them the truth, but he couldn't let me be punished for Gibson's actions.

They reached the level Gibson's bunk was on and surprisingly found him in the hall, with a bloody cloth against his face, smoking from an old pipe. "Goin' t' toss th' monster o'er board yet?" He turned and actually looked at Daric, stepping back quickly he asked, "Wha' did th' bastard say? Are ye trustin' 'im o'er me?"

"He said nothing." The Captain growled.

Only then did Gibson see Iggy catching up to the

Captain and Daric, panting, sweat on his brow. He laughed uncomfortably, "Are ye goin' t' side wit' th' pretty cur, o'er me?" He could already see that wasn't working in his favor, "He asked fer it!" He tried to claim as he nearly tripped as he backed up. "I be goin' t' murder ye," He threatened as his eyes locked on Iggy. He pushed past the four of us rushing up the stairs. "I've been here longer than this squiffy strumpet, 'n 'tis how ye be treatin' me?!"

The Captain spoke angerly, "This is my ship, my rules and I do not take that behavior lightly!" She pushed past Daric, grabbing hold of Gibson's arm as she pushed him through the door onto the main deck, "You are getting off my ship." She growled stepped out to the rain-soaked deck.

Iggy grabbed Daric's arm as the man went to raise it to Gibson, "Stop, you don't have to do any of this. It's fine, it's now dealt with we can leave it at that." "No, Iggy." The Captain snapped.

He sunk low, trying to make himself small as now the whole night crew was listening in, watching from their posts, "I will not have someone who'd take advantage of a fellow shipmate like that on my ship."

In that moment, Daric and the Captain had turned from Gibson to face Iggy, giving Gibson a chance to act. Pulling a blade from the back of his pants he charged through Daric at Iggy, "You fuckin' cur," Iggy stepped back, raising his hands up in defence, closing his eyes.

I stepped forward, grabbing the blade, holding it in my hand and Gibson pushing back.

He grabbed hold of me as he tore the blade, slicing through the skin of my hand. I attempted the wrestle the blade from him with no prevail. In the dark heavy rain, I didn't pay attention to where Gibson and I were fighting. Only when he slammed my back against the railing, did I realise how dangerous it was getting for the two of us.

My blood soaked my arm and along with the rain, my grip slipped on Gibson and he took the chance turning me around, wrapping his forearm around me and placing his blade to my throat.

Iggy went to push through Daric and the Captain to rush to my aid, Daric grabbed him by the waist, pulling him in. Being careful not to hurt him yet keeping him secure at the same time.

The Captain's own weapon was drawn, and Victor was coming up the side, silently as Gibson hadn't yet noticed him.

I had. The blade pressed tightly against my skin; Gibson's hands shook. "One more step 'n I'll slit th' bastard's throat."

The Captain took a step back, lowering her sword. I pushed back against Gibson, he didn't move much so I knew his back was pressed against the railing. I turned my gaze to Iggy and gave him a weak smile. Iggy must have understood what I had planned as he tried to pull away from Daric franticly. "Axel!" He called out, as I kicked back, the force of my body causing Gibson and I to topple over the ledge of the ship towards to crashing ocean surface.

Gibson flailed, his knife slicing my chin rather deeply. We hit the dark, stormy water hard.

The second the two of us had gone over board Jane rushed to the ledge. She threw off her night coat as she searched the surface ready to dive in after me.

"Captain, no!" Daric called out, but his words weren't going to stop her.

She went to dive in when Victor snapped her right out of the air, she flailed and went to protest, but before she had the chance Victor handed the Captain off to Karlic who had stepped in to assist. Victor jumped in after me.

After Victor disappeared over the ledge the Captain pushed Karlic back and ran over looking, watching for a sign.

It was in the late hours of the night, even on the calmest night it would have been difficult to find a man overboard, and this wasn't a calm night as the waves crashed viciously against the boat.

"Victor!?" The Captain called down, scanning the waters, no one had yet to surface.

Iggy held his breath, he studied the Captain looking for her reactions, Daric refused to let him anywhere near the ledge.

"Karlic, get me lanterns and lots of rope."

Quickly the man obeyed the Captain's orders, she tied lantern after lantern to the rope and slowly lowered them one by one, handing the end of the rope to a different crew member. Once she tied the last one, she swayed it back and forth. Hoping that this would be a beckon for Victor and me to follow. Something to lead us back to the ship. Back to them.

This time when I hit the water, I didn't even attempt to hold my breath. I welcomed the water into my lungs knowing I could not drown. Kali's voice sung out to me, "Axel, come back to me. You know I will find you." But strangely it wasn't as loud as the first time I fell into the waters, as if she wasn't talking to me, but she was. She was still searching for me in the untamed sea, maybe her sight was off this night. So, I laid there as the water took me. Was this how I was going to let them be free of me? Was I just going to sink here? Let Kali find and take me? But Kai popped into my head, what was he going to do without me? Didn't he deserve a bit of an explanation? At least a goodbye, he'd been looking for me for a very long time, it was the least I could give him. So, I tried to look for the surface, but I was all turned around and the dark stormy waters above looked as dark as the sea below to me. I had to look for something, a sign to tell me which way to go. But it seemed that I had lost Gibson as well as the ship, I had nothing to go on as I just was there in the water.

Something or better say someone caught my eye as they broke through the surface of the water. That was my sign, I swam towards the disturbance. I hit the surface and cleared my lungs of water. I treaded looking around, finally spotting the ship in the slight distance, slowly drifting away from me.

A man surfaced a few feet from me; I was expecting Gibson, only to see the dark-skinned Victor who waved for me to follow, "Come, we must move smartly."

I nodded and followed his lead, I clearly wasn't as adapt to swimming as the man was, the waves knocking me back under the waters surface multiple times. If I could drown, I would have while trying to keep up with the man. Victor must have gotten annoyed with waiting for me and hoping that I would not drown as he took my arm. Pulling me into him, he wrapped his large arm around my chest, now keeping both of us afloat. Victor placed his fingers in his mouth and whistled, inhumanly loud when he got close enough to the massive ship. He knew that the crew would be searching, listening for a sign. He knew that little sound would reach someone's ear as he repeated ear-piercing noise.

Two ropes were tossed down, Victor tied mine around my waist after securing his own, before he whistled loudly once more, as the crew began to lift the two of us back aboard the ship.

Daric and Karlic helped both Victor and me over the ledge as I dropped to my knees, my body now shocked and numb from the cold. I couldn't help but shiver while the rain and wind pounded against me. Blood soaked the deck were my hand supported me.

Iggy knelt down painfully, next to me as he placed a warm blanket over my shoulders.

Victor amazingly, unaffected by the cold, the Captain offered the warmed blanket to the man with a scowl as she scowled back at him.

"Are you psychotic?!" Iggy asked, helping me wrap

the blanket around me.

Daric inspected the gash on my face as blood smeared down my neck. "That was reckless, another inch 'n that could 'ave been fatal."

I looked up at him, I could see the anger disappearing from his face. I nodded and looked back down pulling my bloody hand into my chest, it didn't hurt, but felt like it should.

The Captain stepped up to me and smacked Iggy and me upside the head. Iggy a lot lighter then she did to me as my head rang, she spoke down to us. "Go get your wounds tended to and rest, but this conversation is not over." The anger was still burning in her eyes as she waved her finger in our faces, but I could also see relief hidden in the sparkle of her eyes.

Chapter 15

Daric led Iggy and me to the infirmary in silence. I tried to read him, but he had gone cold and stone-faced. I couldn't tell it he was just so furious that he couldn't process how mad he was, or if it was just pain from betrayal?

Iggy and I sat down as Daric dug around for some needle and thread, he inspected my chin, jerking my face to the side so he could see the large gash better in the light. "Ye were lucky," he grumbled, more to himself then me. He dropped my face and inspected my hand, without giving me much warning of it, he stuck me with the needle as he began to thread the wound close. Lucky it wasn't painful for me, because Daric wasn't in the mood to be nice about it. Daric was bitter and hurt. He had known Iggy for two years, and yet Iggy wasn't brave enough to tell Daric what he was suffering through? Yet, I had only been here for just a few months and he had confided in me to keep this terrible secret. It wasn't fair to Daric;

all he ever did and all he ever wanted to do was protect Iggy from the exact thing he was keeping hidden from him.

I had come to understand that Daric and the Captain somewhat knew what was happening, but they didn't know it was as bad as it was. Daric felt guilty that he wasn't the one there to protect him from that. He was wondering what he did wrong. As he continued to stitch and bandage me up. I could tell the bitter anger was melting away, as the hurt, the guilt was building behind his cloudy eyes.

He couldn't look at Iggy as all he could think was *Why had Iggy been so afraid to tell me the truth? Did he really think that I would be disappointed that he needed help?* As the shame and guilt kept building in his mind, he found it hard to focus. Daric never criticized anyone for needing help and it hurt that Iggy would think that lowly of him. After inspecting the stitch work on my chin, he looked at my hand and grumbled. Turning away he went to search for clean bandages. He was about to say something to Iggy, but the words didn't come out of his mouth.

Iggy also was starting to let this night's events sink in, guilt and shame was written all over his face. Guilt of not saying something sooner and shame of letting is go as far as it did tonight. Iggy looked up at Daric who hadn't looked him in the eye since storming out of the Captain's chamber, "I'm sorry," he tried to get out only to have Daric snap back at him.

"Don't even start that shit wit' me, lad." His voice was scarily stern that froze and sent chills down both Iggy and my spine. We sat up slightly taller, Iggy silenced. He wrapped a clean bandage around my hand, Daric thought about what he wanted to say. How to voice all of what was running through his head, "I be sorry I failed ye, Iggy,"
Iggy tried to protest but Daric didn't give him the opportunity.

"I somehow made ye feel that ye couldn't come fore about this. That be me mistake. Me burden I now 'ave t' keep,"

"That was never my intention," Iggy argued but Daric waved him to silence. Iggy wanted to protest to explain himself, but the words wouldn't form in his mouth, the bitter pain Daric was feeling silenced all.

"Lift yer shirt. I'll wrap yer ribs 'n adjust yer shoulder." Daric bit down his emotions as he spoke. Iggy just nodded, doing as Daric asked looking away from his friend.

Daric wrapped Iggy up as gently as he could in silence, "Both o' ye go rest, I be done wit' ye."

Iggy tucked his arm into his shirt, creating a slight

sling so he can rest the weight from his shoulders. He motioned me to leave the medical bay along side him as we made our way to our cabin.

His hand was on the handle before he spoke, his grip caused his knuckles to turn white. "Why did you do that? Defend me," He turned to me with genuine curiosity, I was a god, and now I know I am a god, why would I do anything out of my way to protect a mortal, was running through his head.

I tried to think of a jester to explain my train of thought; he was my friend, it didn't matter if I wasn't mortal, so I placed my hand on my chest, above where my heart laid, before reaching out and placing my hand in the same spot on his chest.

It took him a moment to understand, but he smiled. "I care about you too, Axel."

We entered the room as he laid himself carefully down on the bed, propping himself up right, he attempted to get comfortable. He looked back at me as I sat sadly on the bed.

"Even though you are a god, and I suppose you can't get hurt, by mortal mean. I was afraid that you were going to be lost for good, that Gibson was going to hurt you." I turned to face Iggy who refused to look back and meet my stare, "Be more careful next time you try something stupid like that." There was something behind his words that he nor I understood, I smiled at him. He caught it, and somehow, he understood that I would do it all again in a heartbeat. He punched me on the shoulder lightly, before closing his eyes and resting his head against the wall. I curled up in my cot and watched over my friend as he drifted into a deep sleep, snoring softly.

Unsure of how long he had been in the water the cold was already numbing his limps. Gibson had been lucky so far as the waves finally settled around him. Though he was a fool; thinking that the goddess of sea had favored him with her blessing, no. She was waiting patiently.

Gibson suddenly knew he wasn't alone in the dark waters, he could feel something had awoken, something was trailing for him. Gibson could see in the near distance, land, and he forced the numbness away and used all his reserved energy to escape the monster that was awaking at his feet. The creature that was slowly, yet surely catching up to him. His guess was a great white, or something mortal, he would have never guessed that the creature perusing him for its mistress was the great, Leviathan herself. He was finally in the home stretch, no shark would venture this close to land, he figured himself safe as he continued, wishing for the feeling of the sand on his frozen toes.

A horrid, screech filled his ears, and his heart with fear. He now knew his mistake in slowing, his mistake in thanking Kali for not allowing the sea to swallow him whole. Bubbles formed behind him as he turned his head and watched the sea sway and part as the massive creature lifted her head from the depth, her eyes locking onto her target. She screeched again.

Gibson screamed and turned away from the beast, he thought he had to make a break for it, he had to reach the shore, maybe the shoreline would protect him from the giant Leviathan, a creature many sailors spoke of, as in myth and yet now the creature was hunting him!

He swore that the creature giggled at him, as she watched him swim away in terror, but her snake like tail reached for him, wrapping around his body, she brought the tiny human to her face, and inhaled the man's scent. She growled as the mortal, clawed at her tail, praying that doing so would free him from her grasp, but there was no point. Once the great creature had her pray, there was no fighting it.

She dove back under the water, dragging the flaying

and screaming man behind her, as she took her captive to her mistress.

Kali was waiting on the shore, just far enough out the city's light that no one would see her beautiful pet, as much as she wasn't worried if they had. The Leviathan would easily enough eaten, any and all bystanders who dared continue watch. But she didn't needlessly seek the death of mortals, they were partly her children, creatures she grew to love. She only wished harm on those who stood in her way of her own happiness. She sometimes had to act like a monster, but she wasn't always that.

Finally, her precious baby returned, dropping the mortal at her feet. The man shivered, now in fear rather then the cold that still numbed and pained his entire body.

Kali looked down at the man and glared coldly, firmly grabbing the man's chin with her hand, forcing his gaze up to hers. "Why did my creature bring you to me? When all I seek is my brother," She yelled more at the beast, then the unknowing mortal before her.

Gibson's lips chattered, "The Goddess of the sea," He stammered, his eyes wide in awe, "I know nah o' wha' ye ask." The words foolishly pooled from his lips.

She eyed the man up and down, familiar was his face. "Where have I seen you?" She asked herself, the man went to answer, but she waved him off, closing her eyes she took in the mans scent. She smiled, "That is why," She could smell the clear scent of her brother, as his blood traced on his clothes and under his finger nails. "Why is my brother scent all over you?" She asked with a wicked and angry smile as she studied the pirate. "His blood?"

"Yer brother?" He stammered, the clued had yet to piece together in his mind.

She grabbed his hand, bringing it up to her face as she used her nail to scrape out the skin imbedded in his.

Finally, it clicked. "Th' mute? Th' stranger?"

"Mute?" She questioned, placing her hand on her chin, "Guess fear wasn't the reason he dared not speak to me when we last met. Maybe my binding enchantment backfired on him when he escaped and that was his curse? Or something else," She thought aloud. "Where is my brother now, mortal?" She finally spoke to him.

Gibson shrugged honestly, "If ye brother is the man I suspect he maybe, then lost as sea. He doesn't seem to be the best of swimmers."

Kali laughed, bitterly. "If he was at sea, my child would not have brought you to me." She thought for a moment, "You are no use to me then," She whistled to her creature who was waiting patiently for her command.

"Wait! Please, goddess of the sea, I can help you find him!"

She snapped as the creature's mouth was inches from her pray.

"If he is not at sea, then they must have found him and brought him back aboard. I can help you find them, I know which way they sail." He pleaded with the goddess, who twirled her hair with one finger, tangling the braid.

She pondered his usefulness, her baby was ever so hungry, but at last, she smiled at the pathetic trembling mortal who knelt before her. "Inform me of where to send my child, if you are determined to be of use to my quest for my dear brother, you will be greatly rewarded."

"Thank you, Goddess!" Gibson groveled at her feet, thankful for her mercy and thankful to be on land once again.

He told the Goddess everything, yet the sun was coming on the horizon, she was to wait, patiently for the moon to once again rise into the skies, only then would she sent her creature out to hunt again.

Chapter 16

I woke to Iggy; he was sitting on the floor with his back to me as he washed his shoulders, back and neck. Bruising went all the down his arm, fully around his neck, and if his chest hadn't been wrapped up, I would have seen the thick yellow and green bruising that covered. It was by far the worst I had seen, and yet he seemed unfazed as he stretched the stiffness out before throwing a long-sleeved shirt on. He went to tie a bandana around his neck when he paused.

I quickly wrote down, "You'll need more then that to hide those." I waved my book in his face.

He turned around and smiled with a shrug, "Habit's die hard." He still knotted the red fabric around him as I gave a small smile and the shake of my head.

I had been expecting things to be different on the ship, but it wasn't unfolding as I had pictured it would.

The Captain informed the crew of Gibson's removal,

without going into details as the crew didn't ask. They all knew, either in first hand experience or the rumors and even though the crew hated Gibson as person. He was a vile, angry drunk, who before Iggy came aboard would fumble around with the women of the streets whenever they docked, getting banned from brothel after brothel for his 'abusive tendencies'. But to his credit he was a good cook, so his departure angered most of the crew, that morning their bitterness showed as they eyed both Iggy and I throughout the day. We sat away from everyone, as we always did. Iggy knew that this would happen, I couldn't believe it.

Iggy's back was towards everyone as he sunk into himself, all he wished was for the events of last night to be forgotten, there was a darkness in his heart that wished that last night didn't happen. He would have suffered through more of Gibson's abuse if it meant these hateful stares would dissipate, especially knowing that these weren't going to be the worst, as they had yet to encounter Daric this morning.

I wanted to comfort him, but my lack of understanding the situation caused me to pause, I couldn't wrap my head around their anger towards Iggy. He hadn't done anything wrong.

Iggy pulled himself out of his own head as he

inspected my face, the large gash had already practically healed over, "Wow, I thought I healed fast," He thought as he leaned in slightly to get a better look at it, "Does it hurt?" more wanting to ask if it could hurt a god.

I shook my head no as he smiled, but it was short lived.

Victor stepped into the dining hall; the room went silent and everyone seemed to turn to mind their own business. He walked over to Iggy and me, his bare chest flexed as he towered over the two of us sitting down, "Crows nest, Captain's orders."

Iggy nodded, "Yes sir," with that he stood up and headed for the door.

I followed his que, I could feel all eyes on, me? As we walked away, maybe the stares weren't as directed to Iggy, as they were to me? I began to question my time aboard this ship. Maybe it was more limited then I had imagined.

Jane had given Daric the day off; he decided to somberly walk through the inner halls of the ship, dragging his feet as he swung his nearly empty bottle of whiskey. He took a swig as he vividly remembered the night they had met Iggy. The night they made a promise, a promise he failed to keep.

They had picked the perfect night to board the slave ship; the moon was black as they waited for the darkest hour. The Crew of the ship was either oblivious of the Shadow's Blade's advances, or they didn't care to inform their slave drivers.

Jane tried to push her way to the front of the assault, only to have Victor and Daric push her back as they advanced at the head of the pack. Together they incapacitated the first two guards, silently binding their hands to the railing, and gagging them so if they woke, they couldn't call for alarm. Turning back to the rest of the crew of the Shadow's Blade they waved them forward, lifting the Captain over the railing as her crew got ready to climb over at different vantage points of the ship.

There were four quiet bird whistles; that meant the rest of the crew were in position, Victor with a loud and powerful last whistle told the crew to advance and take out the rest of the guards.

The crew of the Shadow's Blade began their assault of the Slave ship, Daric, Victor and the Captain had another mission. Jane made it a personal vendetta to hurt every slave master who dared to share the same waters as her. While the other members of her ship were to free the slaves and kill all the slave drivers and guards by the end of this siege.

Today the Slave Master she had in her sights was a name by the name of Stealio Thorne. She had the plan of removing his head from his shoulders and sending it to the capital as a message. Jane had a personal, undying hatred for Stealio Thorne. She had suffered first hand to the man's brutality, and that was early in his Slave trading career, word of mouth had been that he had become even more of a monster once he claimed the title of Slave Master aboard his own vessel. "Perfecting" his craft.

The Captain had her own twisted plan running through her head, while Daric's focus was on keeping her safe and out of more trouble than she could handle.

Victor cornered a Slave in the hall as they made their way down, he tried to soften his voice, not to scare the poor barely dressed woman, but his thick, grumbly accent caused her to freeze and cry. "Where are th' Slave Master's shillin's?"

She was petrified as she shook her head as if she didn't understand the question.

Jane pushed him aside and rolled her eyes with the motion. She smiled sweetly to the young girl, with large brown eyes as short cropped red hair. Jane pulled up her sleeve revealing her slave mark to the woman, "Please, where is Stealio Thorne?"

She still paused, almost in disbelief that this, confident woman had once been in her shoes, but finally she looked around nervously and pointed down the hall, "Two floors down, the room at the very end," She had a strange accent that Jane had never heard before, making her almost hard to understand, "You will know when you get there."

Jane grabbed the girl's hand softly, "Go up to the deck, my men will help you." With a smile they were off.

The girl was correct; when they got to the door, they knew that it was his. His name was engraved with gold into the solid oak door was a dead giveaway, but even more so was the armed guard standing at the ready. The slave Masters' second hand, Quill. The tanned man upon seeing the three drew a large curved blade from his belt, cocking his head at the strange intruders.

Daric spoke, "We're not here fer' the likes of ye', ye' no longer have to serve that monster." He tried to reason with the slave, but even before Daric was able to finish, Victor drew his sword just in time to parry the man's blow.

Victor and Quill's eyes met as the Slave stepped back regaining his footing.

Quill attacked again with more ferocity, in an attempt to catch Victor off guard, but he was also quick footed and again parried his attack, swiftly and easily.

Quill charged again, this time catching Victor heavy in the shoulder, but to Quill's surprise, Victor raised his knee up into the man's stomach. Quill stumbled, while Victor then grabbed the blade of the sword, seemly unaffected by the deep wound, Victor than gave the man a strong right hook to the jaw, knocking the stumbling man out cold.

Victor grumbled as he looked at his wound, "Another scar fer th' books, Captain."

Jane smiled and shook her head, "Deal with him and head up. Help the rest of the men with the Slaves and crew, Daric and I can handle this creep."

He glared at his Captain, hesitant to follow her order, but Daric nodded. Victor understood that she was safe in his hands as he nodded back as he begun to bind Quill tightly before dragging him up to the main deck.

Daric and Jane pressed their heads against the door before continuing, they knew that the Slave Master would have heard the sword fight. They looked at each other, drew their weapons and pushed forward into the chambers.

Stealio Throne was no where to be seen, but a secret passageway had been left open. They could hear the faintest sounds of hastened footsteps, quickly getting out of ear shot.

Daric and Jane would have rushed after him without a second thought, but someone caught their attention.

In the room, on a large plush bed, laying barely conscious was a very, thin, naked boy. His ankle was chained to the bed frame, his hands bound in front of him, bloody from rubbing his skin raw. His unnaturally crystal blue eyes looked up to them just for a moment. They were red and puffy from tears and tiredness. His body was thin and covered in bruises along his pale legs and stomach, where his near perfect face was unblemished by Stealio's brutality.

Daric's stomach dropped as he had to fight the urge to be sick, never before had he seen a boy being used in such way, it disgusted him. Even more, seeing that the boy before them couldn't be that old.

The boy on the bed covered his face with his arms and cowered to the sight of the strangers unsure of their intentions, but it was the only thing he could do in defense, his body was too weak.

Jane slowly stepped forward kneeling at the end of

the bed, still keeping some distance to not scare him anymore than they had already done. "It's okay," she tried to stay calm, even though her anger was building as she wanted Stealio's head. She showed the boy her brand, which was identical to hers, "My name is Captain Jane Far'mel, what's yours?"

The red-haired boy uncovered his face, resting his still bound hands over his lower half to cover himself as much as he could, while trying to sit up. His voice was broken from dehydration, but he managed to say weakly, "Ignatius,"

She smiled softly and waved Daric to approach, which still took him a minute for his feet to respond to the command. "We are here to help. My Friend here is Daric, he's a very nice man and will never do anything to hurt you. He's going to unchain you and take you up to our ship."

Daric approached and unchained the boy's ankle, the boy stared nervously at Daric who took the hint and took a step back.

Jane smiled again, "Trust him, I did and I've never regretted it." She rushed off after Stealio Throne, giving Daric no choice but to let her go as he was now entrusted with the well being of this young, terrified boy.

Daric stepped forward, "I'll untie yer hands," he said

softly as he took off his trench coat draping it over the boy as Ignatius offered his hands to the man.

The boy began to cry as he dropped his chin, his voice was broken, cracked an barely a whisper as only Daric heard his plea, "Please, just kill me."

Daric got choked up as he dropped the young slaves binds, cupping his hands, he gave a reassuring smile, "Ye will ne'er suffer like this again as long as I be around. I promise ye this."

Ignatius looked up at the man and nodded, trusting the man completely in that moment. Daric than asked as he helped wrap his trench coat to cover the boy, "Can ye walk?"

The boy took a step off the bed, only to fall as Daric caught him, "'tis okay, I got ye." As Daric lifted the boy up, young Ignatius wrapping his arms around Daric's neck as he rested his tired head against the pirate's shoulder. Feeling safe for the first time, his eyes closed, and he fell asleep in the man's arms. Daric never told anyone this, but instantly he felt the urge to protect and care for him. He was instantly connected, and he knew in his heart and soul that he would die for this boy if needed.

While Daric carried Ignatius up to the main deck; Jane had cornered her prey. She bound him, dragging him up to the main deck as she then proceeded to carve the mans chest, flay his arms clean of flesh before watching him bleed out before decapitating him and mounting his head on the mermaid that road on the front of the ship.

Many of the slaves came aboard the Shadow's Blade that night, getting dropped off as freemen and women at the next port, but the bulk of the slaves took the slave ship and sailed off. Ignatius, Iggy was the one only to stay aboard.

Daric was thrown from his memory as he stumbled up on the Captain who was charting a new course. She was also lost in the same thought Daric was focused on, and hadn't yet heard him come in until he spoke, "Care fer rum?"

She looked up as she pulled her own mostly finished bottle, "Got myself covered."

Chapter 17

The moon finally showed itself on this dark cloudy night, luminating the angry, stormy waves that crashed and pulled at the ship. I looked passed the bow of the ship, while Iggy looked passed the stern, glancing at the map he had unfolded, keeping the ships position.

Now the thing that scared me wasn't something I saw that night; it was what I felt it in the air. I felt her awaken. I felt it in my soul.

There was a rumble from the ocean dept's, in the chaos of the night before I had somehow missed her being awakened. But this time I was unable to miss it. I could almost hear Kali's twisted giggle in the wind as it whispered its soft warning in my ears. My heart began to race as I scanned the sea, *maybe we still have time?* I questioned as I shook Iggy's arm in a panic.

Iggy looked back, trying to see what I was so panicked about as I tried to communicate the danger to him, but I gave up rather quickly. Jumping down from the crows-nest, my hands burning as I slid down the rope's not wasting my time with the ladder. Iggy in confusion followed me, yet down the ladder, which was a far more intelligent move as my hands ached. I rushed over to Victor, as I scribbled in my note book, Iggy decided not to follow me up to Victor who was steering the ship. Iggy entered the ship, I rightfully assumed going to find the captain.

Victor looked in confusion at my four words, in very bold letters. *Get to shore, now!* I tapped the paper furiously, trying to imbed my warning in his head, finally, if ever so hesitantly he turned the wheel turning the ship in the direction of land.

Yet, sadly my warning was too late.

Iggy had retrieved the Captain and Daric just in time to hear the creature shriek, the great Leviathan broke the water's surface. Her body left a dark, shadow over the ship, the creatures teeth glistened, a low growl sent fear in the crew's bones.

The Captain's jaw dropped, all words escaped her. Daric was just as stunned and sobered up instantly, he was had to work quickly. He rushed to the wall and rang the bell, signalling all hands to stations, they were under attack by one of the great creatures of myth.

The creature was many times the size of the ship in length; her serpent like body slithered from the depts and towered over the ship. She screeched again, diving causing a small tidal wave to over come the seemingly tiny ship.

Daric grabbed hold of Iggy and the Captain as the wave over took them, some how he managed to keep his footing while Iggy and the Captain were swept off their feet. The ship rocked and creaked under the force.

I had been completely knocked off my feet, Victor tried to grab hold of me, while tightly holding on to the wheel, but I was swept away. Hitting my back hard against the railing, I barely managed to hang on as the ship steadied herself.

The Captain rushed up the stairs towards Victor and I, "How far to shore are we?"

"Still a while out, Captain." He as he continued to turn the ship.

I could see her getting lost in thought as she plotted in her head the best course of action.

Victor grabbing a hold of the Captain's waist as the creature knocked the ship with her behemoth of a body, knocking the Captain and many of the crew who were arming themselves and manning the ship off their feet once again.

Finally, the Captain spoke, "We aren't running." She realized they couldn't outrun the beast that was already upon them, and turning their back to her would leave them defenceless, so she turned the ship back around facing just to the side of the creature, they were going to circle it, and attack with everything they had.

"Daric, get the black powder barrels into the water on my marks!"

"Aye, Captain!" Daric called out; he waved Morgan, Jackal, Jessie, and Iggy, as they all rushed down through the inners of the ship.

The Captain turned to me, "Go to the bell, and on my order ring it."

Victor handed me one of his swords as fear struck me, but I did as I was told, with a nod and a salute. I ran down the stairs.

The Leviathan's eyes caught me as she went in for an attack, her large head crashing into the side of the ship, missing me. Only narrowly. My heart pounded, I held out Victor's blade, waiting for the Captain's orders.

She rushed to the railing, leaning mostly over to see if I was alright and in place, Captain yelled out to me, "Axel, now!"

I rang the bell on her order as three large barrels fell

into the water, once they were far enough from the ship and close to the creature, the Captain ordered me again as I rang the bell. Canon's fired, igniting the barrels as they went off in a large explosion.

The Leviathan screamed in pain, but it did not cripple the creature as it merely angered her. Her tailed whipped up, slamming hard against the ship, the force sending two crew members flying from their post, the creature reached in and snatched one in her jaws, she must have been sniffing for me, as it took her a second before she crunched down on the man, he was a tiny speck in her mouth as blood sprayed in every direction as she ate him in two quick bites.

Victor used his body to cover the Captain from the creature's gaze as everyone looked up in horror.

"Axel, again!" She barked. I jumped. Ringing the bell once again.

Again, more barrels floated from the ship. She called to me again, and as I rang the bell, the canon's fired.

The Leviathan flailed, screaming in pain, her head colliding with the mass, tearing it wide and deep.

This time the canon's fired without order, the creature swept her head over the deck, crushing and crashing into crew, and pinning me against the wall by broken crates.

I freed my hand and sword as I just caught the corner of her cheek with my blade. The metal rather ineffective against her crystal hard scales. I had missed my target, as I was aiming for her eyes.

I tried to squirm my way out of the rubble. Victor and Karlic thankfully had rushed to my aid, tossing the wood scraps easily enough, as they then jumped in to help the other crew members who were caught.

I grabbed Taylor, one of the younger, newer men aboard, placing his hand on the bell. The man nodded understanding what I was trying to ask as I rushed inward the ship, I had to find Daric. They had to aim for her eyes.

The bell rang again and the four of them rolled out three more barrels, Daric the only one soloing barrels down the open ramp.

Four other men maned the canon's, they waited for the Captain's orders.

The door opened, and I rushed in the room straight to Daric, the creature crashed into the side of the boat, knocking everyone but Daric off their feet.

Iggy nearly fell out the ramp, but Jackal grabbed hold of his arm pulling them both out of harm's way as they steadied themselves.

I stood up and pointed to my eye, then pointed in

the direction of the Leviathan.

It didn't even take Daric a second to understand what I was saying, he ordered, "Aim fer th' eyes!"

Morgan and Jackal hit their target easily enough, while Jesse had missed. They reloaded the canon's as fast as they could, but the monster now knew where the fire had been coming from. Her strong tail swept across the opening, wood smashed, leaving a large gap in the ship, knocking everyone about again. Iggy lost his footing and tumbled towards the opening in the side of the ship, "No!" My voice broke as the word left my mouth, the sound startled not only myself but Daric and Iggy. I grabbed hold of my friends' hand while pulling him into my chest and tossing us to the ground, the force of hitting the ground stung and sent pain through Iggy's chest, his broken rib ached, as I pressed my body against him. He gasped as the breath knocked out of him for a second, but he was okay with the pain, he knew how close he was to going overboard.

Our eyes met, we were face to face, barely inches apart. In that moment I was breathless. He smiled up at me in thanks. I could taste iron as if my throat ripped open with the word that had escaped my mouth, I smiled back at him before helping him off the ground.

Daric didn't have time to respond to the new development of my voice. He poked his head out, trying to follow the monsters war path. He waited for her to steady its great head, and at that moment, she regained her footing and located her pray Daric yelled fire. This time all three of the canon's aimed for the creature's eye and fired, Jesse, redeeming herself as she was the only one to hit their mark.

The Leviathan pulled back from the ship as she cried out in pain, one eye bloody and closed. Her nostrils flared angerly as she sniffed the area, she was scanning for me. I wonder if I had just thrown myself into the water if she'd leave the ship alone, leave the rest of the crew alone, but I knew better, so I stayed put. Daric signaled for the three to fire once again at the creature, this time they all hit their target, blinding the creature completely. She flailed, screeching in pain, her body tearing apart the foremast, as the large pillar crashed into the deck.

The three fired again, the creature stumbled backwards. She screamed defeated, as she sunk back into the sea. We had won this battle. Today at least.

Daric wanted to address the fact I managed to speak my first word since boarding this ship, but he knew that he had to first, check on the Captain and second assess the damages done to the ship before he could even begin to unwrap the mess of me.

I helped the other few shipmates patch the large gaping hole in the side of the side, pushing Iggy out of the way when he tried to help. Morgan, Jackal and Jesse all agreed with my decision as Iggy was even finding it hard to hide the amount of pain he was in.

It wasn't the best patch job, but it was the best that we could manage at the time.

Finally, I rubbed my throat and the group of us emerged onto the deck to see the damage done above.

Only two crew members were lost this night, one who horridly got eaten by the Leviathan, while the other disappeared under the waves. The crew took a long moment of silence as they worked to clean up the massive mess and assist injured crew members, seven had minor injures, and one crew member had his leg crushed by the foremast beam. As much as it pained the crew to have to do this to their friend, but the only option was to remove the leg.

They had already removed the leg and cauterized the wound of the fainted Jayson and were now moving him down to the medical wing by the time I and the others from the canon room made it back to the main deck.

The Captain barked orders as her crew worked quickly, her gaze finally turning to us, "Iggy, go help Echo in the medical wing. You aren't any use to me on deck at this moment,"

"Captain, I'm fine." He tried to protest, but before the sentence left his mouth she had already waved him off with a cold glare.

She snapped, "I don't care what pain you have pushed through in the past. I am giving you a direct order to go help Echo in the medical wing." She growled angrily. Iggy just nodded, turning on the ball of his feet knowing his error in judgement to question her.

"Axel," She snapped at me, if I could have I would have let out a small yelp in fear, "Go find Daric or Victor and help them with whatever they need, I will come to find you later."

I didn't dare hesitate as I began to obey her order even before she had finished addressing me. I now knew why she was one of the most feared Captains in these waters.

Her ship was in disarray, Jane looked over her ship as her crew attempted to pull her back together, a very stressed sigh left her mouth. Jane rubbed the temples of her forehead; never before in her life sailing had some come face to face with a monster from legends such as that. It made her begin to question a lot of things that she didn't believe in, she wondered now if she was cursed or blesses. That creature if she wanted too could have torn the ship to pieces and left them to drown or feast upon them. That's when her eyes locked on me, as I helped lift the mast back into place. *Was he the reason for all our trouble? Lilianna and Angela didn't fear him,* she didn't want to admit it to herself that she liked the mysterious naked man they had found on the beach all those months ago. But so many questions were piling together, and all were pointing to the fact that I might not be a good thing for the Shadows Blade.

Chapter 18

Kali was standing with her legs in the warm ocean waters, her hem of her white dressed soaked and stained by the dirt and sand, her feet bare, her toes sinking into the soft sand. She was beautiful there was no denying that; as the morning sun luminated her perfect face, but her bitterness overtook her calmness as she looked out to sea. The morning light was here, and yet her Leviathan had not returned with it's pray. Kali knew that she had failed. She knew that her creature had sunk back into the depths to rest, to heal. Her Leviathan had failed her. "Axel," She whispered angerly to the wind as I had caused her 'trump card' to fail. Kali closed her eyes, feeling for her creature's pain, her frustration; she would be fine, but she needed time. She needed the oceans to heal her and bring back her strength. Kali had to think of a new plan to bring me into her clutches.

She stormed from the beach, where Gibson was washing the marble floor of her temple.

The man must have felt her anger as she stormed up to him. He jumped up from his knees and backed away quickly from the angered goddess with his hands up in defence. "Me goddess, wha' be wrong?" She grabbed him by the throat pinning him against the back wall, he felt real fear, he was defenseless, "How did your Captain's ship defeat my child? They are mortal's!" She screamed her head tilted to the side in question.

"Maybe yer brother used his god magic?" He trembled as she squeezed tighter, her nails digging into the man's neck, blood trickled down.

"I have all his godly powers! He more useless than a mortal at this point." She growled.

"Well," He stuttered trying to thick quickly on his feet. "I dunno why or how yer creature could 'ave failed, but," his words stuttered again, "I know how ye can lure 'im right t' ye! I swear,"

She released, just slightly as he peaked her interest again. "Explain yourself? But know this if you fail me, I will feed you to my child." She leaned in her lips brushing against his ear, "I will enjoy hearing your bones crunch under the force of her jaw."

"Thar be a lad on th' ship, his name be Ignatius. Axel has grown mighty attached t' 'im, his affection fer 'im be why we got into a fight that night, why I got tossed o'erboard." He explained to her.

She squeezed him tighter, "He's the god of death, he doesn't care about mortals. He in the reason our creations have limited life spans."

"But he does! I swear t' ye, me goddess!" She cocked her head to the side inspecting him for lies, "I dunno why, but yer brother has a connection wit' 'im. He also be fond o' th' Captain, Jane Far'mel 'n Daric Greymorn th' second in command. But that Ignatius, he would risk his life in a heartbeat fer that wee bastard."

He could see the puzzlement in her eyes as she released him, Gibson dropping hard to his ass, placing his hand on the red mark from her hand. He wondered if he would have a bruise there.

Kali bent down, leaning in very close to him, her hand cupping the side of his face, "Do you swear on your life?" She smiled coyly, she didn't believe his words, but you don't swear your life to a goddess and lie. Her brother was a soulless god of death, was it even possible for him to have feelings for a human? She questioned. Did this boy have a secret power? As she thought of Kai, the only person close enough to being mortal that I had ever cared for. In her mind at least.

"I swear t' ye on me life," He swallowed hard as she

brushed the side of his cheek.

"Where would that ship be traveling?"

"Dunmore," he whimpered nervously, "'tis a pirate hot spot, they be goin' t' needs some new crewmembers 'n stock up, possibly repairs aft fightin' wit' yer beast."

She stood tall and crossed her arms over her chest, "I wonder, could it possibly be true that a mortal stole my dear brother's heart?" She smiled, wanting to laugh at the thought, "Dear Gibson, you have a new task ahead of you." She gave a toothy grin as a plan began to fall into place in her mind.

Hours had passed, and the ship was starting to look as good as she was gonna get until we get her to a pirate port for repairs. My shoulder and face were burnt from the sun as I fell to the deck, arms out as I closed my eyes for a moment of rest.

We had managed to scavenge enough to patch the large hole in the hull of the ship, and partially fix the mainmast, but the foremast had been destroyed beyond our ability. Luckily, we had enough sail power to get us moving, but it was going to be a crawl.

My muscles melted into the hot wood; I was pushing my mortal frame past it's limit. I could feel myself slowing down as if I was disconnecting from this body. I thought back, I had realized, I had never remained in a mortal frame for more then a few hours before this all happened. I wasn't born to stay I one timeline for so long, I wasn't made for this luxury of bonding with mortals and I could feel it taking a toll on me. My time to stop running from Kali was coming quick, quicker than I realized. My heart ached at the thought, *I'm not ready for this to end.* Iggy's face flashed before my mind, his smile, his nervous ticks. Daric, Jane, I wasn't ready to leave them either, I was invested in their lives. *I don't want to just be a bystander anymore. I don't want to be alone anymore.* I opened my eyes and looked up at the now clear blue skies above me.

Iggy, the person I was thinking about leaned over me, sticking his head in my view as he smiled down at me. His smile wiped away my somber thoughts as I smiled back at him.

He was back to just wearing his vest and his bracers as his one arm was tucked into the arm hole of the vest, still using it as a makeshift sling, his ribs still tightly wrapped, "Day dreaming?"

I shrugged as I pulled myself to a seated position, Iggy taking a seat down next to me. "You're like a guardian angel for me. With all that chaos last night, if I would have fallen in, there would have been no chance of me getting back to the ship." There was a nervousness in his voice as he recalled how close that call really was, "I owe you a lot over this short time of knowing you," he brushed his hair back with his fingers smoothing the knots out.

I just smiled, I hope he understood I'd do anything in my power to help him. I would do anything he asked of me. I studied his face as he looked up at the clear skies, in that moment I thought I understood how Daric felt about Iggy. I thought that I felt the same way for Iggy as Daric did.

"Have you tried to say anything else?"

I bet he had been thinking about that all night and day, my throat still burned painfully and the subtle taste of blood was still at the back of my throat. I tried to force the word no to my lips, but it turned into a very painful growl, as I placed my hand on my throat.

He placed a reassuring hand on my back with another smile, "One word is still a step in the right direction,"

I didn't meet his smile, I just nodded. I tried to think back, tried to place why I lost my voice, somethings just still weren't completely adding up in my head...

Bound by chains I tried to convince Kali that I couldn't bring him back, I tried to tell her this wasn't going to change anything as she dropped the anchor into the water off the small boat, a few yards away from her temples dock, "Kali, please. I can't do anything more; it was his time. Taking my cloak, my powers, torturing me it won't bring him back," But that was all she heard as the chain dragged me off the boat. I plummeted into the water, I struggled, fought, but it was no use. The salt filled my lungs as I tried to call out to Kali, I tried to plead with her, but my words fell on deaf ears as my calls were muffled by the sea.

I shook the image away as a realization arose, I couldn't remember escaping my binds... I couldn't pick her magical locks; I couldn't wiggle free. A question dawned on me, how long was I actually down there? Was I just calling for my sister and broke my voice? Could that really be the simple answer... Did the ocean finally corrode my binds that I broke free? I shivered thinking back as Iggy placed his arm over my shoulder and rested his head against me, "Don't stress, I got you."

I managed to smile back at him this time, but it was a sad one as I knew it was the time to think about saying my goodbyes.

That night, while most of the crew slept a small chunk gathered in the mess hall, Jorgen stood up to address them. His greasy graying locks stuck to his face. His voice cracked as he spoke in a loud, raspy whisper, "Axel be a curse upon us all. First, he corrupts Ignatius 'n Gibson's minds, forcin' them t' quarrel t' gain a better standin' wit' th' Captain 'n Daric as a secret hero in waitin'." The crowd was clearly unconvinced, they all assumed Iggy had just grown tired of the man's abuse. So Jorgen continued to sell them on his theory, "Ignatius ne'er complained afore, 'twas wha' he was bred t' do! Th' only reason he fought back was th' Stranger bewitched 'im!" He growled, pointing at everyone seated around him, he was self aware enough to realize he was getting too loud as he placed his own finger to his lips, "'n then he sends his monster t' come 'n attack us. We be lucky t' be alive here today."

Taylor was the one to question him, "If he was a curse, or if he sent th' creature t' attack us, would we 'ave survived that attack?" He went to comment on the obvious about Iggy and Gibson, but Jorgen jumped on that, his finger pointed inches from Taylor's face.

"In all yer years o' sailin' 'ave ye ever faced a creature like that?" The group all mumbled no as Jorgen jumped on the opportunity. "'n now that he had come aboard, we 'ave? I've been sailin' fer twenty plus years 'n I 'ave ne'er seen a monster like that. I tell ye all, he be a curse, we should rally together 'n rid ourselves o' 'im afore 'tis too late 'n he takes our lives." Still, most of them weren't convinced, "Do ye really believe he has no voice, no memory? He was found naked on a beach, maybe he's a siren!" As the thoughts formed in his head, he caught their attention.

"Aren't sirens girls? There job is to lure men to their deaths?" Morgan asked scratching his ear.

"Usually, but our Captain be a lady, maybe they can change thar appearance? A Captain's soul be a siren's fav'rit." Heads started to turn as they looked around at each other, this story being told was beginning to make sense to them as they nodded, "That's why he be tryin' t' get on th' Captain's good side, he jus' didn' know th' Captain ain't into scallywags." Jorgen was in a stride, "Ignatius 'n Gibson 'ave always been questionable in thar preference, clearly, both 'ave laid wit' men, so that be how Axel was able t' manipulate them!"

"What about Daric?" Reefer questioned.

Jorgen rolled his eyes as he had to think quickly to come up with a reasonable explanation for him, "Daric listens t' whatever th' Captain says, 'n he has a soft spot fer Ignatius as he be a surrogate fer his late son. Ye get Ignatius 'n th' Captain, ye 'ave ensnared Daric as well."

"Daric be still sceptical o' th' stranger," Vendell added.

It was true, Daric wasn't completely trusting of me at the moment, he knew better then anyone that I was hiding somethings from the crew, and that may have been my downfall with these men who were now on Jorgen's side, believing me to be a creature of myth, which he wasn't completely wrong.

"How are we goin' t' stop 'im? We needs t' protect our Captain!"

The group sounded in agreements.

Jorgen smiled as he finally took a seat, ushering the crew to huddle closer, "We got t' figure a plan out together,"

Chapter 19

That night I found that I couldn't sleep. I wanted too, I really needed it as all I wanted to do was dive headfirst into the darkness. My head was flooded with thoughts, haunting me. I laid, resting my warm hand on my still sore throat, it was strange, both my cuts were completely healed, but still my voice, my throat ached as if someone burned the inside of my throat, was not healing. Would I ever fully recover my voice? I tried to audibly sigh as it turned into an agonizing growl. Iggy's words popped into my head as I rolled over and looked at his sleeping face, *one word is better than nothing.* I could help but smile.

There was a very quiet rapping on the door, I sat up, rolling my feet off the bed as I watched Daric open the door slowly peaking his head through the crack, "Axel, ye awake?"

Surprise lightened his face, as he wasn't actually expecting me to be awake, "Ye up fer joinin' me fer a walk?"

I shook my head yes. I tied my boots before throwing on a thick shirt, following Daric as we managed to not disturb Iggy from his slumber.

We walked in silence, Daric's hands deep in his pockets as we hit the main deck; morning was already coming over the horizon. Had I really been tossing and turning for that long? I had to laugh at myself; as the god of time, my awareness of how quickly the time went by seemed to escape me. Ironic.

I followed him up the steps towards the helm, were Victor was standing steering the ship. He for the first time since meeting seemed tired, as his stern, composed expression was drooping off his dark toned face.

"Get out o' here, Victor, get some rest." Daric dismissed the man who took the offer happily. Daric turned to me and waved me to the helm, "Take th' wheel,"

Confused, I did as I was told, my hands gripping it so tightly my knuckles went slightly pale.

Daric tried to hold back his laugher, a small chuckle left his mouth, "Ye aren't tryin' t' strangle a chicken, relax."

I looked down at my hands and smiled, doing as he suggested.

It took him longer then I expected to start to tell me what was really on his mind, why he asked me to join him here, but finally he did, "'twas ne'er me intention t' make Iggy feel like he couldn't come t' me wit' his issues, somehow I made 'im believe he couldn't trust me wit' th' truth about Gibson. Th' Captain 'n I knew somethin' had been goin' on fer a wee while, even afore ye came aboard, but he was far better at hidin' how bad 'twas than we realized. I should 'ave tried t' push th' truth out o' 'im, but I was ne'er good at natterin' t' people about th' bigger issues." He grumbled a sigh. He wasn't used to getting personal with anyone, let alone someone he barely knew. Daric watched the ship sail ahead smoothly across the waters, refusing to look towards me while he continued to speak, "'ave ye heard th' tales about me past? Afore meetin' th' Captain?"

I nodded, remembering what little Jorgen was able to tell, unsure if that was even the truth as all storytellers tend to add exaggerations to their stories, something even I was prone to do.

"Me wife's name was Ashe, we had a wee lad, Demetrius. He was eight at th' time o' his death."

He remembered that day too well. He had been gone at sea for just over a year, under the flag of Captain

Bastion. A man who Daric had sailed with for many years. The man was the most feared Captain in these waters in his time, he loved to strike fear into the eyes of all those who dared sail in the waters alongside him.

Ashe before Daric's last sail begged Daric to stay, to end his career as a pirate alongside Bastion. To stay with her and their son. Daric had promised her the night he left that this would be his last sail, that after this he would take her and Demetrius away, where they could be together always. If only he listened to his wife's plead.

Daric stepped off the boat, his pack in his hand as he nodded to the sailors who wished him well, as this was the last time they would sail with Daric. Though Daric didn't understand the dark plot that was hiding under their knowing eyes.

He had been looking forward to this day for many, many weeks as he knew they were sailing for home. There was a pep in his step as he made his way through Coraline, his home was just on the outskirts, far enough away from all the noise, and most of the danger that came around the pirate port. A spot in which he thought Ashe and his son would be safe.

He could now see the door in the distance, a warm smile formed on his face as he thought of his wife and son's warm embrace. He reached for the handle; his heart paused. Blood on the handle? He opened the door, his bag dropped as he froze. No words. No emotion. Just disbelief. Horror. The inside of the house was sprayed in blood; his wife, Ashe laid with her face down on the wood floor her hands out reaching. A foot from her grasp laid another lifeless body. He had grown so much in that year that Daric wouldn't have recognized the boy if it wasn't for his red hair, identical to his mothers. Demetrius laid dead in a pool of his own blood; fear frozen on his still tiny face.

Daric finally was able to move as he fell to his knees in between his wife and son, pulling them into him. "No!" He sobbed, "Please no." His lips trembled as their bodies were ice, cold. He pulled his son into his arms, rocking back and forth, tears pooling down his face as he brushed his now deceased wife's hair. "Please no." He repeated.

He could still remember the last day he saw her alive, so clearly in his head.

Her long red hair tossed wildly as the ocean air wisped through it, she was trying hard to keep the tears from the corner of her eyes, but Daric could see them. He brushed some away with the back of his hand.

"Daric, you don't have to leave anymore, we have all we need now." She begged.

Demetrius clung to his father's leg but did not say a word.

Daric knelt down and kissed the young boy's forehead, "Ye behave fer yer mother 'n when I get back we shall leave this galleon, maybe go live in th' big city. No more piratin'." He promised her; he would have left it all for her. But he needed to do this last sail, this one last year would make them set for life his Captain had assured him.

Demetrius looked nothing like Daric, or so Daric believed. He could only see the innocent, beautiful eyes of his wife in his perfect, innocent face. A face that was forever tainted with the memory of his twisted, bloody, horrified, lifeless face.

Daric sat in his wife and son's blood as it stained him and his clothes. He didn't snap out of his comatose trance, until the town guards had come to take him away. Only then did he realize as he was cuffed and dragged away from the corpses of his family, he was being framed. Why? Who would kill them and blame him for the deaths of the only people he cared about?

"Do ye know who framed me that day?" His

question snapped me back into reality as Daric was slightly helping me control the ship. I shook my head no, "Captain Bastion, th' monster I had served under."

Realizing that I was controlling the ship, I didn't look at Daric, but he could see the disgust and painted frustration that he knew exactly what I wanted to ask.

"Captain Bastion had a secret rule, somethin' only his second in command was privileged t' know. Th' only way a scallywag could be freed o' thar service t' 'im was by death aboard his ship or a trip t' th' gallows." Daric paused letting me absorb the information before he continued, "About a month afore we were t' reach Coraline he in secret put a hit on me beauty 'n son, orderin' fer th' scallywag t' wait 'til closer t' when we were supposed t' dock. I was only hours behind thar killer." His somber expression was slightly lifted as he pushed the image of his dead wife and son, "'n while I waited fer me death, I met that spunky wee Jane Far'mel, th' lass who promised I'd ne'er forget. I was ready t' give up 'n let me life end, see me beauty 'n sprog in th' next world or however it works 'til I met that young one."

Seeing Daric's late son so clearly in my head, I now understood the instant attachment to Iggy. If

Demetrius got the chance to grow up to the age that Iggy was, they could have looked near identical to each other. I was heart broken as I thought about it, Daric was so protective over Iggy and Jane because he adopted them as his family, he couldn't stand losing them again, or seeing them hurt. *What Gibson did wasn't your fault,* I wanted to say aloud.

He seemingly knew what I was thinking as he studied the expressions of my face, "Aye, but I should 'ave known. When he first came aboard, we had a lot o' issues wit' th' crew that we had t' address 'n we thought we did a good job at it, but clearly we jus' put them more into hidin'." He clenched his fist, "He's lucky that 'twas ye 'n nah me he got into a fistfight wit'. I would 'ave made sure he was dead long afore he hit those waters."

Daric wasn't really talking to me in that moment as he thought back. He uncomfortably scratched the back of his head. He was about to admit something he was now ashamed to admit, "I started t' wonder if ye were th' one Iggy was havin' issues wit', I reckon 'twas jus' be tryin' t' deny that he was able t' hide somethin' like that fer so long behind our backs."

I looked down as I swallowed hard. Daric caught it as he placed a soft hand on my shoulder, he assumed that I was feeling guilty for keeping Iggy's secret from him, but this time he was wrong. As the guilt of hiding my truth from him began to boil. Iggy, Daric and the Captain were trustworthy, they had shown it to me many times over these months. I started to question if my original assessment of them being safer in the dark about my truth? Was I protecting them from it, or myself...

Chapter 20

It had been about a week since the Leviathan had attacked, and Iggy this morning was feeling one hundred percent. He stretched his shoulder out; it cracked, the stiffness was getting stretched out, but what little pain that was still lingering was nothing compared what he was used too. His bruises were nonexistent, even his ribs weren't bothering him anymore. The only thing that was still dampening his brightened mood was the fact that the Captain and Daric were still bitter and mad about the extent of his lying. He couldn't really blame them, thinking back.

He sat on the edge of his cot as he tightened his bracers; he was wearing his tan leather vest with nothing underneath, I wasn't sure why I was just noticing this, but all over his slimmed tone chest and stomach were countless small scars, nail marks, or from a blade? I wondered, it seemed now that the summer sun had been beating down on us that his tanned skin luminated the tiny marks all over his body.

He clearly noticed me staring at him, he pushed me playfully, "Don't dwell on the past, it's a brighter future a head of us, right?"

I nodded. I couldn't help but smile back at him. I tightened the strap holding my book and quill to my belt. Iggy tied his bandana around his forehead, combing his hair back into place with his fingers. "Let's get out there before Daric has to come find us," He smiled as he looked down, scratching at his bracer as he readjusted it, hiding the tail of the serpent that was sneaking out from the bottom of the leather. It was a brand that no person should ever have to wear, a brand that he and the Captain, as well as many other souls had to wear every day of their lives. *I wish I could have protected you from that past...* I thought as I managed another smile, I knew I had to push those thoughts aside; Iggy wasn't dwelling on the fact, so neither should I.

The Shadow's Blade was still a good week sail from the port as she clunked across the waters. Everyone aboard knew that we were lucky to even still be a float, but this put the Shadow's Blade in a very compromised situation, she was easy pickings for any pirates in the area.

Jane and Daric tried to keep close to the shoreline, as

most larger ships wouldn't dare sail that close to inland unless they knew these waters well enough; the risk of catching themselves on small landmasses or coral-reefs was too high. Jane wasn't worried about scratching her already beat up ship.

Mattias and Jesse hung out over the ledge of the ship keeping a closer eye out for possible collisions, while Jorgen and Jayson kept an eye out from the crows'-nest.

The Captain placed her hand on her dusty old hat, as she looked up into the bright morning sky, summer was shinning down on them this morning. Jane had even tossed off her thick coat as she was slowly roasting. She was dressed in a self cut gray blouse; she had removed the sleeves and loosened the top few buttons revealing her cleavage and her corset as she strutted around her ship, inspecting everyone and everything. She was returning to the helm where Daric was in control. She placed her hand on Daric's shoulder as she walked passed him and walked to the stern of her ship, leaning he elbows on the railing, she held onto her hat with one hand. Jane looked down at the water as she could clearly see the bottom, which would under normal circumstances make her uneasy, but she thought if the Shadow's Blade was going to sink today, she'd rather it be close to shore. She leaned back, placing both her hands on the back of hcr head, that was when she saw it. Jane turned her gaze up to the crows'-nest as Jayson was looking at whatever she had spotted in the distance, she called out as his heart began to race, "What do you see?"

"Another ship, Captain."

Iggy and I had just reached the main deck as those words left Jayson's mouth.

Jane rushed to the stairs leaning on that railing as she ordered us, "Ring the bell and prepare for the worst."

The crew once again had been forced into action, yet we were still unsure if the ship now trailing us was going to be a threat or not, but wasn't long for that to come apparent that they were a threat as the first cannon fired, just narrowly missing us.

"Are we runnin' or are we fightin'?" Daric called out to the Captain who was now at the stern of the ship watching as the enemy ship closed in.

She only had a split second to decide, "Turn her around, let's face them head on." She walked towards the center of the ship as she looked over her crew who were preparing for her orders, "Ready for battle, we shall not be taken this day!" She called out, raising her sword above her head.

Everyone cheered loud, raising their own swords above their heads as Daric did as he was told, turning the ship to face the enemy, before handing the helm off to Karlic.

The Captain rushed up to Iggy and me as she took my hand and gave me a sword, "Axel, you are with me. Iggy keep and eye on Daric for me." She smiled with a wink as Daric stepped down beside us, having heard her comment.

I gripped the handle of the sword as already my hands were getting sweaty as I was not ready for another fight, Daric and Iggy with all the chaos that has been these short months neither of them had time, and even with my memory returned I now realized that I had never wielded a sword before stepping foot on this ship, and with how well it went last time, I wasn't hopeful this would go well for me.

Jane could sense my unease as both ships dropped anchor as the Shadow's Blade got ready to be boarded. "Stay close to me, keep your sword up. If you get into trouble put your back against mine, or Victor's." She shook me as I nodded, "I'll keep you safe." With a quick smile, that was the only time we had as the Shadow's Blade was now being invaded and the battle had begun.

It was absolute chaos. We were all already tired and beaten down by the Leviathan and were now face to face with a well armed ship.

Jane and Victor worked well around me, as I fumbled around like a new born deer, knocking enough of the invading pirates into their clutches to feel like I was being of some help to them. I knew I couldn't kill if I wanted to continue being any help; last time when I killed that man, I had become incapacitated. I wasn't supposed to kill; I was a creature of time as much as I am a god of death. I am to preserve the soul, I was never supposed to interfere with the lives of mortal's, as I was now.

I brought my blade up as a pirate swung at me, our blades clashed together. He pushed me back against the helm as I struggled to push back against him. The man smiled as he pulled away, going in for another swing, but Victor came to my rescue as a knife flew into the side of the pirate's head. The pirates eyes rolled back, and his corpse stumbled forward, I slipped out of the way just in time. Wiping some sweat from my brow I nodded with an uneasy smile to Victor, who nodded before rushing down the steps as some of the crew needed assistance.

I turned my gaze towards the main deck, looking for where Daric and Iggy were. They had been tag-teaming as they made their way through their opponents easily and swiftly. Daric using his brutal force to knock them back as Iggy would then slip in for the killing blow. I got so distracted, so mesmerized by their tactic that I didn't hear the pirate coming up behind me. Her blade cut across my back; slicing deep into my skin snapping me back into the moment. I stumbled, rolling out of the path of the woman as the she fell to her knees. She had missed with her second more devastating blow.

Jane charged the woman, and before the enemy pirate could even pull herself up from her knees Jane's blade dove through her spine, exiting her chest. The tip of the Captain's sword, sticking into the deck of her ship, she tried to wiggle it free. Jane grumbled, "Keep your head in this battle, Daric and Iggy can handle themselves."

I wasn't even listening to her words, because as she put her foot on the dead woman's back, trying to pop her blade free another man was charging for her. I just reacted. I jumped between her and the man, his sword slipped through my stomach like butter, I grabbed hold of the hilt of his sword with one hand and the blade with my other as I held the man and his sword in place. I stared at the pirate; whose face was twisted in confusion.

"Axel!" Her head whipped around so fast, she called out my name, but it was a distant echo, as I'm not even sure I really heard it.

There was so much blood. I was dizzy, had to fight the urge to vomit, my head felt weird and my legs could no longer support me as I fell to my knees. Blood pooled out of my mouth, I went to take a breath as I dropped to the side like dead weight, the side of my head cracked painfully against the floor with an audible thud. I choked on my blood as I laid there bleeding out onto the deck. *How many times had I cleaned that spot?* I wondered. It was a strange thing to wonder as my body shut down.

Jane was frozen in disbelief, and that was her moment of weakness. She went to raise her sword against the man who had *slain* me as she gripped the hilt of her sword tightly. The man kicked me over, easily removing his blade.
"You bastard," she went to take a step forward, when a knife was placed against her throat, and lower chin.

The foul breathed pirates whispered in her ear, "Drop yer blade, doll. Don't wants t' 'ave t' ruin that pretty face o' yers," She didn't do as the man said, holding her ground. He grabbed her wrist and twisted it back, forcing her to drop it anyways. He turned her around, slamming her hard against the helm as he pressed his body against her, trying to keep a strong hold on her.

The man who had run me through with his blade, stepped up beside his ally and Jane as he whistled loudly as it echoed across the main deck. The crew from both ships, turned to look in the direction of the noise, as they all turned to see the Captain of the Shadow's Blade in distress.

The pirate holding Jane twisted her wrist more, causing her to grunt, "Tell yer crew t' back down," "Go fuck yourself," She growled, baring her teeth as she tried to break free.

The other pirate placed his blade against Jane's cheek, smearing my blood across her face as he spoke, "Stand down,"

She growled again, "Fine," the man put his blade back to his side as my blood dripped down the metal. Jane straighten in the mans grasp as she hollered out to her crew, "Take no prisoners!"

The man holding her grabbed her hair, his knife knotting in her long hair as he pulled her head back, "Ye stupid cur!"

My body needed to recharge itself… But I had to do something. My vision became slightly clear again. Blood was still oozing from my wound, my whole body practically soaked in crimson. I forced my body to obey me as I pushed myself to my hands and knees. I grabbed my sword that I had dropped a foot away as I stumbled pulling myself to a standing position. The two pirates didn't even turn around to the sounds, even thought I knew I was not silent in getting up.

My blood pooled down my body as I stepped up behind them, still unnoticed. *So much for my speech.* I stabbed the man holding the Captain, the blade went through him, not as easily or cleanly as the other man had done to me, but clean enough that the tip of my blade, tapped Jane's back. She turned her head slightly, catching a glimpse of me in the corner of her eye. The man's grip loosened on her, the other Pirate still oblivious to his dying friend next to him.

Jane lifted her knee as she grabbed a hidden knife from her boot, swiftly she drove the blade deep into his head, through the soft underbelly of his chin. She pushed the dying pirate away from her as he fell to the floor. She looked at me terrified at what she was seeing, I had risen from a fatal wound, soaked in my own blood.

Boom... one, two, three, four. Boom... One, two, three, four, five, six, boom. The pirate I had stabbed heart finally stopped beating, as my heart stopped. I dropped to my knees again, hand on my chest, as I gasped for air, spitting more blood.

Jane forgot her fear of me in that moment as she rushed to my side. She ripped the leg of her pants as she bunched the fabric into a ball, pressing it against my stomach, as if that would do anything to a normal person with this wound.

Daric and Iggy came up one side, as Victor and Jorgen came up the other.

There was a second of relief in Daric and Iggy's eyes before they saw the blood. All colour drained from both their faces as they rushed to our aid.

My eyes rolled back as the world around me went dark, even their voices were fading away in the moment as the last thing I heard was Jane's voice ordering her men, "Finish those bastards and get them off my ship. Iggy and I will take care of Axel, Daric join us when the job is done."

Iggy and Jane carried me down the stairs as Victor and Jorgen protected them as they entered the inside of the ship. Finally reaching the Captain's quarters they dropped me as carefully as the two of them could onto her now ruined cot.

Iggy wanted to ask why they had taken me to her quarters rather than the medical bay, but as she sliced off my blood-soaked shirt, it began to make sense, as much as it didn't.

Jane's concern melted away as they both could clearly see me subtly breathing, she was now angry. She turned to Iggy with her arms crossed, nails digging into her skin, fury in her tone, "What is he?"

He wanted to play naïve, but she saw right through him as he reached out and untied my note book from my belt. He offered it to her with no other explanation.

She took it and began skimming through the pages, looking for something, anything that would explain the how's and why's of what was happening here. She looked up from the book, her jaw slightly dropped as she flipped back and forth between two pages. She shook her head no, what she was reading couldn't be true.

Iggy stood there uncomfortably as she tried to come to terms with the truth about me, "I told him it would be best to keep this from you."

Daric barreled in, huffing and puffing, covered in blood and sweat as he took a deep breath, "Is he?"

"Alive," Jane spoke as she handed Daric the book signaling him to read those same pages.

He was finishing the last sentence as I finally jolted awake. With a quiet, growly groan I placed my hand over the hole in my stomach and forced myself upright. Only then did I realize that Iggy, Daric and the Captain were staring at me, in disbelief, and slight fear, well at least two of them were. Iggy still just stared at me with concern as the colour in his face had yet to return.

Jane tore the book from Daric and tossed it at me, I caught it as I coated the cover with blood. "Are these pages the honest truth?"

I nodded. I wanted to turn my gaze from her, but I didn't dare let my eyes even wonder from her face to Iggy or Daric's. I held my breath.

She studied my answer, and in that moment, I realized she had more balls than any man I had come across in my years as the God of Death. She cupped her hand and struck me HARD upside my head. I was shocked. Stunned. It was not the reaction I was expecting, especially as her face lightened. She let out a bitter laugh, "I hope striking the god of death doesn't curse me more than I already am." She turned around and struck Iggy on the side of the head, not going easy on him before pointing her finger at both of us as she scolded us like small children. "I should toss you both off my ship and leave you stranded on a beach, that is two very dangerous secrets you two have been keeping from me."

"Sorry Captain,"

"So-" *Sorry Captain,* I tried to say as I winched adjusting in the bed, the blood had finally begun to slow.

Jane turned around and fell into her chair as she sunk, with her hand on her face. "Is there anything else I need to know?"

Iggy and I looked at each other as he just handed her my book, "Just read,"

Daric came over and read over her shoulder as they were both trying to understand the entire situation, once they were both done, she closed the book, handing back to me. "Iggy, can you go get Axel some new clothes?"

Iggy nodded and did as he was told. The second the door closed the energy in the room changed as Jane adjusted in her seat, "I need to re-evaluate if it is in my best interest, and in the best interest of my crew to keep you aboard. I am a sea Captain, having the Goddess of the Sea against me isn't the best thing,"

"Aye, but havin' th' God o' Time 'n Death on our side might counterbalance that." Daric defended, to both the Captain and my surprise.

I wasn't going to let them contemplate over it long as I scribbled words in my book, turning the page for them to read, "I will leave, it's for the best."

The Captain shook her head no, "I don't want you to

leave." My face lit up with a slight puzzlement, "As much as you are a god and clearly out of our league. You are one of my crew, for as long as you wish to be here, you are welcomed aboard my ship," I couldn't help but smile, she added a warning, "No more secrets, or I will toss you over board."

I nodded. I didn't express this too them, but I knew our time was limited, and nothing we could say or do would change that...

Gibson found himself in a mercenary club; he removed the hood off of his bald head. He was a large, powerful and intimidating pirate, yet still he felt uncomfortable and exposed while walking through the sea of trained professional killers. All eyes were on him as he was the outcast.

At the back of the room was a large naturally shaped oak table, a toned man, dressed in all black sat with his arms crossed over his chest, legs up, showing off his dark red leather boots, a large black hat with an eagle feather sticking out of it and a pipe lit, puffing smoke, in his mouth. The man's eyes were locked on Gibson as he walked towards him.

The man took in another long puff, he let the smoke just pool out of his slightly parted lips. Speaking to Gibson who finally stopped before the table. "Aye, what do we have here?"

"I be here t' forge a contract wit' th' Mercenary Captain who goes by th' name Lucard. Captain, Patrick Lucard?"

"Aye, that is me." The man dragged his feet off the table, leaning against his elbows, fingers crossed. "Ye of all people should know it's disrespectful to call a Captain by their first name, pirate."

"Aye, I do. Me apologies Captain. Now," he pulled a large sack of coin out and dropped it on the table, "I be here t' offer you a job. Interested?"

Captain Lucard studied Gibson, then pulled the sack of coin closer studying the contents. "What does a pirate need of a Mercenary? I don't usually work for other sea fairing persons as most pirates do their own dirty work." He dumped the coins on the table, stacking them as he counted them suspiciously, "What is so dirty about this mission that you, yourself do not dare take it alone?"

"Odd fer a mercenary ye ask a lot o' riddles," Gibson reached for the coin, indicating his annoyance.

Captain Lucard snapped Gibson's hand, "Aye, I know when to stop. Tell me what I need to know." Rolling a gold coin in between his surprisingly, clean fingers.

Gibson eyed the Captain for a long minute before

replying. "I needs th' capture 'n transport o' two scallywags." Clearly Captain Lucard wasn't impressed as Gibson had to elaborate, clearing his throat, "They be crew o' th' Shadow's Blade,"

He laughed lightly, "Under the flag of Miss Far'mel, still?"

"Aye, th' scallywag I be actually aft; be a stray th' Captain has kept, like a pet. He be a powerful, he jus' doesn't know his owns strength, so I wants some insurance that he behaves, why we needs th' other."

Captain Lucard cocked his brow as Gibson finally stopped speaking, looking back down at the pile of gold before returning to Gibson's face once more. "I personally don't like messing with well a known Pirate Captain's such as Miss Far'mel," He thought about it once last time. Finally, he stood up from his seat and extended his hand out to the pirate, with a sinister smile across his face, "Well, then my friend, you got yourself a contract."

Gibson smiled back as he shook the man's hand. A deal was struck.

As hands were shaking and that deal being laid out, questions were being asked around the Shadow's Blade. Things were piling up against me with the rest of the crew.

Daric and the Captain tried to shut down all talk about what happened that day with me, but they couldn't, there was no stopping the wheels that were turning on this ship.

Jorgen commandeered the storage room, along with a few other crewmembers; Reefer, Mattias, Vendell, and Jackal.

Vendell and Reefer sat on the corners of the table with their arms crossed, Jorgen paced back and forth around the room, while Matthias was told to wait at the top of the stairs keeping an eye out for Daric or Victor.

Jorgen finally spoke aloud, "We needs a plan t' get rid o' this stranger, 'n quickly, he's a danger t' us all."

To Jorgen's defence, he was right to be afraid of me and what having me aboard meant for the crew, even though his conclusion was off. He still tried to convince them all that I was a siren sent here to seduce them and the Captain with my dirt coloured eyes. There memory of the day in the pub with my sister was hazy, but Jorgen was convinced that they were bewitched, as they were right, Kali is the mother of Sirens. Her beauty is what gave the creatures their allure in the first place.

Vendell spoke scratching his head, "Are ye sure, ye saw wha' ye saw?"

"Aye! Right through 'im!" Jorgen snapped shaking Vendell's shoulders.

Reefer grumbled, "If 'twas that obvious, wouldna th' Captain, Daric 'n Ignatius 'ave riddles?"

"Haven't ye been listenin' t' me? They be all under his enchantment!"

Jackal spoke up, "He's a bad omen, I'm not saying I believe he's a Nix's or anything, but he is a threat to our ship. A massive storm, a sea monster, and two raids from enemy pirates since he's been aboard,"

There was a mumble in agreement of everyone, including Matthias who kept his ear to the door. Matthias spoke up, "He's in favor with the Captain, ain't no way she's going to kick him off. He saved her."

"We jus' needs t' make 'im leave on his owns accord or make it seem that way at least."

Jackal questioned, "if he really is a creature of myth, what would we have to use against him?"

Reefer and Vendell were the ones to answer Jackal's question, as Jackal and Mattias became really uncomfortable with this conversation in one word, "Ignatius,"

I woke up finding myself still in the Captain's chambers. I went to place my hand over my stomach, which Iggy had bandaged and cleaned while I had rested, only to find resistance? I turned my head to find Iggy asleep, leaning against the cot, holding my hand loosely in his, his head rested against our hands pinning me to the bed. I smiled as I rolled on my side, trying to not wake Iggy as I scanned the room.

Daric had left, keeping a handle on the crew and the condition of the ship, the Captain was asleep in her chair. Her face resting on her desk, as much as she was usually a very beautiful, graceful woman, it was entertaining seeing her face squished against the hard wood, drool pooling out of the corner of her lips as she snored loudly.

I don't know why I did it, but I reached over and brushed Iggy's hair softly, watching as he lightly slept. He shifted, and I quickly pulled my hand back acting as if nothing had happened.

Iggy released my hand and rubbed his eyes as he turned to face me, his face slightly blushed red as he smiled, "You look awful," He wasn't wrong.

Chapter 21

Crippled, beaten and blooded; the Shadow's Blade finally pulled into the port of Dunmore, having taken an extra week behind schedule. She must have been a strange sight as she struggled into the docks. The Port Master removed his glasses at the sight of her, the Captain threw herself from the deck, landing next to the old man, gracefully with a smile. She swung her arm over his shoulders, "As you can see good man, I require some work on her." Jane patted his shoulder.

"Aye, miss ye do." He tipped his hat as he flipped some pages, pointing at a line, as Jane signed her name promptly. "Captain Far'mel," He tipped his hat to her. "I can't even begin to estimate how long thee repairs will take, ye understand?"

Jane nodded with a smile, "Men need a good leave anyways and where better to have a good enjoyable time then here?" She winked. "I'll have men on shifts to help of course and to keep an eye on things."

"I'd have it no other way, Captain Far'mel."

Vendell and Victor dropped the plank as most of the crew shuffled off the ship, ensuring to tip their hat to the Captain as they rushed off to the local pub and whore houses.

Daric, Victor, Vendell, Echo and Jesse took the first shift on ship, helping explain what needs done and making sure that everything starts smoothly.

Jane tipped her hat and waved Daric off as she wondered off towards the town.

Iggy and I were the last to leave, he seemed hesitant to leave the ship, but as Daric ignored the two of us. He finally shoved me down the plank, tightening his wrist bracers; a coin pouch jingling as we made our way towards the town.

Iggy didn't enjoy this pirate port like the other members of the crew, he had unfavorable memories associated with this place. This place was just a bitter hellhole. He tried to push it aside this day, the summer sun was shinning brightly down upon them; they had survived. Iggy was feeling lighter, no more secrets. No pretending to be okay when he wasn't, no more fear every time he walked through the ship alone. No more being tossed around and broken, having to hide it in shame. He was free. And it was a lot better of a feeling then Iggy ever realized. He closed his eyes and took a breath, stopping right in front of me as I nearly walked straight into him. He shook it off and smiled at me, "Sorry, was lost in a thought." He could see that I was curious about what he was thinking about, but he just smiled again, sticking his hands in his pocket, "Nothing to note on," even thought he knew that I would have enjoyed hearing the thoughts that were running through his mind, he didn't feel like dwelling on it. As much as he believed it was selfish, he wanted to keep that cheerful thought to himself, which he had all right to. He took a whiff of himself as we pushed our way through the crowd, "There is a bath house, nice hot water sounds really good to me right now." Iggy said, he turned to look back at me. I nodded, following his lead through the dirty, smelly crowd of pirates and town's folk.

It was a while out of town, but being a perfect day, it didn't bother either of us; it was a large building of stone and dark oak, old and worn down, it clearly wasn't commonly used, by the condition it was in. "There is another bathhouse that is more commonly used. I avoid that place at all cost," He scratched his wrist uncomfortably, a dark memory flash to the front of his mind, "This place is old, run down, but the water is hot, and no one really comes here."

Iggy opened the door, leading me in, he dropped a

couple coins in an old woman's hand as she led us to a room. She had a raspy voice, her boney hands pointed to a wooden door across the large steam room, "Through there to the baths, if you need anything just ring the bell."

"Thank you," Iggy replied as he pulled off his vest and she left with a nod. Once the door was closed firmly, Iggy untied his trousers, I began to uneasily follow suit. Iggy wrapped a towel around his waist as he untied his bandana from his hair, tossing it to his feet, before running his fingers through the tangle mess of a mop he had today.

I placed the towel around my waist before untying my trousers and removing my shirt. I couldn't help but stare at Iggy, who was just standing there, his hand against his leather bracer. There wasn't even a thought that ran through my head, my body just reacted as I reached my hand out and squeezed his hand softly, supportively? I smiled sweetly.

He broke his concentration with his wrist as he untied the bracer, dropping them into the pile with his clothes, "Thanks, Axel." He smiled back at me as he turned and faced me, "Others may fear what you are, but I am thankful for you,"

There was something powerful filling the room and neither of us understood it, as neither of us seemed to be in control of our actions for that moment. We faced each other, our eyes locked, our mouths went dry as we reached for one another.

I could feel his breath against my face just before our lips pressed against each other. His hand on the back of my neck, as I ran mine through his hair. Mouth's slightly parted, I could taste his lips as his tongue was slightly pressed against his bottom lip. It was only just a fraction of a minute that we were together, but nothing mattered in that moment, nothing made sense and yet everything did? I couldn't, I can't wrap my head around what happened. Finally, we pulled apart. Iggy placed his hand over his mouth, stunned and shocked as if he had offended me, as I stood there frozen with my hands out in a defensive pose. Both our faces were blushed pink.

Iggy bit his lip under his hand and turned around embarrassed, without a word he rushed out of the dressing room into the bath area.

Still frozen, I waited for the door to swing close before I finally took a breath. Never before had I kissed someone in that way. My heart pounded as I finally regained the ability to move, slowly I now followed after Iggy, who was already in the water at the far side of the pools hand over his face, back towards me. Shame was written all over him, as he shrunk into the pool, adverting his eyes from me.

I wondered if I should advert my eyes from him, but I couldn't, I stepped into the water as my body was flooded with a good burn. My barely tanned skin turning a darker shade of red then my cheeks that were still burning hot. Now what ran through my head, *I did something wrong.* As finally I adverted my eyes from him, biting my lip and bringing my knees up to my chest.

Iggy spoke, "It's not you," he was uncomfortable, and he couldn't hide it. "My body," He tried to think of the words, "has never been my own. I've," he paused again, crossing his arms over his chest, trying to make himself small, "I've never kissed someone on my own accord. I'm sorry I pushed that on you, I don't know what came over me." Tears were in his eyes.

I wanted to say something to comfort him, but I couldn't, he didn't force anything on me, and I wanted him to know that. I treaded through the water and sat down next to him, keeping a bit of distance, giving him the option to move in closer or farther. Our eyes met again, and I smiled softly. I slowly reached my hand out and placed it against Iggy cheek. It was the best I could do at this time and

I found out, it was all I needed to do for him. He hesitantly took my hand in his, entwining our fingers together. Iggy leaned in a rested his head against my shoulder. A small smile broke out on his face as we both leaned back and enjoyed the warmth of the bath, relaxing in silence with each other as both our hearts pounded with a new, dangerous emotion.

We finished at the bath house, both of us still wrapping our heads around our own actions as we made our way to the inn.

The Captain and about half of her crew were already well into the liquor, making a ruckus and disturbing the peace, and yet the barkeep continued to fill their drinks and bring plates of food out for the rowdy crowd.

Jane saw the two of us walk in, she waved high above the crowd, beckoning us over. We did as she requested, making our way through the mess of pirates.

"A round for my friends!" She hollered at the barkeep. He brought out a bottle of hard liquor and two glasses. "What have you two been up too?" She smelt the air around us leaning her elbows on the table, "bath house?" We both nodded, she smiled drunkenly.

Iggy downed his glass before taking mine and finishing it off just as swiftly, "I'm going to get some rest, it's been a long few days," he wiped access from his lips, trying to keep his gaze from me he continued, " and I got the early morning shift." He placed his hand on my and the Captain's shoulder as our eyes met for just a moment. He swallowed nervously, fighting his urge to blush, "Farewell,"

The Captain pouted as she tipped her hat goodnight to Iggy, pouring more liquid into a mug before pushing it to my lips, nearly forcing it down my throat as she tipped it in my mouth, "Drink!"

I did as I was told and she continued to pour the strange tasting liquid down. The room became a blur and I had the nearly uncontrollable urge to tell everyone everything that crossed my mind, if I could, but all I could think of were Iggy's lips against mine, his hands on my neck, his breath against my face.

I couldn't even tell how many drinks I was given as every time I had looked away Jane had filled my cup once again. When I found my self unable to stand on my own two feet, Jane had to carry me up the stairs to my room. I was too drunk to make it on my own.

She giggled, red faced and tipsy she rolled me into the bed, throwing the blanket over me Jane brushed

my hair back out of my face. "Sweet dreams, Axel."
She said, but I was already long gone.

Chapter 22

Iggy got up just before the crack of dawn; stretching his arms above his head, his back and shoulders cracked and popped, letting out one last yawn as he then wiped the sleep from his eyes. His hands brushed against his lips; he went to drop them to his side only to pause as the memory of my warm lips against his flashed before him. He let out a long breath, running his hands through his hair; a strange tingling sensation went through his body. He thought about me in a way he never imagined he could think about anyone.

He tried to push the thoughts to the back of his mind as he started down the hall, grabbing a chunk of bread and an apple, he continued his way quickly to the docks.

Reefer, Jorgen and Jackal were the others joining Iggy for the morning shift on the ship as they sluggishly crept up on the Shadow's Blade, as the group had enjoyed the drink along with the Captain into the late morning.

Iggy waved to Daric as he stepped up onto the deck, large black bags hung under his eyes as he seemed unfocused and frustrated.

Daric grumbled, with an uncontrollable yawn as he walked up to Iggy, "Thar be still a lot t' be done here, I fear we may be stuck two weeks at least," he scratched his beard, fighting the urge to yawn again, "Captain ain't goin' t' be happy t' hear th' news."

"Lets hope she doesn't have too bad of a hangover after last nights drink when you tell her the news." Iggy said with a smile, crossing his arms over his chest as he inspected what had gotten done, which to his eye nothing.

"Well, thar isnt anythin' we can do about th' waitin' on th' mass, which th' carpenter said would be a few days 'n a week at th' latest." Daric turned to the others as they now assembled onto the ship, "Th' sail needs t' be sewn 'n thar be still a large hole below deck that needs properly patched up, th' woodworkers will be droppin' off supplies any time now." Daric pulled a small book out of his pocket, "If ye manage t' get those done afore shift end, mark it off 'n start th' next thin' on th' checklist." He handed the book to Jorgen before turning back to Iggy, "Captain wants ye t' begin stock if ye finish repairin' th' sail."

"I'll just do a double shift and get that done for her, if we are going to be here as long as you think I don't mind working away a couple extra nights."

Daric raised his bow, but didn't question it, "if that's how ye wish t' waste yer time," and with that he waved them off, finally falling way behind his shift group who were almost out of sight seeking and craving a good rest.

"I'll start on the sail," he chose this knowing the others wouldn't want to help, as it would give him some quiet alone time to continue to think.

His assessment of the other shift crew was correct as he sat crossed legged on the deck the fabric draped over his legs as he began to work.

Jorgen, Reefer and Jackal had finished up their shift; leaving Iggy to finish up whatever he was working on while the next shift began their work. They had a date with some lovely brothel maids.

With their wagging tongues barely contained in their mouths they walked through the dark, dingy inn.

There were many old, dirty sailors with beautiful, scantily clad women. As well as a few women perched on the bar table, revealing their goods as the three new customers entered their den. They licked their ruby red lips, suggestively as the men walked past them.

A dark skinned women in a short purple dress, stockings and a corset, her long curly black hair was tied up in a messy bun. She batted her eye lashes at the men, placing her hands on both Jackal and Reefers arms before stroking Jorgen's chin with her pointer finger with a smile. "Welcome to my establishment," she bit her lip as she looked past them eyeing a few of her girls to approach. "And what draws your fancy?" She snapped her fingers as five girls appeared beside her, "Blondes, brunettes, redheads, exotic women." The last she said with a strong roll of her tongue as she stepped into the men more. Making direct eye contract with Jorgen as he looked the Mistress of the Brothel up and down. Then she looked away turning to Jackal, "Or are you into some of the more, interesting sexual adventures, she ran her long nails over the strong mans throat, her tongue pressed up against the roof of her mouth.

Reefer stepped up to the petit redhaired girl, she had orangish freckles that spotted her face and her chest. She wasn't fruitful in the chest as some of the other women, but her tiny physic against Reefer's excited him. He took a stand of her hair, spinning it around his finger as he leaned in and kissed her neck.

She giggled playfully as she then took his hand leading him away.

Jackal took a tanned woman with dark tattoos into another room.

Jorgen was just about to choose a lady of the night himself when a voice called out to him, calling him by name. Jorgen turned around, annoyed only to stand there in shock as Gibson approached.

Gibson smiled as he then spoke to the Mistress, "I need to borrow my friend here, Mistress."

The mistress nodded and snapped her fingers as the free ladies dissipated, disappointedly so.

Jorgen was in disbelief as he placed his hands on his old shipmate's shoulders, if feeling to see if he was a phantom haunting him from his sea grave. "How did ye survive? I was sure th' sea would 'ave taken ye. Ye know if th' Captain sees ye, she will surely 'ave yer head fer wha' went down wit' Ignatius 'n th' Stranger."

Gibson waved him down, "That be partly wha' I wish t' speak t' ye about. Come, come, I had a tale ye will surely enjoy." Gibson lead Jorgen to his room he had rented in the brothel as he knew Jane and her closer allies wouldn't step foot a place like this.

Once they were behind closed doors, he locked it and beckoned Jorgen to make himself comfortable.

"How did ye nah drown that night? 'twas only a miracle that Victor was able t' find th' stranger 'n 'ave th' two make it safely back t' th' ship afore th' sea had swallowed them whole."

"Miracle me arse," He spoke convincingly, "I was saved by th' goddess o' th' sea herself!"

Jorgen was about to laugh, but noted the sincerity in his eyes that caused him to hold back.

"She saved me so that I could assist her in a task, a task t' reveal th' dark secrets o' that same stranger who sent me into th' sea. Ye were close t' bein' correct, that be no mere stranger," Gibson paused as he knew he had Jorgen locked into the story already, "he be more o' a threat then even ye could 'ave imagined!" He shook Jorgen's shoulders as if trying to sink the last bit of his point across. "He be no creature o' th' sea, Jorgen. He be a god," he took a long dramatic paused as Jorgen stared deep into the mans eyes, "he be th' god o' death."

Jorgen's eyes lit up as he stood up from my seat, "I knew it! I knew it all along, he needs t' be taken out! Revealed t' th' Captain as t' wha' he really be!" He looked as if he was about to run out of the room to proclaim this information straight to the Captain that second, but Gibson grabbed his arm and turned him back to his seat.

"Kali, th' Goddess o' th' sea said that he has entranced th' Captain, she will nah believe ye 'n even if she does she will nah maroon 'im. She believed 'im t' be an ally."

"If she knew that he was th' god o' death she surely would change her mind, wouldn't she?"

"I fear 'tis too late fer that,"

Jorgen seemed confused, "Why 'ave ye come then? T' tell me somethin' that in me heart I had known from th' beginnin'? T' taunt me wit' more facts?"

"No, o' course nah," Gibson laughed at the thought, "I 'ave a better plan. Kali has missioned me t' brin' Axel t' her, at any means necessary."

"'n?"

"I 'ave procured a mercenary ship wit' cabin fer two captives, I jus' needs help gettin' them 'n meself close enough t' procure them."

"Them?"

"Axel be a god, I be nah goin' t' risk jus' tryin' t' take 'im. Kali has ordered me t' ensure his arrival, Iggy be that insurance."

Finally Jorgen understood what Gibson was saying, a twisted smile formed on his face as he looked upon his friend, "When would ye be ready?"

"I can 'ave them ready in days notice if we sort out a plan smartly."

Jorgen thought for a moment, "Ye needs Iggy as bait t' brin' Axel t' ye rather then ye hunt fer th' two o' them 'n I can reckon o' th' perfect opportunity when t' do that."

Jorgen and Gibson smiled at each other as a plan was now unfolding.

Chapter 23

Iggy and I hadn't spoken, or really even seen each other since returning to the inn after our adventure at the bath house, and now the following day was nearly coming to an end. I had just finished my shift on the ship and the sun had just set when I was about to make my way back to the inn. I could smell myself as the wind blew around me. I was drenched in sweat and dust as we had been crawling around in the lower levels patching some of the smaller holes that were found.

I took a deep breath and wiped the sweat from my brow, stepping off the dock, that's when I finally noticed Iggy waiting just beyond. His hands in his pockets, dressed in a light green tunic he smiled at me as he stepped forward, "Hey, Axel," he spoke softly, nervously.

I smiled back at him as we were now awkwardly face to face, I could see his cheeks flush a slight red, he looked away, kicking the dirt at his feet, "You have a good shift? Is she starting to look like her old self?"

He smiled again looking back towards my face as I just nodded and turned back looking at the Shadow's blade. We were making good time, possibly better then what carpenters suggested.

"Do you want to get a drink? Maybe at the actual pub rather then the inn, get away from the noise of the rest of the crew."

I nodded, but placed my pointer finger up as I then pointed at the dirty mess that was me.

Iggy laughed, "Yeah you should clean up a little bit, even though you still probably smell better then most of the people wondering around these streets." He laughed again, and I just smiled at him, letting him lead the way.

We both entered my room as I emptied a pitcher with cold water into a bowl with a cloth. I looked back at Iggy, he wasn't trying to pay attention as I untied my shirt and tore it from my sweaty body, straining the cloth as I washed my face.

"Do gods, um, never mind." Iggy started to say something but stopped before the question ever finished, taking a seat, leaning against the door frame.

I turned my head to face him as he had peaked my curiosity, I now saw that he was trying his hardest to not look upon my bare back.

Iggy rubbed the back of his neck; something was clearly stuck on his mind. I dropped the cloth in the bowl and walked towards him kneeling down next to him, our eyes met, beckoning him to tell me what was on his mind. I silently waited for him to speak, hesitantly I placed a soft, reassuring hand on his knee.

He ran his fingers through his hair as he thought about what he wanted to say again. This time my face flushed red, I stood up crossing my arms over my naked chest, backing away slightly.

Finally he swallowed hard and spoke, "Is it normal for someone like you to be," He thought of his words carefully, "physical with someone like me?"

I was thrown off by the question as I actually stumbled in place thinking about it. The truth of the matter over the thousands of years that mortal's have been in existence many gods had prayed on humans for physical companionship, but I did not believe that it was the question Iggy actually wanted answered. I pointed to my chest and shook my head. I had admired many mortals over the years, for their strength, their humanity, and their sacrifices of course, but it was just that, admiration. I never before had these complex emotions and feelings that were running through my mind about Iggy ever appeared, and I don't think it was because I never got the chance, just Iggy was one of a kind.

Once I knew that Iggy understood my response I turned back away and walked back over to my washing table, sticking my hand in the water; my heart was pounding, my face was hot and red. I held my breath, I tried to stop the pounding beating in my chest, but it was fruitless.

There was a strong urge that beckoned Iggy to step towards me, but he held strong as he continued to sit, failing at keeping his eyes off my naked back.

I finished washing myself and placed a clean grey tunic over my head before turning and smiling at Iggy signalling that I was ready to go.

With that we shared one last smile before silently we wondered out of the inn and down towards the towns center. Where we entered a slightly larger pub then that of the inn's, it was just as full, but these were all people Iggy and I did not know, we were both strangers in a sea of many faces.

We sat far away from the noise both with a large pint of ale as a beautiful, yet filthy women walked around filling empty mugs.

Iggy sat with his back against the wall as he could keep his eyes on all that was happening around us, while I sat with my back towards the many rambunctious pirates.

Iggy downed half his drink, scratching at his bracer, answering a question that had popped into my head before I had even finished thinking of the words.

"It's all in my head, it never really physically itches, anymore. Captain wears hers as a badge, that she fought a war and won. I've never felt that way. I hadn't successfully fought for my freedom out of that cage." He tugged again at the strings loosening it just slightly. "In crowds where I don't know people, I feel safer with it hidden, in the past people have tried things after seeing my mark." He smiled anxiously, "Just makes my life a little easier."

Even in the dim candle light I could see the red and white marks left on his skin as it was too tight, just slightly pressing too deeply into his forearm.

He drank the rest of his ale, as he raised the glass placing another coin on the table was the woman approached filling his glass and mine, I downed the still mostly full glass. The liquid bubbling back up my throat slightly, I forced it back down with a pat of my chest.

Iggy laughed slightly as he sipped the foam from the top, watching the woman take the coin and continuing on her way.

Now out of ear shot he asked, "I've been wondering

for a while now, are the stories true, about the gods?"

Some, I waved an iffy notion towards him, as most were peppered with truths, though many of the gods liked to boast of their greatness.

Iggy looked around suspiciously at the crowd before leaning in and whispering yet another question, "How about your story? Did the gods really hate and fear the creation of, you?"

I looked down the pale liquid in my mug and drank it down quickly as I thought about it. It was the most truthful of all the stories I remembered, I remembered their hatred all too well.

"And the god wars? Are those stories true?"

I was hesitant in answering this question, but I nodded sadly as the mood between us shifted.

Iggy spun his cup on the wooden table, shamed by his questions of curiosities, "I'm sorry, Axel."

I waved my hand with an impressively faked a smile, as he then smiled back at me.

"We need to drink much more," Iggy laughed uneasily, he raised his glass once again as the woman came back around. Iggy placed a few extra coins down on the table as she left the large pitcher on our table. He filled his up, downed it once again before filling it another time, yet only drinking half as he left out a burp.

I matched his drink, as I downed my still near full glass and two more.

I was a light weight when it came to the alcohol of mortal's it seemed. Already my head was fussy and my body uncomfortably warm as Iggy was barely even beginning to feel the drunkenness from his drinks.

I had lost all sense of time after three more mugs of ale and there after lost count of how much we had consumed as pitcher after pitcher was placed before us. I, to Iggy's surprise kept up, drink for drink with him. He laughed as he knew I would regret that decision greatly once the morning came.

Iggy poured himself one last drink as I went to reach for the pitcher he moved it out of my reach as my head was resting on the table, my eyes were barely opened and my stomach ached, painfully.

He drunkenly laughed at me as he finished the last of the ale, "I should have cut you off a while ago, my poor friend, but now you are definitely cut off."

I smiled, my eyes closed, I lifted my head from the table and took a nauseated breath. I couldn't tell but my head bobbed, and if you asked Iggy that night he would tell you that a small amount of drool was dribbling down my chin. It grew harder and harder to keep my eyes open as Iggy got up from his chair laughing at me once again. "Okay, big fella, let's get you back to the inn."

I painfully hiccupped as Iggy tossed my arm over his shoulder. He wrapped his arm around me, lifting me from my chair.

Standing up was a mistake as I nearly toppled the two of us to the ground, staggering trying to catch my own two feet.

The fresh sea air did not help as we made our way out on the street. I went one way and Iggy the other causing him to stumble and trip, we both tumbled to the dirt. I rolled onto my back as I stared up at the stars and the blackened skies. *That was once my home. Banished from my home, from my family.* I reached my hand up as if reaching to pluck one of the stars from the heavens. I let out a painful sigh, but my drunken mood lifted as Iggy leaned over me blocking the stars from my view with a smile. His perfect, innocent smile on his handsome face. I couldn't help but smile back at him as I brushed the side of his face softly with my hand.

He shook his head with a chuckle, taking my hand and pulling it over his shoulders lifting me back to my feet as I already began to force him to tumble. He groaned, "One step at a time,"

It took longer than Iggy had imagined, but we finally

made it back to the inn. He carried me up the stairs, pushing the two of us through the door to my room, he closed the door behind us, before I unintendedly tripped Iggy with my sloppy footwork, sending the two of us tumbling onto the bed.

I fell with my back against the bed, catching Iggy, his chest resting against mine, our faces inches from each other, lips seconds apart.

His face blushed red as I couldn't help but smile. I swallowed hard and reached my hand slowly up, brushing his cheek and neck tenderly. "Stay," I managed to say in my broken, drunken voice.

At first, he recoiled, his heart skipping a beat. He turned and looked away from me, adjusting uneasily on the bed, only to cave and lean into my touch with a still uneased breath. He finally took my hand and placed it on my chest, standing up from the bed.

I nodded. I understood his hesitation and didn't take offence as I adjusted myself in the bed resting my head on the pillow. I was turned towards him as I tried to keep my eyes open, to keep watching him, but it was futile.

Iggy went to the door, his hand on the handle when he paused looking back at me. Turning back to the door. He thought and thought, trying to fight what his body was telling him to do, but his fear failed that night as he let his heart decide in a momentary lap of judgement. He locked the door and turned back towards me. He laid next to me in the bed, looking to the ceiling, scrunched up uncomfortably.

My arm wrapped around his stomach as I unconsciously pulled him into me.

Iggy jumped, but then eased into my arms, his nature and his past was telling him to run. It was telling him to fear this moment, but he couldn't move away, and he didn't want too. He rolled into me, placing his head against my chest, he took a deep breath. Listening to my sleeping heart beat, slowly beating away, my lungs inhaling and exhaling as he slowly calmed himself and fell asleep in my arms.

Chapter 24

The morning sun warmed the room as I woke. I went to stretch my arms up above my head, but one was still trapped underneath the undisturbed Iggy, who was asleep tucked into my chest. I smiled as he seemed so peaceful; it wasn't faked, he wasn't hiding any pain. He was just calm and content laying there beside me. I smiled as I brushed his hair out of his face before slowly removing my arm from under him.

I must have not been slow enough as once my arm was free; Iggy shifted his eyes blinking awake, he instinctively rubbed his face. Looking around, confused as he almost forgotten where he decided to sleep that night, his drunken memory was slightly blurry. Finally, the pieces clicked together as he looked at me. Shaking his head free of his hungover grogginess, he focused on me and turned his head in shame, "I'm sorry, I don't know what got over me," he panicked, going to stand up and leave, but I grabbed his hand gently, not forcing him to stay, but it caused him stopped and looked at me.

We both sat on the edge of the bed, eyes locked on each other.

I was the first to turn away this time. Iggy swallowed as his mouth went dry, he reached his hand out and placed his hand on the side of my face turning me to look back at him. He leaned in, and I didn't control myself as I leaned in with him, our lips brushing each other's; so soft, his breath, so warm. We both pulled back slightly, looking each other in the eye once again, calculating this scenario in our heads. *I was a god, he was a mortal, there was no way this could work, this shouldn't work. I should pull back; I should stop this before it goes any farther!* I told my self that, even though I leaned in and pushed my lips against his. Iggy pushing back against mine as we both placed our hands around the others face falling into the moment. He rolled me down onto the bed, his body pressed against me, his heart pounding through his chest, as mine pounded back at him. My hands traced down him, stopping at his hips, Iggy was straddling me when he suddenly pulled away again a boat of shame filled his mind. He looked away from me his face flushed red with so many emotions that were racing through his mind. Iggy's breath was panicked, he clenched the bed sheets as now I looked away embarrassed, wondering if I had somehow pushed him into this. If he thought this was what my goal was and that he couldn't refuse me because I was a god.

Again it was as if he knew what was running through my head, he placed his hand on my cheek and smiled sadly, "No," shaking his head, "It's all me," He laughed uneasily, rolling off of me, legs now hanging off the bed once again, "I want this so badly," He exhaled a large breath, fiddling with his fingers, "I've never been attracted to anybody, male or female," he paused and looked back at me with an uneasy smile, he was fighting back tears. Growing more and more frustrated with himself, "but you. You are the only person who I've ever wanted for myself, and I don't know how to feel about that. I don't know how to act or react to these emotions." Iggy pulled his hair in frustration, before brushing his hand softly down his face pulling at his lips as I sat up next to him. Giving him the space he needed to process his train of thought, "Touching, kissing," he paused again looking away as shame filled his eyes, "fucking, it was always a disgusting reminder of what I am."

I forced a grunt.

He smiled looking back at me, placing a hand on my leg, "Was, correction, I'm sorry."

I smiled, sadly back at him.

"You don't make me feel that way, but I get lost in the moment and it just everything floods back to me. I've never done anything like this because I've never wanted too," He sighed again and leaned his head against my shoulder, "I don't want to feel this way anymore, I want to get over these feelings."

We both jumped. There was a pounding at the door, only to calm once again as I stood up from the cot when a familiar voice called out, "Axel, are you in there?" It was the Captain.

I hurried over opening the door as Jane leaned up against the door frame speaking to me with an eased smile, "Aye, no one saw Iggy or yourself last night or this morin' just wanted to make sure everything was all good? Iggy's not in his room so," She was about to ask if I knew where he was, when she spotted him behind me, standing beside the bed trying to not look guilty of something. She smiled and raised her brows looking me up and down, "I see,"

In that moment I realized my shirt was mostly undone, I covered myself and looked away, my mouth went dry.

Iggy spoke from behind me, "It's not what you think, Captain."

She punched me lightly on the shoulder with a not so

subtle wink, "No shame from me, you know that."

Iggy pushed past me, "It's not that," he said more firmly, he shook his head as he spoke. Making his way around the two of us without another word, he walked to his room and closed the door tightly behind him. Both the Captain and I heard the click of the lock.

She looked in the direction of Iggy's door and held it for a moment before turning back to me with a death glare, pushing me through the door she closed it behind us. "Did something happen between you two? Ever since we got here Daric and I have noticed things have been a little tense, should I be kicking yer' ass?" She asked non-sarcastically as she crossed her arms over her chest, blocking the door with her body.

I shook my head no, but she didn't believe me as she stepped closer to me, asking me again.

I tried to think of how to explain it to her without any words. I finally placed to fingers to my lips, tapping them three times, before taking that same hand and patting it on my chest, as a quickening heart beat.

She cocked her head to the side as she tried to analyse what I was trying to explain to her, it took her a few seconds, but she got the idea. Finally asking, "You two kissed?" I nodded, "But that's all?" She almost wanted me to say that more happened, but I nodded again.

Jane thought she saw the whole picture and nodded, as she eased up on her imposing stance and thought about what she was to say next. The Captain leaned back against the door. Thinking back, she sighed, "I wish I could say I knew what he was going through, but really, him and I had different lives in that hellhole." She looked broken hearted as she thought about what she had to say, and it was another thing that was trailing in the back of my mind, "Axel, you need to be careful with whatever you are developing with Iggy,"

I looked away rubbing my arm uncomfortably.

"I know you want to stay with us on my ship and you are more than welcomed too, but you and I both know it will eventually have to come to an end. You are going to hurt Iggy in the end when you have to leave." She paused, letting me absorb her words, "I am grateful for how much you have helped Iggy, even from outside this bubble you two have created. I can see how much he has grown in these short months with you, but you know I am right."

I wanted to explain to her that this was never my intention to get involved with someone's life as I had with Iggy, I never expected, and I never even believed developing these feelings were possible for me. Gods have fallen for humans before, even Kitari, the hot-headed mortal hater had fallen for a beautiful maiden or two, but I was different. I wasn't made to live in this world. Yet, as much it was never my intention to fall for Iggy and have Iggy fall for me, it happened, and it was a problem I needed to deal with. I knew my already limited time was dwindling down, Kali could be around every corner and I was putting them all at risk having them defy the goddess of the sea, the one god/goddess a sea baring Captain should have on her side at all times.

Jane scratched her head, she looked apologetic even though everything she was saying was true. "This is not how I expected the day to start. I am sorry, I just am looking out for Iggy, and yourself. You may be a god, but I imagine at least you of all the gods can suffer from a broken heart. You are an immortal, he is not. He's fragile,"

I understood that more than her, but I gave her a reassuring smile, trying to convey that I was alright, and I understood where he was coming from, as she smiled back and left my room without another word.

I closed the door behind her and sat down with my back against the wood. I had forgotten in the momentary happiness the threat that I was to them. I needed my cloak. I needed my powers back. That means that I needed to face my sister. I stood up and walked towards the window opening it up as the ocean breeze poured in, filling my lungs with its salty air. I closed my eyes, *soon, Kali. I will be in your clutches again. Just give me a few more days and I will come to you.*

I just wanted a few more days, to say goodbye and then I would leave them for good. Go back to my darkness, that was if Kali didn't just kill me the second she had be in her grasp.

Chapter 25

I had changed and was laying on the bed, still lost in thought as I looked out the window on that beautiful day.

Iggy knocked loudly before opening the door without hesitation, he poked his head through the doorway and smiled as I had turned to look at him. His hair was still dripping, as it was smoothed back by the water, his bandana damp; wearing a tan vest, his wrist guards as always and dark coloured trousers. "Aye, come spend the day with Daric and me, Daric has pretty much been working almost non-stop since docking here, I thought we might drag him away from his work for a while. What do you say?"

I smiled and nodded at him, rolling off the ledge, cracking my back loudly before catching up to Iggy who was already making his way down the hall towards Daric's quarters.

I caught up just in time to watch Iggy dragging Daric out of his bed like a child tugging on their parents arm to move faster. Iggy hadn't even given Daric the curtesy of a knock, he just barreled in hollering Daric's name. "Come on ye Seadog!"

Daric grumbled as he pulled his arm free, standing up and adjusting his shirt and rubbing the sleep from his eyes, "Aye I'm up," he grumbled giving Iggy and I the stink eye. "Wha' do ye 'ave in mind?"

Iggy placed his hand on his chin thinking through the ideas in his head as Daric and I waited for his reply. He must have saw Daric's blades in the corner of his eye as an idea finally solidified in his head, with a smile. He pulled a dagger from its sheath on his belt, "We are going to teach Axel a game."

Daric seemed to approve, he understood what Iggy had in mind.

Daric grabbed a few extra knives while Iggy lead us out the inn and towards the woods.

We walked on the outskirts of the woods, along the beach, the sand marking our track clearly as we made our way without worry. The sun bore down on us, and the waves crashed on the shore.

Iggy was running through the sand bare footed, far ahead of us as Daric called out, "Ye better nah find any more strays t' brin' in," Daric nudged me playfully, he tried to hold back his smirk. I nudged him back, matching his smirk with one of my own.

Iggy turned and yelled back, still moving quickly

through the waves and sand, "Without our lil' stranger think about how boring our lives would have been these last months!" Even from that distance we could see his perfect, white smile.

Daric waited until Iggy was turned back away before he spoke, just me and him, "Ye been a good addition t' th' crew. We owe ye a lot, I may nah know how much time we 'ave left together, but this may be th' ole scallywag in me speakin', but I be grateful fer ye comin' into our lives. Iggy really needed someone, 'n that someone happened t' be a god." He laughed lightly as he patted me on the shoulder.

His words made me sad, but I managed to smile through it. I think all of us, besides Iggy, knew our time was coming to an end.

We looked a head as Iggy had finally stopped, having found what he thought was the best tree for what he had planned. He pulled out his knife and began to carve a target deeply into the trunk. Daric and I caught up when Iggy finished his last touches before wiping the blade clean on his trousers, stepping back, Daric and I followed.

He placed the blade between his thumb and his index finger, rocking the blade back and forth just slightly, eyes locked on the target. He whipped the blade at the tree; hitting just to the left of the marked-out bullseye.

Daric nodded stepping up next to Iggy. He pulled his own blade from its sheath, this time I focused solely on Daric's hand movements.

The knife whizzed through the air, I lost track of it for a second before it hit dead center, with how fast it moved through the air.

"Show me up why don't yah'," Iggy grumbled playfully with a smile.

Iggy handed me one of his blades, beckoning me to take a shot at it. I took the blade and held it between my thumb and my index finger just as Daric and Iggy had. I focused on the target and released the blade. I had the image of my blade digging into the trunk of the tree between Daric's and Iggy's; my imagination was way off. The blade made it just over the halfway mark, sticking limply into the sand.

Iggy busted into laugher at the pathetic attempt. Daric on the other hand fought really hard to hold his back as he patted me on the shoulder in an attempt at being supportive. I finally let out a painful chuckle, the second the sound left my mouth Daric lost it, he let out a gut filled chuckle. We all wondered over to collect the knives as they continued to laugh at my expense.

This time both Daric and Iggy instructed me as I

readied my throw, making it all the way to the tree, but missing it by an arms length. Iggy hit the bullseye and Daric was slightly below mark.

After my fifth throw I finally managed to hit the target, Iggy cheered me on from his seated position in the sand, raising one fist in triumph for me. I smiled before taking a seat on the sand between Daric and Iggy.

Iggy laid back, uncaring that sand was sticking to his body and getting into his hair. He closed his eyes, basking in the warm sun-soaked ground. "I do love the sea, but nothing feels better than the warm sand on the skin."

"I can reckon o' a handful better," Daric noted slyly. Iggy sat up and shook his head with a look.

That day I was on Iggy's side as I ran my fingers through the sand, trying to hold back my smile while they bickered around me, arguing on situations that were better then now. Which even through Daric was good at convincing people and I did make it a thing to not disagree with the man, I had to here. I couldn't ask for a better last few days with them.

We got back up and continued throwing knives until the sun was well over the treeline and the onset on purple skies as the sun slowly began to set.

We wondered back to the inn, in search for a drink.

Iggy promised to cut me off long before it got near the point of the night previous. He wrapped my head in a lock, messing up my hair with his knuckle before pushing me away with a chuckle. I combed my hair back into place with my fingers before hip-checking him playfully back.

Daric smiled softly at the two of us fooling around; our actions, or the subtle tension slowly lifting between us, had tipped him off that something happened between Iggy and myself. By the small smile he tried, so hard to keep off his face, I knew he was approving.

We entered the pub to find Jane sitting with her elbows on the bar making eyes with the bar maid, who was blushing furiously at the Captain's smooth compliments. Before that day I would bet that woman had never considered being bedded by another woman, but Jane knew her art well. With her silver tongue and beautiful face, she could nearly convince anyone to be bedded by her.

Daric stepped up to the Captain, wrapping his arm over her shoulder tipping his head to the bar maid with a sly smile, "Ye can steal our Captain later tonight, but fer now I be needin' her."

Iggy added in, "When you can ma'am, bring us over some food and a few pitchers of ale." He smiled as

Daric lead the Captain away from the beautiful woman.

Jane pouted but didn't fight while Daric lead her to a table at the back sitting her down before taking his own seat. Iggy and I just a step behind, all with smiles on our faces as we watched her sigh. She looked back at the woman, "I was so close to taking her away for the night, Daric!" She sighed sadly.

Daric patted her on the back, "Aye, ye still may, Captain."

"You have about a week to woo the beautiful barmaid," Iggy added with playful smile when the woman began to approach, dropping a platter of food on the table and two pitches, leaving only to return again with mugs for us all and a third pitcher; she knows well how much a group of pirates can drink now.

Jane gave the woman a wink, the bar maid blushed placing everything down before actually continuing her other duties as there were other patrons in the pub.

Jane poured everyone some ale, while chugging her first of many this night. Placing her foot on an empty chair and her elbow on her knee, leaning back in her chair. "Aye, I still have a little while yet to seduce her, since my poor ship is still in disrepair." She grumbled as she drank more from her mug. "What is the occasion?"

Iggy shrugged drinking his glass down as I just looked down at the amber substance with regret before taking a long drink, "I just thought it would be nice to drink and be merry together."

Jane's eyes locked onto my face, her eyes read seriousness as the rest of her face read enjoyment. Her conversation with me refreshed in her and my own mind. I nodded subtly to her, and she then eased up on me.

Once again, I had lost count of how many drinks I had consumed that night, Iggy was being truthful about cutting me off long before I got close to the amount from the night previous, but he still allowed me to get drunk to the point I wasn't able to stand up unassisted.

Jane and Daric had been laughing at me as my head bobbled around trying to make sense of their conversations. Iggy finally took mercy on me, "I think Axel, should call it a night." The three of them were barely buzzed from the alcohol. I nodded to Iggy's insight and stood up from my seat, only to fall down as my legs buckled themselves. Iggy caught me just before my ass hit the floor, pulling me back up. I knew Jane was eyeing me as I tried to push him away, but she just crossed her arm over her chest while taking a drink, "Just let him get you to bed, you're drunk." Daric and Jane began to chuckle again.

Iggy tossed one of my arms over his shoulder, he spoke to the two giggling drunken fools, "I'm gonna' call it a night as well, going to hit the bath house before my shift tomorrow, you all are welcome to join."

Jane tipped her mug to Iggy, "I may just have to take you up on that Iggy," She smiled as she finished her drink, beckoning Daric to catch up.

"Goodnight, kids." Daric subtly waved in our direction.

I waved obnoxiously, I felt a hiccup building in my chest, as I prayed it wasn't going to be more then that.

Iggy dragged me up the stairs; I caused him to drop me a few times as he just tried to muffle his laugher. He continued to pull me up by my arms, "Come on, you got to put some effort into this!"

Finally, he dropped me on the bed as I rolled onto my back, eyes barely open, with a dumb smile on my face.

"Good night," Iggy laughed, he was about to leave the room, but I stopped him, my hand intertwining with his.

I managed to say, "Stay," With a drunken but sweet smile.

I could see him hesitating, so I pulled him in towards me, weakly enough that I wasn't forcing him, but strong enough to actually move him.

Iggy laid down next to me as I wrapped my arms around his shoulders; Iggy swallowed. He got himself comfortable in my arms, he now rested his head on my chest, arms tucked in between us. I closed my eyes and held him close, placing a small kiss on his forehead. I already found myself drifting into the darkness. I could feel Iggy's warmth, his breathing, his heart beating, his breath on my chest as slowly but surely sleep caught him as well.

I was back home in the darkness of time while I slept. Is Kai here? I wondered as I stood there with my eyes closed, taking in the comforting feeling of the black, soulless dimension of time.

I began to wonder, my hand out tracing the emptiness around me, the air was thick as fog. Even through you couldn't see anything, you could feel the strands of time weaving through and around each finger. If I had my cloak, I could grab hold of a single thread and it would lead me through that lifetime, that soul's lifetime, I could watch life after life, until the soul darkened and finally turned black.

But, I still felt like a guest in my own home. I was here, but I wasn't allowed access to my own things. I smiled, thinking back, even before Kai it wasn't really that lonely of an existence, I hadn't seem what I was missing. I had all these memories; all these mortal's lives at my finger tips. If I wanted too, I could relive the memories of heroes, poets, kings or queens. I could see anything I could ever want. I could feel as if I was a part of something; I was part of something, I am the keeper of their stories. It was my only true connection with the world of mortals.

A dark thought ran through my head as I found myself standing still again, *what would happen to this world if I did die? Would Kai be able to maintain it alone? Or would it, as everything does, come to an end?* The truth was gods were not truly immortal. They all had an end, so that means so should I, right? Never before had I questioned myself, never before had I considered my own death. But I believe that may be the only end with Kali this time. Would she destroy my cloak? Or would she allow Kai to take on my mantle? To preserve all what I've created, all these stories, all these lifetimes... Or is her bitter anger towards me going to destroy everything in her war path. These were questions I did not know the answer too. These were questions I couldn't find with the snap of my finger. I chuckled to myself, *it was something I could only learn in time.*

Time was passing as I wondered aimlessly; was I secretly looking for Kai? If Kali did end me when we met again, I wanted a chance to say goodbye to him. Maybe subconsciously I was telling myself that I wanted to see him again. I wanted to tell him that he was just as important to me as he felt I was to him. But all I could do was hope that he already knew that.

I took in the moment; trying to lie to myself that I was ready to be forgotten again, as it was supposed to be as life intended me to be. Falling back into the nothingness that holds the fabric of everything together. Everyone will move on without me, as they are supposed too, as they were destined too...

Chapter 26

Morning broke; I didn't want to wake, as I tightened my embrace of Iggy, nestling my face in his hair as he also began to shift awake in my arms.

Iggy groaned, he rolled his shoulders and stretched his neck, pulling himself from me as he rubbed his eyes free of sleep with a wide yawn.

I rolled onto my back, I stretched my arms above my head before propping myself up on my hands, looking at Iggy who was now cross legged on the cot next to me.

He blushed and looked away, embarrassed that once again he had slept next to me.

I reached out and placed my hand softly against his cheek. He turned and smiled back, removing my hand, and just holding it, pinned against the bed, our fingers intertwined.

Iggy pulled away, rolling off the bed as he did another stretch, adjusting his vest and retying his arm bracers. "We should get some food and head to the bath house, I want a couple hours to relax before my shift this evening. Knowing Daric, he's already been to check on the ship and the other crews progress from that night."

I nodded as I pulled on a new tunic, before tying my book to my belt.

Together we made our way down to the pub where we had a quick breakfast with Jane and Daric; of meat, cheese and bread, washing it down with bitter coffee. We then together as a pack made our way to the bath house from our first day here.

Today we weren't alone, two older men sat in the pool, conversing of their sea fairing days.

Daric, Iggy and I walked up to the pools edge only then dropping our coverings as he quickly stepped into the steaming water.

The Captain took a few extra minutes, she came out with her cloth draped over her shoulder, baring all to everyone who dared stare.

Daric and Iggy had must have seen this view many times before, the two of them were unfazed by the beautiful, toned and tanned woman before them. I unsure what to do, turned my gaze towards Iggy who was sitting next to me, his eyes closed, resting his head on the edge of the pool.

Jane dropped into the water, bending her body so her breasts were under. Taking a seat next to Daric, she dunked her thick, curly hair into the water, running her fingers through the tangled mess. She blissfully sighed, relaxing into the water. Straining her hair, she threw it over the side of the pool, allowing it to dry with her head rested against the edge. "This has been a very interesting few months for us, hasn't it?" She opened her eyes and stared at me. As much as I was ashamed of the harm, I had put them all through, there was no more anger or hatred in her voice, she smiled looking away.

"Wit' ye Captain 'tis been an interestin' lifetime." He propped himself up on his elbows, not fighting back his grin any longer.

Iggy gave me a soft smile as I turned away in fear I may continue to blush, I sank into the water. My skin already turning pink from the heat. Why was the universe trying to make leaving harder for me? It's like somehow Mother called out to them from beyond her death, whispering to them that our time was coming to an end. Telling them to leave with no regrets of words left unsaid. But I had to push these thoughts to the side. Enjoy the moments for what they were and think of what was to be when that moment came. For now, I was surrounded by people who actually cared about me, and who I cared deeply for.

Jane could see that I was trying to shake a train of thought as she wrapped her arm around me, shoving me under the water playfully. I flailed like a fish out of water. She finally released me as I wiped the water from my eyes and face, shocked and in disbelieve Daric and Iggy busted a gut laughing at my expense, again!

Iggy took the chance as Daric wasn't expecting it to push the back of his head dunking him face first into the water, he scurried away out of arms reach of retaliation. But by moving away from Daric he crept into my path as I tackled him, knocking us both under water.

Together we came up for air, wiping the water from our faces. Iggy tossed more water at my face as he swam even farther away, trying to hide his smile. Jane had Daric now in a head lock, messing his hair in her hands as he just stood, arms crossed over his chest, attempting to hide his smile, but it was without prevail.

The four of us were so obnoxiously, loud and rowdy that the two other men who were trying to enjoy their bath in peace, left in a huff.

Jane kissed Daric on the fore head, wrapping her arms around him, "Oh, I love you ye ol' pirate." She laughed as he tried to pull away, but she just held on tighter.

Daric grumbled as he gave up trying to break free of her grasp, Iggy and I chuckled at her affection towards the old sailor.

We had been in the waters so long that our skin had begun to wrinkle and grow uncomfortable. We all decided it was time to get out as Iggy had to ready himself for his shift on the ship.

If we had known that this was going to be the last time that we all smiled, we all laughed together, we would have savored this moment just a little bit more. But that wasn't how fate would have had it...

Chapter 27

I had decided to crawl back into my bed to rest my eyes for a few more hours, Daric having agreed to wake me before it was time to take over on the ship. Captain took her free time to finally persuade the beautiful bar maid to her quarters, while Iggy rushed off for his shift on the Shadows Blade.

The mass was finally being installed this evening, so while Jorgen, Reefer, Vendell and Matthias worked on that, along with the wood crafters and hired carpenters, he finished stitching up the mast before heading down to the storage room, checking for the damage done to their stock supplies.

It wasn't long when Iggy began to feel that something was going on, something was wrong. He couldn't wrap his finger around it, but he could feel Jorgen and them watching him. Every now and then Matthias, or Vendell would enter the storage room, acting as if they were searching for something, or just peaking through the open door silently, as if to check that he was still working.

He would never admit it, but it made his stomach churn with a slight fear, but he just shook his head, and pushed the feeling to the side, suspecting it was just past memories while he continued his work without pause.

Hours had passed, and Matthias came down to the storage room, "Iggy, the next shift is arriving, time to head off."

"Okay, thanks Matthias." Iggy called out with a small wave. Tying the storage logs together and placing them down on the table before heading up to the main deck.

Daric and I were looking at what still needed done, Daric directed Taylor and Morgan to their tasks for the night.

I smiled and waved as Iggy emerged, he smiled back, pushing his earlier feelings aside, he still believed it to be nothing.

He walked up to Daric and put his finger on the paper, "Storage room is complete, the list is there."

Daric nodded, "Good t' know."

That feeling built again in Iggy's stomach. He looked around the boat, this time he couldn't push the feeling away as I saw it on his face. "I'm going to head out," Iggy tried to push past me, but I grabbed his hand lightly and raised my brows in curiosity as I could see something seemed up with him. He squeezed my hand tightly and smiled, before pulling apart, "I'll come see you after your shift, maybe we can relax, just the two of us."

It took me a second, but I nodded as I watched him leave, only for Daric to distract me with orders. If only I had looked a little longer, maybe I could have stopped the wheels that were already in motion...

Matthias came up next to Iggy once they stepped off the dock, consciously leading Iggy off the main path.

Matthias finally branched away from Iggy as Jorgen, Reefer and Vendell appeared behind, trailing, they slowly gained on him.

Iggy swallowed hard. He looked behind him, turning into an alleyway as he clutched the hilt of his dagger, thinking he could easy lose them, but little did he know this was exactly where they wanted him.

Vendell and Reefer rushed to the entrance of the alleyway, blocking the exit, while Iggy spotted two men blocking his path ahead of him. He came to a halt, still not understanding the why to this situation.

Iggy held his breath, studying his surroundings, looking for ways to even out the odds. He placed both hands on his weapons as he went to continue forward, hoping for just another second if this was all in his head. Only when Vendell took the first move, reaching for Iggy's wrist, Iggy to slap his forearm with his blade, a small, yet deep cut. Reefer charged Iggy; slamming him up against the wall, his face connecting with the hard brick. Iggy dropped one of his blades, only to tighten his grip on the other. Iggy tucked himself into the wall and rolled out of Reefers reach swinging his blade low, slicing the first stranger's abdomen, as he stepped forward joining the assault.

 He was a towering dark-skinned man, unarmed; he didn't need a blade to fight. After it cut through his skin, he grabbed Iggy's wrist, twisting it back with a snap as he broke Iggy's wrist, cleanly. Iggy kicked back against the man, only to stumble into Vendell, who tried to grab him in an attempt to hold him down.

Bending low, dodging the large man, Iggy pulled another blade from his boot and jabbed Vendell in the thigh, as the blade struck, the other stranger took advantage of the moment. He was a large tanned man with dark hair, grabbed Iggy by the back of his shirt and smashed the side of Iggy's head with great force into the wall. Instantly he was dazed, blood pooled down his face, he tried to react, but it was too late, the man locked his forearm around Iggy's throat and clasped a firm hand over Iggy's mouth to keep him silent. The force of the man around Iggy's throat cutting off oxygen, Iggy tried to claw himself free, gasping under the man's firm hand.

Vendell and the dark-skinned man grabbed both of Iggy's arms, twisting and tying them behind his back as he tried to fight. Jorgen finally stepped forward as he took one of Iggy's knives that had fallen to the dirt and cut off one of his leather bracers, slicing through his skin, he began to bleed profusely. Iggy cried out under the man's hand as Jorgen then untied Iggy's bandana that was holding his hair in place, tied a knot in it before stuffing it in Iggy's mouth, Iggy bit down catching Jorgen's finger, breaking skin. Jorgen punched Iggy in the face as the large stranger held Iggy still, placing his hand back, firmly over Iggy's mouth, just to be safe as another hooded figure entered the alleyway.

Iggy's nose flared as he kicked and fought watching the man approach. He placed the back of his hand on Iggy's bloody cheek with a sickening smile. A smile that Iggy knew too well, formed on Gibson's face. "Ahoy again, me wee pet."

Iggy lunged at him, the gag and the mans hand muffling his growl and profanity.

Gibson snapped his fingers and turned to walk back the way he came, "Let's hurry, we don't wants t' raise attention."

They dragged Iggy through the town, being careful to keep a hand clasped over Iggy's mouth just until they made it to the woods. Iggy wasn't going down without a fight. He gave it all he had, but he was fighting a losing battle as the concussion slowed his movement even more in his already hindered state. Once in the woods the man dropped Iggy to the dirt as they beat him into submission. The tanned man pulled one of Iggy's legs out as he crushed his ankle under his boot, crushing it painfully. Iggy cried out under his gag, tears streaming down his face. He was rolled onto his side as the other man kneed him hard in the ribs, before lifting the now limp Iggy back to his feet. The two men dragged him the rest of the way. He was dazed and confused, blood covered his face and filled his mouth, his eye swollen, barely left open.

Finally, they reached the Mercenary camp as they dropped the limp, beaten Iggy to their Captain's feet, forcing Iggy to his knees. He looked up at the mercenary captain, utterly defeated and in agony, he struggled to breathe behind his bloodied gag.

The Captain, Lucard shifted uncomfortably in his seat, turning his gaze from the beaten boy at his feet, "Our contract didn't mention he was just a boy," "Does it matter?" Gibson chucked, he tossed a bag of coin to Jorgen, not even turning his proudful gaze from Iggy.

Lucard stood up and walked up to Gibson, "I don't traffic children."

Gibson met the mans angry gaze, "He's nah a sprog," he growled, "he be jus' th' bait, if ye knew about th' scallywag we be trappin', ye would be thankful t' 'ave somethin' t' keep 'im in check." Gibson rolled his eyes and turned back to Jorgen, "Make sure Axel, gets th' message."

Jorgen fondled the sack of coin in his hand before informing Gibson, "His shift be o'er at daylight, so ye 'ave th' night wit' 'im."

"Perfect," Gibson smiled.

With that the traitors of the Shadow's blade left Iggy in his captor's hands.

Iggy was bound to a small tree, his hands being retied around the trunk, and another rope wrapped a few times around his chest. Unfortunately, the adrenaline from the fight had warn off and his still bleeding head and broken, swollen ankle and wrist throbbed, his ribs and faced were bruised and ached. He bit down on his gag trying to fight the pain away, tasting blood; the gag continued to keep his lip wound open as they rubbed against each other. Tears of pain and frustration formed in his eyes. He wanted to close his eyes, sleep, in hope that this would end, and I wouldn't come to his aid. He prayed that I wouldn't come, but he knew that I would. He had no doubt that I would. But at this moment he had other things to worry about. He could feel Gibson's presence even before the bald man approached; kneeling in front of him with a sick smile stuck on his ugly, face.

He grabbed Iggy's chin, trying to turn him to face him. Iggy growled behind his gag and tried to shake the man away, but his binds were too restricting. Gibson traced his hands down Iggy's neck and chest before placing it firmly, uncomfortably on his inner thigh. "I've missed this," He jerked Iggy's head to the side as he kissed his now exposed neck. Iggy closed his eyes; his fight and his fearlessness began to fade. Gibson grabbed Iggy by his hair, holding him still as he placed his lips on Iggy's gagged mouth.

More tears now fell down Iggy's face as a sick, disgusted feeling built up in him, Gibson's hand on his thigh moved upwards.

A voice came to Iggy's rescue, "What do you think you are doing?"

Gibson snapped, teeth bore as he spun around, "None o' yer concern!" he than realized his mistake. He turned to face Captain Lucard. He bit his tongue thinking of his next move carefully.

The man grabbed Gibson's arm and tossed him forcefully away from Iggy. Gibson was unable to keep his balance as he was spun, stumbling to the dirt. "I do not stand for that kind of treatment to prisoners, not while you sail under my flag." His voice was firm, final.

Gibson stood up and stepped towards Iggy, entranced by his urges towards him, "He's a strumpet, he likes this attention." Lucard placed his hand threateningly on the hilt of his blade, blocking Gibson's path to Iggy, "I said, no."

Gibson growled under his breath, but stepped back, retreating, knowing that he had lost this fight tonight.

Lucard knelt in front of Iggy who recoiled, quivering still in fear. The man reached in his pocket, pulling out a handkerchief to Iggy's relief. The Captain spoke, "Fear not, the man Gibson assured that once the man who goes by Axel is delivered to our client, that you will be released, unharmed." Captain Lucard was telling a lie, but he wanted to ease his mind, even if it was with false hope.

Iggy fought back his dread-filled tears as the Captain cleaned Iggy's wounds and bandaged his ankle tightly and attempted to tightly wrap his wrist. Iggy turned his gaze away from the man who now sat across him, his back against another tree as they waited for day light. They waited for the moment I'd find the ransom letter. The moment I'd come to his rescue. The moment he was dreading most.

I was exhausted, for a few moments I was happy that Iggy hadn't come to meet me after my shift. My body was heavy as I dragged it up the steps. All I wanted was to crawl into that bed, close my eyes and rest. But as I pushed my door open, instantly I knew something was wrong, the door wasn't latched. I blinked in confusion, as it just swung open to my touch. Entering with hesitation I looked to the table next to the bed, blood? That was when I saw Iggy's sliced leather bracer, soaked in blood, a folded letter placed next to it. Instantly I woke. My heart raced as I picked up the note and his bracer bringing it into my chest, I clenched it tightly, my hands now coated in the blood as I read.

We have your friend, Iggy. Come meet us in the
woods, north of the old pier. If you inform Daric, your
Captain, or anyone else about this, we will kill him.
Come alone, come unarmed, or we will kill him.
Do not test us. Your friend's life is in your hands.

In that moment of panic, I made a few grave
mistakes. First off in my whirl wind, I dropped the
note and bracer to the ground, I rushed out of the
door and down the stairs that the room was left wide
open for anyone to stumble upon the ransom note
and blood. As well as I rushed down passed the pub,
Daric had called out to me, asking where I was
rushing off to in such a hurry. I just ignored him, not
even hearing or seeing him as I had passed him.
Nothing mattered, expect for Iggy's safety.

Chapter 28

The skies were orange from the early morning sunrise and the wind was oldy course and cold for this summer morning. It wasn't hard for me to find the old pier as two days before Iggy, Daric and I had passed it in search for a spot, but I had no time to think back. I rushed through the woods without thinking, without assessing the situation. Nothing else mattered.

Stopping suddenly. My heart was pounding, my breath visible as I tried to catch my breath in the cold, biting air.

Six pirates stood around Iggy who was bound, forced to his knees with a dagger firmly pressed against his throat. The man holding him forced Iggy's gaze towards me, tugging him by a handful of hair, revealing that the whole of the left side of his face was bruised and swollen, still covered in dry blood.

Iggy finally focused on me, dread-filled and ashamed as he tried to fight against Captain Lucard who just gripped tighter, pushing the blade into his skin.

I put my hands out, trying to tell him to stop, my eyes pleading for Iggy to stop struggling.

I could see it in his eyes that he just wanted me to turn around and leave him there, but he listened to my silent plead and froze, closing his eyes for a moment to collect himself.

Turning my stare to Captain Lucard; I pointed to Iggy than away from the group of men before pointing to myself and placing my hands out, wrists up and together. "Ig," I tried to speak, forcing the words out, tearing my throat, "Iggy goes free." I spoke in broken words.

Iggy pleaded under his gag for me not to do this, but it was hopeless, I wasn't going to leave him in the hands of these men.

I repeated brokenly, the iron taste filled my mouth, "Iggy goes free." Still my hands out.

The men looked at the Captain, waiting for him to respond, Captain Lucard snapped signalling for them to move in. Two men from the back stepped up and approached me. I did not move, they took my arms, twisting them behind my back, the thick iron cuffs and a neck cuff were placed on me, cutting into my skin, but I dared not react.

Eyes locked on Iggy who had tears in his eyes, he knew what at the time I did not. I went to repeat that

Iggy was to be set free in my minimalist wording, when they shoved a gag in my mouth, I had to fight the urge to struggle.

Captain Lucard removed the blade from Iggy's throat and released his hair. Iggy now leaning forward, head dropped as tears streamed his face.

"What is the next move, sir?" One of the men asked.

As he spoke, Gibson approached from his hiding spot in the trees, he smiled at me, stepping closer to Iggy. "Get them both to the ship,"

In that moment, I had no self control as the pirate mercenaries were lucky that they had a strong hold on me, or I would have been on that snake of a monster in seconds. Teeth bore behind the gag he smiled as the two men struggled to hold me back.

Captain Lucard stepped between Gibson and Iggy, as he finally ordered, "Get them both to the ship,"

Two men grabbed Iggy lifting him to his feet, he fought sluggishly, stumbling as he tried to tear himself from their arms, but he was already defeated.

I'm sorry Iggy... What did I expect to happen?! I was furious with myself as my legs got weak.

To the left of us the trees shifted. The men stopped, the few with their hands free pulled out their weapons, eyes locked on the direction of the sound.

Daric?!

Daric entered the small clearing with his blade drawn, face filled with determination as his eyes scanned between Iggy, Gibson and me.

He made the mistake of not finding more help before charging into this fight, but he saw the distress on my face, and he was sure whatever was wrong he didn't have much time to assess the situation, he just thought that I needed help. If he understood the situation more, he would have found the Captain, he would have gathered the crew, charging in as one. But instead he stood alone. Blade drawn and determined, blood rage building in his eyes as Gibson backed up, cowering in fear at the mans presents. He stammered, "We said alone! We said we would kill 'im if ye informed Daric or th' Captain!"

Captain Lucard snapped his fingers as three men charged Daric, he dropped Iggy to the dirt, placing his foot firmly between his shoulders, holding him in place. He knelt down; knife once again drawn.

Iggy was still disoriented and sore, he wasn't strong enough to fight the weight of the man.

It was almost laughable, sending three men up against Daric; these three weren't nearly as talented with the sword as the older man faced before them.

Daric swiftly, as if still a young man began to

dispatch them one by one.

I fought wildly against the two men holding me down, but I was no match for their grip, and even if I did free myself from their hands, what help would I be? I wasn't getting free of these binds on my own accord.

Daric slit the throat of one of his attackers as the man fell, blood spraying across the field, Daric charged at the next man.

The last man standing jumped away from Daric, their hands bloody and weaponless. They shook fearfully, as Daric plunged his sword into the other attackers pelvic. The man screamed in agony, he dropped to the ground. Daric ripped the blade from the man's body, with no remorse for the mercenary, fury filled his eyes. He stepped forward towards the man running away.

Daric raised his blade to the man and was about to attack when the Captain's whistle caused him to freeze. He held his breath even, he didn't dare test the man's impatience.

Captain Lucard had Iggy's head pulled up, his neck exposed as his blade was pressing deeply into his skin, "Drop the weapon. I don't want to hurt him, but I will."

Iggy called out from under his gag, this time the

muffed words could be understood as the gag slightly loosened, "Daric, don't!"

The Captain clamped his hand over Iggy's mouth and adjusted the blade as the soft skin of Iggy's neck began to bleed as he cut through. The Captain turned back to Daric. "I said drop the weapon."

Daric didn't move; his fingers just opened, and the blade dropped at his feet.

The last of the men who stepped in to fight now hesitated, but he stepped forward.
"Gibson, assist him." Captain Lucard ordered.

Gibson went to refuse but the Captain did not seem in the mood to be tested, so he stepped forward as well, grabbing Daric's sword and tossing it out of threats way. They twisted Daric's hands behind his back. Daric took this as an opportunity, believing it to be one of his last; he knocked Gibson in the mouth with his head, spitting in his face, as the other man knocked Daric down to his knees. Daric now behaved as Captain Lucard cleared his throat, showing Daric he still had Iggy's life in his hands.

Captain Lucard looked between Daric and Iggy, something was running through his mind, as he then turned and looked to Gibson who stood behind Daric, fearful. "You mentioned that Ignatius wasn't the only one who would work as collateral?"

"I suppose, but" Gibson spoke with an unease as he knew what the man was thinking.

He sat Iggy on his knees, tossing Gibson some rope to bind Daric. "Bring him here."

I fought even harder against the two men, *please don't, please don't.*

This man had a decision to make. Bringing both Iggy and Daric would be a mistake, he knew. Gibson said that I was most fond of Iggy, 'most' being the key factor but, he was unpredictable and so far, fought them tooth and nail. Daric on the other hand, who again I was fond of, was a very strong and smart man, the key being smart enough to know when he had been beat. He knew what battles to fight and what battles to step down from. Captain Lucard respected that. He suspected that if he kept Iggy alive that Gibson had his own plans in mind for the boy once I was dropped off at the location. Daric might have a chance as Gibson didn't seem so fond of the older man as he did the boy.

Daric was knelt next to Iggy, his head straight, his face unmoving, emotionless.

I was not calm, or emotionless. My face was red with frustration, anger at myself. Red hot tears ran down my face, I wanted to beg to them to let them both go, plead that I wouldn't resist, but I knew it would have been a futile argument. If they know what I am, they don't know what power I could possess. They don't know what they are dealing with.

The Captain nodded sadly as he had made up his mind. "I will make it quick." He told me. "Take him to the ship, he doesn't need to witness this." Captain Lucard said, he didn't seem happy about what he had to do. It killed me inside as they turned me away from Daric and Iggy. I tried to turn my head, tried to fight but eventually I was out of sight. Out of ear shot of the cries and possible screams from the surviving ally. *Iggy, Daric, no! No! NO!* I repeatedly screamed inside, tears drenched my face, my lips trembled behind the gag. I was too weak to save them, I was too selfish to give myself to my sister those many weeks before and because of my fear of my sister, one of my friends were dead because of me! I knew the moment they were gone... I could feel it, as my heart stopped. My legs buckled, and I lost the will to fight. The two men gave me a moment to regain myself as I now allowed them to lead me to the ship. My fight was dead, along with my friend.

They took me down to their brig; two cells, one took up three quarters of the far wall, while the other was just big enough for a large man to lay comfortably. They placed me in the larger of the two;

chaining my ankle to an anchor in the floor, before grabbing large weighted chains that they wrapped around my body tightly. I tried my hardest to stay up right, but as I assume the point of all, I toppled to the floor. I couldn't move my arms, and I could barely move under the weight of it all, not that I would have tried... I laid my head against the wood planks and bit down on the gag.

Once they were satisfied with their job, they left the brig after sealing the door to my cell with three extra locks.

I laid in wait with my eyes closed. Alone, for the answer to my nightmare were to be revealed.

Chapter 29

Hungover, or should I say still drunk for the night before Jane sauntered out of her quarters and across the hall knocking loudly on Daric's door. She waited. No response. Rubbing her tired eye's, she banged harder, "Daric, you awake?" She questioned, finally turning the handle and peeking in quickly as she spotted an empty room. Not thinking anything odd of that, but when she turned around and saw that my door was wide open. She paused, now her gut was telling her something was terribly wrong. "Axel? Iggy?" She rushed through the open door with panic, swinging it open the rest of the way as the door hit the wall with a large bang, a small whirlwind causing the note I had dropped back to the floor to lift up and skip across the ground. She picked it up, reading it quickly as she crumpled it in her fist turning from the room, banging on every door she knew her crew occupied. "All men at attention." She yelled, drawing her blade as it grinded against its sheath.

They must have known that she meant business as

even all of the other hungover men rushed to attention. She spoke no words of explanation as she now rushed down the stairs, grabbing the few strangling men who were still in the bar and followed the vague directions. She was running through the now busy streets, pushing her way passed other sailors and pirates with no regard for them.

With the entirety of her crew falling behind her, she finally reached the clearing, to find the corpse laying in the grass.

She was speechless, horrified as her body trembled, she clenched her fists, her nails digging into the skin of her palms, she tried so hard to hold in her emotions, but they over came her. Her men behind her took a long moment of silence, removing their hats as their Captain rushed over to her fallen friend and their fallen crewmate. She cut his binds before rolling the corpse, so they faced the sky rather then resting in the dirt, grabbing his face pulling him into her chest as she held him tightly. She was kneeling in his blood, her hands now soaked in it as she tried to hold back tears.

Victor came up to her placing his hand on the Captain's back in comfort.

Her sorrow had to be pushed aside as fury and determination for retribution filled inside her. "Bring him back to the ship," She handed Victor the note that was crumpled in her pocket, as she looked him straight in the eye, "I want answers, now, and if you find any man who is even partially responsible for this, you bring them to me and I will show them what happens when they cross Captain Far'mel." She growled, clenching her fists once again. Standing and looking away from her fallen friend, a wave of nausea washed over her, but she swallowed back, turning to her men. "If anyone has anything to do this with note," Pointing to the note now in Victor hands, "I will find out, and when I find out their will be hell to pay."

She studied her men, studied them carefully for even the slightest flinch, as did Victor.

Victor whispered to the Captain, "Jorgen, Matthias, Taylor, Jackal,"

Jane nodded and snapped her fingers, repeating those names Victor whispered to her. "Take them to the brig, I will break them and find the truth."

Jorgen and Jackal tried to run, but the non-traitorous men grabbed them, as well as grabbing the others mentioned by the Captain.

Jane stepped up, inches for Jorgen's face, "I will find out everything I need to know." She waved for the men to move, as the traitors were forced back to the

Shadow's Blade. A few stayed behind to help; they lifted their fallen ally carefully.

Every minute that passed we got father out of Captain Far'mel's reach, she knew she had to work quickly, to find her answers and get her ship ready to sail.

I waited; alone for far longer then I had expected too. Only lifting my head when I caught the sound of the keys to the brig jingling. They turned the lock and a small crash as something, no, someone was thrown with great force against the wall.

The door swung out and the prisoner was tossed down the stairs, they rolled and tumbled, my stomach tightened as all I could do was watch. Their shirt was soaked in blood, but I knew it wasn't their own. His face was bruised as he clearly put a resistance after watching our friend have their throat slit by our captor. He rolled hard into the side of my cell as he went to stand; still wanting to fight, but only to stumble to one knee. He tried to steady himself, but the men where back on him, placing him in a headlock. The man lifted him to his feet, while the other unlocked the cell, forcing him in by throwing him against the back wall. He hit the wall face first and stumbled for a moment. This give the pirates just enough time to lock the door before he rushed them, slamming his body against the locked cell.

My heart broke all over again as I saw the anguish in his face. Apparently, Iggy wasn't always the best at hiding his emotion from the world.

The mercenaries left without a word. Iggy slammed himself against the bars three more times before his broken ankle twisted, forcing him to crumble to his knees. He placed his forehead against the cold wooden floor, teeth bore down on the gag as he failed to fight his furious, tears back.

Iggy... I curled into myself the best I could, as I thought about the late Daric.

Iggy twisted his wrists, the broken bone twisting painfully, cutting the rope deep into his skin as he caused himself to bleed. He screamed behind his gag, in frustration as he kicked the bars, finally, his thumb twisted uncomfortably enough as his hand slipped out of his binds. He tore the gag out of his mouth, standing up, he shook the bars and screamed in frustration. He laid his head against the bars and crumbled back to his knees, eyes closed as he tried to hold back the tears, but it was hopeless, "I will make them pay for everything they have done!"

Unable to do anything, I finally looked away from

the grieving mess, that was my friend. I had caused all this pain. I had caused Daric's death. After all they had done for me, this was their fate. Ruin because they tried to be good people and help someone in distress?! Sadly, the stranger in distress had to be the monster that was me. Death as a person has no place among the living. I am just a creature of time and destruction.

Iggy wiped his red, raw eyes as he placed his hand good through the bars towards me, "Are you alright? Come here, I can try to help,"

I turned away from him in shame.

"Please, Axel. Just come here." His voice sadly broken.

I looked up, I expected to see anger towards me as I had placed us in this situation, I placed Daric in the situation that caused his death due to my stupidity, but Iggy's innocence, his naive innocence, and possibly his love he developed for me, made it so he didn't blame me for his situation. He gave me his sweet broken smile as he beckoned me over, again.

I hesitated, but I did as he asked, pushing myself to a seated position as I scooted over to the bars next to him. He untied the gag from my mouth and he pulled it out. I placed my back against the bars and strained the words, "Thank you," out of my mouth as I tipped my head in silence. *Daric, the second I can, I will find your soul and send you where you need to be. You will be reunited with your loved ones and maybe you will be given a better life then this one you suffered through.*

Iggy tugged on my chains, the locks rattling loudly, finally I turned my head and caught the determination written on his face.

I tried to shrug him off, "No use."

"I'm going to TRY anyways." He snapped, only to quickly apologize. "This ain't over." He breathed loudly, "I am going to fight them, every bloody second until I take my last breath. I will not let Daric's sacrifice be for nothing."

If they kill you, it will be for nothing. Tears silently fell down my face.

Iggy continued to speak as his hands finally fell to his lap, realizing it was no use to try to loosen the chains that bound me. "Somehow I always knew Daric would sacrifice himself for me." He chuckled sadly, "He would have done the same for the Captain, or even your life. But I just knew in my heart that I would be the one to have to carry that burden." Silence fell. We held it for a long moment as Iggy tried to compose himself and his words. "I know you want to blame yourself for this," he corrected himself, "I know you are blaming yourself for this, but so you know, I don't blame you for Daric's death, in his last moments he didn't blame you for his death, and he wouldn't want you to blame yourself. He made it his choice." Iggy grabbed my hand and squeezed it tightly, leaning against the bars he admitted. "They were going to kill me instead." He confessed.

Chapter 30

I turned my head to face Iggy, shocked by what he had just said. He had pulled his legs up to his chest, with his free arm wrapped around them as he still continued to squeeze my hand, we both needed a human touch at this moment as he revealed what happened after I had been dragged away.

Daric and Iggy watched while I was dragged away unable to do anything. Fighting was futile for all of us and the two of them understood that; they accepted their fate.

Daric sat tall on his knees; he concluded that the smartest decision would be to eliminate the strongest, biggest threat between Iggy and himself. That was his reasoning for being so sure that this would be his end, that Iggy would have the best chance for being rescued. He had hope that the Captain would track down who ever did this and find Iggy, find me, even if it was going to be too late for him. He had accepted that fate. He was ready to die.

Iggy had come to the same conclusion as Daric; Daric was the stronger, he was smarter, he was the one of more risk to keep alive. As well, they had picked him personally to kidnap, knowing that Axel would risk everything to rescue him, not Daric. But Iggy wasn't going to sit there and let Daric die for him.

The Captain dug his blade into the palm of his hand as he looked between his two prisoners, he was mostly certain who he should kill and who he should take hostage, but the decision plagued him still as he asked himself again and again, looking at them both; two men who were equally prepared to die for the other.

Gibson approached, whispering in the Captain's ear, "save the boy," he suggested.

The disgusting man's ulterior motive was what sealed the deal for Captain Lucard as he knelt down in front of them his eyes now locked on Iggy, sympathetically he spoke, "I always regret killing someone so young, but I feel it would be the more merciful move to make." He spun the knife around again, before turning his gaze to the man holding Iggy in place, giving him a nod, he grabbed Iggy by the hair and forced his head back. Iggy was shocked as he froze, unable to close his eyes, he looked up, waiting for the blade to slice through his now exposed neck.

He heard Daric whisper, "I'm sorry bout' this, kid." *Wait, no!* Iggy turned his gaze to Daric as he could only watch in horror. He tried to call out to Daric, tell him to say no, but it was too late to do anything, it was too late to save Daric from himself.

Daric jerked his head back into the man who was attempting to hold him in place and charged the mercenary Captain, slamming the man with all his force in the chest causing the man to stumble. But the man easily found his ground again and toppled the now off balanced Daric. The man growled as he placed his knee into Daric's back, he wasn't going to waste anymore time, he wasn't going to give them anymore chances.

Daric looked away from Iggy, as he didn't want the boy's devastated expression to be the last thing he saw, he wanted to try and remember the light that was once in the boy's eyes as the mercenary slit his throat. It was quick and clean.

Now both the men held Iggy back who kicked and screamed behind his gag, tears of anger and disbelief pooled down his face.

The mercenary Captain stood up and wiped his blade clean on his jacket before making a cross with his hands over his chest. "You deserved a death greater then that. May death grant you peace, sailor." He gave Daric a long moment of silence, with a tip of his hat, before snapping his fingers and ordering his men to take Iggy back to the ship.

They had to rough Iggy up quite a bit on the way to the ship, his strength that returned with his anger. He fought every step of the way as the Mercenary Captain assumed he would.

Iggy placed his head in his lap, squeezing my hand tighter, as I squeezed his back.

Daric...

"It hurts," Iggy spoke with a long, pained sigh as tears pooled down his face again.

"I know." I managed to say.

Captain wore her fury well as she sat in her throne like chair, her legs crossed, fingers brushing softly against her pressed lips as she fought with every urge in her body to just sit and watch while Victor interrogated the traitorous scum that now occupied her brig.

Jorgen was strapped down to a chair, tightly as the leather binds cut into his skin. He was crying, begging and pleading, trying to convince Victor and the Captain that of course he had nothing to do with Daric's death, he had nothing to do with the capture of Iggy and myself. He was not a good liar, and Victor had yet placed a hand on the pitiful excuse of a man.

Mattias, Jackal and Taylor we also in the brig chained to the bars as they had to watch in horror what was about to be preformed on their traitor ally. Matthias' face was drenched in sweat, while the other two attempted to keep their poker faces straight and strong. Captain's eyes locked on them, they went pale, with a loud gulp as she crossed her legs the other way adjusting in her seat, she got even closer to the show.

Victor was now ready as he tossed is now sharpened, and red-hot blade back and forth in his hands, the blade shinning off the lanterns light. He placed one hand on Jorgen's elbow keeping the mans forearm still as he placed the still burning blade against his exposed flesh, slowly, peeling back the skin as it seared and sizzled. The smell that filled the air was of a roasting pig and piss. Jorgen screamed louder, Victor holding a four-inch long piece of the mans skin before his face.

"Please Captain! I had nothing to do with what happened to Daric, I swear it's the truth!" He lied between his clenched teeth, his tears streaming the dirt down, leaving streaks.

 Captain said nothing as Victor dropped the bloody scrap and continued. Re-heating his blade on the open flame every now and then, as the smell of burnt hair and skin now fumed the entirety of the lower deck.

  Victor had peeled the skin off Jorgen's left forearm, he placed the blade on the right forearm, something finally clicked in Jorgen's head as he confessed, "Daric was ne'er supposed t' be harmed! He wasn't part o' th' plan if Axel would 'ave listened Daric would still be here!"

"What plan?" Victor asked as the Captain stayed silent letting the man do this work.

  Jorgen hesitated as Victor stabbed his knife through Jorgen's palm, pinning his hand against the wooden arm rest of the chair. He screamed and cried, in panic and fear. "Gibson's plan, he approached me shortly aft dockin' here," he spilled his guts to the Captain and Victor as Jackal, and Taylor sat silently, praying to the gods they would not face the same fate as Jorgen.

 "I dunno where exactly, I wasn't part o' that plan, ye 'ave t' trust me, Captain. 'twas ne'er th' plan fer Daric t' be harmed, let alone be killed, that was all Gibson. I did this all fer ye! Axel was corruptin' yer mind! He be a monster, he ain't a mortal like ye believed 'im t' be!"

Her lip twitched. "I knew exactly what Axel was, and he unlike you was not a traitor on my ship." She pulled a knife from her boot and plunged it into his groin as she placed her free hand over Jorgen's mouth, muffling his screams of agony as she stepped even closer, whispering in his ear. "You are the reason that my closest friend is dead, I am going to make you wish you had that swift of a death." She twisted the blade, digging it even deeper into him. She pulled another knife from hiding as she repeatedly stabbed Jorgen again, allowing him to scream, cry and beg her to stop as the three other traitors in her clutches now knew they were not going to spared.

Jane wasn't entirely sure when Jorgen had passed out from blood loss, honestly, she couldn't have been sure if he was even alive. Her blade slipped from her blood-soaked hands. She was exhausted and drenched in sweat and her victim's blood. She fought back tears as her composer was finally starting to fade. She threw her knives across the room and held her breath trying to hold it in just a little bit longer.

Victor who had been standing there in silence watching the Captain work finally spoke again, "Do ye require anythin', Captain?"

She just shook her head and went to leave.

Matthias spoke up, he was sobbing in fear, "Captain, there are others, responsible for this."

She stopped in her tracks and turned and looked at him, waiting for him to continue.

"Reefer, Vendell, Jorgen and I were the ones who lead Ignatius into Gibson's trap. Jackal and Taylor placed the note and have been planning this alongside Jorgen for weeks."

Her strong shoulders dropped as she asked, "Why," "Jorgen convinced us that Axel was trying to hurt you, he was trying to steal your soul or something." He sobbed into his bound hands, "I didn't agree to giving Iggy to Gibson, but I knew to much that they said they'd kill me."

She let out a long sigh as she picked up one of her knives, cleaning it off on a small section of her pants that were somehow clear of blood. She knelt in front of Matthias with a sad smile, "Thank you, for your honestly." She stabbed the blade up through the soft flesh of his under chin. He was dead instantly as he fell limp against the cold wet floor. The Captain retrieved her blade from her dead crew member and turned to Victor. "Go find Vendell, and Reefer, skin the traitors till near death, then call for me. I will be in my quarters."

Once the Captain reached the main deck all work froze as they turned to their blood coated Captain. They swallowed hard as she called out to Karlic, "Is she sea ready?"

"Aye, Captain she be ready." He dared not explain what was left to finish, as he knew she did not care that this moment.

"Set sail, we head east. Keep eyes out for a mercenary ship." That was all as she turned away. She was strong enough to make it to the door of her personal quarters, close the door firmly before she crumbled to her hands and knees, sobbing uncontrollably, smearing blood over her face. She spent the majority of the night there on her floor back against her door as she cried everything out, knowing that when Victor would come for her, she had to be the strong, un-waivered Captain her crew needed, the same Captain that Iggy needed to save him.

Morning was near when Victor came with a soft knock on her door.

"I shall be a moment." She called back as she quickly washed the blood off her face and hands, and changed, remerging from her quarters as the strong Captain her crew knew her to be, the strong Captain Daric had conditioned her to become. She placed the dusty old hat she stole from Daric those many years ago back on her head and strutted to the plank, where her six remaining traitors stood, blood dripping and staining her newly replaced deck. They were well out to sea now as the sun began to rise above them. Even in the sun, the waters were dark and deep, hiding all the monsters that lurked below its surface.

Victor held a bucket, of the collected pieces of the traitor's flesh, he waited for the Captains orders as she nodded to him, he dropped the bloody mess into the waters, calling the sharks. Before one by one the six were led to the edge of the plank and forced off with a large push. All of them tried to fight it, but with their hands and feet bound, their bodies broken and bloody, they stood no chance against the waves, as each and everyone sunk deep into the dark black waters.

The Captain went to the back of her ship as she watched the shark's fins circling, happy as they ate, blood staining the sea. Silence. The wind howled in her ears. She closed her eyes and breathed deeply.

Hours had passed, and night was falling. Captain Far'mel handed her ship off to Victor. She needed some time alone after playing the part of strong unaverred Captain all day.

Jane found herself sitting below decks staring at the draped corpse of her late mentor. Daric's passing had only been two days ago, and already she knew that time was limited and soon she would have to send her dearest friend's mortal body to the frames, freeing his soul from this world. She now knew the god of death… She wondered if all these things people do for the dead, did it help? Does it do anything? Or is it just to make the living feel a bit better about the loss of their loved ones? Jane signed sadly. Daric didn't deserve to die the way he did. He didn't deserve a burial at sea, he deserved to be buried along with his loved ones. Jane bit her lip as she fought back more tears. She was not ready to say goodbye to him.

Laid upon Daric's corpse she had placed his dusty hat, his sword and a necklace that was once his wife's. It was the only thing of his wife's that he managed to find after her murder and his near execution.

Jane spoke aloud, hoping that somehow Daric could hear her, "Victor is now officially my second in command. I swore him in this morning after the executions, and Karlic is taking over Victors position." Her hands were together, elbows on the table, head looking to the side. She couldn't look directly at him as she spoke, "I'm going to have to start looking for a new crew after Iggy and Axel's rescue. We've lost a few good people over these weeks. I feel that there are more people who have questioned my judgement over the course of these short months with Axel being aboard. I can't have that on my ship." She swallowed hard, "If you were still here, you'd be able to get them back on my side, but I've never been the one to rally men to my side as well as you. Honestly, I question if I should just give up my command." She sighed, turning to look over his corpse, "You were the reason I became a good Captain, a great Captain you would say, but only because I knew I could always rely on you to help, to stand up alongside me. Now, I don't know if I can Captain my ship without you. I never thought the day would come, it never occurred to me that it would happen so soon." She placed her hand on Daric's chest, taking another deep breath as she composed herself, she let out a bitter laugh, "I need your advice on how to deal with the loss of you." Taking a moment, she spoke again, "I know I didn't say it enough, Daric. But you meant the world to me, you saved me from myself all those years ago, sent me on a path. I will stick to this path for you, and only you. I will make you proud and I will never forget all you've done for me. I love you Daric." She placed her hand on the table which he laid, "I'll find Iggy, I'll save him." Jane could feel the tears forming in the corner of her eyes as she pressed down on her tear ducks forcing the water away. She finally stood, no longer a grieving woman, but a strong, determined Captain. "I can figure out where to go, I can find them on my own." She grabbed Daric's hat that had been resting on his chest and placed it on her head with a weak smile, "Wish me luck, ol' friend."

Jane rushed off to the map room below decks. A large detailed map unrolled on the table as she chartered where they were currently sailing, placing her hand over the spot she scanned the shores. Speaking aloud, "Jorgen confessed he was not told of where they were taking Axel and Iggy, but maybe we can figure this out." She paused, looking up from the map remembering that she was alone. "I can figure this out." She sunk down into her chair as she brushed her fingers against the parchment, biting her tears away with a heavy-hearted sigh. "Gods' are real..." She closed her eyes and clenched a fist into her hand and began to pray. *Send me a sign, tell me where to go. Axel, help me save Iggy, help me save you.*

She rubbed her tired eyes with her hands before shaking herself awake, she believed she had the answer to her riddle of finding where she should to go, she just had to sit down and process what she knew. It would lead her to the truth, it was just a matter of time.

Chapter 31

It was their third day at sea, and Iggy was struggling to stay awake. His stomach ached, his body was weak, hungry and dehydrated, but he had been afraid to sleep. He laid on the floor, facing me, with his hand through the bars still reaching out holding my hand, his eyes almost closed, his cheeks still wet with tears as he breathed softly. Uncomfortably, I leaned against the bars, resting the back of my head against them I closed my eyes. I dared not rest; untrusting of our situation under good instincts as I knew Gibson was lurking, waiting for an opportunity.

Iggy's fingers went subtly limp between mine, I smiled as sleep took him, a sweet dream of something so much better then this had hopefully taken over. I smiled, slightly envious as I tried to stretch my confined body under the presser of my chains. I had lost feeling to most of my body by this point, my bare arms were red and white from the chains digging uncomfortably into my skin. I twisted and turned, hoping that I could shift them, but I knew of course it was useless to battle against the locks. I let out an audible sigh, dropping my head defeated. I closed my eyes again, as the wind whispered in my ear, a prayer? *Axel help me.* Shocked, confused, my eyes shot open as I looked around the brig, as if I expected Jane to be there standing next to the cell, asking for my help. I was about to shake the voice out of mind as a wishful delusion, but she called out again, *help me save Iggy. Help me save you.*

I looked around again, *Captain?* I could hear the desperation in the sound of her voice, that's when I knew that she had found Daric, deceased. I turned my gaze back to the sleeping Iggy, who was curled up against the bars, reaching out for me as I had drifted slightly away from his reach. I closed my eyes again, focusing on Jane, on the Shadow's Blade. Nothing happened. I clenched my eyes closed and focused on the darkness, I focused every last inch of power I had into my body, I knew where we were heading, I knew where Kali waited for me, Jane just need to know, I just needed to tell her that one thing, that only thing. I needed help... I wasn't strong enough on my own, only now did the thought ever cross my mind, I'm not alone. Even before Iggy, I haven't been alone for a long time, I just needed to call him. To ask Kai for help...

I opened my eyes and looked over at the sleeping Iggy, I had to drift into the darkness, which meant Iggy would be defenceless against those on this ship who may wish to pray upon him. With a heavy heart I had to take the chance, the longer Jane wondered the seas without a destination, the longer Iggy was unsafe aboard this ship. I didn't have the heart to wake him from his dream as I closed my eyes, resting my head on the cold floor, I drifted into the darkness.

He was waiting for me. He smiled playfully as he read the confusion on my face. He rushed over to my and wrapped his arms around my stomach. I could never be sure if my form in the darkness was just so large, or it was his form was always that of a child.

"I never realized how lonely this darkness is until you've been gone." He finally pulled back from me his face now more serious, "Have you found a way for me to help you yet?"

I nodded.

"Tell me the plan!"

He looked up at me as I placed my hand on his forehead, closing my eyes I focused my thoughts on him. I could feel his eyes on my face. Finally, when I opened my eyes again, he was gone. I silently sighed with relief as I fell to my knees, rubbing the tiredness from my eyes, I had to wake up now. It was time to wake up!

Jane rubbed her eyes, yawning and stretching as she stood up from her chair, she didn't even recall falling asleep. She finally looked a head at a young boy who stood at the edge of the map table. Shoulder length curly dark hair, dark skin the young boy smiled at her.

More confused than startled Jane stepped back studying the boy. "Who are you?"

He looked down at the map on the table, picking up a marker and tracing from the Shadow's Blade location, "Just an ally," He looked back up at Jane, with an innocent, childish smile on his face. He tapped his finger on the map again before placing the marker down in the parchment.

Jane ruffled her hair stepping forward and placing her finger next to the marker the boy had placed down before her. "The temple of the sea?" Things clicked into place, "Gibson is taking Axel and Iggy to Kali's temple in deep cove?"

"Beautiful and smart," he winked, tapping the

temple of his forehead with his index finger.

She laughed, feeling that she was still asleep, and this wasn't all really happening. "You literally marked the map for me,"

"True," He smiled and appeared next to Jane, he took her hand in his and brought it to her chest, allowing her to feel her own beating heart. "He's not gone, your friend, he is there," he tapped her forehead with his index finger again, with a soft laugh, "and here," placing his hand over her heart. "But that is all the time I have," he said sadly as he disappeared from her side reappearing back in front of the map table. Tapping his finger again on the marker he had placed down. "Till we meet again, and may it be many, many years from now, beautiful lady." He said with a bow as again he disappeared into smoke.

Jane woke up in a panic throwing herself from her chair, as she laughed, realizing that it had just been a dream. She scratched her head, brushing her hair with her fingers and resting down back in her chair. She groaned groggily, dismissing it as just a dream, her eyes traced over her map with her fingers, where did he tell her to go again? It was hard for her to remember, she remembered the boy so clearly, but his words became a jumbled mess as she yawned. Her finger hit a bump in her map, a marker. The marker the boy in her dream had placed; Deep Cove. The Temple of the Goddess of the Sea.

Without a moment to lose she jumped from her chair, scooped the map in her hands and rushed to the main deck, they had a course.

She took the helm in her hands and steered the Shadow's Blade out into deeper waters; this was no longer a search. This was a hunt.

Now that Jane had informed the crew of their destination, she knew they still had a four-day sail ahead of them, three if the wind favoured them.

She then asked to be left alone unless absolutely necessary, or to tell her they have caught up with the mercenaries. Locking herself in her cabin, hidden away where she didn't have to pretend that she was okay. She didn't have to hold in her tears, her sorrow. Day four had come and gone. The wound of Daric being gone had grown as she sat alone. Daric was always there with the answer, or even just with words of encouragement, he always knew what to say. And now she was alone with her own mind, her own self-doubts. Daric was gone and there was nothing she could do to bring him back to her. She now had a lead on where to find Iggy and I, but she couldn't even be sure if it was real. She still had doubt. Her ship was barely holding up against the waves as the carpenters had just narrowly finished patching her up. Jane was stressed, angry and depressed. She clawed at her head, screaming as tears pooled. She punched her desk, so hard, the wooden table shook, sending papers and bobbles tumbling to the ground, her hand instantly ached in pain. She ignored the pain, she crumbled to the floor hands over her face as she began to sob. "Daric, I need you." She pulled her legs into her chest and held herself tightly.

There was a knock at the door.

Jane took a long, deep breath, rubbing her eyes raw.

She knew exactly who was at her door, and she knew exactly what they had to say. She cleared her throat and checked that her voice was unaverred and collected before speaking. "Come in," the Captain ordered.

Victor cautiously opened the door and stepped in, closing it shut behind him. His usual expressionless face was oddly peppered with some form of sorrow. He tried hard to hide the fact that he also was feeling the loss of their shipmate, but Jane could see it in his distant eyes.

The Captain puffed out her chest, playing off her strong, composed self. Victor wasn't stupid, so even if he noticed the red, tear-stricken eyes, he dared not to take note.

Victor cleared his throat, "Captain, 'tis been at least four days since,"

"Aye, it's been about five days since Daric's passing. We can't wait any longer. Have you prepared a boat for him already?"

"Aye."

"Is the rest of the crew ready?"

"Aye, Captain."

She sighed, taking another deep breath. Steadying herself, "I'll be ready shortly, make sure everyone is in attendance."

He nodded and turned to leave, only to stop once he reached for the door handle. Turning back towards his Captain, he struggled to find the words. "Captain, I hope ye know that none o' us expect ye t' act unaffected by this tragedy." He licked his lips and looked away from the Captain, ashamed of what he was about to confess to her, "even I 'ave found meself affected greatly by his loss. Daric was a good pirate 'n a better scallywag. He was th' type o' sailor that scallywags like me 'n th' rest o' yer crew should always strive t' be more alike." Victor cleared his throat and settled his own composer, "He was a good second in command, a great ally 'n an even grander, friend."

Jane stood there listening to him speak as tears fell uncontrollably down her face even though she fought hard to keep them at bay.

"I know I can ne'er replace Daric, I could ne'er truly be everythin' he was t' ye, 'n I can nah pretend I shall even be half th' scallywag he was fer ye. But, always remember this Captain. I shall be thar at yer side 'til th' day I die."

Jane smiled with a nod. Trying to dry the tears

from her face, taking a shaky breath. "Thank you," she groaned annoyed, "I'll need a couple more minutes to ready myself now."

Victor managed a smile. It seemed odd on his face. He left without another word as the Captain readied for their final goodbyes.

Chapter 32

Iggy woke up to the door to the brig being unlocked, he rubbed his eyes clear and leaned out to shake me awake, he couldn't be sure how long he had been asleep. "Axel," He called out to me, shaking me harder as the door finally opened. "Axel, wake up." He called out again, a hint of panic in the sound of his voice as Gibson entered the room. The door getting locked behind him by another man.

I began to stir as Gibson walked passed, leaning against the wall, he looked Iggy up and down with a smile. "Pretty soon 'twill be jus' as 'twas afore, ye 'n me. No interruptions, no gods comin' t' yer rescue." His eyes traced over to me, his arms crossed over his chest.

My eyes finally opened; I rolled onto my stomach, using as much strength as I could muster to pull myself upright onto my knees. I bore my teeth at Gibson.

Gibson licked his lips and smiled, he felt he had won.

Iggy was frozen. In fear was what Gibson and I had assumed, but we were both wrong as he was fueling his anger. He pulled himself up to his feet, hands clenched tightly into fists. His eyes locked on his tormenter, "Touch me again in that way and I will ensure that is the last time you ever touch anyone." Iggy took a step forward, while Gibson took a step back, he genuinely felt afraid for a moment. Iggy took a deep breath and continued, trying to keep his emotions in check. "The only reason I never fought back as hard as I could, was fear of Daric finding out and hurting him." His words, his face was cold and bitter. Gibson was speechless and nervous. "You killed the only father figure I've ever had, and I dare you to try me now. I dare you." He spat.

Gibson was searching his face, his words for even the slightest hint of a bluff as he swallowed hard taking another step backwards.

"I've never been afraid to die," Iggy laughed sourly, "death doesn't scare me. You do not, scare me." There was a growl in his voice that neither I nor Gibson had never seen from him. It scared me.

Gibson licked his lips uncomfortably and turned his gaze from Iggy, shifting in his spot. He rubbed his face and turned back to Iggy, taking a hesitant step forward. He puffed his chest out, cocking his head to the side he studied his "pet," "I see yer bluff, lad." He waved his finger at Iggy, a smile formed on his face, "Ye haven't grown, ye haven't suddenly found th' strength t' defend yourself. 'tis in yer nature t' please whoever holds yer key." Gibson dangled the key to the cell, "I hold yer key. I owns ye, Ignatius. Remember that next time ye try t' act brave fer yer scallywag."

Iggy stumbled backwards, his back now against the wall. He tried to keep a brave face, but he was afraid. He was breathing heavy; fighting between his fear and his anger. Some how he managed to keep eye contact with Gibson as he processed his next move.

I tugged and fought against my binds. Gibson ripped the bars, one hand just over the lock to Iggy's cell. He was so tempted to unlock. We could see the temptation in his eyes, the desire to take his reward. His eyes traced over to me as his smile twitched sadistically. I yanked hard in his direction, the chains digging painfully into my throat and wrists, but I didn't care as I growled at the man as he spoke. "Jus' reckon, ye would be inches away 'n unable t' do a thin' about it." He turned his gaze back to Iggy, "All this big natter, this game ye be tryin' t' play Ignatius. It doesn't fool me fer a second."

Iggy clenched his fists even tighter, before lunging

at the door, gripping the bars as Gibson jumped back quickly, stumbling, he dropped onto his ass, holding the keys tightly to his chest.

"You will never own me! Never again will you take advantage of me. Fuck you," tears streamed down his flushed face, "if I get a chance, I swear to you I will send you to the afterlife myself!" Iggy spat in Gibson's direction.

Gibson jumped up and rushed towards the door to the brig, only turning back with a trembled voice, "Once we reach Kali's temple, ye will 'ave no choice but t' fall in line wit' wha' says I. Ye be me prize fer brin' Axel t' her." He tried to play off calm and collected, "I dunno wha' she has in store fer ye, Axel, but do nah worry I shall make sure ye 'ave a front row seat fer a preview o' wha' I be goin' t' do t' yer heartie once ye be out o' me way fer good."

He knocked on the door, as he was allowed out without another word spoken.

Iggy waited for the door to the brig to be locked securely before he finally broke down to his knees, hands over his face he sobbed uncontrollably.

"Iggy," I croaked. I wanted to reach out, show him he wasn't alone. Do something, but all I could do was kneel here. I wanted to tell him everything was going to be okay, but I didn't know if it was...

Iggy voices shook as he tried to dry his eyes, "Is your sister going to use me against you, as Gibson is using me against you?" He asked emotionless.

His words didn't make me uncomfortable, but how he said it did. He stared at his binds that laid scattered on the floor next to him.

I couldn't have known sure certain, so it didn't feel like it was a lie, but it was, when I shook my head no. Telling him that she wouldn't use him against me. I knew deep down if she thought it would get her what she wanted; she would definitely use him.

"I don't want to continue on, Axel."

I pulled myself next to his cell, being unable to say anything to comfort him, I just let him think and talk it out.

"Since the moment I was born, this life time has been hell. My mother even tried to smother me when I was first born," he struggled to yell me this, "she was beaten to near death and sold off. I was then groomed as a child to be this pleasure object, for sick rich monsters. I tried to take my life to escape from it and I even failed at that. Captain and," he took a long pause, more tears falling down his face, "Daric, rescued me from that life and still I found myself stuck in it. Even now, if I wasn't around none of this would have happened. If I had died on that slave ship you would have stayed on the beach, probably wondered to the nearest town and stayed away from the sea as your memories slowly came back. But because I saw that you were alive, Daric to brought you back to the ship. Since I helped convinced the captain to keep you aboard, Daric is dead. You got captured because you were afraid of what they might do to me, and still I find myself trapped by my tormenter." He was filled with frustration, anger, bitterness and depression as he continued debating on grabbing the rope, still inches from his reach.

There was so much I wanted to say to him, to comfort him, to tell him some how I'll make this all right for him, but there was nothing I could say that could convince him of this and I knew what ever I managed to voice wouldn't be what he needed to hear. Even the thought of telling him that I was here for him, I knew he would twist into a bad thing in his state of mind, so I just sat there in silence as he poured himself out to me.

He had stood up and stomped around the small cell, punching the walls till his knuckles bled and his already broke wrist, twisted and swelled with pain once again. His ankle broken ankle twisting multiple times, tumbling him to the ground. Finally, in a fit of rage he crumpled the ropes that had bound him and tossed them out of the cell, taking away his dark temptation. He sighed bitterly before sitting down against the bars reaching out for my cheek as he placed his hand so softly against my face.

Our time was slowly coming to an end. I could sense, not just Kali, but I could sense a piece of myself approaching. I could feel my missing power, my cloak so clearly now, I could almost reach out in the darkness and touch it. I could feel some energy seeping back into my mortal frame as I closed my eyes and just enjoyed Iggy's soft skin against me. I knew it might well be the last. He spoke softly to me, fighting back his sadness. "I'm not ready for this to end, Axel." He bit his lips as more tears fell down his face.

"Neither am I," I horsed painfully as our eyes met. Tears falling down my own face. The two of us laid like that in silence, no words could fill the space, no words could explain these emotions.

Jane found her formal best; black trousers, an unsoiled white blouse, that she correctly buttoned up, the first time doing that, and she wore her dark, black overcoat, with the red embroidered ship on the back, threaded with gold embellishment's. She tightened the straps on her dark leather boots that went all the way up to her knees. She looked up at hat that laid resting on her desk. Daric's hat. She picked it up and traced her fingers against it's rim thinking back to the first few weeks of knowing the ol' pirate. She had never imagined that he would become so important to her. She never imagined it would hurt so much to lose someone. Before him she had locked her heart up after losing her family, Jane never expecting to find a new one in a dusty ol' pirate who was ready to die. Jane spoke aloud, hoping that Daric could hear her from beyond, "I always imagined I'd go before you. Me with my recklessness and all, or at least we'd go down fighting alongside each other." She only allowed one tear to escape, only to quickly wiped it away, "I hope that when you passed you at least knew that we all loved you, I hope you knew how greatly you would be missed y dear friend." Jane shook off her pain. "It's time to send you off."

Captain Jane Far'mel stepped out onto the

main deck of her ship as the crew of the Shadow's Blade stood at attention. Most of her crew were struggling holding back their own emotions as they stood around the small boat holding Daric's body. The crew had lined it with fabric to keep him in place, and comfortable, as odd as that may seem, and each member of the crew placed something in alongside him. Bottles of liquor, hand written notes, food, and other symbolic gifts for the man they were surely going to miss.

The Captain stepped up to her deceased friend and took a small breath, removing her, his hat from her head. She bit her tongue to keep her emotions in check as she placed his hat on his chest. The Captain spoke loud enough for her entire crew to hear her clearly, "Daric, deserves so much more than a burial at sea. He deserves to have been buried alongside his wife and child, he deserved to be honored, to be remembered and to be celebrated as the great pirate, and the great man, friend and family he was to all of us." She took a moment to process her words, the crew chimed in with an "aye," raising their hats.

"But our friend, our ally was taken from us, due to disrespecting traitors who plotted behind our backs, snakes in the grass. Now besides honoring Daric's life, his wisdom and sending his body off there is nothing left we can do for him. But we still have allies in danger. Allies Daric cared greatly for, and sacrificed himself to protect. Together we will avenge Daric's death!"

"Aye!"

"We can make all who caused Daric's death pay for what they have done, for what they have taken from us! And I swear to you, we will make everyone, and anyone regret the day they trifled with the Shadow's Blade!"

"Aye!" the crew called in a up roar.

The Captain had clenched her fists so tightly, imbedding her nails into the soft of her palms. She lightened up and managed a small, soft smile. "If Daric was still here, he would grumble at all of us and say, "Stop yer mopin' around 'n get back t' work." The crew was silent. The Captain closed her eyes and lowered her head, taking a deep breath, "But he isn't with us. So, together let's take a moment of silence for our fallen friend." The crew joined her. She whispered to herself, "Goodbye dear friend."

After a few long minutes she placed her hand on Victors shoulder, he nodded. It was time. Victor and three others positioned the boat over the side as they slowly began to lower it.

Jane had a small change of heart as she reached over and grabbed Daric's hat, holding it tight against her chest. She refused to let it go with him, she fought back tears as they continued to lower him out of sight. "Technically it's my hat." She grumbled, again as if talking to Daric.

Daric's small boat drifted off and away from the Shadow's Blade. The crew all watched from the railing, singing softly their goodbyes. Once he was far enough away Karlic handed the Captain a bow as she readied her arrow. Notching the bow and lighting the arrow ablaze. Exhaling, she released. She let Daric go. The boat easily caught aflame as they watched the smoke. The Captain allowed her crew a few more moments of goodbyes as they continued to sing, before turning on her heel and barking commands, "Now is the time for action. Make haste men, we have an ally to avenge.

Chapter 33

A few more days had passed, and we could now hear the mercenaries hustling around the ship; they dropped anchor, the ship slowly came to a halt. We had reached out destination.

I breathed out sadly as Iggy sat up, recoiling his hand from me as we awaited what was next. "Axel," He said as we could hear them coming towards the brig, "I love you, and no matter what happens I don't regret knowing you." He smiled weakly at me.

"I love you." I forced the words out; the pain was nothing to me as the words slipped somewhat easier from my lips.

Captain Lucard was the first to enter the room, followed by his second mate, then Gibson and a few other large crew members. They all walked passed me stood in front of Iggy's cell, the Captain's second in command holding new binds. The Captain ordered, "Boy, step to the door, hands behind your back, towards us."

Iggy spat in Gibson's direction arms crossed over his

413 | Page

chest in protest. "Fuck you,"

The mercenary Captain was not in the most patient moods this morning, you could see it written on his face.

"Iggy," *don't fight.*

Iggy saw me in the corner of his eyes but didn't budge.

Captain Lucard scowled, "I have no issue with making our client wait another hour, if you'd like I'd lock Gibson in there with you and let him have his way if you'd prefer that to my request." He snapped, cocking his head to the side. There was no bluff in his face, or in the way he stood. You could tell the excitement in Gibson's eyes at the threat, he was begging for Iggy to protest.

"Iggy," I said with more conviction.

Iggy growled angerly, but took a deep breath, he stepped to the cell door. Turning around and placed his hands behind his back, the second in command placed his arms through the bars binding Iggy's hands tightly before the cell door was unlocked. Gibson and another large man stepped forward grabbing Iggy by the arms and leading him from the cell.

Iggy lifted his knee into Gibson's groin when he stepped forward. Gibson crouched in pain, trying to collect himself. The large man still holding onto Iggy, punched him in the face, before slamming him against the bars, pressing his face in as he waited for Gibson to collect himself. Gibson grumbled, straightening himself, and dug his nails into Iggy's arm, gripping him tightly.

The second in command as well as three other men stepped into my cell, while two unchained the weights and binds around my legs and ankle, they kept the weights around my chest and arms, precautions. I wasn't going to fight. I had already lost, I looked down, allowing them to lead me away. With every step down the old, rickety dock towards the Temple of the Goddess of the Sea, I could feel my tired mortal frame regaining its power, the power I had lost. Every step forward to Kali and possibly my death, was at least a step forward to my cloak and my powers. I was ready to face my sister, now I realized that our quarrel couldn't be avoided. She wasn't going to forget or forgive. *Kali and I are fated to have this battle, this war until the day she dies, or I somehow make her understand.* I was doubtful to the latter. *Mother, if you can somehow hear us still, help her understand.* I walked with my head held high, unafraid of the fate that was laid out for me, the only regret, the only unease was that of Iggy's fate. He didn't deserve to be punished for my deeds.

Kali's temple was the spitting image of what the majority of the temples to the gods resembled now. Crumbling, forgotten, they had all been left to rot. The stone structures that held the building up on top of the seas surface were drained of their colour; only the very tops, could you still see a soft blue of its once vibrant colour. Thought you had to look closely through the ivy and lily vines that had tangled their way up, and into the cracks of the walls. Even the dock that we walked on was decayed, boards missing after being eaten away by the ocean, uneven as some of the mercenaries found their footing off, stumbling uneasily.

Now that I was standing in Kali's home, everything flooded back to me. I took a deep breath and looked over the edge of the dock. *If I dropped off the edge, would I find the anchor that held me down?* Was it still waiting for me? *Waiting for the moment Kali would return me to the ocean deeps to continue her torment upon me? Or does she have something new in mind.*

I hadn't realized it, but I had stopped in my tracks as I had focused on the ocean and my memories. It wasn't until one of the impatient mercenaries leading, pushed me forward causing me to stumble on an uneven board. I turned my gaze towards him, our eyes met; I gave him a dead, cold glare.

The now nervous man unintendedly loosened his grip on my arm. I could feel his heart racing, his voice shook, "Keep moving." His confidence was broken as he pointed out, "Or your friend gets hurt." Their trump card, their only saving grace.

I turned to look back at Iggy, who was still fighting at Gibson's touch. I wanted to break free and beat the life from that man's body, but I controlled my urge. I sadly looked away from the scene, it was too late to help him now. As I hoped Iggy remembered what happened the last time he had met with my sister.

We stepped through the threshold; I questioned if the mercenaries really knew who they were here to meet. If Captain Lucard really knew who he had made a deal with?

Kali had destroyed large chunks of the floor, leaving wide pools open, and strategically exposed. Against the back wall of the temple sat a large marble throne; once upon a time there stood an equally large, marble carving of Kali. The statue long gone, as Kali herself, now sat upon the throne. She sat impatiently, picking at the crumbs protruding on her arm rest. She looked up and smiled excitedly, she tossed a handful of blue, beaded dreadlocks behind her, adjusting her dark blue dress. Revealing even more of her beautiful, long tanned legs, in the slitted dress. "Welcome to my sanctuary." I knew she wasn't talking to me as she gave her new playthings a toothy grin before biting down on her pale cracked lips. I looked around as everyone except Gibson, myself and Iggy were entranced by her spell. Iggy's eyes were closed, and he looked down.

She skipped from her seat as she finally turned to speak to me alone, "Axel, dear brother. You look dreadful. That mortal frame of yours really takes a toll on your soul doesn't it?" She ran the back of her hand down my cheek, while she did a full circle of me. I could feel her breath on the back of my neck as she whispered in my ear. "Should I kill them all before we get started?"

"Don't," I horsed.

She giggled playfully, "No voice, still? That was weeks ago that I last saw you. Ha, how pathetic your mortal frame really is. I guess it's a crude reminder that you aren't one of them, or one of us." She rolled her eyes turning away from me, hands behind her back, fingers once again entwined. "I really want to kill at least some of these men. How should I do it, dear brother? Slit his throat," she pointed between a few of the mercenaries, "feed him to my pets? Make him slit his throat?" Her face went cold as the words left her mouth, "Have him drown himself?" She walked up to Captain Lucard's second in command tapping him on the shoulder. Kali spoke seductively in his ear, "Be a dear and go place your head in that pool of water until I say enough." The man entranced did as she said.

Captain Lucard and the other men where now fully aware of what was happening but had no power of will to fight it as Kali, if she willed it could have them all drown themselves by just a simple command.

"Stop," *Kali, this is between you and I.*

"I know that." Kali answered, "I just want to remind you who holds the power in our little relationship. I want to remind you how killing these mortals means nothing to me as it does you. Just think, these men gave me exactly what I asked for and yet I have no problems with killing them. A small reminder of what I will do to you, do to your cloak. I am not afraid to drown and slaughter every last living soul on this pathetic mortal realm, destroy every, last strand of your cloak, your source of power, your source of being before feeding every shred to my serpents!" Her anger showed, her nostril's flared.

I can't give you what you want, Kali. I never could, and all this won't change the fact that he is gone.

"No!" She screamed like a child having a tantrum, "You can, I know you can, but you wont!"

Kali, lets just end this, you and I. Let the mercenaries go. I'm sorry he is gone, but I cannot bring him back, I don't have that power, no god does.

"Enough!" She cried as the man removed his head from the waters, gasping for breath, he panted. Kali's eyes twitched with anger as she stepped up to me once again. Placing both hands firmly around my throat, squeezing, her nails scratching against my skin, her eyes questioning, "What do I have to do to get what I ask of you?"

I didn't speak, I didn't breathe, or swallow.

She caught Iggy in the corner of her eye as Gibson, nodded to the Goddess, with a small bow.

She stepped away from me, her eyes locked on Iggy, like a predator to her pray, placing her hand on his chin. He still dared not to look up at her. "You," she brushed the side of his cheek with her long fingers, her nails scrapping against his skin, "I remember you." She smiled sweetly.

It took every ounce of willpower for him not to look up at the stunningly beautiful, yet deadly goddess. "Ignatius is what Gibson calls you. Your friends call you Iggy, if I am not mistaken? You introduced yourself as Iggy to me, you seemed so sweet and kind."

Kali, enough of this. Please! I pleaded with her,
unable to hide my emotion.

Kali ignored my cries as she was entranced by her
prey. She placed her soft hands on the side of his
face, turning his gaze to her. Iggy was unable to fight
her, their eyes met. A twisted smile appeared on her
lips as she licked them, moist as she inspected him.
"You are a pretty thing, aren't you?"

Iggy swallowed hard, his heart raced, he was afraid,
but stood strong. Her breath was warm on his cold,
sweaty face. "You are the one who broke my charm.
The one who stepped between my brother and I last
time we met. I'd never forget such a pretty face like
yours."

Iggy held his breath, in a failed attempt to settle his
pounding heart. He still looked her straight in the
eye, she had not entranced him, even thought he was
in her grasp, she leaned in brushing her lips against
his.

She brushed his hair back, now speaking to Gibson,
"This is the one my brother is fond of?"

He seemed uneased by the way she had asked it, but
he dared not lie to her. "Yes, goddess."

"You must care a great deal about my brother to
be able to break my enchantments."

He swallowed hard and nodded. He wasn't entirely sure if it really was a question or not.

She hummed, her tongue tracing around Iggy's lips as she could see me growing more and more uncomfortable. I tried but failed to hide my weakness.

"What did he promise you for this love and devotion?" Her and Iggy's eyes locked, Iggy swallowed hard, feeling Gibson pressing his body against his backside.

"He promised me nothing,"

Kali smiled and laughed cynically, "You are just in love with the god of death, because what, he wooed you? Death cannot love someone, death cannot have friends," she paused thinking of the right word, "he just has projects." her tone darkened again, "I could rip your chest open with my bare hands and he would just watch, helplessly. Even if he had his full powers, powers that could heal your wounds, he wouldn't. He would sit by your side and hold your hand as your blood drained from your body. As you bled out, slowly and painfully. Is that the type of lover you seek, pretty one? Is that the kind of person you'd risk your life for?"

He kept his eyes on her, "Yes I would, because you're wrong about him."

Kali growled as she slapped him hard, his lip began to bleed.

"Kali," *he isn't a part of this, stop, please!*

I tugged with all my force from the men attempting to contain me, I broke free only to fall to my knees turning my body to face her. I stayed on my knees pleading with her.

Iggy swallowed hard again, his lip quivered just ever so slightly, she breathed in his fear. His eyes darted to my face, just for a moment as he fought back fear filled tears.

The two mercenaries quickly rushed to recover me, one hitting me in the back of the head with the hilt of his sword, blood was drawn as everything went blurry for a second.

"Axel!" Iggy called out, forgetting his fear and trying to pull away from Gibson.

Kali turned on a dime, forgetting Iggy and in an instance, she had her hand around the man who dealt the blows throat, lifting him off the ground, "You dare strike a god, in a holy place for the gods'?!" She was enraged as he dangled, gasping for air, but the mercenary could not reach for her arms to even being an attempt to pull her away.

Kali, please.

She looked down at me and for a moment, just one,

I saw humanity shine back into her eyes as she dropped the man.

Kali straightened her dress, snapping her fingers, the mercenaries now no longer under her spell, "Leave my brother and his friend, your reward will be on your ship as we speak.

The mercenaries ran away without questioning the goddess.

Gibson, remained wrapping his forearm around Iggy's throat, keeping him in place, "Goddess, our deal?"

Kali turned to the man.

Do not let him take Iggy.

Kali hesitated, contemplating as she watched Iggy recoil to the man's touch, there was a moment again, where her humanity came to the forefront. She brought her hands to her chest and thought about her next move carefully.

"Me goddess, our deal." He repeated, he wrapped his forearm around Iggy's throat, tightening his grip. "I did everythin' ye asked. I brought ye yer brother, I brought ye th' god o' death. I deserve this."

Kali, please don't let him hurt him. Please!

Kali looked back at me, biting her lip. She shook her hesitation away and waved us all to silence, "I promised you nothing, but for you to leave with your life, pirate."

"Wha'? No, ye 'ave no needs fer 'im. He be me reward, I helped ye!" He tightened more, Iggy gagged, gasping for some air.

"Iggy!" I called out, watching him struggle. I tried to rush to his aid, but Kali grabbed me by the arm and pushed me hard to the ground.

Stay. She threatened in my head.

In Gibson's anger towards Kali's betrayal, he hadn't felt Iggy struggling to loosen his binds.

Kali took a few steps forward, stepping between them and I, "You dare question my honor, in my own temple, mortal?" Her voice echoed through the walls, the pools around us rumbled with the growl of her fury. Something was building beneath the waters surface.

"No, me goddess," he tried to backtrack his words, "I mean no disrespect, but yer brother be here, ye 'ave no more needs fer Ignatius!" He let go of Iggy, as poor Iggy dropped to his knees, finally taking a full breath. Gibson brought his hands together and tried to beg for forgiveness from the mighty powerful, goddess of the sea.

In that moment of Gibson groveling, Iggy had a chance to finally break free of his binds, he rolled out from under Gibson.

Gibson was confused and didn't have time to react as Iggy punched him once, hitting the bridge of his nose. Blood pooled down his face, stumbling backwards, but he recovered quicker than Iggy had anticipated. Iggy went to throw another punch, Gibson dodged it, throwing it a punch of his own, getting Iggy in the ribcage.

Iggy gasped; the wind momentarily knocked from his lungs.

"Iggy!" I managed to get back to my feet, once again attempting to charge in to help my friend, but Kali tightly held me in place, she struggled but held strong.

Gibson tried to take advantage as Iggy keeled over, trying to catch his breath. He reached to grab a tuff of his hair, only for Iggy to lung forward, knocking Gibson off his feet. Iggy jumped onto Gibson's chest, pinning him against the floor. There was no self control in Iggy's mind. He repeatedly punched Gibson in the face, as hard as he could. "You don't own me," Iggy growled. Gibson's blood splattered; coating his fists, face, and the ground around them.

Gibson managed to break one punch through, it knocked Iggy right off him. Iggy was crumbled on the ground, spitting blood that was pooling in his mouth. It took Gibson a second to recover, wiping the blood from his eyes he grabbed the binds that Iggy had freed himself from. Stepping over to Iggy he wrapped them tightly around his throat, the ropes digging deep into Iggy's neck. Iggy was pulled up onto his knees, trying to claw at the tightening rope.

Kali please stop this! Help him, please! I begged with tears in my eyes, I furiously fought against her hold on me. Though, I stopped fighting with the sound of a grumble. Both her and I knew what it meant.

Iggy's eyes were clenched shut, he tried to catch a breath, his lips turning a pale shade of blue.

A hungry roar filled the room, everything around us shook, and water sprayed everywhere.

The rope loosened around Iggy's neck, and something cold and wet soaked his back. He gasped taking in a deep breath, falling to his hands, coughing violently as fresh air was forced back into his lungs. Finally, when the sound of bones crunching under a great force filled Iggy's ears and he turned his head to face what had just happened.

Gibson's feet were still dangling out of the great Leviathans mouth.

Terrified, Iggy stumbled away from the creature, his eyes locked on the hungry beast as she watched him squirming on the floor before her.

She lifted her head and swallowed what remained of

the bald pirate, before turning away and disappearing back into the depth.

Iggy was petrified. Soaked in Gibson and his own blood, he turned to look at me, "Axel," only to find himself face to face with Kali.

"Stand," she ordered, standing over him with her arms across her chest.

Iggy nodded, struggling to stand, but did as she asked of him.

Kali was clearly struggling to be the bitter monster that she had become accustomed too, while she studied the bloodied boy before her.

Kali, just let him go. Iggy has nothing to do with this, do whatever you want with me, just let him go. He's been through enough already; can't you see that?

I could see her considering it, but she shook her head, snapping herself out of her sympathetic mood. Kali grabbed Iggy's arm and pulled him along with her, "If you even try to fight me, I'll make you do unforgiveable things," she threatened Iggy as he followed her lead without hesitation, looking back at me. "Come brother," she snapped, leading Iggy to the back wall, "No funny business from you either, dear brother. I will not hesitate to slowly bleed your lover out." She waved her hand as the mirage hiding her magical spiral stairway, that lead down into the darkness.

I followed as ordered.

Iggy was in as much awe as he was in terror. The walls that encased the stairwell were clear, Kali's magic keeping the water from caving in. If his hands weren't bound, he would have been able to reach through and snatch a creature from the sea as it swam by.

We reached the bottom step, it opened in to a grand chamber.

Kali was unspoken, she dragged Iggy to the far corner of the wall, placing him in a large cage, locking him inside. He did not protest, he was still slightly in shock.

I remembered this room well; potions, charms, spell-books and more littered the far-right wall, a cauldron and crystal ball on a stand made out of braided pickerelweeds, a white cloth covering it from view. In the upper right corner was a lounge chair, draped in royal purple and deep blues, as well as a small table for two. The rest of the room was cluttered with tools she used to torment and punish, tools she had used on me. Iggy's new cell was on a pully system as she lifted the cage off the ground, Iggy being unable to keep his footing when the ground shifted around him. He fell to his knees and decided it be best to stay there as his eyes kept focused on me, concern and dread glued to his perfect, but bruised and bloodied face.

Kali locked the chain in place and walked to the center of the room, she reached her hand down through the floor, an eel, swam towards her, holding a chain in it's mouth. I knew too well that at the bottom of that chain was a very old, very large anchor. She beckoned be forward with the twist of her finger, I did as I was told.

She attached my already shackled wrist, and once she let go, the chain began to sink back towards the oceans floor, dropping me once again to my knees as I struggled to stay like that, it was pulling me down with great force. She unlocked my neck brace, and inspected the back of my head, the large wound that was left by the mercenary was still bleeding. She grumbled, "Mortal bodies." kali waved her hand over me and I could feel the skin recovered instantaneously.

Was she feeling conflicted? *Where is my cloak?* I asked hesitantly.

Kali who had walked over to her crystal ball, removing the white cloth as she swirled her finger over the top, the clouded crystal swirling in sync with her finger. "Safe." She replied.

This was the first time in a very long time her cynical nature towards me seemed gone, but for how long I wondered to myself.

Let him go, Iggy has done nothing to you. This is a problem between gods.

"Actually no, it really isn't, Axel." The way she spoke my name, I could feel the bitter hatred coming back to surface. "This is a problem fixed by a god, caused by a god, between a god and a human." Kali turned to Iggy as she placed one hand firmly on her crystal ball. "Do you know how the god wars started, pretty one?" She asked, but he knew that she didn't want an answer from him, so Iggy remained quiet. "Axel, technically started it." She walked over and traced her hands down the bars of Iggy's new cell, "Our brother Kitari, the god of fire proposed that humans needed to restart from the beginning. That they were cruel monsters, only getting worse as the years went on. Most the gods agreed with our older brother. Axel protested. Saying that because he spent the majority of his time in the mortal planes, watching and observing their lives, that he understood them better then the rest of the gods. He felt that he the kindness and the love humans could feel towards each other, he believed they needed more time. Another chance to grow and learn from their mistakes of the past after they had brutally burned and murdered our mother, a goddess." Kali kept eye contact with Iggy as she told her tale. "I stood up for my brother that day, against my better judgement. That protest, that small ripple in our time, was the god wars. Axel was banished from the heavens. It made no difference to him, due to the fact he never belonged in the heavens with us to begin with. But I, as well as every other god who stood alongside him was banished as well, our brother Kitari and many others recoiled to the heavens forgetting about all you mortals."

Iggy remained silent, and un-swayed by her words, but he knew she was going to make a point of her story.

"Axel, hurts everyone who stands with him, he himself is never affected by his actions. He is death, he is every living thing's end. Including yours and mine."

Iggy held his breath as their eyes met.

Kali walked towards the lever that had Iggy suspended in the air, unlocking it as it, and he dropped, the bottom of the cage now slightly sinking through the floor as the water seeped around him, soaked from the waist down. Iggy fought back the urge to panic, but it was written all over his face.

Kali bent down slightly and smiled cynically, "How

well can you hold your breath, pretty one?"

"Kali enough!" My voice no longer broken and pained.

Chapter 34

The shadow's blade came around the bend, the
cove which hid the Temple of the Goddess of the Sea
just as the Mercenary ship was exiting. The Captain
rushed to the bow of the ship as she studied the
mercenaries, Victor at her side. "Inform the rest of
the crew that they are to take control of that ship.
Kill anyone necessary and search the decks for Iggy,
there is a chance he could still be on board."

"Aye, Captain. Do ye reckon 'tis best that ye charge
th' temple? Karlic 'n I could go alone."
Her glare told him his answer, he nodded and
stepped away calling for them to drop anchor, as the
large ship slowly came into the dock.

Jane didn't wait for the ship to come to a stop as
she catapulted herself over the ledge, landing on the
mossy planks with a thud.

"Captain!" Victor called out with a grunt, as he now
had to meet her brass action, throwing himself over,
Karlic followed along cheerfully.

Captain Far'mel tripped her hat to her crew as they

lifted anchor and dropped sail, heading off as quick as they came, charging after the mercenary ship.

She didn't wait for Victor and Karlic to regain their footing, rushing off towards the temple, sword now drawn. She did not know what to expect once they passed the threshold, but she knew there was no turning back.

They entered the temple to find it deserted. Blood streaked the floor as Jane's heart sank slightly, unsure of the source, as who ever it belonged too, was clearly not living any longer. She placed her hand down in a small pool of blood, feeling as it was still warm to the touch. If she didn't know better, she would have told herself they were in the wrong area, but she did know better. This was where she needed to be. Studying the back wall, her eyes traced around the large marble throne, some how she saw the subtle distortion in the far corner of the room, "There," she pointed it out, rushing over, carefully placing her hand through the wall.

Victor and Karlic jumped back, uneased by the dark magic before them.

Jane took a deep breath and turned to her crew, "I cannot force you to face this with me, you can turn back. This is not an order."

Victor and Karlic didn't need a second to think

about it as they smiled at their Captain, "We shall go t' th' depths o' Davy Jones' locker wit' ye."

She smiled, they might as well be. She stepped through the distortion and rushed down the spiral staircase, Victor pushing a head of her, while Karlic took behind, all of them now with their blades unsheathed.

Pooling out of the stairwell they were met with a voice of confusion, "Captain?" As confused as Iggy was, he was fearful and thankful for their arrival.

Kali's face twitched with anger as the humanity that had been building in her eyes dissipated. "Oh, your pretty Captain, Axel, you didn't tell me you had invited more guests to our little party."

I turned my head to face them as I tugged even more furiously against my binds, "Captain, no. This is too dangerous!"

Kali purred as she spoke, hand stroking the leaver, "Who do you care for more?"

"Don't,"

But my words were too late as she released the chain, the cage sunk through the floor. Iggy didn't have a chance to catch his breath before he was fully submerged and sinking rapidly.

"Iggy!" The Captain and I yelled.

The force of the water hitting Iggy's chest, forced most the air out of his lungs. He already only had a partial breath to spare, he held what was left, and tried to keep himself from seer panic. He realized that his survival rate was slim, but he had to fight for it. Iggy wanted to help me, he wanted to help the Captain, Victor and Karlic, he wanted to fight for Daric's sacrifice. Iggy tugged and slammed his body against the door to his cell, but it was too late, he couldn't make the momentum and his body forced him to take a breath. He coughed, gagged as the salty water filled his lungs. He continued to fight through the pain pulling and banging against the door. *It can't end this way! Not after all of this! It can't!* It was hopeless for him to continue fighting. His lungs screamed for air as he swallowed again. Iggy's eyes began to close, as his body refused to respond. He went limp, his body was shutting down. Iggy was slowly dying, slowly leaving the mortal realm, I could feel it. *Boom. Boom. Boom. Boom. One, two. Boom.*

Jane charged forward, only to stop in her tracks as Kali herself summoned a sword of ice to her hand and cracked her neck, she stepped up to Jane. "You dare enter a goddess's chamber, armed and uninvited? You my beautiful pet, must have a death wish." Kali knew she could have enchanted the three of them, but she decided against it. She already had the upper hand.

Karlic charged up the side, and with an easy swish of her sword, their blades connected, and the force knocked him into the air, flying hard into the book shelves. Kali continued forward as if she had just shooed a fly.

Jane stopped, she would never admit it to anyone, but she stopped in fear. But that moment of hesitation was caught by Kali, and in her moment of over confidence, it gave me just enough time to make my own move against her.

Kali was blinded by her confidence and Jane was blinded by her determination as fear left her once again. They stepped towards each other, blades at the ready. Jane went to swing high and down across the goddess's chest, while Kali was going to run her victim right threw.

Jane's attack was deflected, her sword tumbled across the floor and she was thrown to the ground. Kali's blow was strong and true, as it pierced through flesh and bone, blood staining the magical weapon, and dripping on the floor, yet Kali's intended target was safe and sound behind me.

I used my reserved strength and energy from the air around me. I had forced myself to my feet and dove in front of Jane, using myself as a mortal shield. Kali's blade went clean through the center of my chest. I coughed blood as I choked, spitting blood unintendedly in my dear sister's face as I gasped.

Shocked and confused, the startled Kali pulled her blade forcefully from my body and dropped it to the floor. Her hands trembled, backing away from me.

Blood pooled down me as I looked at the large hole in my chest, a hole that would not heal this time... "Kali," I wheezed, gagging on my own blood, falling back to my knees.

She shook her head, her eyes went wide, "No," her lips trembled, unsure what to do, "no this wasn't supposed to happen." She turned and ran to the back of the wall as she waved her hand, my cloak appearing from behind a magical wall. She tore it from its binds and rushed back over to me, falling to her knees before me she placed it over my shoulders.

The chains that bound me corroded into the sea as I placed my now free hands on the hole that was my chest.

"Axel," The Captain whispered in disbelief.

Kali's limps trembled, "Brother, I'm..." I could see that she wanted to apologize, but the words escaped her as tears filled her eyes, tears of regret. Tears of the unknowing.

Victor finally pulled the cage through the floor as Iggy's body laid limp, and lifeless on the steel floor. My heart ached, I for once was unsure of his fate. My own heart was beating too loudly in my chest that I couldn't hear his any longer... I could feel the finality of death filling the room, was it for my own, or was it sent for Iggy? I feared the worse. I could feel Jane's confliction. She was clearly torn between staying with me or rushing to Iggy's side. I wiped blood that was drooling down my lips on my shoulder before turning my head with a soft, reassuring smile to my Captain, "Help Iggy, please," She still paused, "I will be fine." I lied. There was no longer any pain, my body slowly went numb to the world around me.

Jane did my request of her as she rushed to the cell. Kali waved her hand and the door opened.
Victor rolled Iggy onto his back as Jane placed her ear against his chest.

He wasn't breathing, and his heart had stopped beating. She placed her hands together and pumped his chest in the count of three, "Come on Iggy, come back to me." She breathed into his mouth, again at the count of three, before checking for a pulse, she repeated.

Even through my powers were now returned to me, I knew it was too late for me. My time... Was now limited.

Kali was trembling, sobbing uncontrollably. She had never planned to go this far, she never wanted to kill me; she just wanted the love of her life back.

My time was precious, my energy was weakening still, and she need to learn, she needed to understand why I couldn't give her what she wanted. I took her hand and held her tightly. She looked me in the eye as the world around us froze, before we faded into the darkness.

"No," She shook her head, "You need to recover, your body needs to rest! Axel, what are you doing?" I pulled her in for a hug, *doing something I should have done years ago. Showing you what I've tried to explain.* I now had my voice, but no energy to waste to use it. I was spending what limited energy I had, focusing on one soul, one body. But I had to do one last thing for her, my dear beloved sister. Even after all she put me through, when it came down too it, I loved her with all my being.

A quaint little cottage on a hill, over looking the great sea appeared around us. It was like looking at a reflection in a pond, rather then being there in form as I couldn't muster the strength to place us there.

Kali wanted to question on why I had taken her here, but it was answered before the words came to mind. Her lips trembled, "Hector,"

She went to take a step towards her lost lover, but I held her hand still. Even through my grip was weakening as blood oozed, draining from my body.

The Hector that stood in the distance, wasn't really the man she had loved all those years ago. As she watched, she could see it now.

The man resembling her late lover, the man who held his soul called out, "Kali, come here please." As a small blonde child came up to the older man. He lifted her up in his strong arms, wrapping her in a warm embrace as he kissed her cheek.

A blonde pregnant woman stepped out of the house and placed her hand on the man, he kissed his wife as the three of them returned together into the little cottage.

If I had the power to bring back that soul to the body of the man you loved, he would forever be cursed. You would have deprived his soul of all these opportunities to live on, to become a husband, a father. Gods were never meant to fall in love with the mortals you helped create. Their souls need many lifetimes to develop, their mortal frames can't hold up as yours can. An extended lifetime would have corrupted him and destroyed the man you had fallen in love with, with the man you are still grieving. It's okay to love, it's okay to feel pain when they leave, but that is the life of mortals. Mortal's die, and their souls move on to hopefully better lives. I coughed more blood as I tried to hide it with my hand.

Kali wiped her tears from her face and turned to me, flustered with too many emotions to control. "Why didn't you tell me this, before I went too far!"

I placed one hand on her cheek wiping at her smudged makeup. *I tried. But you were not ready to listen until this day.*

"Am I going to lose you now too, brother?" her voice cracked as she spoke. She entwined her fingers in mine, I gave her a reassuring squeeze. But I dared not give her the answer to that question even though I knew the answer.

We returned. No time had passed as the Captain's lips were still pressed against Iggy's. Time resumed, I dropped to my hands and knees. Blood dripping from my lips as I gasped trying to catch a full breath. Fluid. Blood was filling my lungs. My body was dying. I was dying. I could feel my soul fluttering away.

The Captain was still working frantically on Iggy,

trying to resuscitate him, she forced her breath down his throat, she fought hard trying to bring him back to her.

I looked up at Kali who had crumbled to her knees, her faced buried in her hands as she continued to cry.

My head was aching, and my mind was going fussy. I couldn't help Iggy. I watched as my friend, the only person I loved lay dead across the room from me, and there was nothing I could do to bring him back.

Kali looked at me, she could see me looking at him, helplessly. She finally shook her distress and stood up, walking over to Iggy.

Jane stopped as she reached from the dagger in her boot.

"No, Captain." I managed to force out as I collapsed to the ground, fighting to keep my eyes open.

Kali kneeled next to Iggy and placed her hands on his chest. She found the water in his lungs, and traced her hands up, over his throat and out his mouth. Water flooded from his lips.

We all waited, as Jane pressed her lips back to Iggy's breathing once again into him, but it was too late. He was too far gone and there was nothing anyone could do to bring him back. Kali turned to me, tears fell from her face, "I'm sorry, dear brother,"

The pain consumed me, all I could do was watch my grieving friend sob, and my dead love lay lifelessly out of reach, my body began to deteriorate into nothing.

I found myself in the darkness of time. I didn't feel like myself, but I was there with my cloak wrapped around me. Everything was different now and I couldn't figure out why. I placed my hands over my face, and fell to my knees, crying knowing the suffering I had caused. *Iggy, I'm so sorry... Daric, I'm sorry I failed you both.*
"Remember? I told you not everyone is afraid of death."
My eyes opened, and I looked up to see Iggy basked in a warm glow, reaching his hands out to me with his usual innocent smile.
"Iggy?"
"Why are you so surprised?" He asked as I finally took his hands, he pulled me to my feet. I wrapped my arms tightly around him. I just held him as I sobbed onto his shoulder, he wrapped his arms around me too, squeezing me tightly nestling his face in my neck. He tried to play the brave face, but his cracked voice gave away his subtle desire to still live, "No one can hurt me anymore, I'm finally free."

He pushed me away, placing one hand on the side of my face. He wiped away my tears, swallowing his pain away. Iggy managed a saddened smile, turning his head as Daric appeared alongside us.

"Keep an eye on th' Captain fer us, she'll be needin' it." He smiled, keeping his distance, kicking at the darkness around his feet.

Iggy knew it was time as he placed his hands on the side of my face, leaning in; our lips touched again for one last perfect kiss. My eyes closed as I took every second in. It was a bitter goodbye because when I reopened my eyes, I was alone. Iggy and Daric had moved on, hopefully to a better happier life...

The END

Epilogue

It had been two months since that fateful day. Things still hadn't fallen back into normality for Captain Jane Far'mel. Her ship was now back in full running order, she had an almost entirely new crew, they even had a destination for their next sail. Jane planned to sail back to Tasyrn, disrupt military slave ships, they were all prepared, but something was holding her back. Her heart wasn't in it at the moment. She was still mourning the lost of three great allies, great friends, people she had called family.

Jane was sitting alone in an old rundown bar, just in the outskirts of the Capital, Stormwall. She had just polished off another bottle of hard liquor, while the barmaid tried to make a move on the Captain, but even for the affections of a beautiful maiden she wasn't in the mood for it.

People had been coming in and out of the bar all day and she hadn't lifted her head from her drink, but this time as the door slowly creaked open, Jane turned her gaze towards the door.

A young girl entered, attempting to hide her appearance with a red coloured hood over her head. She tried hard to seem like a normal girl, but the gold jewelry around her wrists, neck and daggling from her ears that she tried to hide, peaked from behind the rich cloth and the deep red coloured fabric of her cloak clearly stated she wasn't just a normal girl. Yet Jane didn't care about that.

Jane was frozen as if staring at a piece of her past, this young raven-haired girl, with crystal blue eyes scanned the room. She looked exactly how Jane imagined her sister would have looked at that age.

A few older pirates spotted the young girl and got up from their seats to approach her, twisted grins on their dirt covered faces.

Jane placed her hat on her head and quickly stepped up to the young girl, placing her arm over the girl's shoulder with a smile. "Ah, there you are, I've been waiting for you."

The girl went to push Jane away and protest in confusion, when the Captain whispered, "Someone like you goes for a lot on the black market if you talk to the wrong people."

The young girl swallowed hard and nodded, "Sorry I'm late."

Jane lead the girl to the back of the bar, away from

everyone else.

The young girl sat down, there was a second as she scanned the area where she seemed nervous, but that vanished, very quickly. She sat up tall and readjusted the hood of her cloak around her head.

"What brings a thing like you here? You can't even be old enough to drink."

The girl placed her hands on the table and pulled a jeweled, gold ring from her finger. "I need passage to Tasryn, I was told there is a Captain here who might be able to help me." The girl put the ring in front of the Captain, "I was told to look for a red-haired woman. I can pay you handsomely, half before, half when I safely get to Tasyrn."

Jane inspected the ring, she knew where it was from, but wondered how far this young girl was willing to go, "What's your name, girl?"

"K-," She stopped herself, thinking quickly, "Castriel," *Castriel,* shifted uneasily, she studied Jane's raised brow, "Castriel Far'mel."

Jane scrunched her brows and leaned in, whispering, "That I know is a lie, but where did you get that name from Princess?"

The girl swallowed hard, "If you knew who I was why ask?" She snapped with a pout. The pout of a real princess.

"Tell me where you got that name from, first."

The girl looked around, leaning in, "Okay, I am Katherine Ironfist, betrothed to the Prince of Stormwall. That name was my mother's."

Jane's heart began to pound in her chest, *her mother's name.*

"Well, Katherine, why don't we take this conversation somewhere safer, away from peering eyes?"

Katherine Ironfist looked around and nodded, following the Captain's lead, "I never got your name."

Jane smiled turning to face the young girl, "Captain Jane Far'mel."

Hearing her late mothers maiden name shook the young girl as she froze in confusion.

"I think we have a lot to talk about."

Had fate brought a small piece of her past to her? Or was it someone else.

Made in the USA
Middletown, DE
05 June 2019